49

McSWEENEY'S 49

COVER
STORIES

© 2017 McSweeney's Quarterly Concern and the contributors, San Francisco, California. ASSISTED BY: Annie Julia Wyman, Brian Christian, Molly McGhee, Theodore Gioia, Stephanie Steinbrecher, Moss Turpan. PROFOUND THANKS: Vendela Vida, Heidi Julavits, Brian Dice, Beverly Rogers, Joshua Wolf Shenk, Kellen Braddock, Andi Winnette, Jordan Bass, Jeremy Radcliffe, Jed Repko. WEBSITE: Chris Monks. PUBLICITY: Ruby Perez. DEVELOPMENT: Shannon David. ART DIRECTION: Sunra Thompson, Dan McKinley. COPY EDITOR: Daniel Levin Becker. POETRY EDITOR: Dominic Luxford. ASSOCIATE EDITORS: Jordan Bass, Daniel Gumbiner. PUBLISHERS: Brian Dice, Kristina Kearns. Executive Director: Kristina Kearns. MANAGING EDITOR: Claire Boyle. EDITOR: Dave Eggers.

MCSWEENEY'S PUBLISHING BOARD MEMBERS: Natasha Boas, Kyle Bruck, Carol Davis, Brian Dice, Dave Eggers, Caterina Fake, Gina Pell, Nion McEvoy, Isabel Duffy-Pinner, Jeremy Radcliffe, Jed Repko, Julia Slavin, and Vendela Vida.

MAJOR SPONSOR: Mailchimp. SPONSOR: Amazon Literary Partnership. FURTHER SUPPORT: Thank you to all of our Kickstarter backers, members, donors, and subscribers, individually acknowledged on pages 210–221.

Printed at Thomson-Shore in Dexter, MI.

McSWEENEY'S 49

COVER STORIES

INTERIOR ILLUSTRATIONS: Aesthetic Apparatus
COVER ART CREATIVE DIRECTION: Gary Burden; ART DIRECTION, DESIGN, & COLLAGE: Jenice Heo

DEAR MCSWEENEY'S,

I was finally able to steal WiFi. Thankfully, the guards are usually on their smartphones, alternating between PornHub, online gambling, and ESPN. Every night, when we hear guards Jolene and Biff excuse themselves from their station to patrol the yards, Jawad scours the disposal containers for spare electronic parts. (Jolene and Biff actually go have sex in the commissary. Both are married. They think they're discreet. They're not.) Jawad only has four minutes and twenty-one seconds—that's the length of this sad tryst of ennui, self-loathing, and middle-aged, fleshy friction. It cumulates in Biff emitting a slow roar, sounding like a beagle with emphysema, which signals to Jawad to race back to his tent and slip under the sheet (made in Egypt) and blanket (made in Mexico until the trade war, but now made in Bangladesh) before they come with the flashlights for their nightly check.

But I digress.

Brushing off his college computer science skills, Jawad has somehow created a few starter phones. He gave me this one to return a favor. Recently, I gave him a lead role in my play, "Me at the Camps." Jawad said the experience reminded him of the first video he posted on YouTube: "Me at the Zoo."

I was just grateful my English major came in handy. But, who knows? Maybe the South Asian aunties and uncles were right. I should have pursued one of the holy trinity: doctor, engineer, or dubious businessman who runs an import/export factory. Maybe those skills would be handier in here.

Two years gives you plenty of time for regrets. The Executive Order was inevitable. They waited for that one lone extremist who shouted *Allahu Akbar* before ramming his pickup through the thick crowd waiting at the TKTS booth in midtown. The ban, the vetting, the registry were all just prelude.

"The need to protect against terrorism outweighs individual rights and the rights of American Muslims…" read the Supreme Court ruling. It was déjà vu, a dubstep remix from hell. But, when a President tweets out threats using 140 characters and hijab emojis, when only terrorist attacks by Muslims are covered by the media and the ones by white supremacists are ignored, and when the so-called judges who tried to uphold the Constitution disappear or suddenly fall sick, well, I can't say I was surprised.

Americans will always rather feel safe than be free.

So, we drink chai here and keep chill, because there's no Netflix. But, we do have chai. Also, biryani. And shawarma. And sheesha and tarneeb. And an underground trading market. And exquisite weed, which I don't partake in, but can smell every Saturday night near the hipster quarters. (Yes, all the men have big beards. Some stereotypes remain the same inside and outside.) Necessity breeds creativity and resourcefulness, which leads to excellent sushi rolls made from lumpy oatmeal.

I tell myself I have to remain chill. Anger will only create resentment. And how will that help me and my children inside these walls? But, I won't lie, McSweeney's. At night, when the generators fail— at least twice a week—and my feet become brown popsicles, I see the faces of all the people who told me, "Naw, he'd never do that. Congress will never allow it. This country will never stand for it," and I curse at them. I'm talking *Wrath of Khan*– level vindictive rage. I'm talking Ricardo Montalban quoting *Moby-Dick*, "From hell's heart, I stab at thee!"

Real dark, Evil Eye shit, invoking the full might of all Celestial Powers to damn your privileged, complacent ass.

But, by morning, it passes. We wake up and take our Russian classes. Я мусульманин! I get to do my Ivan Drago accent for one hour. The teacher, a leggy blonde brought in from Moscow, chuckles. I pass by the refugee quarters and they give me Chobani yogurt for breakfast. Hamdi Ulukaya is generous here, just like he was outside, creating a massive trough for first come, first served. I take my kids over to Ibtihaj, who teaches us fencing. I go to the library, skip the *Art of the Deal* sections (notice I said sections, plural), and head over to Russian literature. Tolstoy and Dostoyevsky's piercing understanding of the human soul is always relevant, now more than it was two hundred years ago. We mostly skip TV, which consists of Fox News, Breitbart, and reality shows. There's only so much state propaganda one can take.

Dave and Aziz keep testing out material in different sections of the camps before premiering a new show for everyone every few months. Salman has started a teaching co-op. The Khan Academy is reborn without the internet.

It isn't perfect, of course. Some of the Sunnis don't mix with the Shias. There's the African American quarter and the Arab quarter. I wish they'd interact more, but there's still lingering bad blood. The Indians and Pakistanis share recipes and food but have somehow created a Line of Control near the latrines. However, all of us feel bad for The Miscellaneous. They're a ragtag bunch of non-Muslims who look Muslim-y and were accidentally thrown in with the rest of us saps. By my last count there's at least seventeen Iranian Jews, ninety-eight Arab Christians, fourty-two Sikhs, and Colin Kaepernick.

Despite the divisions, each night, as the sun sets, a young woman named Tahera stands up and does the *adhan*, the call to prayer, in beautiful, classical Arabic. We all come together to pray, each in our own way, as one: Muslim and miscellaneous Sikh, atheist and weed-smoking hipster, standing shoulder to shoulder, feet to feet.

And for those brief moments, we feel grateful that even though we're inside, we stand next to each other, for each other, as one, as the melodious sounds drown out the carnage beyond our walls.

Until I break out,
WAJAHAT ALI
CAMP FDR, WASHINGTON D.C.

DEAR MCSWEENEY'S,
On the September 23, 1970 episode of *The Johnny Cash Show*, Johnny and his wife, June, are onstage talking. She says that she regrets having missed time from the show after giving birth to their son, as though she were talking about a cold she caught from running around in the rain. She then recites a strange poem about milking a cow, first confusing and then eliciting a laugh from the audience. When she finishes, she looks deep into Johnny's eyes as he gives her encouragement. "Was that okay?" she keeps asking. Johnny keeps saying, "You did good." "Was it?" she asks again. "You did good."

Johnny announces that the next guest will be Ray Charles. Johnny sits on the piano bench next to Ray. He reveals that it's Ray's fortieth birthday. "On behalf of the Country Music Association," he continues, "I want to say thanks to you for taking country music around the world and introducing it to a lot of people. Nashville welcomes you with open arms." Coming from a man who was the king of country music at the time, it must have felt like being knighted, not that Ray Charles needed to be knighted.

Ray looks very touched and says he has something to play for Johnny. He begins an impromptu solo version of "Walk The Line." After a verse and a chorus he stops and says, "Did you hear that?"

"Yes, that's something else," Johnny says.

Then Johnny mentions that Ray has a new album of country songs called *Love Country Style*. Ray Charles laughs and says, "You know that city love ain't quite like country style."

"No, it's a little bit different," Johnny says, and everyone laughs knowingly.

For a place that once endured an actual, bloody Civil War, it's strange to think that the real divisions in the United States have always been more about country versus city. It's even stranger to think that something so fluid and ambiguous as music could be caught up in those dividing lines, but as Ray Charles is about to demonstrate here at the Ryman Auditorium in Nashville, those divisions have nothing to do with words, chords, or melodies.

Ray says, "Well, here's a little song called 'Ring of Fire.'"

He says the title of the song like it burns his mouth. He supposedly kicked heroin in 1966. The way his body is pulsing, it looks more like he's on cocaine. You can see the electricity coursing through his body, and every word he says is delivered with a delicious joy. If he is on drugs, it is quite an argument for doing drugs.

The song begins with a large unseen band backing Ray. They have a very groovy '70s feel, light years away from the mariachi-influenced country-folk of the original. When Ray sings one line and leaves a space that was normally occupied by a horn line in Cash's version, there's just this big deep groove into which we can push all of our secret physical urges.

The most compelling moment comes at the breakdown after the first chorus. Ray stops playing piano and looks up with joy and just spasms for a few seconds as the bass line keeps going. He lets out an "Aghh," and then comes in right with the band. If you notated this moment musically on a score, there would be nothing in Ray's part except for several rests, and yet it is one of the most fascinating things I've ever seen a musician do. He is just silently convulsing with the rhythm as though doing so were more important than any notes he could play. Wherever he is, the invisible bass player seems taken aback and begins to lose the tempo, but then Ray comes back in and syncs up with the big brass hits.

He delights in every word of the lyrics, reveling in the sensuality of them. It's odd to think that the song was written by June Carter after seeing a page in her uncle's book of Elizabethan poetry. The burning referenced the fires of hell that you fall into when you succumb to desire, the kind of desire she felt for Johnny, who was married at the time.

Or did Johnny actually write the song? Johnny's first wife, Vivian Liberto, claims as much in her book *I Walked the Line*: "To this day, it confounds me to hear the elaborate details June told of writing that song for Johnny. She didn't write that song any more than I did. The truth is, Johnny wrote that song, while piled up and drunk, about a certain female body part. All those years of her claiming she wrote it herself, and she probably never knew what the song was really about."

It's pretty unusual for there to be a question of song ownership between two lovers. It's not like you ever have to wonder whether Eric Clapton or Pattie Boyd wrote "Layla."

If the subtext of the song really is about a certain female body part, Ray takes that subtext and explodes it all over the Ryman.

On the last chorus he gets really quiet and starts to sound a little unearthly. "That ring of fire, that ring of fire," he chants. Then his voice falls to just an ominous whisper: "It burns, burns, burns, that ring of fire."

As the band behind him dies out, Ray is still going, like he doesn't want the song to end, and he lets out one last shudder and cackle like he just invented the orgasm. "Burns. Ah ha ha ha."

The crowd gives a standing ovation and Johnny returns to the stage, looking like a man who just watched someone have sex with his wife but was so in awe of how good he was at it that he could only thank him.

Best,
NICK JAINA
BOGOTÁ, COLOMBIA

DEAR MCSWEENEY'S,
I want to tell you about Trumpmania from the perspective of a black woman, lesbian, child of civil rights activists, mother of a black man, living in Prague.

I arrived in the Czech Republic

in spring of 2014, fresh off a four-month backpacking trip through South and Central America, Mexico, and Havana, our departure point for the Czech Republic. My Czech partner and I met and fell in love in San Francisco. Now we would make a life in Prague.

For the first year, I bragged to friends that I didn't feel the weight of my blackness in Prague as I did in the U.S. because the Czech people saw my black grandfathers as their liberators from the Nazis. Then the shift. The refugee crisis unfolded in startling TV images and things began to change.

Czechs strongly opposed letting anyone in. It pleased Czechs that refugees bypassed their country and headed to Germany, by way of Austria. Perhaps the refugees knew that Czechs, as citizens of one of the world's most atheistic countries, weren't having any of that religious bullshit, or that the language was just too hard, a fact of which Czechs are very proud.

On the day of the U.S. election, when I walked about the office in a daze, my coworkers' sweet smiles of sympathy could not hide the look in their eyes: "The U.S. is going to fuck us over, again." (See history of U.S.-Czech relations.) But, it wasn't my fault. I voted for Her, by absentee ballot.

It stunned Europeans that the U.S. could generate someone fouler than Europe's own crop of white male extremists. (Poland's women had to march en masse to protect their right to abortion.) For Europe, it was like the brother you looked up to suffered a mental breakdown and joined a cult. What could you do? For me, it was an out-of-body experience.

Now I was a refugee from my own country, and the Women's March in Prague was my way to reconnect. I was curious to see who would show up, since here, *feminist* (usually spoken in a whisper) is literally a dirty word. We stood in the cold (-12 °C), the calls to action crisp and sharp in the winter air. In Czech and then English, the speakers described the parallels between our governments: the Czech president supported Trump and visited Mr. Putin, a man whose country had sent tanks through these very streets to crush rebellion in the Prague Spring of 1968.

A speaker rallied the crowd: "We will not go back to the days when neighbor turned against neighbor, friend informed on friend, just to survive." I stood among people whose lives were still etched with memories of a man called Hitler, and the Trump experience was not new to them. There were cheers and shouts, and as we sang Katy Perry's "Roar," I released a howl into the frigid air, one with this small mass of people, most of them Czech, some from other parts of the world, who believed in hope.

Sincerely,
ROBIN TERRELL
PRAGUE, CZECH REPUBLIC

DEAR MCSWEENEY'S,
I've always believed that even in the darkest, saddest times, humor has its place. Maybe because I'm cynical or wildly inappropriate, or maybe there's just something wrong with me. Regardless. I think often of the time my grandmother, who was modest and declining, wheeled herself out to the nurses' station at her nursing home and asked, "Is it time for bingo?" The thing is, she had no shirt on. She was topless. My grandmother was topless in public, asking about bingo. And while that certainly was sad and awful, I envied my aunt for landing the punch line: "well, that's when I knew something was really wrong. She hated bingo."

I see it as the timeless battle between darkness, darker darkness, and a li'l bit of reflected light. So you can imagine my disappointment that trying to write funny things hasn't really seemed to be saving me since the election. Every time I write a piece or a tweet—and I know this is going to sound crazy—it just doesn't feel like I'm actually *doing* anything. Preposterous, right? But I just can't shake the feeling that being a smart aleck isn't going to deliver us from fascists.

For example, I had an idea for a funny sign for the Women's March: OH HEIL NO. Right? It's good. Original, catchy, a couple layers of meaning in there, brief. All signs (pardon the pun) of a winner. And while my co-workers in advertising are always saying stuff like "There's nothing original anymore," I was thinking, Well, pretty sure my sign is fucking original. And although I didn't actually go ahead and make that sign because I was super busy sharing depressing articles on Facebook and napping in the middle of the day, I did go to the March (with a pre-printed sign with someone else's design and words on it). While I was there I scrutinized every sign and guess what? Not a single OH HEIL NO sign! Not one! I rest my case. Actually I don't even remember what case I was making. Something about originality, humor, politics. It'll come back to me.

Anyway. I'm starting to wonder whether this is how people with terminal illnesses feel. For example, I used to bitterly joke about winter a lot. I mean, a lot a lot. But now when I see snow swirling outside my window or my kids trying to pat together a pathetic slushy snowman in our front yard, I just want to lie down and weep. Nothing funny about that!

Lately, I've been bursting into tears at the sight of a fishtail braid in my ten-year-old daughter's hair. Or flowers from the supermarket, even the crappy ones that are obviously dyed, like purple roses or orange carnations. Really any sort of sign of vibrancy or vulnerability or change makes me put my head down in my hands. I start to think that maybe I never fully tasted cinnamon before or appreciated how the crows in the trees yawp back and forth. Things that used to annoy me now seem heartrending. And most terrifying of all, definitely not funny.

If this is what knowing you're about to die is like, then no thank you. I want to stay annoyed at crows. They're always doing creepy side-eyed shuffles or blackening the skies in their big crow gangs. And *yes, I know it's called a murder*. Gives me the damn willies. And I want to make fun of those shitty orange carnations. They totally deserve it. I don't want to have an existential meltdown over my daughter's hair, because how will I fight Nazis if I'm crying over her braids and not writing something funny?

I know it's taken me a while to get around to this, but I thought that, as an outlet for humor yourself, you might know how I feel. Next time I see you, I would like to cry together and perhaps nap in the same bed. But let's make fun of some dying people first, just so I can feel a little bit better. Down with fascism! Ha ha!

In solidarity,
KIMBERLY HARRINGTON
SOUTH BURLINGTON, VT

DEAR McSWEENEY'S,
For the longest time I thought my uncles wrote "Stagger Lee." I was in my twenties when I found out they hadn't, which was a huge disappointment and shows you how little I know about music.

My uncles and aunt were on Sun Records in the late '50s (recording under Bobbie and the Boys when my aunt sang and the Cliff Thomas Trio when my Uncle Cliff sang). They met Johnny Cash, shook hands with Elvis, and still blame their failure to make it big on Jerry Lee Lewis.

After every holiday meal, we'd gather around the piano and sing their songs, each of us straining at the tops of our lungs to be heard. Apparently they'd throw in some covers, but at the time I just assumed that everything my Uncle Ed played on his piano was a song they had written.

I loved "Stagger Lee" most of all. I loved it when Stagger Lee went home to fetch his .44 and then ventured out into the night to find Billy. I loved how poor Billy begged for his life but Stagger Lee just shot him anyway, breaking a bar glass in the process, and we got to cheer for him even though he was a murderer who killed a man with three young kids and a sick wife over a little bit of money and a Stetson hat. Go Stagger Lee! Go Stagger Lee! Of course my uncles couldn't have written this song. Their songs were about picking wild mountain berries and Popeye.

So one day I'm riding in the car with my mother and sister when it comes on the radio. I interrupt our sing-along to say that it is definitely their best, by far the best song they ever wrote, and they're like, "Who?" and I'm like, "Ed and Cliff," and they give me sad looks and feel sorry for me like they do sometimes because I'm always gazing out of windows and swallowing pills I call vitamins.

After I discovered that my uncles had not, in fact, written "Stagger Lee," I set out to learn more about them. One day during happy hour, I went over to my Uncle Ed's house to ask him some questions. I took notes as we sat in his kitchen drinking wine from party cups. The stories he told me were ones he had always told. After a while, we went into the den to watch old videos of all of us gathered around the piano. I didn't know what I was looking for. I thought I'd write an article but I didn't know what it would be about. My uncles and aunt had been on *American Bandstand*. They

had met famous people. They still received BMI checks, but they were not famous and had never been famous and they had not written "Stagger Lee." In one video, my cousin and I wore matching maroon velvet tracksuits, our hair piled on top of our heads in ringlets. My uncle took his gold record off the wall and handed it to me. I held it. I had no idea what I was doing on his couch asking him questions about things that had happened sixty years ago. I felt bad for drinking his wine and delaying his dinner.

I spent the next week trying to write an essay about my relatives' brush with fame, but it was directionless and shitty and I never published it. My uncles did not write "Stagger Lee." They didn't write "Blue Monday," either. No one has ever heard of them and no one ever will. The older I get, the more I think they aren't so special and the more I believe that there are a lot of us out there like them, those who very nearly made it. We nearly did something that would make people remember us but we weren't lucky enough or we gave up or we chose different paths. Or maybe fame is just plain scary and when it gets too close we retreat and choose to tell the story of almost instead.

My Uncle Ed has lived a good life. He married a woman he loved. He has four children and many

grandchildren and sometimes he stops by my parents' house on his way to get frozen yogurt with the woman he still loves for no other reason than to say hello. Hello, Uncle Ed. Hello, Aunt Barbara Ann. Rest in Peace, Uncle Cliff. I remember you.

Sincerely,
MARY MILLER
JACKSON, MS

DEAR MCSWEENEY'S,

I intend to describe to you a particular tribute album, one that had an impact on me at the time of its release—*Rubaiyat: Elektra's 40th Anniversary* (1990). However, before I get to that, I want to briefly sketch out the context.

Tribute albums go way back, you know. In fact, from a certain vantage point, there were tribute albums from the moment there were recordings, if you count a great many classical albums: *Horowitz Plays Liszt* or Glenn Gould plays all of the Bach fugues, or what have you.

In modern times, in a way, Dylan and the Beatles repudiated the commonplace tribute album because they (and the Stones, the Kinks, the Who, et al.) insisted on writing their own material. Music publishing was always the power center in the world of recorded music. That was where you made the money, and so, in post–British Invasion rock and roll, it just wasn't the business model to record other people's material. Tribute albums in the '70s were fairly embarrassing, like Art Garfunkel's *Watermark*. In rock and roll those days, most frequently, people wrote their own songs, and the production machinery, the apparatus that got between the performer and the track selections for a record, was at a minimum.

However, a couple of indie rock albums changed my own attitudes about the worthiness of the tribute album. One of these was *Famous Blue Raincoat,* by Jennifer Warnes (1987).

Part of the reason *Famous Blue Raincoat* was so perfectly calibrated to be a *succès d'estime* was that Leonard Cohen's own fortunes were at a low ebb in 1987. He hadn't yet released *I'm Your Man* (on which Warnes sang), or made his late-life conversion into a gruff, baritone spoken-word artist. But people who knew about good songwriting knew that those early songs were masterpieces (despite the complicated feelings most people had about *Death of a Ladies' Man).* They knew that despite his weak standing around the time of the record's release, Cohen's relative obscurity wouldn't last long. Warnes took advantage of this moment and sang the great songs. Not to advance her own career, exactly, but to show off Cohen's

songs to the greatest possible advantage. From a certain angle, an album of Cohen songs sung by a woman would seem impossible. Yet here was the album, and suddenly we heard Cohen's songs in a way we hadn't before. Warnes made Cohen's songs into contemporary period pieces, with jazzy lounge aspects and added up-tempo discofications, all without seeming reckless about it. Warnes's voice, as others have noted, is sensitive and thoughtful. She served the songs on *Famous Blue Raincoat* without genuflecting, and that was why the album had such an impact (it recently got its twentieth-anniversary re-release, in fact, with a few additional tracks).

There were other great tribute albums in the '80s, but this one suddenly made the tribute album a conceptual treasure as far as I was concerned. There was a great glut of them in the ten or fifteen years after that, a tribute album for anyone who had ever recorded a song, sometimes multiple per artist. Tribute albums good, bad, and indifferent. And this tribute-album glut gave way to other conceptual approaches, such as album-length covers, like Mary Lee's Corvette covering all of *Blood on the Tracks* (2002).

All of this preliminary thinking about covers and tributes is meant to lead us to that particular album we're all gathered here for— *Rubaiyat: Elektra's 40th Anniversary.*

Rubaiyat was organized around a simple but potent principle. Elektra Records, at the crest of its fortieth-anniversary wave, was sitting on a *gold mine* of amazing songs and a lively roster of contemporary artists. Why not simply ask some of the contemporary artists to cover the chestnuts of Elektra artists past?

As you can imagine, this idea could be either remarkable or rather horrifying, depending on the performer and the song. The ideal match would be hard to quantify on paper, because it depends on so many imponderable issues. Can an ironic cover ever be good? Can certain songs, forgotten by history, sound incredibly different in new historical circumstances? Are there classics that are now impossible to cover? All of these questions come into play on *Rubaiyat,* and now and then the results are shockingly bad. They point out how difficult it is to marry the historical with the contemporary across a broad spectrum.

As I say, there are some astoundingly bad covers on *Rubaiyat,* this I cannot deny. And some of them are made worse by the twenty-four years since this compilation's release. For example, "Motorcycle Mama" by the Sugarcubes is pretty bad. I love Björk as much as the next person, but it now appears that the Sugarcubes were a rather unlistenable band, a sort of cheeseball imitation of the B-52s, who were themselves cheeseball imitators, and it's a miracle that Björk ever got out of that straitjacket alive. Also, there is Teddy Pendergrass singing Bread's "Make It With You." I mean, it's too easy to hate Bread. Once, I heard "Make It With You" while parked in the town square of Paris, Texas—they were *broadcasting* Bread in the town square—and by virtue of feeling decontextualized and momentarily unable to identify the artist, I suddenly understood that there was real songcraft taking place in the soft-rock juggernaut of Bread. All the same, Pendergrass did not, on *Rubaiyat,* believe that he should shrink from the sentimentality of the original, which slew him just as it slew Bread. Even if the transmutation of Pendergrass's white-bread folksiness into R&B slow jam is somehow fascinating, it's only worth listening to once.

The mediocre covers on *Rubaiyat*—by bands that time has forgotten, of songs that time has forgotten—do not require extensive cataloguing here. Let's not bother. Instead, let's talk about what's *amazing* on *Rubaiyat*! And there are so many things that are amazing. For example, Jackson Browne singing "First Girl I Loved" by the Incredible String Band. You have to be a real music weirdo, a sort of obsessed person, to understand fully how unsurpassed this

song is. I would say it's one of the very greatest love songs ever written. I really would. And almost no one knows it. It's up there with "Tangled Up In Blue" and "Something" and "Chelsea Hotel No. 2." However, unlike those songs, which have been covered extensively (Sinatra!), "First Girl I Loved" is incredibly difficult to cover, not only because it is so eccentric, but also because Robin Williamson's slightly Moroccan guitar playing in the original and his love of vocal grace notes are impossible things to recreate. Jackson Browne, with his New Orleans inflections and gospel feel, would seem an unlikely interpreter. But Jackson Browne, even in 1990, has the capacity to *feel* the original. Even if he is no Celtic/Moroccan bard, he somehow manages to bring something American to this saddest of stories: the relinquishment of the loves of one's youth. It's an honorable and creditable cover of a very important song.

What else is great? "Going Going Gone," by Robin Holcomb, Wayne Horvitz, and Bill Frisell. This is a Dylan cover of a song from *Planet Waves,* the only album Bob Dylan released under the auspices of Elektra. (I think he was feuding with Columbia at the time.) This recording is essentially a jazz supergroup covering Dylan. Robin Holcomb is an astounding singer,

with an Appalachian vibrato that sounds like an eighty-three-year-old woman warbling on her front porch in Kentucky. Bill Frisell, meanwhile, plays the distorted electric guitar, winding himself around Holcomb and Horvitz's organ until the end of the song, when he uncorks an astounding solo that goes on and on and on. Look, it is hard to say this, especially when Dylan religionists are potentially going to read this letter, but Holcomb's version is *far, far better* than Dylan's version. In fact, I cannot listen to this song without weeping, most of the time. It is sung with a sense of remorse and acceptance that is unapparent on the original, and with a truly adult worldview. That Robin Holcomb never got quite the attention she deserved is one of the cruel tricks of time, and if you have never heard her, you *must* listen to this recording.

How about the Kronos Quartet covering "Marquee Moon" by Television? This is the most strategically brilliant piece on *Rubaiyat*. The most clever. The most alarming and mesmerizing mix of performer and track. Kronos dispenses with the lyrics entirely, and cuts the whole thing down to pop-song length (4:14, to be exact). And they play it like this: part old-time hoedown, part legato romance, and part post-minimalist tract. But it all hangs together, especially when they get to the guitar solo, which they reconfigure into some kind of interlocking field of string arpeggios before the big crescendo. I, of course, admired other popular covers in the Kronos songbook (their "Purple Haze" *is* kind of great). But somehow this is more than all that. It's not show-offy, but rather has real appreciation for the original. Any time anyone asks me for a favorite cover, I offer this one, and have been doing so for years. It's geeky, it's original, it's loving, it's unexpected. All the things a great cover should be. But there are also hints of the sublime in this recording, a thing that classical players are allowed to tilt at but rarely show up in popular songs.

Those are the three best tracks, but there are others that are very nearly as great, like Metallica playing "Stone Cold Crazy," by Queen; an astounding Danny Gatton instrumental called "Apricot Brandy" (originally by Rhinoceros), sort of a jaw-dropper, really; a cover of "Hotel California" (please, no!) by the Gipsy Kings that *almost* ennobles all the parties involved; Ernie Isley doing a completely improbable cover of "Let's Go" by the Cars; Michael Feinstein doing Joni Mitchell's "Both Sides Now"; and, believe it or not, Howard Jones doing "Road to Cairo" by the cult hero (ask your indie-rock friends) David Ackles. I'm telling you, the

Howard Jones track is far better than it has any right to be.

That only begins to describe this overlooked gem, *Rubaiyat*. I would say fully half of the album is bad, some of it even awful, and I would say that a lot of the performers on *Rubaiyat* have been left behind by the march of history, and this is as it should be. I would say that *Rubaiyat* was probably not worth its list price at the time, and that's why it is not so widely remembered, as it should be. But it also has a great number of masterpieces on it, some of which I haven't even gotten around to describing this morning, and it reveals a laudably canny idea of what the tribute album might have been and could be again. More labels should do this!

But, more importantly, when you listen to the whole of *Rubaiyat,* you start to get a feel for what a cover is, what it can accomplish, and why the tribute is, when it works, such a beautiful thing. Because, at the end of the day, the songs are the thing. They are the coin of the realm, and often the songs reveal their glories in the improbable refractions, not *just* in the original.

Okay, time to get outside, McSweeney's. I can't spend the whole day with you.

Best wishes,
RICK MOODY
ASTORIA, NY

DEAR MCSWEENEY'S,
I would appreciate it if you could issue the following corrections:

1) When my band played the song "Motownphilly" recently, our drummer was accidentally playing the beat from Bell Biv DeVoe's "Poison." We regret the error.

2) Also—same song—some people were singing "east coast swing" and some were singing "east coast fling." Also, I think some people were singing "swing" but were tired and not enunciating well, so it kind of came out "shwing."

3) Also, nobody sang the walking bass line during the a cappella breakdown. I technically could have done it, but I lacked confidence.

4) When we were playing Ramones songs later that night, whenever there were lyrics about "Nazis" or "the Fatherland" I mumbled them. I feel uncomfortable singing about the Nazis, especially these days. Good Lord. I apologize for being so square.

5) On November 11, 2013, at a show in London, I sang the song "I'm So Bored With the USA," by the Clash. I'm not actually bored with the USA. I lived in Montreal for 10 years, and I pined for America. American

culture is my culture—Melville, Elvis, DuBois, Public Enemy, chili cook-offs, the customer always being right, George Washington on the money, our stupid bicameral national legislative body, our history of atrocity, our history of beautiful and noble action—I love my country deeply. I'm deeply invested in how we exist and act in the world. I feel personal responsibility. And I feel a collective responsibility—with my neighbors, my son's school teachers, the people waiting for the bus on the corner, the weirdo who runs the weirdly empty deli, the flight attendants, the cab drivers. And—pardon the cursing but jeez louise, the complaint about America these days is not that it's boring.

6) Additionally, I'm preemptively annoyed that someday I'll be running for public office, and some idiots unaffiliated with my worthy opponent will put out a video of me singing "I'm So Bored With the USA" when I was in my early 30s with a tagline like: "William Butler—Bored with the USA? Bad for the USA. Paid for by Facebook Robot Dads United for Freedom."

7) Also—and this, too, weighs heavy on my chest—in the second half of the first verse of "Motownphilly," I changed this one particular jazzy bass note to a less jazzy one. I knew it was wrong, and yet I played it. The jazzy note was just too hard to sing over. Maybe with more practice we could have done it properly.

Thank you. *Avec beaucoup d'affection*,
WILL BUTLER
BOSTON, MA

DEAR MCSWEENEY'S,
On November 12, 1955, Marty McFly, sitting in with Marvin Berry and The Starlighters, stepped up to the microphone to introduce his cover of "Johnny B. Goode." "This is, uh, this is an oldie…well… it's an oldie where I come from." With that, he turned to the band, gave them some quick instructions, and launched into one of the most famous guitar riffs in rock and roll history. Not a single member of the audience had ever heard it before.

A little over two years later, on March 31, 1958, the original release of "Johnny B. Goode" performed by the song's writer Chuck Berry appeared on the Chess Studios record label. The song about a country boy who "could play the guitar just like ringing a bell" was a top ten hit.

How could Marty McFly cover "Johnny B. Goode" before Chuck Berry released the original? Anyone who has seen *Back to the Future* knows that Marvin Berry called his cousin, Chuck Berry, during the performance Marty gave when he traveled back in time, and Chuck Berry heard his own song over the telephone. That made Chuck Berry's original 1958 recording a cover of a cover of his own song.

As a child, this blew my mind. Whose song was it if the original came second? Ignoring the time travel paradoxes created by the scenario (and the sticklers' discussion of exactly what part of Marty's performance was heard by Berry), *Back to the Future* highlights the implicit understanding that a performance of a song is considered a cover based on when it took place in time. If someone else performed it first, all subsequent performances are covers. Which is why, by fixing performances in time, the advent of recorded music seemed to establish that chronological distinction. Before recorded music, the notion of a cover didn't really exist.

It should be remembered, however, that in Chuck Berry's 1950s milieu, it was still common practice for an artist to record another artist's song without any concern for copyright. Big Mama Thorton's 1953 hit "Hound Dog" (recorded by Elvis Presley in 1956) was covered seven times within a month of Big Mama Thorton's original release, and that number does not include answer songs or parodies, which began appearing the same week of Thorton's release. With new recordings coming that quickly, contemporary audiences might not have known which one was the original and which were covers. For listeners, the historical facts of the recordings were irrelevant.

And then there is the possibility that the original recording isn't really the original. "Hound Dog," while written for Big Mama Thorton, was written by the songwriting team of Jerry Leiber and Mike Stoller. According to Leiber, when they handed the song to Thornton, she began crooning it in the style of Frank Sinatra. The songwriters envisioned the song as a moaning blues number, not a crooner, and it was only after Leiber sang the song to Thornton that she began to sing it as it appears on the record. So, in a way, the original Thornton recording was a cover of Jerry Leiber's performance. The "original," never recorded, no longer exists.

So while recorded music might have introduced the idea of a cover, perhaps it does not actually serve as the definitive measure of primacy. After all, when Chuck Berry performs "Johnny B. Goode" now, fifty-six years after recording the song, people do not consider his performance a cover. He has ownership of the song, whether it is as the songwriter or as the performer. His own recording doesn't make his live performance a cover. Just as the hundreds of covers of "Johnny B. Goode," some of which have been hits on the charts, diminish Berry's ownership. But, financial considerations aside, does that matter?

When *Back to the Future* was released, it was criticized by some for the suggestion that Chuck Berry needed to learn the "new sound" of rock 'n' roll from a white kid. Filmmakers Robert Zemeckis and Bob Gale, of course, meant it as just a gag, but the criticism highlights the attitude that the "original" version of a song has more value. But if a cover is defined by time, and if time for every individual is relative, then the sequence of original to cover becomes personal.

Which goes back to my blown childhood mind. *Back to the Future* was very likely the first time I ever heard the song "Johnny B. Goode." It certainly became the way I have heard the song the most in my life. So for me, it can be said that Marty McFly's version is *my* original, just as it is for the kids at the Enchantment Under the Sea dance, and that Chuck Berry's recording is a cover in my personal musical life. (On top of that, Marty is a fictional character played by the actor Michael J. Fox, who lip-synced Mark Campbell's vocals, and mimed Tim May's guitar, making the facts of the recording truly immaterial.) For me, *Back to the Future* got the chronology right, Marty played "Johnny B. Goode" and then Chuck Berry did.

This means, for a song, there is the "original" for the songwriter, the "original" for the performer, the "original" for the record company, and the "original" of a song for the listener, considered individualistically instead of historically. Anyone who has loved a song for years before finding out it is a cover has had that experience. In fact, "Johnny B. Goode" even serves as a good example of this, because the opening riff of the song comes note-for-note from the horn introduction to "Ain't That Just Like a Woman," a 1946 song recorded by Louis Jordan and His Tympany Five, making the beginning of the song a cover. But almost no one knows that now, so Berry's rendition of that riff is the "original" as far as the world is concerned.

So in my timeline, when the television replayed a pre-recorded audio track synced with a filmed video that purports to be set in a specific time in the past before the song "Johnny B. Goode" existed, and I heard it before I ever knew it was a song, that layered experience defined the "original." Everything else, regardless of historical facts, was a cover.

Reflectively,
ARIEL S. WINTER
BALTIMORE, MD

INTRODUCTION

by THE EDITORS

The first time we printed a cover story was back in 1999, with Issue 4 of this journal. Then, we asked Rick Moody to take a classic story he loved and do his own version of it—in the way a musician might cover another songwriter's song. Moody chose Sherwood Anderson's "The Egg," and the results were so extraordinary that we figured we'd invented some thunderclapping new literary form, and that we would do a cover story every issue. Then, for reasons mysterious to us now, all these years later, we didn't. Occasionally we remembered that we wanted to do cover stories, then we would forget. Then we would briefly remember again. Then forget. Then, during Obama's second term, when all was very quiet at our San Francisco headquarters as we worked through a rough period, we began this project in earnest. Now, seventeen or so years since the initial inspiration and two years since the project's inception, it emerges into a moment of racial, social, and economic reckoning and imminent fascism. This issue is being born into a country that looks much different from the one in which it began, fronted now by a meek and dangerous imitation of a president. Tucked between these thirteen beautiful renditions of thirteen classic stories is an instance when a cover is not an homage but rather a perversion of its predecessor. We hope these stories, though, will bring you back to the originals and remind you, as they did us, the value and possibility of building something new from that which came before it.

NOBODY KNOWS

an autobiography by GARY BURDEN

(Gary Burden, creator of some of the most iconic album art of the past sixty years, was the dream art director for our cover stories issue. He brought in his partner, Jenice Heo, to make the front and back collages, and also shared with us his extraordinary life story, some of which we're proud to present below.)

EARLY LIFE AND WWII

I'm telling my story assuming my life is of some interest to others mostly because I was a part of something big that happened when important changes were afoot led by rock and roll. I'm also telling my story because I think someone somewhere might find it helpful to read where I came from and where I ended up. I didn't have a plan, but I believed in myself and in the presence of a guardian angel or spirit guide who looked out for me. Because of that, I was able to endure some awful times and emerge to build a remarkable life.

My strongest memories begin from December 7, 1941 when I was eight years old. It was a Sunday and I was at my job at the feed store and hatchery near my mother's home where I was taught to sweep the floor with torn, wet pieces of newspaper that would pick up the dust. The man running the store was a very quiet and kindly old man named Mr. Calhoun. On that afternoon the tranquility of the rhythmic strokes of my broom and the music on the radio was interrupted by a loud panicked voice coming from the speaker yelling something I could in no way grasp: "Japanese sneak attack on Pearl Harbor." Suddenly, the mild-mannered Mr. Calhoun became irrational, crying and yelling at the radio. It scared me badly. I started crying too, dropped my broom, and ran out of the store. I ran all the way home and came in breathless and panting to find my whole family crying and yelling. It was utterly frightening. Finally my mother quieted down enough to try to explain what had happened. War? Bombing? Pearl Harbor? Japanese? Just words I didn't understand.

World War II had a profound effect on me in many ways and I have vivid memories of that period of my life. I was living with my mother in Miami. At night when I was in bed and I heard military planes feathering their props and making loud noises overhead, I was scared we were being bombed. As I came to understand the meaning of war and what we were up against, I found heroes in the brave soldiers, sailors, and marines of the United States military. The good guys and the bad guys were quickly defined in my young mind by the propaganda that pervaded every phase of life from the radio to magazines and films. War was the subject of every conversation I overheard the big people having. As a scrawny kid growing up without a father around very often, the soldiers became not only my heroes and my idols but, in some weird way, my big brothers and my father whom I could look up to.

I have a funny recollected image of this perpetually barefooted skinny kid in shorts and a polo shirt, trying to be a part of his heroes' lives. It is very touching and also pathetic how much I needed to be a part of something—to have some kind of family, anybody's family, because I didn't really have one of my own at home that I liked or could relate to. That kid never intellectualized about his life, but underneath was fueled by the overwhelming desire for a place to fit, a family to embrace. Instead of reflecting on his life, that kid just responded to it and, more often than not, got in trouble for his fearlessness and desire to absorb everything. I look back with a full heart for that little barefoot boy who was so free and unfettered and brimming with love.

MARINES

In 1950, when I was sixteen, I convinced my mother to sign papers saying I was seventeen so I could join the U.S. Marine Corps. Everything I knew about the Marines from movies and the propaganda that had shaped my life during WWII was that they were the best of the best. I dreamed of being a fighter pilot like the ones I had seen in the movies. In those days it was possible for an enlisted man to work his way up through the ranks to become a pilot. I would go through boot camp then to a basic airman's school and later be shipped to flight school at the Navy base at Pensacola, Florida. In my mind I was already sitting behind the controls of a Corsair shooting down enemy planes.

But first there was boot camp on Parris Island in a swamp off the east coast of South Carolina. Our days started at 4 a.m. with the screams of drill instructors and were filled with scrupulous inspections of our beds and foot lockers, scrubbing of the wooden planked floors and "decks" of our barracks with toothbrushes, training classes, calisthenics, and tons of marching and close order drills with our rifles. We would spend days doing hand-to-hand combat drills, climbing ropes, and running obstacle courses as training for a forced march at night in the swamps of South Carolina. We'd be given a compass, told where our rendezvous points were and be expected to get from point to point in the dark. I remember hearing a story about a group of recruits who years before had gotten lost in the swamp on this night march

and some of them drowned. It was a cautionary tale meant to strike fear.

I graduated from boot camp in the spring of 1950 and was assigned to the US Marines Air Station at Cherry Point, North Carolina. While I was waiting for a full class to be made at basic airman's school, I was shipped off to the Naval Air Station in Jacksonville, Florida. There, I did guard duty at nights, protecting the hangars at the air base. I did get to go on weekend passes and sometimes I would wait by the control tower and hitch rides on USMC transport planes going where I was headed or just somewhere to spend some time, then catch a flight back to base. We would sit on the floors inside the fuselage of the big transport planes or roll out blankets and clothing and go to sleep. No seat belts. If the plane went up or down radically, well then, so would the men in the cargo hold.

Sometimes, I would try to get hops to Miami. If I couldn't get a hop I would hitchhike or, on some crazy occasions, I would steal cars to drive down to Miami. My specialty was stealing cars from used car lots. I started doing this one night when I hitched to a small town where I was dropped off very late and there was no traffic and I couldn't get a ride. I saw a car lot, had an idea, and hot-wired a car that I would drive until it ran out of gas. Sometimes I would steal another one and continue on my trip. If I ever wanted to go into town and didn't have a pass I would just go to the boondock edges of the base, jump the high chain-linked fences, hitchhike into town, and then try to get back before morning, climbing back over the fence and sneaking into the barracks. I can't believe I never got caught doing that.

In the fall of 1950 I was transferred to the Basic Airman School at the Naval Aviation base at Millington, Tennessee, just outside Memphis. Rock and roll was just starting to get big and there was a lot boiling under the surface. I was there around the time Sam Phillips started Sun Records and Elvis Presley, Jerry Lee Lewis, Carl Perkins, and the rock and roll Johnny Cash were soon to follow. I was seriously dating a young woman who was from Memphis. She was my first experience with a "cool" chick. She and her friend who hung out with us were involved with a guy who was a very early DJ and in the radio and music business. I have no idea who that guy was. It could have been someone I would now know of but I had not a clue then. Looking back as someone who has spent 40 years up to my neck in rock and roll I see some parallel magical prelude connection that could have happened, though it never did. At that time in my life, I wouldn't have had any idea where or how I would fit into the music business.

I started going into Memphis nearly every night and hanging out with my girlfriend and her friends, who exposed me to marijuana for the first time. In 1950, for the most part, white guys didn't smoke pot unless they were jazz musicians. This behavior was certainly rare and totally unacceptable for the Marine Corps, who began to take notice of my changed lifestyle. The late nights with my girl smoking pot were starting to take their toll on me and I began falling asleep in class. The Marines sent me to see the medics and after an extensive battery of tests, including broad blood testing, they got their answer. I had marijuana in my blood. I was interviewed a few times by the FBI, who had been brought in to support the USMC provost marshall and the MPs, and then I was unceremoniously dropped from the Basic Airman School, my dreams of being a fighter pilot crashing and burning because of my stupidity.

I was assigned to the second Marine air wing at El Toro, California and lived in a quonset hut waiting to go to Korea. I had asked to go there and serve and that request seemed to have been granted. On nights off, I used to go into town or to Hollywood and sometimes into downtown LA on weekends. One late night I was out with a bunch of Marine buddies drinking beer in a seedy part of downtown and we met a young woman who was hanging out on the street. She was very willing, so a couple of my buddies and I got a hotel room and took her there, sex being the obvious objective. Things heated up and I had sex with her. I never gave it another thought until a few weeks later when I was visiting one of my Marine buddies who was part of a contingent of Hawaiian Marines had been with me when we encountered the young woman downtown. As it turns out, she was an underage runaway. Somehow the police tracked us down and arrested all of us for statutory rape. She was fifteen. I was still a teenager myself at the time, just eighteen years old. I was crushed and my world came crumbling down around my shoulders. Even as I write this I am getting emotional because it signals the beginning of the end of my service in the Marine Corps and the big changes coming to me that would affect me very deeply for the rest of my life.

A representative of the Marine Corps came to the LA county jail where I was serving a six-month sentence and delivered my UD, undesirable discharge. I certainly was an undesirable boy. It was an awful way to end my service. I was so depressed and ashamed of the way I left the Marine Corps that I entered a long period of denial. I could never admit to anyone how my service actually ended. I started lying to cover up the facts and telling people that I had actually served in Korea. Once that lie was told it was difficult to get out of. I had to lie to support the original lie, which is the way it is when you tell a lie. Now I realize how gross that was to do. It is an affront to all the good men and women who were there and died in service to our country. As I read this now, some sixty-odd years later, I still feel ashamed and embarrassed.

How does anyone survive growing up and becoming who you ultimately are? God only knows and he ain't telling. But I am, and I am certain that the revelation of this lie will impact many of my friends who think I did go to Korea. I apologize to them and ask for understanding. There is nothing else for me to do. For me a weight has been lifted and I am free of living a lie for so many years. It feels good.

POST MARINES

When I got out of the county jail with nothing but the clothes on my back, I fell in with a very shady crowd and managed to dig the hole I was in even deeper. Someone introduced me to heroin and it was the perfect drug for me at the time because I could shoot up and find relief by surrendering to the blackness and the void of mindlessness.

None of us had much money and all of us needed it to buy drugs so, in desperation, the gang started robbing stores, often at gunpoint. My job was sorting through the loot and figuring out how and where to turn it into cash, keeping the best drugs for ourselves. We would go into pharmacies and intimidate innocent working people who stood between the drugs and our needs. Once we strong-arm robbed a pharmacy filled with people. One of our guys had a gun and held the people while the others went through the shelves of drugs behind the counter of the pharmacy and emptied the cabinets of anything we could take, snort, or shoot. When I think of these moments, it is nearly impossible to believe that I was actually a part of this. It's like remembering some make-believe horror movie, but I'm in it.

By 1955–'56 I was back in Miami, trying and failing to get clean. I was dealing hard drugs. I had two customers who regularly bought drugs from me, a young woman from a wealthy Miami Beach family who was strung out in a big way and her boyfriend who was a former professional baseball player and also a heroin addict. The woman always bought plenty of drugs and introduced me to other dealers she knew. I was starting to make money from dealing drugs and I was meeting some larger-scale wholesale dealers who were noticing my successes.

After getting an introduction to a big-time drug wholesaler I decided to take a trip to visit him in Monterey, Mexico. This guy was importing super high-grade heroin from West Germany. I was being drawn into the world of dealing drugs and, though I didn't stop selling, I never felt good about doing it, or about my role in feeding and exploiting other people's misery. Even though

I had a rule of never turning anyone on for their first time, I went with the flow and didn't try to get out, in large part because it was a way to take care of my own habit. I decided that I would renew my efforts to try to get clean before I went down to Mexico.

I knew little or nothing about crossing the border to make this connection, but I knew I certainly wasn't going to transport drugs myself. At the last minute the woman from Miami decided that she would like to be a part of the deal, investing some cash up-front in exchange for a share of the shipment and then continuing on with me as a partner. I thought about it and decided that partnering with her could lead to big problems down the line, especially because she was strung out on heroin, so I politely refused her offer. In the end, though, against my better judgment, I agreed that she and her boyfriend could come with me but they would have to be clean and could not create any problems by letting their addiction get in the way.

I had a newish black-on-black 1955 Ford Thunderbird that was my pride and joy and the three of us squeezed into it and took off for Mexico. When we arrived in Monterey I called my connection and he told us where to stay and we made plans to meet up the following day. At his home we were surprised to find a number of imposing, armed guards in place outside the high steel bar fencing. The dealer was a heavyset Mexican man with a big smile and an imposing, even threatening demeanor. Because I speak fluent Spanish, we hit it off instantly.

We drank beers and smoked pot with him and began to outline our plan to import heroin to Miami, beginning with the modest quantity of a kilo to see how things went. Our meeting was successful and we agreed to go into business together. He would have the kilo shipped to me in Miami and I would pay half of it upon arrival and the second half soon after. He offered us a taste of his heroin. The woman and man with me were both instantly interested in doing that but I politely refused on the grounds that I was cleaning up in order to be a more reliable businessman. As we were leaving, I asked him if he was ever concerned about people coming to his house to rip him off. He smiled and lifted the corner of a mattress in the room revealing a US M1 carbine automatic rifle with a large clip filled with .30-caliber rounds, a shotgun, and several pistols. He pointed to his several "assistants" who were also packing pistols. I don't think he had anything to worry about from three dumb gringos.

The next morning we loaded into the T-Bird and headed back north to the border and on to Miami. We had planned to arrive at the border in the evening when the traffic would be lighter and cross back into the US. I was sleeping in the passenger seat when we arrived, sick from kicking the heroin. The moment we stopped, I was awakened by loud voices telling us to keep our hands where they could be seen and large-caliber pistols being pointed into both windows. We were herded out of the car, handcuffed, and led into the office where we were interrogated. "Do you have anything to declare? Are you bringing any contraband into the US?" Of course I said no because I had made a point to clean out the car and be certain there was no residue or roaches from the pot we had smoked. I argued we were legitimate tourists who went south of the border for harmless, legal fun and adventure. I was a college student on break. I had several props in the car including textbooks with University of Miami book covers on them. We were taken into separate rooms to have full body searches. I was, of course, clean. Not so much my wannabe partner: she had concealed an ounce of heroin in a condom inside her body. Obviously the person she had bought the heroin from was an informer and had turned her in along with the description of us and the car we were traveling in. Hence the reception committee at the border.

We were transported to the county jail in Laredo, Texas, where we were charged with smuggling heroin into the US. In those days the Feds had just introduced a new law that provided for anyone charged in a drug smuggling case to receive a mandatory five-year sentence, with no possibility of parole or probation. If I live to be a thousand I will never, ever forget the day I was sentenced and the judge said five years in federal prison with no possibility of parole or probation. Five years! It was very sobering news for a young man at the beginning of his life. I was 23 years old. Yet, though I never really had the remotest chance of receiving a fair trial, I finally came to accept my punishment. I thought to myself, five more Christmases and I will be out of prison. I had gotten away with so many illegal things in my young life that I figured this was a balancing out of my debt to society. Karma! I believe that this was God/my guardian angel's way of protecting me and telling me that the life I was headed for as a big time heroin dealer was not what I was destined for. I accepted my fate.

It was summer and the Laredo, Texas jail was hot as hell. The June bugs were out in full force and the jail was filled with the huge black cockroach-like insects. They were everywhere, walking over me in the night as I slept. Mexican border music played constantly on the radio with loud commercials blaring "Sin enganches" repeated over and over along with a telephone number. It means no down payment.

In 1964 after my second wife, Annette, and I moved to Los Angeles, where I was working as an architectural and interior designer, a friend who was a finish carpenter told me that the singer Mama Cass of the Mamas and Papas had just purchased a home in Laurel Canyon and needed architectural and interior designs. He set up a meeting with Cass Elliot. It was love at first sight. She was such a wonderful person and we clicked immediately. She was so warm and beautiful, it made me feel good just talking with her.

We agreed we wanted to work together and I went with her the next morning to look at the house she had just purchased. It was going to require major work, including taking off the roof in one section to create a guest suite and extensively remodeling her bedroom and bathroom in the master suite. I went to work making drawings and meeting with potential craftsmen to work on the job for her. We were rolling.

I had some very good design ideas for Cass's home. In particular, I came up with a bedroom that was perfectly suited to her lifestyle. Cass loved to be in her bedroom and lounging in bed so I made it amazing for her. I had craftsmen build a custom bed that started with a king-size mattress and was surrounded by a canopy framework of ancient hand-carved Indian wood posts and beams with elaborate carved details of animals and human figures. I had tie-dyed heavy, high-quality velvet drapes that hung on the frame and tie-dyed a velvet bedspread to match. When the drapes were closed, the bed became a dark, separate environment unto itself. It was like a cocoon that Cass could close off and be isolated from everything outside her bed. I also built a television into the ceiling at the foot of the poster bed frame. This was before flat screen TVs, so it was an engineering challenge. The coolest thing was the built-in storage at the base of the bed frame and, best of all, a built-in refrigerator that could be filled with late-night snacks. The bed was a beautiful piece and Cass loved it. It became our place to lounge, smoke pot and talk.

As the plans for her house evolved, Cass and I began to spend most every day all day together starting with a breakfast at Nate & Al's deli in Beverly Hills or The Old World on Sunset Boulevard. That spot was owned by Jim Baker who also owned the Aware Inn, the first organic restaurant I ever went to. Later he opened The Source, also on Sunset, which became famous when he established his notorious cult there. At the Aware Inn we'd be joined by one or another of Cass's musician friends, including David Crosby, who I was immediately the best of friends with. I remember once after a long day of tripping on STP we went there for dinner; Cass, Crosby, and me. During the dinner Crosby fell asleep, with his face nearly in his plate. Cass and I got up quietly, slipped out, and left him there… with the check.

I loved Cass's house. If you know about Gertrude Stein's salon in Paris in the early 1900s where she brought together the crème de la crème of the art world during that period, including Picasso and his gang of painters, Cass's house in Laurel Canyon was much the same but it was the crème de la crème of the world of rock and roll music. Nearly every day and night there would be people hanging out in the house or by the pool, talking, playing music, or just absorbing one another. I remember many days taking acid and floating in the swimming pool and tripping to fantastic places inside my head. It was an idyll in a time when magic was the normal order of the day. Everyone was opening and blooming like exotic flowers and there was so much creativity coming from every direction at once. All of the possibilities were amplified. It was easy to believe anything was possible and people accepted that and operated in that way. Amazing things happened then.

I remember one particular afternoon when David Crosby and Stephen Stills were there. Stephen was at liberty because the Buffalo Springfield had broken up and David had been fired from the Byrds. They were talking about what they would do next and wanted to do something together. Cass said she had an idea and placed a call to Graham Nash who she'd met when she was in London and he was still a part of the Hollies. They didn't immediately get him but later, when we all cruised over to record producer Paul Rothchild's house, they called Graham again. Cass knew that the three of them would make amazing music together. She heard it in her head. Stephen and David liked the idea too. Graham was in, and from Cass's head the world-famous band Crosby, Stills and Nash was born. They weren't originally called that. They started out calling themselves, half jokingly, The Frozen Noses.

From the very beginning, it seemed like I was fulfilling my destiny to be a part of this group of friends who were doing big things. And, though I didn't really know it at the time, I could sense that Cass's house was the doorway into a new life. At first, the friendships I made there were strictly social. I was not making album covers yet. I was the architect guy. The cover designing came later and happened quite organically. One afternoon, Cass and I were sitting out by her pool talking and she told me she had decided I should make album covers. She knew me to be a good artist, capable of overseeing a job and getting things done, whatever the task. She loved my "eye" and how I could see beauty in the world around me, she said. I protested that I knew absolutely nothing about graphic art or printing

or any of the myriad other things needed to produce an album cover. I never had any real interest in that kind of artwork. I was into more substantial and lasting forms of art, like designing architecture and beautiful interior spaces or fine art, painting and sculpture. Yes, I was a good drawer and spent a lot of every day drawing and dreaming up things, but not graphic art. She insisted that she knew I could do it and wanted me to make the album cover for a new Mamas and Papas album they were currently working on. She finally convinced me that I could and should do it, and my career born. Here I am, more than forty years later, still making art for music.

Looking back, I realize how amazing it was that by some circuitous and random route, I had arrived and was fulfilling my destiny. I believe Cass knew that and understood her role in this moment. Anyone who ever knew her would say she was their best friend, and she was. There is no way to describe how much I loved, and still do. She was a special human being and we shared something extraordinary in our friendship. I made a point of telling and showing her how much I appreciated what she was doing for me. She gave me a good life that I would not have had otherwise and I know that. I really miss her and wish she were still around to hang out with, to laugh with, and to share things in life with. Cass was deeply and seriously funny, super smart and magically intuitive. She just knew things others didn't and couldn't because she was the one and only.

JIM MORRISON

In the summer of 1966, I was going to the Whiskey with some frequency. It was just up the hill from my home so it was easy getting there and back, even half drunk. In this period the Doors had become sort of the house band there and played every night for more than a month, until Jim Morrison got too deeply into the Oedipal section of "The End" and the parents and authorities raged against his "lewd" performance. The Doors were fired! The owner of the Whisky, Elmer Valentine, had a business to run. For all of the new-found freedoms of the '60s, things were not so much changed that there were no remaining guardians of strict rules of behavior. The first time I saw the Doors live it was at a house party off of the Sunset Strip. I was standing right next to Jim, not a foot away from him. Now that was *experiencing* a band up close and personal. Not a bad house band for your private party. I didn't really know Jim then. That was to come later. We became the best of friends and serious drinking buddies around the time when I made the art for *Morrison Hotel* in 1970.

That gig came about when I was in the recording studio at Elektra records with an artist named Joel Scott Hill. Joel was a well-known studio musician, and a great guitar player and singer. I was making his album cover art. The record was being produced by the famous Paul Rothchild, a good guy who I never knew that well, but traveling in the same circles made us aware of each other. Some years before, Cass, David Crosby, Stephen Stills, and I had gone to Paul's house so they could call Graham Nash in London and convince Graham to join them in the new band. He was also the person who brought me in to make the cover for Joel Scott Hill. While I was shooting some images of Joel, I started talking with Paul about another project he was working on at the time—the Doors. He said I should meet Jim Morrison and talk to them about making their new cover.

As it turned out, Jim had a small room in the Clear Thoughts building, where the Geffen/Roberts offices were, that he was using as an editing room for a film he was working on, *HWY: An American Pastoral*. I had seen him there at the Clear Thoughts building off and on and got to know one of Jim's best friends, a guy named Babe. I don't know Babe's last name, never did, but he was a cool guy, a big biker-looking dude who had a very good heart and was easy to talk to. To discuss the album cover I met with the Doors to discuss their album cover at their office, which was just down the street from the Clear Thoughts building on the corner of Santa Monica Boulevard and La Cienega. Whenever I pass by that old building I think of those days and of Jim, who I really came to love.

As Jim and I got to know one another we discovered lots of things we shared in common. A major one was that his girlfriend, Pam Courson, and my wife, Annette, were lifelong friends. They had gone through elementary, junior high, and high school together as rebel girls, with the bond of 'weirdos' who believed outside the mainstream. What were the odds of that happening? Once Jim and I connected we began spending lots of time together, drinking and going to films. You could find us quite often at Coogies on La Cienega, a restaurant bar named after the band leader Xavier Cugat, who was a big star from the forties. His wife was the coochie-coochie-coo girl, Charo.

The Doors always had incredibly cool album cover art for each of their albums. When we got down to talking about what we would do for this cover, Ray Manzarek brought up a place he and his wife Dorothy had discovered one day when they were driving around downtown LA—the Morrison Hotel. A few days after our meeting, the band and I, along with Henry Diltz, went to shoot the pictures. We all loaded up into John Densmore's VW van and went to this location to see what photos we could get. The hotel offered great possibilities. It was a pretty seedy place. Jim said it felt like a place where you could plot a murder or start a revolution.

The name of the hotel was painted on the front window looking into the lobby and that seemed like a pretty good place for a cover shot. Everyone stood around the sidewalk in front of the hotel while we scoped out the inside. There were chairs just inside the window where the band could sit and be framed by the Morrison Hotel lettering. Perfect! Henry spoke to the guy behind the front desk and told him we wanted to shoot a photo of the band sitting there, but the desk clerk denied our request. When Henry came out and reported the news, and we were discussing alternatives, we noticed the man leave front-desk, get into the elevator and disappear. Quickly, the band went inside and sat in the window and Henry started shooting. I noticed that he was too close to get the full effect of them inside and I told him to use a longer lens and back up so as to get everyone in the frame and flatten the image. I like the effect of shooting with a long lens, the way everything is flattened and graphic-looking. We shot a roll or two of film and felt we had gotten it, so we loaded back in the van. Just like that we made history with the famous image.

We continued driving around downtown and wound up in the seediest part of skid row—lots

HAVING A COKE WITH YOU*

by REBECCA LINDENBERG

for my sister

is even more fun than going to Berlin, Vernazza, the Barceloneta, the wine cellars of Eger,
the Turkish baths, being lightheaded with mirth on the Hop On Hop Off in Budapest
partly because in your hot-pink scarf you look like a better cheerier Grace of Monaco
partly because of my love for you partly because of your love for pâté
partly because of the Aperol-orange tulips around the churches
partly because of the secrecy our smiles take on before hipsters and boulevards
it is hard to believe when I'm with you that there can be anything as mundane as
unpleasantly earnest as hipsters when right in front of us the warm 4 o'clock light is
tangoing with the waves coming out from under the Oberbaumbrücke and we with our feet
on the rail of the boat are drifting back and forth
between each other like a language known only to the astronomers of some obsolete
dynasty, or to our unique zippering of chromosomes, or swans

and the posters laquered to all the walls and the billboards at the tram stations and on the
sides of buses seem to have no faces in them at all just looks you've given me like Don't
you dare invite these lads to sit down with us, or I would push you in front of traffic for a
sandwich right now, or Hey listen to this bicycle bell, or whatever

I listen to you and I would rather listen to you than all the catchy tunes in the world
except possibly for Lou Reed occasionally that melancholy one about the right kind of day
which thank heavens you also love so I can watch how you listen like when in high school we
got a little tipsy backstage with the opening band at a Los Lobos concert and the fact that
you laugh so gloriously more or less takes care of nihilism
just as I never think about Nietzsche at home or
on a bike ride a single line by Chekhov or Nine Inch Nails even though I'm kind of wowed by
both and what good does all the machismo of the avant-garde do them
when they never got the right person to wink back at them over a cup of tiny coffee
or for that matter poor Possum when he didn't consider the notion as carefully
as the words

it seems they were all cheated of some splendid experience
which is not going to go wasted on me which is why I am telling you about it

---

* after "Having a Coke with You" by Frank O'Hara

of bum bars and people lounging on the streets looking for a handout to get a drink. We turned a corner and there was a bar called The Hard Rock Cafe. It looked like a possible location so we parked and scoped things out. The minute we were on the sidewalk we were surrounded by bums looking for money. Every one of them had a sad story to tell about how they wound up on the street. Jim, ever the poet, wanted to hear all of their stories.

It seemed like a good time to go inside and get a drink. We bellied up to the bar surrounded by all of our new friends and started buying rounds of drinks for the bums. Jim, more than anyone else, was deeply engaged in conversations with these men. He had sincere empathy for them and seemed to find all of their sad stories of great interest. We had a few beers and were shooting pictures all the while. Jim was the center of attention, perhaps because he was the one buying the drinks, or maybe because he was the most generous of heart. We shot lots of pictures both inside and outside the bar and finally moved off towards the van, trailing a small crowd of new friends still looking for more money from us.

Shortly thereafter I got a call from the record company looking for some publicity photos of the band. So Henry and I met up with the Doors, loaded back into John Densmore's VW van, and headed to Venice. Venice was the Doors' natural habitat because when they first got together both Jim and Ray were living in Venice; actually, Ray was living there and Jim used to crash on the couch at Ray and Dorothy's place. We started out shooting group pictures against a wall mural of a street scene then moved down to the beach itself where we got some wonderful photographs of them on the sands and on the monkey bars. Jim swung on the swings and climbed up on the lifeguard stand. We stopped in a liquor store and Jim got a bottle of rotgut wine that he wrapped in a brown paper bag, hobo-style, and continued swigging. Someone came up to him and offered him a joint, which he and I shared. Turns out it wasn't just pot but pot laced with PCP and both Jim and I got totally ripped and pissed off about being dosed unexpectedly. Suddenly, we were both tripping whether we liked it or not. There's nothing worse than a cheap psychedelic trip with some shit drug like PCP. I hated it, but we still managed to enjoy our time in Venice and got some great photos of the band. The afternoon wrapped up with a giant lunch of Mexican food at the Lucky U, a well-known Venice restaurant and that was the capper to a wonderful day.

Jim and I continued hanging out and drinking together. He was something very special. I know he has been cast as an addict, a drunk, and a wastrel but from my perspective he was a real poet, someone who was unafraid of delving deeply into life irrespective of the personal cost. He wanted to taste life to the fullest as a way of feeding his poetry.

NEIL YOUNG

By 1969, I was making album covers for some of the most prominent artists of the time, many of whom became my family. That little barefooted boy in Miami who longed to find a more monumental love than he had known in his own family found it in the friendships that began true expression of that love through the friendships that began at Cass's house and eventually expanded out like a galaxy to the wider musical universe. Cass was my center, the matriarch of my burgeoning soul family, and eventually Neil Young was to become my brother. At first, though, he was more like a shadow figure appearing on the edges of my life like a fantastic dream.

Long before I actually met Neil, I was a fan and saw him play at the Whisky when he was in the Buffalo Springfield. They were my favorite band. I have always thought they were America's answer to the Beatles. Every bit as good! In those days Neil was rocking his Native American western look with his now-famous fringed leather jacket. The music was simply amazing and when Neil and Stephen traded guitar licks the walls of the Whiskey would pulse and threaten to explode. The beautiful young chicks in the go-go cages would get so caught up in the music they would space out and forget to frug and gyrate.

I was spending most of my days at Cass's house, designing her rooms, floating in the pool, smoking pot, meeting and sharing ideas with the endless stream of friends that congregated there. One day, I saw an old 1948 black Buick hearse parked in Cass's driveway. I took note of it since it was quite a unique ride. A guy came out of the house wearing a fringe jacket just like Neil Young's. *Hey, holy cow, it was Neil himself!* He smiled and said hello, very friendly like. I was stunned, but I played it cool. He got into his hearse and was gone.

I didn't see him again until I was working with Crosby, Stills and Nash. By then I had become the album cover guy and the architectural designer guy was gone, faded into history. David, Stephen, Graham, and I were very close, spending almost every day together, beginning with breakfast and trailing on into languorous afternoons of laughter, pot-smoking, and music. How sweet it was! When it came time for CSN to make their second album they decided they needed a second guitar player and songwriter. Neil was the obvious choice. Not only was he already a friend of and partner guitar slinger with Stephen from their Buffalo Springfield days but Neil and CSN had the same managers, Elliot Roberts and David Geffen.

I clearly remember those days when I first met

Neil formally and we started hanging out and bonding. Stephen was renting a house in Laurel Canyon from Peter Tork of the Monkees. The house was owned by Wally Cox, otherwise known as Mr. Peepers. It was a large old rambling ranch-style place on a big plot of land with a commercial kitchen, many bedrooms, and a large swimming pool. Before Peter Tork, the Rolling Stones had rented the place to rehearse for a tour or an album they were working on at the time. In one of the large rooms, CSNY set up their studio. They draped Indian fabrics over packing pads hanging from the walls for soundproofing and brought in a 16-track recording board so they could learn each other's songs, rehearse them, and then put them down on tape.

I spent nearly every day, all day at that house. There was a cook who made food for us all day long and, of course, there was a robust cadre of David Crosby's "groupies," beautiful young women who floated about all day, skinny dipping and indulging with the rest of us in one excess or another. Oh boy!

In this setting, little by little, Neil and I began hanging out together and becoming friends. Our first bonding was over our love of cars. Though the hearse was probably a better fit for his tall frame, Neil was now driving a funky little white Austin Mini Cooper. Coincidentally, I was driving one too,; mine was an amazing 1967 souped-up chocolate brown mini that I bought from Hollywood Sports Cars, tore apart, and rebuilt as a hot rod. I used to drive it over Mullholland so fast and dangerous that I could taste burning brain cells on my tongue.

If we weren't at the rehearsal house, Neil and I would head over to my house in West Hollywood. I had an old wooden three-car garage out behind my house that I used as my art studio. Neil was often distraught in these days over the break-up of his first marriage, to Susan Acevedo, and I think he found some comfort from this emotional hell by escaping Topanga and hanging out with me in my studio. Eventually, after he and Susan divorced, he found land and moved up north, offering to sell me his house in Topanga for exactly what he paid for it. It was a beautiful thing he did for me and my family. It was worth much more than the forty grand I paid for it. Nowadays it would easily be worth millions. The house had been set up for Neil to make records and so the bottom floor housed the studio where *After the Gold Rush* was recorded. I turned that room into my art studio. It was pretty trippy working in the same room where Neil had made records. The house itself was really cool; it was two towers, each three stories tall, connected by bridges, all made of redwood. Sort of an upscale hippie pad, it had been built by the man who owned the Topanga, Corral, a famous club in the canyon where many bands played, including Neil. Later, when I was living in Topanga I put together a benefit for the local Chumash Indian medicine man Semu Huate, who was a friend of mine. The Eagles, Neil, and Joni Mitchell played there and we used the monies raised to hire a lawyer to stop Pepperdine University from destroying the canyon with a housing development.

In 1970, after a painful fiasco involving a documentary tour film I directed for CSNY, Neil asked me to make the album art for *After the Gold Rush*. For that cover I decided to use one of the photos that Joel Bernstein had taken on a day when Neil, Graham, and I were walking around the streets of New York during the CSNY tour. I was filming Neil and Graham for my documentary and Joel was snapping away. There was this great shot of Neil going one way and a little old Italian lady passing behind him going the other way and it looked like their bodies were one. I wanted to use that photo and also emphasize something in the cover that spoke to the title of the record. I thought, what would be left after a gold rush? Rust! So, I made the lettering look like rusty metal. I spent a lot of time getting the rust lettering just right. It turned out okay, but if I made it today I could do a better job. I have learned a lot in the nearly fifty years since I started doing this work and I like to think I have gotten better and better at it. As for Neil and I, we've been friends, artistic collaborators, and brothers for most of those fifty years. He was my best man when Jenice and I got married and we are in each other's lives daily and that too has gotten better and better.

SECOND ACT

Few people are given a second act. Back in the day, I met Cass and subsequently Crosby, Stephen, Joni, Neil, and all of the other artists from that time who became my family and gave me an unbelievably amazing life. I'd be a fool to ask for or want anything more. But here I am, getting more. At eighty, after many years of work, I'm finally fulfilling a lifelong dream of being a film producer. *The Monkey Wrench Gang*, by Edward Abbey, which I have been trying to get made for twenty-six years, is finally happening and starts production soon. More importantly, I've been reborn into yet another musical family of artists and best friends like Conor Oberst and Jim James who are living the same connected life of music friends and family, just like we did in the '60s and '70s. How sweet it is to have yet another opportunity to make art and have a family with people you love. Not too shabby for an outlaw Florida "cracker", dope fiend, armed robber, ex-convict, criminal with little or no formal training. For that I thank the Creator for my gifts and hope I have made him/her/it proud.

THE BABYSITTER

by EMILY RABOTEAU

after "Some Women" by Alice Munro

The night before Thanksgiving, someone whom I had not been told about arrived at Mrs. Fagan's house claiming to be a family member. I was upstairs singing the little girl to sleep when I heard a car roll into the driveway blasting the Grateful Dead, and then someone charging up the front steps to yank the handle of the front door. Finding it locked, the person called, "Ellie!" which I had never heard my employer called. The voice belonged to a teenager, or a man, and it was mocking and sure of itself.

I went downstairs, suspicious of the stranger now drumming on the door. I opened it a crack after putting on the chain. He stood so close that even in the jaundiced porch light I could make out every pore, every tiny red vein in the sclera of his eyes. Darkness expanded behind him like a never-ending cape.

"Oh shit! Is this the right house?" He named the address.

"Yeah."

"Who are you supposed to be?"

I told him I was the babysitter, and that Mrs. Fagan would be back any minute. Immediately, I worried I shouldn't have let on she was gone. The young man said that his name was Dennis.

"I'm the son."

I looked at him blankly, without undoing the chain.

"Dennis."

I didn't say anything, and he could tell I was stumped.

"The stepson. Ellie was married to my dad. She didn't tell you I was coming for Thanksgiving?"

I shook my head. He didn't look a thing like the dead man in the picture. Philip.

"Oh, man. That's just like her to forget. She's a total airhead sometimes. But check this out."

He held a frozen twenty-pound turkey hooked on his finger by its trussed legs. "Open the door, please, kid? It's cold as a witch's tit out here."

He wore a baja hoodie that smelled of cigarettes and made him seem young, as did the ripped knees of his acid-washed jeans. But his face was deeply

tanned in a way that made him look much older, like the tan went down to his skull. He could have been eighteen or thirty-five. I couldn't tell. He wore a Birkenstock sandal on one foot and a navy blue Aircast on the other. Something told me not to trust him, and he perceived this, too.

"I'm not gonna hurt you, if that's what you're thinking. I just want to start cooking this bird."

"Mrs. Fagan will be back any minute," I repeated.

"She's paying you to watch the kids while she's out, right? Maya and Eddie? See, I know their names and I already told you mine. Dennis the Menace. What's yours?"

I didn't want to say. They were always warning you not to talk to strangers in those days, when they printed images of missing children on milk cartons and ran public service announcements at the top of the nightly news: *It's 10 p.m. Do you know where your children are?*

"Now you're just being rude. Did anyone ever tell you you're cute when you're being rude?" he tried.

"No."

"Well, you are. I'm going to call you Rudy the Cutie."

"That's not my name."

"How 'bout Rudy Two Shoes?"

"Stop it."

"Okay, Rudy Huxtable."

Flustered, I told him my name.

"Nice to meet you, Dana. Let's start over and play nice." He batted his eyelashes, which were thick, like he had on mascara. I noticed the crow's feet at the edges of his eyes. A faint sense of alarm buzzed through me.

"You're the babysitter. I'm the big brother. Right?"

"So?"

"*So,* you have to babysit me, too."

"What do you mean?"

"Open the door, now, sweetheart. It's your job."

I can hardly believe I'm the same age now that Eleanor Fagan was when I began to babysit her children. At that time I was myself a child. Though there is much I have forgotten in the intervening years, I can conjure everything about myself in her house, as through a viewfinder. I felt in the wing of a stage I might as well call womanhood, on which a great drama was about to unfold. I can still remember all the games my girlfriends and I used to play: light as a feather stiff as a board, spit, cat's cradle, cootie-catcher, and M.A.S.H.; games that foretold which boy in the sixth grade we would grow up to marry, how many kids we would have, and whether we would live with this family in a mansion, apartment, shack, or house. I remember the words to all the songs we used to sing, the *smack-smack*

of the jump rope against the blacktop, and the thrill of rushing under the rope when it peaked in the air like a raised eyebrow. *Cinderella, dressed in yella, went upstairs to kiss her fella. Made a mistake and kissed a snake. How many doctors did it take? 1, 2, 3, 4, 5...* We girls believed equally in fortune and misfortune in those days. Either you could become magically rich in some way that involved a man or you would remain poor and turn out miserable like the woman who raised you.

It was because of Eleanor Fagan's misfortune that I got my first babysitting job in the summer before seventh grade, when I was twelve years old. I was paid ten dollars an hour. Back then that was two and a half times the going rate.

Mrs. Fagan lived at the end of a cul-de-sac on the opposite side of town near the graduate school and the private swim club. I could not call her Eleanor, as she asked me to do on my first day. My mother, who called her "the widow," would have smacked me for such familiarity. Nor did it ever occur to me to address the woman as Professor Fagan. That was her title, but not even the media called her that. Instead, they referred to her somewhat mockingly as Lady Jones, after the Indiana Jones movies. This was because Eleanor Fagan had been to East Africa, where she had allegedly witnessed the Ark of the Covenant. She'd authored a controversial book about the content of the tablets, for which she'd appeared on public television and in *Time* magazine. The book was banned in parts of Florida, and in Texas, where it was also burned. At some point during Eleanor Fagan's glowing career, or prior to it, she'd married her mentor, an archaeologist twenty years her senior with whom she'd adopted two Ethiopian children, but this husband had recently died in a mountain climbing accident. She'd accepted a position at the university in our town in order to start afresh. Very little of this information was shared with me at the time. In our neighborhood, Eleanor Fagan was famous for being the white lady with the black kids.

The little girl, Maya, was three. Eddie, the boy, was only ten months old. There was also an au pair named Femke from a place called Belgium. I was hired to look after the children on Wednesday evenings and Saturdays, when Femke had her break.

My simple instructions were to play with the children. In the den were a closet full of art supplies and a shelf of picture books. In the living room were an upright piano, a rocking horse, and an antique dollhouse that had been Mrs. Fagan's when she was a girl. In Eddie's nursery was a chest full of chewable plastic toys. In Maya's room there was a zoo of stuffed animals, and a live albino rabbit named Claude Hopper in a cage. She also had a bed with an enviable ruffled canopy and a ceiling painted with a mural of the sky. I was to help myself to anything I, Maya, or Eddie might want to eat in the kitchen. Two things baffled me since this was so clearly a household with money—the place was filthy and without a TV.

That summer, Mrs. Fagan didn't leave the house. She just shut herself in her bedroom suite and attended her grief by napping, sobbing, or listening to a cassette tape of Glenn Gould playing Bach's Goldberg Variations. The atmosphere of depression in the house grew thickest when you approached her room. Her eyes were so perpetually red-rimmed and bloodshot from crying that in my memory they are pink, like the pet rabbit's. On Saturday afternoons at three o'clock, Mrs. Fagan was visited by a male masseur who carried a padded table that folded in half. I intuited that she didn't want to be bothered.

Since it was too hot outside to play, I mainly rolled around on the crusty Persian carpet with Maya and Eddie, doing peekabo and itsy-bitsy spider. Whether or not they were biological siblings—I never discovered if they were and almost immediately stopped caring—they looked alike with their burnt-umber skin and large, otherworldly eyes. I made it my project to teach Eddie to walk, letting him grab my pointer fingers for balance. Maya didn't want to play with me at first. She regarded me suspiciously while sucking her thumb and tried to bite me when I changed her diaper. Eventually I won her over by grabbing her ankles and swinging her in ellipses until we both grew dizzy—a game we simply called dizzy time. She had a bad habit of withholding her poop until it calcified into pellets, which she would hide about the house like Easter candy. Supposedly she'd been potty trained before her father died but she refused the potty now. Her only ambition was to gain entrance to her mother's room. I learned to bribe her with pretzel sticks to stop her from ramming the door with her head. For dinner I fed her and Eddie Kraft macaroni and cheese and frozen peas, which I cooked in a pot on the stove. When Femke returned at nine o'clock, I helped her to bathe them, dress them in their pajamas, and tuck them in bed, though they were never in the vicinity of sleep by the time Mrs. Fagan emerged from her room, rubbing her temples, to drive me home.

When my mother heard about this arrangement she couldn't understand why the widow didn't impose an earlier bedtime, at a decent hour for little babies. She was also confused about the widow's profession. How could a person be employed if they were at home all the time instead of at their job? And she was critical of Maya's hair, on display when Femke brought the children to town for story hour at the public library. On this point, all the women in our neighborhood agreed. Mrs. Fagan's emotional sloppiness was evident in the untamed afro of her adopted daughter (they never said "daughter"). To them, unkempt hair was clear evidence of neglect.

"Box braids, Dana. Do them tight."

I explained that they did not have the right hair-care products at the house, but I didn't tell my mother that I'd come to know this by spying in every drawer during the kids' random naptimes. The only rooms I hadn't ransacked were Femke's, which was locked, and Mrs. Fagan's, which was occupied, as I've explained.

"Lord, give my child the strength to put that poor white woman's house in order," prayed my mother. Isaiah 38 was among her top five Bible verses. She sent me back with a jar of petroleum jelly, a wide-toothed comb, a tube of Queen Verlene hot oil treatment, and a packet of bright little barrettes from the drugstore.

But that small gesture just showed how little my mother understood about the extent of the mess in the Fagan household. It could not be fixed by such products. The whole place reeked of dirty diapers. Boxes from their move went unpacked, blocking the hallways. Laundry went undone, spilling out of the hamper, strewn about. The trash went un-emptied, the kitchen floor un-mopped. Food grew angry-looking mold. There were ants. Mrs. Fagan was blind to the mayhem, or else she relished the way it matched some inner feeling: the countertops sticky with jelly and juice, the backsplash splattered with old tomato sauce, the

H ere is a mantra, a short one, that I give you.
You may imprint it on your hearts and let every
breath of yours give expression to it. The mantra is:
"Do or Die." We shall either free India or die in the
attempt; we shall not live to see the perpetuation of
our slavery. Every true Congressman or woman will
join the struggle with an inflexible determination
not to remain alive to see the country in bondage and
slavery. Let that be your pledge. Keep jails out of your
consideration. If the Government keep me free, I will
not put on the Government the strain of maintaining
a large number of prisoners at a time, when it is in
trouble. Let every man and woman live every moment
of his or her life hereafter in the consciousness that
he or she eats or lives for achieving freedom and will
die, if need be, to attain that goal. Take a pledge, with
God and your own conscience as witness, that you
will no longer rest till freedom is achieved and will
be prepared to lay down your lives in the attempt to
achieve it. He who loses his life will gain it; he who
will seek to save it shall lose it. Freedom is not for the
coward or the faint-hearted.

—*Mahatma Gandhi, from the*
"Quit India" speech, 1942

The opinion of this so-called judge, which essentially
takes law-enforcement away from our country, is ridiculous and will be overturned!

—*@realDonaldTrump, February 4, 2017*

windows grimy with little handprints, the hill
of unopened mail on the dining room table, the
urine-soaked wood pulp at the bottom of Claude
Hopper's cage. I could never get the advancing
army of Legos, puzzle pieces, and Tinker Toys that
pushed in an aggressive front across the floor to
retreat. And one time I found Eddie munching
on a used maxi pad as if it were a biscuit.

Overlooking this disarray was a framed photograph of the dead husband in a bright yellow
windbreaker. It had been taken on his last expedition in the Andes, by whom I do not know,
minutes before he died, and it hung in the stair-
well. There were rumors that he jumped. I didn't
like to look at it.

My mother was a Jehovah's Witness, so she
was interested in the interior of the house as far
as it reflected Mrs. Fagan's troubled soul. On
the outside, the house was far fancier than ours.
She managed to peek in once, on my second
Saturday there. I was in the kitchen, raking a
ball of Play-Doh out of Eddie's mouth while
Maya whacked me on the back of the head with
a spatula. I kneeled there, mortified, hearing her
signature knock before she trilled out my name.
"Da-na!" Then, the sound of her rifling though
her pleather handbag for a copy of the *Watchtower.*
I didn't dare move. I ignored the doorbell when
she rang it, and rang it again. Finally, Mrs. Fagan
padded down the stairs.

My mother explained that she wanted to be sure I was doing a decent job with the little ones and to bring me my asthma pump, which I'd forgotten. She also wondered how Mrs. Fagan was managing in her time of trial. "Dana's a godsend," Mrs. Fagan said in a chirpily condescending voice, without inviting her in. I had no idea how she'd gotten this impression of me from her position on the second floor. "I'll see that she gets her inhaler," she said.

I knew my mother couldn't see past the vestibule into the wreck and I was glad for that. She wouldn't have been able to stop herself from attacking its clutter and I would have felt even more embarrassed for Mrs. Fagan than I already did. I'd seen the Division of Youth and Family Services called into houses on John Street, where we lived, for lesser infractions. My mother recited some shopworn stuff about leaning on the cross, pushed her literature into Mrs. Fagan's hands, and took off.

That night my mother said that the widow was out of God's favor because she hadn't prostrated herself before Him. What did it matter that she'd laid eyes on the Ark if she didn't bear witness to the basic commandments? Fancy degrees could not compare with true wisdom in faith. She did not even belong to a church. She wasn't humble enough to believe, which was why the Lord had brought her low. (We were having one of our epic battles, this one relating to the worth of Eleanor Fagan's bestselling book, *The Covenant*, which neither of us had read.)

From the au pair's perspective, I must have seemed just as righteous as my mother, just as judgmental about Mrs. Fagan's state of affairs. Soon after I began working there, Femke confided in me while we bathed Maya and Eddie that Mrs. Fagan was addicted to anxiety pills and knew nothing about parenting, which was why the kids were spoiled rotten. Maya fought like a wet cat as Femke roughly shampooed her hair. Femke's own hair was permed into waves that reminded me of Darryl Hannah's in *Splash*, but also of the ramen noodles I ate for dinner on the nights my mother worked the graveyard shift at the nursing home. I tried to tell her that washing Maya's hair so often was drying it out, but I was too timid to interrupt her rant. She couldn't have been older than nineteen or twenty but to me she was an adult. Her accent, which was something like Pepé Le Pew's, added to her authority. In Femke's view, Mrs. Fagan was a self-absorbed snob who didn't care about anyone else's feelings.

As for the house, Femke went on, scrubbing between the baby's fat little legs with a washrag, it was not in an au pair's job description to clean, so she'd put in a request with her agency for a transfer. "It's too difficult with the two," she said. "Truthfully, if it was me in her shoes, I would send back this one." It took me a moment to realize that she was talking about Eddie.

In any case, she continued, I was not to touch any more of the food in the kitchen marked with an F, though it was understandable that I had already done so since I hadn't known that it was hers alone. She was a vegetarian. Also, I should stop cooking the children's dinner on the stovetop since it just added one more pot to the over-crowded dishwasher, and should start using the microwave oven instead. Femke yanked the baby out of the tub. "You know how to use a micro-wave, yes?" she asked, wrapping him in a towel like a butcher wrapping paper around a flank of beef. I told her that I did.

I didn't share Femke's frustration with Mrs. Fagan, or my mother's indictment of her. In fact, I was awestruck that Mrs. Fagan had written a book. It wasn't anything like the paperbacks my mother checked five at a time out of the library, romances with coy titles like *Two in the Bush*, *Slipping into Grace*, or *The Blacker the Berry the Sweeter the Juice*. The only books my mother owned were the *New World Translation of the Holy Scriptures* and the phone book. I must have had the idea then that women didn't write about history, read ancient languages, or travel alone to foreign countries. I was astonished that Mrs. Fagan, who couldn't seem to pick up a sponge,

had accomplished these things. The woman with the daring smile in the author photo hardly resembled the Mrs. Fagan I knew, who stared into the middle distance with reverse paren-theses between her eyebrows, a teacup cooling in her hands.

Usually Mrs. Fagan went about in a brown bathrobe that had belonged to her husband. She was a tall, slim, gray-eyed woman who appeared shorter than she was by standing slightly bent at the waist, like a geisha, or a person who's been slammed in the gut. She wore her graying blond hair parted in the middle and cropped at the chin, and she spoke in such a quiet voice that I often missed what she said. When she reproached the children, she sounded beleaguered. "Please be quiet," she'd beg, where my mother would have boomed, "Simmer down!" Sometimes a stress pimple appeared on her forehead as if she were an adolescent. Later on, in high school, when we read *A Streetcar Named Desire*, Mrs. Fagan was my picture of Blanche DuBois—she had the same moth-like, delicate, desperate aura. By the time I made that association, I was no longer babysit-ting but waitressing at the Ground Round on Route 130, and the Fagan family was long gone.

When she discovered me with her book, she asked where I had gotten it. From the bookshelf, I said. There were multiple copies there along-side books by her late husband about the musical instruments of the Aztec Indians. I showed her to this shelf in the den. What seemed to surprise her most was that someone had gone to the effort of unpacking the books and organizing them. Because I was that person, I hoped she would gift me a copy of *The Covenant*. She didn't. Instead, she told me that her husband, Philip, had been the love of her life. They were equal partners who'd upheld their marriage vows to share every duty, from childcare, to cooking, to editing one another's work, and now that he was gone she hardly knew how to keep going, though she knew she must. But how was she supposed to do that? *How?*

Mrs. Fagan blinked rapidly when she asked me this, seeming actually to expect an answer from a girl of twelve. I blushed. It was as if she'd revealed her naked breasts to me, something that had happened more than once when the robe slipped open.

"I'm very grateful for your help, Dana," she said. "I know how challenging childcare can be. It's one of the most overtaxing but undervalued kinds of work, which is why I pay you what I do." I understood then that she didn't expect me to speak at all, and I was relieved.

I was just as silent in Mrs. Fagan's car when she picked me up and drove me home. She was a terrible driver, overly cautious to the point that others honked when it took her too long to make a turn, or when she inched forward at half the speed limit. Sometimes they rolled down their windows and barked at her to get off the road. *Learn to drive, lady!* or *Where'd you get your license? A Cracker Jack box!?* I was thankful for the car radio, tuned to NPR, filling the discomfiting silence. But one night toward the end of the summer I risked a conversation. She was the only person I'd ever met who'd been to Africa. I knew nothing about that continent except that it had a jungle in it, and the Nile River, and that you were supposed to be insulted on the playground when some kid called you an African booty-scratcher.

"Did you get to touch the Ark?" I asked.

"Excuse me?" I'd startled her, like a car horn. She answered so quietly I had to read her lips. "Oh. No. I wasn't allowed."

I'd mistaken her general timidity for distraction. Observing the way she gripped the steering wheel, I recognized it was fear. I couldn't reconcile my respect for her then with my feeling of pity. How could the person who wrote *The Covenant* be afraid of the road? Was this a part of her character or part of her mourning? Femke snickered about this kind of behavior behind her back, and my mother clucked about it, too. They weren't the only ones who disliked her for her helplessness. Eddie's car seat was in the back, and there was a yellow BABY ON BOARD sign suctioned to the rear window. For the sake of her children, people said, Eleanor Fagan needed to snap out of it and pull her act together. Now.

People were angry that she could afford to luxuriate in her tragedy, to weep in the frozen food section of the supermarket, unsure of what to buy. You don't see us crying about it when we hit hard times, they said. Another thing they said was that her children would be better off with black parents. I defended her, pointing out that plenty of black parents hadn't turned out so great. I didn't dare use my own as case in point.

Midway through August she realized the children needed new clothes. I asked if I could bring them into the backyard to play in the sprinkler and Mrs. Fagan bought them bathing suits. She had a gardener who trimmed the hedges, weeded the garden, and watered the lawn.

The man's name was Floyd. He lived across John Street from my mother and me and in fact it was he who'd recommended she employ me. Mrs. Fagan hadn't hired Floyd, he just worked for the people who lived there before and kept on working there after she bought the house. His own lawn was spoiled with car parts, which he surveyed from a hammock on his porch while swilling forty-ounce bottles of malt liquor and gossiping with passersby. But here he tended the rosebushes with infinite care, drowning the Japanese beetles in coffee cans of vinegar, and

leaving bouquets on the back steps to brighten Mrs. Fagan's day.

Floyd was out there cutting the grass on the afternoon I set the house on fire. I was alone with the children. Femke had changed her tune about leaving after acquiring a boyfriend, an aging punk rocker who worked at the Record Exchange, and was off with him on a date. Upstairs, Mrs. Fagan napped so thoroughly that not even the smoke alarm woke her. I'd been cooking the children's lunch of alphabet soup in an aluminum pot that caught fire in the microwave. Black smoke threaded out the sides, tripping the alarm. The shrill beeping made Eddie cry and Maya laugh. Thinking to put out the fire, I opened the microwave door by pushing the button with a broom handle. It popped open and out leapt the flames, tonguing the cabinets above. The heat came at me like a shove, along with piles of smoke. I stepped back. The sink was too close to the microwave to approach safely. I didn't know what to do.

I stuck Eddie on my hip and grabbed Maya's hand. She was coughing now instead of laughing. "Mrs. Fagan?" I shouted up the stairs. No answer. "Mrs. Fagan?" I looked back into the kitchen, transfixed. The fire spat and crackled with more appetite than seemed possible, consuming the cabinets and flickering up to the ceiling. It mesmerized, like all things that contain the visible spectrum—rainbows, sunsets, peacock feathers—only more so, because it was ruinous. In a spray of embers, the plates and cups came crashing down.

"Fire," said Maya, who couldn't speak more than ten words in English. One of these was my name. "Dana. Fire."

The smoke stung my throat. I felt a pressure in my chest that signaled the constriction of my lungs. All of a sudden, I could barely breathe. In the middle of my panic, I managed to locate my backpack and fly out the back door carrying both of the children. Together, their body weight was nearly half mine. I'd never been so happy to see Floyd, with his familiar Jheri curl, aviator sunglasses, and Vietnam veteran's cap. He choked the mower's motor.

"What's this now?"

I wheezed so hard that I could only point.

"Christ on a bike," Floyd said, wiping his face with the towel around his neck. He dragged the garden hose inside to extinguish the fire while I fumbled in my backpack for my asthma pump and sucked it dry. Floyd entered with the hose coiled at his hip like a green lasso, and I waited. If I had had enough breath in me, I suppose I would have held it.

My mother hadn't made it past the threshold, but I had no doubt that if any responsible adult ever entered the house and witnessed how irresponsibly it was run, someone official would be called in and the whole system would fall apart. I didn't want that to happen, for the sake of the kids, but I did expect something to shift after Floyd saw how things were.

I assumed I would be fired. Part of me looked forward to being let go even though I'd come to love the children, the income, and the reprieve from Saturday afternoons with my mother going door to door to preach her message. The house weighed on me. Hadn't my ineptitude shown that the job was more than I could handle? Maybe the fire would be the wakeup call Mrs. Fagan needed to get back on track. Maybe she would hire a housekeeper, and a nanny who cared. Some no-nonsense Mary Poppins.

Floyd didn't tell my mother what I'd done (though he did take to calling me Firestarter). Neither did Mrs. Fagan. She must have reassured me that accidents happen, but I don't remember her addressing the fire directly. In my memory, she drove me home that evening as slowly as usual and picked up the conversation I'd started two weeks earlier right where she'd dropped it. There was a guard who warned her not to touch the Ark, she said. She spoke as if she were sleep talking. According to this guard, she would burst into flame if she did.

I thought I understood what Mrs. Fagan was getting at. Knowledge comes at a price. Wasn't that the oldest story in the book? We (and by "we" I mean girls) all knew what happened when you bit into a fruit you were forbidden to taste, peeked into the box you weren't supposed to open, or strayed from the path and spoke to the handsome wolf. But I didn't know *why* she said it, or how it related to what I had done, not even the next morning when I woke up with a fudge-brown smear in my underpants.

At first I thought I was injured in some way connected to the fire. I had breathed in too much smoke, and now, because of my asthma, my black-ened lungs were dripping something bad out of me like chaw. Then, it dawned on me what it was. I felt relieved, and very, very sad. To spare myself a mortifying lecture and, I suppose, from shame, I kept my period hidden from my mother. I kept it hidden for months.

I was not fired. In fact, when the school year began I was promoted. As Mrs. Fagan's duties at the university increased, so did mine with her children. She taught two classes and chose to prepare her lectures in her office on campus, where her head could be clear. I was now entrusted with taking care of Eddie and Maya while she was out of the house, and asked to watch them more frequently.

Of course, I was still a child myself. Under my watch, the rabbit choked to death on a piece of gum,

Eddie chipped a tooth falling off the changing table, and Maya broke an eight hundred-year-old clay flute. At night, I raided the refrigerator, shaving delicately at the Frusen Glädjé so nobody could tell how many spoonfuls I'd eaten. I snuck into Mrs. Fagan's closet and her jewelry case to try on her fine things. Still, I was not fired. Femke stayed out later with the boyfriend and so I bathed the children without her. I enjoyed belting Whitney Houston anthems when I tucked them into bed. *I believe the children are our future; teach them well and let them lead the way...*

Indian summer passed into fall. The smell of cut grass gave way to the smell of rotting leaves. Floyd raked up the leaves that fell from Mrs. Fagan's sycamore trees and bagged them by the curb. Eddie's top two teeth grew in. My breasts began to bud, tender as wounds. I felt as if I were on the precipice of a steep cliff overlooking a bottomless gorge, against my will. In October I was persuaded to stay an entire weekend to help out while Mrs. Fagan attended a conference out of state. I didn't want to do it. It meant missing my best friend's birthday party at the roller rink where there would be ice-cream cake, disco lights, and the hokey pokey, but my mother told me that I had to help Mrs. Fagan out of Christian duty. When I bucked against that, she added that she couldn't pay for a school choir trip planned for Philadelphia. If I wanted to see the City of

Brotherly Love, I had better keep on fattening my piggy bank.

"Maya's afraid of losing another parent and you're like a second big sister to Eddie," Mrs. Fagan entreated. It was flattery to pretend I was indispensible. She knew as well as my mother the value of guilt in winning a specious argument. "You're practically family," she wheedled.

Family.

Mrs. Fagan's stepson, too, sized me up, apparently, as somebody who could be bossed around—especially when bossed flirtatiously. Dennis was right about that, though my compliance had less to do with his charisma than it did my own self-consciousness. When he showed up unannounced on the doorstep that Thanksgiving night, I feared he might be a kidnapping murderer. Yet having my throat slit was a less embarrassing prospect than being the cause of his irritation. I let him in with his turkey and his duffel bag.

"Are the kids asleep?" he asked in the foyer.

"I think so," I said, worried for their lives yet curious to see what would happen next.

"That's cool. I brought them a kite from Chinatown. I'll give it to them in the morning. Man, this place is a dump, isn't it?" He kicked at a teetering stack of unread catalogues from J. Peterman and Land's End with his good foot.

"Where's the kitchen?"

I brought him to the kitchen where he washed his hands and face with great splashes of water that puddled the floor. His oily sun-bleached hair reached to his shoulders. He had a cleft in the chin and a nose that looked like it had been broken. He did so much smiling and cajoling that it was clear he regarded himself as good-looking. As to whether or not he was, I hadn't made up my mind. When he took off his baja, the t-shirt beneath it lifted a little, and I noticed the muscles of his abdomen. What my Louisianan grandmother, who grew up using washboard, would have called a washboard stomach. He saw where my eyes had focused, and grinned. I looked away.

"Like what you see? I'm rock solid. Go ahead, punch me."

"No thanks."

"Don't be shy. You can't hurt me," he goaded, so smugly that I wanted to prove him wrong. If he tried to touch me I would stomp on his injured foot. But I would not go near him unless he reached for me first.

"Preheat the oven to 325° and bring me the butter," Dennis said. The kitchen had been partially refinished after the fire and tonight it was cleaner than usual, but not by much.

"I worked as a galley steward on a Carnival Cruise ship for almost a year after I dropped out of school. You learn a lot about people working on a cruise ship. I'm what you call a 'people person.' Where's the roasting pan?" he asked, pushing his hair back. "If we get this done tonight, we can relax tomorrow. I know a trick to keep it moist. You probably don't know this about Ellie but she gets really stressed out about stuff like cooking."

He was wrong about that. I knew she was stressed about everything.

In the time it took him to squeeze droplets of Visine into both of his eyes I learned that he'd just fractured his ankle in a bad wipeout. It was a bummer, but he was rolling with it. Maybe it was his dad's way of telling him to slow down and spend some time with his family. Ellie and the kids were the only family he had left. His real mom had died of breast cancer when he was about my age, fifteen. The following year his father had married Ellie, whom he hadn't seen in a little while.

"I'm twelve," I corrected him.

He rummaged in the refrigerator and pulled out a half gallon of orange juice. Right before taking a series of gulps that made his Adam's apple bob up and down, he said that if the babysitter were still a baby then he'd try his best not to rob the cradle.

"How long are you going to stay here?" I asked him.

"Dude. What kind of question is that?" he asked, wiping his mouth with the back of his arm. He returned his attention to the turkey by spanking it. I disliked the wet sound of him plunging his hand into the cavity and pulling out the gizzards. "Hey. Remind you of anything?" he asked, holding the bluish neck at the level of his crotch and making it wag.

"My dad's dead too," I blurted, to blot the leer off his face.

Mrs. Fagan returned just after that. She rushed into the kitchen in her heels without even bothering to take off her trench coat and scarf. "Dennis? Is that you? Can it really be you? What happened to your foot? Tell me you didn't get into another fight."

They hugged for long enough that I felt I shouldn't be watching. When they pulled away from each other, Mrs. Fagan told him he looked terrific. "That's true," Dennis replied offering her one of his cunning smiles, "but you look terrible and your house is a pigsty."

What I couldn't figure out was why that made her smile back at him. It was hard to make sense of a reunion when you had so little background information. She tucked his hair behind his ears.

"Stop it," he whined, putting his hair back the way it was. Then, resolutely, "You might as well take me to my old man."

I followed them to the living room. Mrs. Fagan pointed her chin at a container on the mantelpiece, the contents of which I hadn't understood were Philip's remains on the day Maya climbed up on the rocking horse and dumped it on the floor. I supposed some of the deceased was ground into the carpet under their feet. The rest of his ashes I'd half-heartedly sucked up with the Dustbuster.

"That's him?" he asked.

"That's him." She unwound her scarf and touched her throat.

He picked up the urn with both hands, testing its weight. I was sure he'd peek inside and find it empty. Instead, he shook it like a snow globe and said, "Uh. Hey, Dad. It's me, Dennis. I'm sorry I missed your memorial service."

He gave Mrs. Fagan a lost look.

"I'm sure he understands, my love," she said.

My love?

"I wanted to be there," he said to the urn, choking up. "It was just a really sucky time for me to leave rehab."

I sneezed then, involuntarily, and they both turned to me in surprise.

"Oh, goodness, Dana. It's nearly eleven. Let me drive you home."

That was one of the last times Mrs. Fagan drove me. After he moved in, Dennis took over dropping me off in his orange Volkswagen Beetle. The rusted-out car with its unpainted passenger door and ripped vinyl seats smelled of his musk, as did the wood-paneled den where he slept until noon. Cooking dinner became a regular thing he did for the family, along with occasional housecleaning. He was talented at neither task but the kids adored him because he carried them around on his shoulders while making believe he was a werewolf.

"Watch out, girlie," he'd snarl at me as I looked on reproachfully with my arms crossed over my chest. "The wolfman's gonna bite you!"

At first I thought Mrs. Fagan wouldn't need me around anymore since she now had her stepson to help out, but she insisted that I stay for a sense of stability in the kids' lives, especially since it wasn't clear how long Dennis would be with them. It seemed to me he overstayed his welcome. The cast came off his foot. Eddie grew one inch taller, and three more teeth. Maya started speaking in compound sentences. I started wearing a training bra. Floyd draped burlap sacks on the hedges to protect them for winter, and Dennis was still lingering on with his dartboard and his bongo drums and his *Penthouse* magazines. He stayed for Christmas and well into the new year with no sign of leaving any time soon.

I have to say that all of them flourished in the man's company: Maya and Eddie, who needed a guy to rough-house them, Femke, who mistook his flirtation for something personal, and Mrs. Fagan, who wanted, I supposed, a piece of her dead husband back. Why else did she laugh so girlishly around him? Why else did she begin to wear perfume and dye the gray out of her hair?

I remembered Femke saying to me when I began working there that Mrs. Fagan didn't welcome conversation. That's how you could tell she was stuck-up, Femke said, because she didn't wish to be bothered by unimportant people. Surely, I thought, if ever there was a time for Mrs. Fagan to be bothered, it was now. Having the skunky malodor of marijuana permeate her den, and the young man who smoked it wandering around shirtless.

But Femke must have been mistaken. Mrs. Fagan didn't retire from Dennis, who must have rated as an unimportant person. Quite the opposite. With men—I had learned Dennis was twenty-seven—she could be rapt, giddy. He convinced her to start playing tennis with him at the indoor university courts. They were friskily competitive about their matches. She dressed for these in a short white skirt and ankle socks with fuzzy balls at the ankle. I admired the muscular backs of her thighs, which weren't dimpled with cellulite like my mother's. One time I saw her swat Dennis's backside with her racket. "I'll beat the pants off you," she taunted. "Oh, you'd like that wouldn't you, Ellie," he said. He returned her from their games flushed, sweaty, and blithe.

I didn't trust him. Every showy gesture, platitude, and pratfall seemed to mask a sketchier impulse. I couldn't figure out what he was up to. I didn't like how he tossed Eddie in the air like a football. I didn't like how he scratched at his chest hair, and invited Femke to feel his biceps. And I especially didn't like being alone with him in the car at night after he'd taken Mrs. Fagan on what seemed like a date. Why did he tease me by asking if I had a boyfriend yet? Why, when I answered no, did he joke, "Glad to hear I'm still your first love"? I doubted he'd try anything, but just in case, I always positioned my left hand on the seatbelt buckle and my right on the door handle, prepared to jump and roll.

Yet the house was indisputably happier with Dennis in it. He was always kidding around. Most of his jokes were about poop. "Did you see the movie *Constipated*?" he'd ask at the dinner table.

"No," Mrs. Fagan would answer, eagerly.

"That's because it never came out."

If I declined to laugh he called me "Rudy Prudy." Mrs. Fagan and Femke always laughed, and so did the kids. Whether related to the poop jokes or not, Maya started using the potty again. Eddie started giving high fives like Dennis, who was fond of saying that his mission on earth was to make people feel good. One time he asked me to lend him twenty bucks to buy Mrs. Fagan a birthday present. He never paid me back. Another time I heard him remark in a friendly way that he hoped Femke wasn't planning on wearing her ugly parachute pants in front of her boyfriend. They made her look fat, he said. I realized something when I looked at Femke's face just then. Something sickening and pathetic. She *liked* being put down by him. His scrutiny was a reward, like a gold star on a spelling test. It made her twinkle.

His other trick to keep things cheerful was to talk about his life—how he had tried peyote and had a vision, snorted cocaine out of a stripper's belly button and bottomed out, backpacked across Europe via high-speed rail, and worked as a sous-chef on a cruise ship before moving to Hawaii, where he was spotted on his surfboard by a scout for his fearlessness, good balance, and angling, and soon found himself placing in the Rip Curl Competition trials (he made this sound like winning an Olympic medal). This led to his eventual job as a surf coach for the stars. He had given a lesson to none other than Kevin Costner, the actor, who had been terrified of sharks. There was a scar for every story, a story for every scar. He pointed to these, lifted his shirt, rolled up his pant legs, and invited us to finger them. There were also tattoos. One said CARPE DIEM. Another was of a sea turtle.

"It's been a wild ride," he said, "and it's not over yet."

I started to see that there were some types of people—men—whom others liked to be around, not because of what they, the men, had achieved but because of their cocksure delivery. A pleasure with themselves, an ease with putting their hand on your shoulder, back, or knee, a confidence that their experiences were more extraordinary or entertaining than yours, and that you couldn't help but take pleasure in their company. There might be some folks—folks like me—who didn't buy into this, but that didn't stop them from selling.

I wondered if he'd been laid off his job for using drugs. How could he manage to stay so long otherwise? And who could be supporting him but Mrs. Fagan?

One Saturday in February, Valentine's Day, Dennis took Mrs. Fagan to a movie at the mall, and Femke returned from her night out before they did. I'd fallen asleep on the couch trying to read *The Covenant* and was awoken by the sound of her key in the lock. I bolted upright to give the impression I'd been awake.

"What movie did they go to?" Femke asked, innocently. The lower half of her face was pink from making out with her boyfriend.

I told her I didn't know.

"It's generous of Dennis to bring her out," she said. "He has a very big heart."

"I guess."

"Does he ever talk about me when he drives you to your house?"

Femke's eyes were glassy and her voice was too loud. I figured she was drunk. I said that Dennis had never mentioned her to me on any of our drives.

"Dennis says he believes I will be an amazing mother. He says I'm a natural woman with the children. More than Eleanor. Dennis says she's depressed. This is why he acts nice with her."

I thought of how Mrs. Fagan tiptoed into her children's rooms when she got home late from campus to kiss them on their foreheads, her face animated by longing. How she sometimes lay down to curl herself around their sleeping bodies, and fell asleep like that without taking off her pantyhose. Even if it wasn't enough, I wanted to prove that it counted for something. I wanted to stand up for her but I didn't know how. Besides, Femke had already made up her mind about Mrs. Fagan and wasn't likely to change it.

"Doesn't Dennis tell you how he pities her?" she pushed.

I did say something then, to redirect her, and to clarify things for myself. "No. He doesn't talk about his mom like that."

Femke snorted. "That woman is a mother to no person. She couldn't get children. Something is broken inside of her. Fibrosis of the uterus."

I heard her say fire in the universe. I tried not to look confused.

"She is having a hysterectomy. You know what this is?"

I hated to admit when I didn't know a word. "I don't care. I think she's brilliant," I said.

"Possible," Femke shrugged. "But how would *you* know this?"

Playfully, she jabbed me in the belly with her pointer finger. "Oops. Better look how many cookies you steal from us."

Us.

On the last Wednesday in March, Dennis leaned in as if to kiss me when dropping me off at home. He held his face very close to mine and lowered his eyelids. "Someday soon you're going to drive the boys wild," he said softly. I sat very still, titillated and enraged. I thought he might kiss me, but he did not. He sighed, unbuckled my seatbelt, reached across my lap, and opened the door. Inside the house, I discovered my mother waiting for me in the dining room. We seldom used that room, with its floor-model dinette from Bob's Discount Furniture and its plastic carpet protector. Now it was lit for an interrogation. She told me to sit down. I thought at first she had seen Dennis almost-touching me. But that was not it. I was to explain the paper bag on the table before her.

I remained silent in my chair, since it was obvious what was in the bag. My armpits and palms prickled.

"When did you get your curse?" she demanded.

"That's not what it's called."

I can't remember correcting my mother before I started working for Mrs. Fagan, but I did it all the time after. What does it matter that I'm sorry for it now? The distance between us terrified her, even as she cultivated it for my own betterment.

"When did you begin your *menses*, Dana?" She said the word with great displeasure, like she had bitten into a rancid melon. "Mind you tell the truth, now."

"A little while ago. I don't know."

"More than one cycle?"

"I guess."

"How many months?"

"I don't know! Just a couple."

"You've been lying to me."

"Technically, I never lied."

"You did."

"No. I never said I *didn't* have it. I just didn't tell you that I did."

"A lie of omission is still a lie," she said, employing her fist like a gavel. My mother had worked as a legal secretary, among other low-level jobs, and could preach legalese as well as Bible-babble. "Tell me where you got these." She shook the incriminating evidence of the bag that held the sanitary napkins.

"From Mrs. Fagan." I kicked myself. Why hadn't I told her I'd bought them myself?

"She gave them to you?"

I hesitated, sensing a trap. "Yeah."

My mother rose from the table and made as if heading for the rotary phone screwed to the kitchen wall. "In that case, I'll just call the widow up and ask how come she overstepped her bounds when it wasn't her place."

"No—*don't*. Please."

"Why shouldn't I?"

"Because, she doesn't know I borrowed them," I said softly.

"Do I look like I fell off the turnip truck? You 'borrowed' them? You plan on returning these feminine products? Huh? After you drench them in blood?"

"I guess not."

"So what you're telling me is that I raised a thief, as well as a liar who hides secrets under her bed."

"Jeez, it's not that big a deal!"

"She says it's not a big deal, Lord Jesus. Do you hear this scheming child who rolls her eyes and takes your name in vain? She says it's not a *big deal* that she could become pregnant."

I was grounded for the remainder of the school year. I hoped this meant I would be free of Mrs.

Fagan's house. But for reasons having to do with discipline, duty, saving for college and, I now understand, influence, the grounding did not extend to my babysitting job.

On my second to last Saturday of work, Mrs. Fagan was out of town at another conference, Dennis was supposedly working out at the gym, and Femke was home sick with the flu. Maya had a touch of it, too. Her slight fever made her more cuddly than usual, and I enjoyed having her on my lap.

"I want to be a butterfly. Do you want to be a butterfly?" she asked me before she and Eddie went down for their naps.

"Yes, I do," I said. We'd been reading *The Very Hungry Caterpillar.*

Once Maya fell asleep, I thought to ask Femke if she needed me to bring her anything. Ginger ale, or crackers. I knocked lightly on her door, not wanting to disturb her if she was resting, but then I heard her moaning and thought she might need help. The door was unlocked.

Inside I witnessed Dennis, evidently not at the gym, masturbating with his penis directed at her open mouth. Both of them were naked. The parts of her that were normally covered were as pale as an uncooked turkey, in contrast with his testicles, which were darker than the rest of

him. Most surprising of all was the rigorously spartan state of Femke's room, bare as the cell of a monk. Both of them turned to look at me. She covered her face with her arm right before I slammed the door.

I fled to Maya's room. Her eyes popped open.

"Shut your eyes," I told her. "Go back to sleep."

"I don't want to," she said. "I'm scared."

I climbed beneath the covers and put my nose in her hair, the braids I'd done. Through the bed's gauzy canopy I could make out the mural painted on her ceiling. Happy white cumulonimbus clouds against a powder-blue backdrop. It looked fake, terribly fake. Someone had torn away the real sky and replaced it with this: cartoon brushstrokes and a light fixture full of dead flies. Then came the rhythmic hammering of Femke's headboard against the adjoining wall. They hadn't even quit their business. All of a sudden the benign neglect of the house felt dangerously purposeful, and I was furious. Maya burrowed into me, and I clung to her hot little form as if I could ever go back to being little, myself.

"Are we butterflies now?" she mumbled, half asleep.

Dennis drove me home early that afternoon and asked me not to mention what I'd seen. "It's not that we did anything wrong, but Ellie's really sensitive and I don't want her to get upset right before her operation," he said. Mrs. Fagan's hysterectomy was scheduled for later that week.

Did I believe Dennis, that she would be upset? I did.

"I won't tell," I swore, staring out the window, with my arms crossed over my chest. That was my posture that spring, my arms crossed over my chest. I didn't think I was being more defensive than usual but Dennis could read my mood.

"Come on, don't be like that. Are we still friends?"

He couldn't read my mind, which was still busy calculating.

"Don't be rude, Rudy Two Shoes."

"You were *never* my friend," I seethed. I kept my eyes on the window, so he couldn't see they'd grown wet.

"Aw, don't be like that. You act like you're mad at me or something."

"Don't talk to me."

"You're not jealous, are you?"

The terrible thing was that I was.

He pulled up to my house. It had never seemed small to me before I began babysitting for Mrs. Fagan. I scampered out of the Beetle.

"Say something, kiddo. Don't just give me the silent treatment. Are we cool?"

What came out of my mouth, haughty and dry, took us both aback and would have done my mother proud. Corinthians 13:11. "When I was a child I spake as a child, understood as a child, thought as a child, but when I grew I up, I put away childish things."

Before he had a chance to turn scripture into a joke, and because I wanted to enjoy the final word, I slammed the car door in his face.

In the end, I got out of my babysitting job by lighting a second fire. I knew it had to be grander than the first, spectacular enough to bring in the outside world like a defibrillator to the heart. The Saturday following the sex act, Mrs. Fagan was recovering from her hysterectomy at a hospital in New York. Dennis and Femke had gone off somewhere, together or apart I cannot say. I had the children to myself. Dennis would swear he hadn't left his bong alight, had not lit up that morning at all, but who would ever suspect a twelve-year-old of the power or vindictiveness of arson?

I waited for the fire to reach the bookcase before I led the children outside. I watched it blacken the spines of *The Covenant,* whose diction was light-years beyond my reach.

It was late April now, the pinnacle of spring. Somewhere in the city, they had withdrawn Mrs. Fagan's uterus from her body like a bedroom slipper, but the rhododendrons on her front lawn were fully in bloom. All up and down her block, the blossoms were a pomp: forsythia bushes, dogwood trees, clusters of tulips, deep purple irises with licks of yellow at their centers and bumblebees daubing their stamens. The day was almost too warm for the little jackets I'd buttoned the children into. There may have been butterflies. If there were, I would have shown them to Maya and Eddie, to distract them from the conflagration overtaking the house at our backs.

"Someone will come for us," I said. I sat them down on the pathway that led from the front door, and waited. The flagstones were dusted with bright green pollen that got on our clothes. Within the hour the lawn would be dusted with ash. The air surrounding the house was already polluted with smoke. As a preventative measure, I took a hit from my asthma pump. This time wouldn't be like the last.

Something burst inside, like a giant balloon, followed by an updrafting *whoosh.*

"Fire," said, Eddie, who was talking now.

"Shhh."

I might have performed a hand-clapping song to keep them calm. "Rockin' Robin" or "Miss Mary Mack." "Look at the flowers," I might have said, picking a daffodil at the border of the path, or buttercups to hold beneath their chins. The properties here were four times the size of those in my neighborhood, the houses spaced farther apart, the grass healthier, and of course, greener. Yet for all the beauty of spring, not one of Mrs. Fagan's neighbors was outside to enjoy it. I'd counted on one of them to notice the smoke, since the alarm was disabled after the first fire I'd caused, ripped from the ceiling and never replaced. Time passed interminably and instantly. Five minutes? Five hours? I was a child, and then I wasn't? *Soon,* I thought, as the children grew restless, *I will have to fetch a grown-up.*

I had the story worked out in my mind, how I had smelled something burning in the den where Dennis slept, and seen the curtains on fire. Just as I was resolving to ring the bell on the Tudor next door, Floyd drove up in his pickup truck full of gardening tools and mulch. I'd forgotten he was coming.

"Holy smoke," he said, with a touch of irony. "Not again." But this time the inferno was too rampant to quell with the hose, and he had to call in the fire department.

Eddie clapped and laughed when the shiny hook and ladder truck rounded the curve blaring its siren, followed by the pumper engine and an ambulance. But Maya was truly afraid. The fire roared in twirling geysers of noise and heat. Floyd lifted us up into the high cab of his pickup, where we watched the firefighters at work. I sat in the middle with my arms around the children's skinny shoulders. One of the men had given us a scratchy wool blanket. It was too warm for it, but I arranged it over our legs anyhow. I wished I could take the children home with me, but I knew I could not

keep them. I also knew the Fagans wouldn't be homeless, even as the blaze flamed out of the second story windows, battling the pressure of the fire hose. There were always security nets for people like Mrs. Fagan. I wished Floyd would flick on the windshield wipers when the ash began to fall upon the car like dirty snow. Through that precipitation, we watched the fire collapse the roof. It dropped on one side, like a falling hemline.

Did I feel remorse? Not then.

I understood fairly well the theatre of neediness staged in Mrs. Fagan's house, but as the babysitter, it was strange to think what small roles the children played in the overall drama, and to discover that I had the power to recast their circumstance. After the fire, Dennis was sent to court-ordered rehab, Femke was reassigned to a family in Brussels, and Mrs. Fagan accepted a distinguished professorship at a small liberal arts college in Ohio, from whence she came, and where her mother (who agreed to help with the children) still lived. I grew up, acquired two degrees, traveled widely, published a book, and had children of my own.

I have often wondered about them—Maya and Eddie. It's easy enough these days to track people down to see what's become of their lives. But so far, for fear of unearthing some damage I may have had a hand in, I have refrained. It is more reassuring to think that, for all I remember about that time, the children I sat for don't remember me at all.

THE LOTTERY, REDUX

by MEGAN MAYHEW BERGMAN

after "The Lottery" by Shirley Jackson

The morning of July 27th was clear to the horizon on all sides of the main island of Timothy, once a large chunk of land but now a series of marshy islets overrun by dragonflies, which moved across town in black, buzzing swarms. The people of Timothy, descendants of men and women exiled from America fifty years ago for crimes against the environment, were gathering by the empty fountain in the square. The place might have been a village green elsewhere, but on Timothy it was sand and rock, the brick paths and buildings calcified. The fountain used to flow with seawater, but they'd given up on piping it in, and although the dry fountain was an eyesore, no one in the square was thinking about that today. The lottery was that afternoon.

The sounds that morning were the same as any: the roar of waves gnawing at the shoreline, the scream of the occasional heron passing overhead, children laughing on the beach, men throwing sandbags or tinkering with the artificial reefs, and Clare Smith leading the women's fishing co-op back from its daily expedition. They walked up from the sea to the picking house, where they broke open crabs with their fingers and skinned fish with rusted bowie knives, gossiping only a little, their eyes on the fish; they wasted nothing. Clare made sure that the women got back on time today, because she and her fifteen-year-old daughter June were in charge of civic duties, including the lottery administration.

The children usually followed Clare and the women from the beach up to the picking house to see what the catch looked like, peering into the handwoven baskets at the flopping fish, not quite dead, and the burlap sacks of freshly dredged oysters. But today the kids—there were only seven of them—were dutifully assembling piles of driftwood on the beach, and mounds of large conches and other shells. Clare, wearing a leather hat with fishhooks slipped over the brim, nodded at them in passing. The children waved back to the women,

who were still dripping with seawater after braving the rough currents and rip tides. They carried spears and rods and threw nets over their browned shoulders like shawls of old, threadbare lace.

The men were gathered at the dry, chalky fountain, smoking hand-rolled cigarettes. The tobacco came from their rooftop gardens; it was burly and rustic and they stuffed it into cones of dried seaweed. It was illegal to use pasture space for anything but food crops, but Clare had permitted the rooftop cultivation of tobacco because everyone agreed that it helped keep things mellow. Now nearly everyone smoked, especially today. Summer Hutchison, the seventeen-year-old golden girl of the island, lit a nori cigarette and held it between her teeth as she walked toward the picking house, bucket in hand. She smiled at everyone she passed, licking her dry, chapped lips. She was always cheerful because she was in love, and no one on Timothy was really in love in these days. Most of them ended up in each other's beds because they were bored or obligated, but not Summer. She was in love and the co-op's women agreed it made her pleasant to be around, and so they began to talk about weddings in the picking house, telling secondhand stories from their own mothers of tossed rice and slow dances.

"We could make a veil from an old net," Jade Sleeman said. "We'd drape it like this," she added, gesturing toward her dark, cropped hair.

Her daughter Lana played underneath the table, stacking empty oyster shells on Jade's toes while the women worked. Jade was thin but strong; her mother had been a horsewoman and a polo player before exile.

Summer smiled. The sun, and there was too much of it, caught in her hair, lit it up like pale stained glass.

"We don't have any nets to spare," Clare said without looking up from the rockfish she was skinning, blade expertly snaking underneath the scaled flesh. When she did look up, gazing out the window, she could see the men at the fountain, smoking, browned from working all summer long on the artificial reef fashioned out of the timbers and iron washed ashore from a shipwreck. They figured that the wreck was just east of the island, that the pieces had tumbled toward them in the strong western current. Though the men rarely wore shirts, they began pulling them on, and though it was forbidden, she knew many of them had stuffed their pockets with gull jerky and marmalade.

But not Javier Lewis, she thought. Javier, hardly twenty, was honorable, and that's why she tolerated this talk of weddings. He and Summer were the future of Timothy. They respected tradition and understood what had to be done. She could see Summer looking for him through the big windows in between feeding empty shells to Lana underneath the table. Clare imagined

Summer and Javier with a child. Surely it would be a towheaded baby, kissed constantly, worn on Summer's back as she waded into the water to fish.

"Okay, girls, let's wrap up," Clare said, rising from the wooden table. She dropped the hunks of rockfish into a bucket of brine. As she stood she ducked the emergency rations—salted fish dangling from twine overhead like strange ornaments, drying in the harsh sunlight. She wiped her hands on a towel and left the picking house. She could feel the men's eyes on her as she made the short walk home, June close behind, the sound of her bare feet on the sand barely perceptible. A mother knows the sound of her own child, she thought.

"You get the basket and I'll get the shells," Clare said. She opened the cabinet and retrieved the large white enamel bowl her mother had brought over on the boat, the only boat to have landed at Timothy in fifty years. For decades she waited, as her parents vainly had, for the boat to come back, with a quiet hope that their exile might be excused after the offending generation had passed. But here she was, living in someone else's vacation home built centuries ago, the last of the books rank and spotted with mildew, food scarce, and many of the villagers suffering from malnutrition and melanomas. Here she was, trying to remember her mother's stories about shampoo, television, and shopping malls.

June, always compliant, had prepared the basket

of food that morning: three salted and smoked gulls, five oranges, two jars of marmalade, and two bottles of boiled rainwater. June checked it over one last time, added another jar of marmalade, and scooped the handle over her shoulder.

Clare paused at the door of her home and took a deep breath, bracing herself. She reached for June's hand and squeezed it, their skin warm, their hands calloused. As they stepped outside into the humid air, the village stared back at them from the fountain. They were talking—she heard bits and pieces of conversation about nori and oysters, a shark that had been spotted near the reef—but she couldn't help but notice the way the conversation died as the door of her house creaked open.

Clare could see Javier standing next to Summer Hutchison and her father, Jim, who managed the rainwater plant. She nodded at everyone and walked toward the fountain with the enamel bowl full of shells balanced on her hip. Without being told, June walked quickly down to the beach to set the food basket by the pile of driftwood and rope, knowing instinctively that there wouldn't be time after the lottery.

Clare looked down at her daughter's silhouette on the beach, skinny and browned, long auburn braid hanging down her back. June had placed the basket next to the driftwood, but she was staring at Hope House, a skeletal structure falling into the distant ocean. It stood on rickety posts and

waves crashed against its front door at high tide. During the second summer of exile, a big storm had come and inundated the easternmost end of the island, washing out a row of waterfront homes on the central beach, including Hope House. The waters never receded and East Timothy was lost forever. No one boated or swam out there; the fishing was good but the sharks were numerous and the boats weren't reliable.

"Let's move on with it, Clare," Jim Hutchison said.

She looked up at Jim. The sound of wingbeats and the black swarm of dragonflies moved over them, there and gone again. The sound jarred her into the present.

"We'll take our time," Clare said, setting the bowl on the edge of the fountain. She wanted to keep proceedings calm; it was the only way to avoid a frenzy.

"Well, we've got a bunch of work to do on the reefs," Huck Sleeman said, "so let's get going." He had one tattooed arm around Jade. Lana played at their feet with a doll made of seaweed, sticks, and a square from an old quilt.

Clare's mother, Jennifer, had saved the exiles with agriculture. She'd coaxed saltwater rice paddies, orange trees, and surprising gardens from the island, which she tended to with rainwater and burlap guards to reduce salt burns. While the men spent their time building a boat that would

POEM FOR KEATS*

by MATTHEW ZAPRUDER

sadly my favorite
poem begins
with him saying
he's sleepy,
but a creature
loud just like
one that for
whatever
pre-dawn reasons
comes to the tree
and makes my wife
roll over say
bird then go
again back into
that place
I cannot follow
won't let him join
oblivion,
not yet,
in the leaves
it creaks,
and now the poet
is to himself some
perfect unseen
melodious nocturne
amalgam like
a wood no one
but he
knows to
sing about,
O he says
he wants to drink

and forget
what no bird
needs to know:
verdurous breezes
pass through
countless novels
and hotels
where we lie
and listen
to numberless
fingers counting
shadow shadows,
all night some
void wakes
us making
every moment
another morning,
it says all you
bright plaintive
fancy elves,
all you medieval
process queens,
you think your time
is so full
of time you can
give it to
the glowing
screen for viewless
thin beautiful
northern Californian
specters to monetize,
darkling we listen

and say yes
we know just
enough to keep
breathing but
some hill
side still puts
its murmurous hand
over our mouths,
while hidden
melody containers
each sing their same
glade bell songs
to each
concerning
all those
similar particular
Februaries
that will happen
more or less
just like the room
next to those
famous steps
you can visit
and sit beside
his bed
lorn and helpless
as a friend.

---

* after "Ode to a Nightingale" by John Keats

never be seaworthy, Jennifer had accepted their plight and started the women's co-op, outlining a rigorous fishing schedule. She was a midwife, a nurse, a leader, and because of her contributions to an improved life on Timothy, Clare and June were exempt from the lottery, their matriarchal line considered the closest thing the island had to a monarchy.

Jennifer. To even think her mother's name harkened to a different time, and a mainland no one but Bruce Haverford knew. Bruce, with his long white beard and rambling stories about baseball. He was seventy-five now, and sat in his flimsy lawn chair with its rusted joints, waiting for her to start. She made eye contact with him as she unfolded the list. He nodded curtly.

"I'll call the heads of each household," she said. "When I call your name, each member of your household will draw a shell."

Just as Clare turned to read the first name, she saw Summer's mother, Beth Hutchison, hurrying up the sandy path to the village square, her thick gray hair tied up with a red scarf. She held her youngest daughter, Kate's, hand. Beth locked arms with Jim and touched Summer on the back. "I let the day get away from me," she whispered. "I forgot. How could I forget?"

Javier nodded at Beth politely, and then his eyes returned quickly to Summer. He was thinking of the hushed nights when he had come to her in the shallow, dark water and they'd stood there alone, looking out at the dim horizon. She worried about her future, as they all worried, and he assured her that if things got bad, she could make it on her own, that he would come join her, that nothing could keep her from him. He reached for her hand and held it tightly.

"Thought we'd have to start without you, Beth," Jade said.

"Kate and I were just hanging up the last of the laundry!" she said. "You wouldn't want us all to be wandering around naked tomorrow."

There was polite laughter, but it died down quickly.

"Dunbar," Clare called out. "Who's drawing for Dunbar?"

"I am," an approaching woman said, and then reached for a shell. She didn't dare peek at whatever was carved into the white, pearlescent inside. She cupped the shell face-down in her hand and receded into the crowd.

"Watson," Clare said. "Watson," she repeated when no one came up.

"He's sick," Huck said from the back. "Laid up with some gut problem."

"Someone has to draw for him," Clare said.

"Fine," Huck said, weaving through the crowd, reaching into the bowl. He held the shell up then laid it face down on the fountain. "This one here's for Bob."

"Bruce Haverford," Clare said, thinking to herself: Dear Bruce. Last of my mother's friends. Last of the original exiles. It was a dubious seniority, she thought. She loved him for his age and experience, and yet wasn't he part of the reason they were here?

Javier helped Bruce rise from his chair and kept one arm on him until he was steady. Bruce shuffled toward the bowl, reached in for a shell with a solemn face, and retreated. "Thirty years," he said to himself. "Thirty years I've done this."

Clare moved down the list of names: "Anderson, Bentham, Hutchison…"

"Sleeman."

"Go on, now, Huck," Jade said. "The moment you've been waiting for." She and Lana followed close behind, taking their shells in turn. Jade held onto Lana's.

"It seems like we had a lottery just the other day, doesn't it?" Beth whispered to Summer, who was still clutching Javier's hand.

"Lewis."

"Get up there, boy," someone said. Javier dropped Summer's hand and went to claim his shell. He was an orphan, the last of his family, and he worked hard to be a valuable member of Timothy. He cleaned the composting toilets, took on risky reef repair work, kept the town calendar.

June stood next to her mother, silent, and watched Javier. She thought he was beautiful and sometimes she was jealous of Summer. There was no one else for her: the other boys were young, too young.

You can see the shells burning holes in people's hands, Clare thought. It had always been this way, ever since the first time her mother had read the names.

"We won't be doing this much longer," someone said. "Next big storm and the ocean will wash right over us."

"Delacroix… Zanini… Dunbar," she read.

"I wish you'd say it," Beth said quietly.

Clare could hear the dragonflies. They weren't far away. She drifted in and out of her body. She felt as if her mother were inside of her, speaking for her, giving her the strength to do the right thing. The right thing, she repeated to herself.

Everyone was quiet because they knew it was time to turn over the shells. In a minute they would know.

Javier sensed a strange feeling in his heart, something dark and irritable, a feeling beyond sadness. Jade Sleeman lowered her gaze and began mumbling a prayer. None of them really knew how to pray but they'd seen the exiles years ago bowing down in front of the driftwood cross, the one bleached by the sun and surrounded by semi-circles of shells, which sometimes people kneeled upon until they bled.

No one moved, no one dared breathe until Clare

SECOND WONDER

by KEVIN MOFFETT

(This monologue will air this season on The Organist podcast, from McSweeney's and KCRW.)

The oldest person in town keeps dying. Yesterday the oldest person in the town died seven times—by the end of this account the oldest person in town will have died and died and died again. Some outlast their bodies, others are outlasted by them. Some dream of escaping themselves, scuttling free of their skin like naked crabs in search of a new body (our town is filthy with new bodies, unblemished, supple, vacant) but they can't. They all die after eating their last meal. The oldest person in town wants you to come closer, he has a secret: you know the giant safari painting hanging in his nursing home activity room? It terrifies him, he always keeps his back to it while doing activities, subconsciously he might connect it to the time he—no, the oldest person in town's secret is now that she never goes a day without smoking a cigar and eating a thick slice of hogshead cheese. Hogshead cheese isn't cheese at all but a terrine of congealed brain meat suspended in aspic. One of her middle husbands wouldn't let her have it in the house because he claimed it was hobo food. A man who ate pickled hardboiled eggs trying to disparage hogshead cheese? No sir. She served it every so often without him knowing, put it in stews and in a noodle casserole she called truck. These chitlins in here? he'd ask. The man had no quarrel with chitlins. She wasn't happy when he died and she wasn't unhappy either. Dying will be easy, it will be like reaching the end of a long day without anything left to dread or shepherd or forecast or unbutton. No more musical chairs. No more music. The oldest person in town pictures Death as a stout nurse pushing an empty wheelchair—no, the oldest person in town now pictures Death as a nice light-skinned usher with a flashlight. Walking patiently beside her with his hand on her back. The oldest person in town still remembers when there were ushers in movie theaters, real ushers, who wore velvet uniforms with piping and epaulets and would see you to your seat. Nothing much of importance has changed in her lifetime except that more people used to wear uniforms. Cats seem a little nicer now and every story is her story: she remembers inventing thunder and laughter and the alphabet and being rescued from a tower and the time the other villagers made her sew a scarlet A to her work shift. She remembers her first unsteady steps on the moon. The capsule door opening, the twin sensations of rising and falling as she hopped out, the agony of being born again. The oldest person in town lost track of her age twenty-seven years ago. She keeps an antler-handled fillet knife under her pillow. Two men come into her room, one with a camera around his neck and another with a vase full of flower-shaped fruit, and he says, You did it, can you believe it?, and she says, No, I can't. She reaches for the knife and says, Put whatever that is down and slowly walk away.

raised her hand. All at once everyone exhaled, except for Summer, who dropped her shell, the one that had the cross etched inside. She began backing away from everyone, staring at them like a startled animal, nostrils flared, mouth open. Her mother fell to the ground, crying. "It isn't fair."

"Everyone took the same chance," Jade said, as her eyes followed Summer down to the beach. "It's always been this way."

"It's the way it has to be," Bruce said from his chair, rising. "There isn't a choice."

"Clare," Beth said, repeating the name over and over again.

June reached for Clare but she was distant, outside of her own body. What if we just tried to get by? Clare wondered, not for the first time. What if we outlawed children and died out gracefully? But you couldn't keep people from getting pregnant, and they had to allow themselves the consolations of joy, didn't they? That had been her mother's thinking. She was thinking of her own mother now, her scent, something like burned skin, cooked onions, and carrots fresh from the earth. She thought of her mother's sins, and the ways she paid for them. The way they all did.

Jim Hutchison crouched as if he might be sick. Someone handed his youngest daughter, Kate, one of the conch shells people had begun to fetch. She looked at it, and then at her sister.

June moved forward, waiting. She'd never cared so much about a lottery. She'd never had such mixed feelings.

Javier stood at the front of the crowd, staring at the beach. Summer was already down there, working to build the driftwood raft, the basket of food by her side. He guessed that she had about twenty minutes left. Jim reached for his shoulder but Javier shrugged it off. He remembered something Summer had said one night as he had held her weightless in the water, kissing her neck. Her legs were wrapped around his body, her pale hair long and loose, the moonlight glinting off her damp forehead, the skeleton of Hope House on the horizon. She'd whispered, "Sometimes I think I'd rather die fast than go it alone and die slowly."

"But you wouldn't," he'd said. "Because I'd find you, and we'd make it. We'd get to Hope House. We'd survive."

But as she looked up from the raft to find Javier's face, her fingers tying the wood together as they'd practiced, Summer saw something in his eyes, something neither of them had expected, and she stood up from the pile of wood. She started back toward the village as she was not allowed to do, and it was an invitation. It was a request. Though she'd never seen a ballet in her life she opened up her body like a dancer, arms out, eyes shut, and thrust her chest forward to willingly receive the rocks and shells that found it.

THE TELL-TALE HEART

by ANTHONY MARRA

after "The Tell-Tale Heart" by Edgar Allan Poe

Your Honor, I stand accused not only of first degree murder by the prosecution, but of mental unfitness by my *own* defense lawyer—the charlatan in the polyester suit over there—and in light of this treachery, I have no choice but to confess to the former charge to defend myself from the latter. Please listen, Your Honor, to how reasonably, how rationally I describe the gruesome business—and then try to tell me that I am not mentally fit.

To begin with, I had nothing against Richard. No, just the opposite. He was my roommate and friend, the cultural and civic leader of our two-bedroom apartment at 2359 Green Pine Ave, #3A. He was a kind, soft-spoken

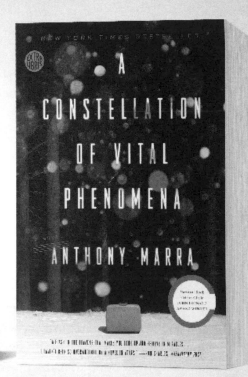

young man. He liked to think of himself as a rebel and had several piercing, which his mother made him remove when they went to brunch—I knew it was Sunday by the studs and hoops soaking in a teacup of his grandmother's Polident denture cleaner.

His only shortcoming, if you can call it that, was his iPhone. Every experience he dutifully engraved via tweet, post, or status in the marble memory of the cloud. Reality was only visible to Richard at 326 ppi. He had thousands of friends on Facebook, most of whom he'd never met, and when I saw the whole of his sturdy frame hunched over that glossy four-inch screen, tapping furiously, there seemed something pitiable about such a tall man submitting to something so small. It was clear he yearned for connection—he was no different than you or I, Your Honor.

The night he signed up for Tinder, I spied him through a crack in the bathroom door. I pressed my eye to the gap and watched as shirtless, stern-mouthed Richard nearly herniated himself trying to dredge a weak wedge of muscle from his padded abdomen. Again and again, Richard pointed his phone at the mirror, snapped a picture, and studied it. I studied him. I expected pride, self-satisfaction, but no, his face reddened in a flush of self-loathing. Not even he would sleep with himself.

I should've backed away and slipped into my bedroom, I know. That would've been the end of it. And I would have, but just when I'd made up my mind to leave Richard to his private discomfort, his eyes flashed to the mirror and I saw—or imagined—that his found mine in the reflection. His eyes were the deep blue of a vulture, and you can call me *unfit*, but if you stood at the cracked door, with those pale blue points pounding into your soul, your spine, too, would have wilted. But he hadn't even seen me, Your Honor. It was only a trick of the light.

When Richard went back to the bathroom the second night, I tried to concentrate on the book I was reading, told myself to focus, but was drawn—propelled, even—back to the gap in the door. This isn't me, I told myself. I'm no voyeur. But the previous evening, I had witnessed Richard's unvarnished self-doubt, had trespassed into an intimate space, and you may call me strange—mad, even—but I felt a greater connection to Richard in those moments than I'd ever felt to another person.

And so, that second night I stood in the narrow slab of light that sloped through the cracked door, and I again watched Richard watch himself. Floss-launched saliva asterisked the mirror. Richard stared into it with carefree composure that lasted as briefly as the camera flash. I pushed the door gently, oh so gently, until the two-inch crack widened to three. Still—still!—he didn't see me. He pressed the red delete button and the phone emitted a crumpled crush as the image disappeared. He sighed, drained of everything but relief. Over the next hour, he took dozens of self-portraits, and every time he deleted them, he sighed. Destroying the Richard of two seconds earlier seemed to fortify him. He wasn't taking pictures for his Tinder profile anymore. He was taking pictures to delete them—and my lawyer says *I'm* mad. It was terrible, seeing him there, at the sink, taking and destroying picture after picture, as if each one brought him closer to erasing his own face. His shoulders loosened as mine hunched. His tendons relaxed as mine stiffened. That was the moment when the idea came to me. Your Honor, my only madness was mercy. I was no more than a forefinger on the red delete button, finishing what he had himself begun.

Each night for eight nights, I stood at the bathroom threshold, and each night for eight nights, I cracked the door a few careful inches wider.

Each night I watched with a kitchen knife hidden behind my back. Not that I was planning anything—no, of course not—only because the presence of the knife pressurized each moment with thrilling possibility. Then, finally, the eighth night. I cracked the door inch by inch until my own face was visible in the corner of the mirror and still—still!—he refused to see

me. He stood shirtless at the mirror and as one photo became ten became twenty, each of which he erased, Your Honor, I swear I nearly turned away. But in that moment I noticed that Richard was holding the iPhone at too wide an angle to capture his own reflection in the mirror. The dark-pupiled camera lens stared directly at me. He took my photo, examined it, and went to press the red delete button, but before he could, a roiling terror uncorked inside my chest; tuning pegs tautened my nerves; what happened next was no more premeditated than your next heartbeat. I stepped forward and raised the knife. When I brought it down, his eyes finally met mine.

We needn't go into the gory details. You've all seen the crime scene photographs. I stoppered the puncture wounds with cotton balls. I checked his pulse, but anyone could see he was gone. I slid his favorite oxfords onto his feet, washed the blood from his face, and clothed him. What does one do with a corpse? I had it worked out so plainly, so perfectly: I pried open the living room floorboards and entombed him within the dusty cavity. For the rest of the night, I scrubbed the bathroom, washing blood from the walls, Cloroxing the tiles. When I finished erasing the evidence of Richard's death, I began erasing the evidence of his life. I trashed his toothbrush and wiped the mirror. I zipped the contents of his closet into

A NICKEL ON TOP OF A PENNY*

by STEPHEN BURT

I am going to disappear in Belmont,
after taking a walk in intermittent rain.
I will vanish one day in Belmont—don't correct me—
on a warm day like today, a Thursday, in fall.

I know it even more than I know how we all want
contradictory things, like security and excitement,
immortality, hang gliders, gumdrops, a home, and all
the space in the world—Eden, Paris, Tokyo, Cockaigne.

My writing hand hurts. To the good friends who asked me to dinner,
I'm afraid I should tell you not to expect me.
When you set the table, say, "Stephanie couldn't be here,
although we were good to her; we gave her presents

for Christmas and such; we answered most of her letters,
importunate as they became; we tried not to offend her;
we sat through her chatter about piano lessons,

and telephoned her in the midst of a snowstorm last year.
We think we could not have treated her any better.
We never believed she'd simply disappear."

_____

* after "Piedra Negra Sobre Una Piedra Blanca" by César Vallejo

two suitcases and cleared them into the dumpster out back. I worked all night and fell asleep in the purple dawn light.

Three sharp knocks flung me into the somber afternoon. I sat up, my face and chest damp, and tiptoed to the door, half-believing I'd dissolve into a puddle of perspiration before reaching it. Could the authorities have been summoned? Had I been too loud? Had Richard shrieked as he died, or had I as I dreamed?

But the woman behind the door wore an expression of cautious optimism. She fidgeted with her hair. I stood back from the peephole, having already spent too much of my life watching the inner dramas of others.

"Yes?" I asked, opening the door.

Her smile was a cheerful breath intruding into the apartment's gloom. "I'm here to see Richard."

"How do you know him?"

The corners of her lips tightened as she tried to parse an answer. "We met, well, we haven't met yet, but we're supposed to hang out."

"I'm sorry?"

"We have a date," she said.

I couldn't believe it. He'd actually met someone on Tinder.

"He isn't here yet?" She checked her watch. "I guess I'm a couple minutes early. You mind if I wait inside?"

She must've been from some idyllic Midwestern province where people leave their doors unlocked and instruct their children to say thank you when accepting candy from strangers. But I had nothing to fear; I'd been too careful, too crafty. Your Honor, you should have seen how sanely I smiled as I invited her in.

A faint buzzing came from somewhere, but I ignored it. I was too busy being convincingly stable, the kind of roommate Richard always wanted me to be. She tapped on her phone while we talked.

There! Again! A murmur beneath the floorboards. Dear God—was he still alive? No, he couldn't be, impossible. I had held him in my arms and felt the soul sigh from him. And yet I crossed the room to stand on the floorboard but my weight wasn't enough to silence the throbbing beneath.

She frowned. Had she heard it too? She must have.

"Is something wrong?" I asked.

"He isn't responding," she said, sending another message on Tinder. "I'll try again."

"No, no, no," I said. One *no* too many.

But I barely heard her because the hum beneath the floorboards had grown to an audible shudder. The vibration pulsed from the wood grain through my shoe soles so that I was not standing on a floor but on the very frequency of Richard's heart. His heart, preserved in that cursed phone, shaking with each message she sent! I'd recognize it anywhere, the two-part clamor so imprinted in my consciousness while I'd lived with Richard that I heard it in foot shuffle, in cricket legs, in my own beating chest. I must have slipped the phone into his pocket as I dressed him—the carelessness! I wanted to shout, to pull my hair, but the woman now looked at me curiously—oh God!—she pretended not to hear, just as Richard had pretended not to see. I had no choice but to maintain the charade.

"Maybe you could call him?" she asked again, checking her watch. "Or maybe better not. He seemed like an alright guy when we were messaging, but man, standing someone up from a hookup app? That's just demoralizing."

"No, it's not that." My voice slipped, my hands trembled. The gears of my dark imaginings spun by the pedal power of my pacing. "He'd never do that. There must be an emergency holding him up."

"Really? Now I'm worried," she said, setting her hand on my forearm. "Please call him."

I reached for the landline and dialed his number. My breaths quickened to gasps. Richard's heart had stopped on the floor in the bathroom—it had!—I had felt the pulse silence beneath my finger tips. Now the short, shimmying pulses grew louder, louder, louder still beneath the floorboards. The clamor resounded and—God, oh God—I was resurrecting him! I was putting the drumbeat back into his muted heart! He would rise from beneath the floor, I was sure of it, and then—I was sobbing—ranting—weeping—he spoke to me from across the chasm of death: *Hi, you've reached Richard. Not here, obviously. Leave your name and number and I'll call back.*

The floorboards beneath me had silenced, but I still heard Richard in the static-laced stillness of his afterlife.

The woman now tormented me with an expression of grave concern. She asked if I was okay, if I was sick, if I needed a doctor. Could she not hear the vibrations of the phone? The beat still thundered in my ears—booming! banging! blaring! How could she just stand there asking if I needed help? Mad—she must be! She knew! She heard! She had! Yet there she stood, torturing me with kindness! It was too much. I couldn't bear it. Anything was better than this anguish. I dropped to my knees, pried up the floorboard, and reached into the dusty cavity to extract Richard's phone. "There!" I howled. "There he is! Take it!"

I thrust it into the woman's hands, and she stared at me, first dumbfounded, then horrified, and before she accepted the phone, before she snatched it and charged outside to call the police, she looked from Richard to me, from Richard's empty eyes to my own, and the three of us shared a moment of genuine connection.

FALLING FAINTLY

by JESS WALTER

after "The Dead" by James Joyce

He told her twice that night that he loved her.

The first time was outside a bar in Brooklyn when they'd gone out to smoke together. Michael had started up again just two weeks earlier, when he saw her step away from the set, shake one from its pack, and go out a side door. He'd followed her out and bummed a smoke.

"Hard to quit," he said by way of introduction.

"Who wants to?" she asked, her accent surprisingly heavy when she wasn't acting.

After that, Michael started making excuses to be on set, hoping to catch her smoke breaks. They always seemed to find one another, a raised eyebrow, a tilt of the head; they'd probably smoked ten times together in the two weeks between their first cigarette and that night at the bar.

Oh, that night. How many times would he replay it—every word, every glance? Dead of winter on a Friday night in Williamsburg, a noisy group from the show was waiting in the bar for a table when he made eye contact with her (*Smoke?—Sure*) and they excused themselves, went outside, and drifted a few steps down the sidewalk. He cupped his hand over hers, against the wind, as he lit her cigarette. She was tall and pale, with lovely brown hair and a thin face that made every other face seem like an error in composition. She drew in smoke and let it go into the sky. A light snow was falling, swirling in updrafts so that the world seemed weightless around them.

"We're in for a night of it," Michael said. "This snow—"

"Pretty," she said in smoke, her accent breaking the word in two.

"Faintly falling," he said.

Michael was a novelist who had gotten—just in time for his forty-fifth birthday—this dream job, a spot in the writer's room of a television show. The show was called *Eight Days* and it was about two detectives investigating a murder over eight days in 1950s Brooklyn. After the pilot had been accepted, they'd written what was called a mini-season, but at the last minute they got an order for thirteen episodes, a full first season. So the cast and crew were taping those first five episodes on a sound stage in a converted bread factory in Long Island City while he and the other writers hurriedly wrote the last eight.

The Brooklyn of *Eight Days* was a very different place from the one Michael found himself smoking in six decades later, in that Year of our Lord in which novelists first found themselves sought after by TV producers (just as God and the Writer's Guild intended). Michael could think of no downside to being a TV writer. The money was great. Prestige was high. And he was free from his Colorado teaching job and tenure limbo stick. He missed his kids, but frankly, having his boys see their dad as a success was better than the alternative: eating some sad sack dinner with him at Red Robin every other weekend. At least that's what he told himself.

And while the job caused him to write dialogue that sometimes made him wince, he was happy to have discovered the secret of "quality television": all the shit you edited out of a decent novel—the overt and sentimental, the contrived and programmatic, the soap-operatic—is precisely what makes for good TV.

The show also introduced him to a world of people who seemed to be his long-lost creative tribe: cameramen, location scouts, makeup artists, audio engineers, designers, various people whose jobs he couldn't quite discern, and most of all, the actors—these ethereal people he longed to be cool around, to seem unimpressed by, but whose attentions left him breathless.

Especially her: Jana De Vos, a Belgian actress, all of 26, who somehow found within those divine lungs, throat, and mouth a surprisingly believable outer-borough accent with which to portray fiery Dolores, wife of one of the TV detectives.

"You were great in the dinner scene," he said as they smoked that night.

"Thank you," she said. He was amazed how heavy her accent became when she wasn't acting. "The writing also was good."

"Thank you," he said, even though he hadn't written that one. He *had* given notes on the episode, though, specifically on Dolores's character. More and more he found himself writing just for her. Once, Jana had even mentioned during a smoke break that she didn't understand why her character seemed so unhappy. He said he'd see what he could do and ended up pitching a scene in which the childless Dolores stands on her stoop watching children play stickball outside.

That night, she did eighteen takes of a scene in a hot-lit corner of the dark soundstage. Dolores's husband, the more stoic of the two detectives, was only two episodes from being revealed as gay. In the scene, the couple is beginning to fight about his coldness, and about her unhappiness. In each take, she yelled at her closeted TV husband in the shell of their dining room, and then slammed china against the table. The china, specially made to shatter, would always be cleaned up for the next take, lighting and sound adjusted, and then she'd be back in the moment, yelling and throwing more plates, and each take, Michael believed the scene more than the time before—so pure was this girl's talent. During one take, she threw a plate but it didn't break, just bounced high in the air. Everyone on set started laughing together at this cathartic break in tension, and that's when Michael noticed that she seemed to seek out his eyes. She's looking for me, he thought. Finally, they wrapped the dinner scene, the crew applauding perfunctorily, and that's when a handful of them decided to go for a drink and a late dinner. Michael had no reason to be on set that day—another writer was in the box for rewrites—but he'd wanted to watch Jana's big scene and was hoping for this very thing: that he'd find a moment to smoke outside a bar alone with her.

And here they were, the snow swirling, floating flakes dancing at their feet, flakes floating in the cold air between them. "'Falling faintly,'" he said, again, "'through the universe and faintly falling.'"

She cocked her head. He'd noticed that when

she didn't understand something, she tilted her head like this, like a woman preparing to be kissed. He leaned in, just a bit closer.

"It's from 'The Dead,'" he said. "Do you know it?" He took a drag. "The Joyce story? From *Dubliners?*" Smoke and steam mingled in his breath while he reveled in thoughts of James Joyce's classic story: snow on the Dublin grave-yards dusting the scant evidence of our time here on earth.

She just stared at him, her head tilted. Michael felt their eyes lock and if he'd been closer he would have leaned in to kiss her. "You should read it," he said quietly. "'The Dead'—it's my favorite story."

They stared, snow in the air between them.

He felt something physical and surprising, like a warm seam opening in his chest, an ice dam giving way, a dam built up after the divorce, after the last few shitty years, the last shitty decade. If he could have named the feeling, he might've called it Grudging Acceptance of Benevolence. His whole adult life, he'd been a member in good standing of this dreary species called novelist, and as such had always expected his fate to be that of the downtrodden, under-paid, unappreciated artist, a path he'd lived duly and forthrightly: forty-five, divorced, midlist, middle-class, suspicious of the thinness of his hair and of his talent. And yet here he was: making money, writing smart TV, standing on a Brooklyn street talking to the most beautiful girl he'd ever seen.

Their eyes linked, and the moment felt elec-trified. And in the heat of such a moment comes the hard awareness of its passing. The best bits are like this—too fast, too hot, a flare arcing over a dark sea. He moved slowly to close the space between them.

"Jana," he said quietly, "this isn't just me, is it? This feeling?"

She tilted her head a little further.

"Jana," he said again, and then the words came in a great rush—the deep hole he was in after his divorce, doubting his lifelong desire to be a writer, his string of bad luck, and his friend Patrick calling him with this opportunity, coming to Brooklyn, meeting *her*, "Oh my god, *you*, Jana!" He told her about the anticipation he felt every time he knew he was going to see her, the thrill of writing dialogue for her, her incredible beauty, the extra care he took with her lines, the way he watched her and came to the set when he knew she'd be there—and too, he talked about his own writing, its limitations against his huge ambi-tions. And he talked about "The Dead," about the snow falling on the graves at the end of that story, about not wanting to waste his brief time on Earth, about living with passion in the furious finger-snap of time.

"Listen," he said, "I know we haven't known

each other very long, but maybe… I don't know, Jana, maybe our feelings can't wait. Maybe they race ahead and we have to run to catch them. Maybe our feelings exist in spite of us, swirling around us, like this snow, like the snow in 'The Dead.' Faintly falling and falling faintly." He whispered, "And us, too."

Her mouth opened slightly.

Fuck it, he'd already come this far: "Jana, I am in love with you. I'm so in love with you I can barely stand it."

That was the first time.

The second time was three hours later, outside her building in Fort Greene, a mere four blocks from his own subleased apartment. Michael stood on the sidewalk. The snow had stopped falling and was already melting. Cabs blew past, combing the dirty slush with their tires, slushy dirt in the creases of the curbs. Michael made a ball of slush and threw it at her window. It took three slush balls before he hit it. He called up from the street. "Jana! Please! Come down! I want to talk to you. I love you!" Ten minutes later, two police officers showed up and wrestled him to the cold, wet sidewalk.

The ankle monitor was a simple black device, the size of a wallet, like a big watch on a black plastic strap around his lower leg. It was waterproof so that he could shower. The bracelet measured his heart beat and sent an electrical signal to a small black power station plugged into the wall like a landline telephone, which, every minute or so, sent a message to the company that monitored such things and notified his probation officer if he so much as left his apartment without permission.

Of course, he'd been fired from the show. He didn't blame Jana for this. *He* was the one who'd struggled with the police officers. *He* was the one with a half-gram of cocaine in his pocket (stupid Freddy the Grip, with his stupid cheap cocaine.) *He* was the one who, after Jana rebuffed him, went back to the bar, snorted a line with Freddy and got really drunk. *He* was the one standing on a street yelling that he loved a girl who, he had to admit it now, he barely knew, a girl who apparently had less mastery of English than he'd imagined.

When he read her police statement later, Michael wasn't sure how things had gotten so out of hand, how she'd misunderstood him so completely. Had all of that eye contact meant nothing? Was the language barrier even worse than he'd imagined? Was she insane?

"The suspect then told Ms. De Vos that he loved her and 'couldn't live without her.' He repeatedly talked about her being 'dead' if he couldn't have her. Later, he threw rocks at her apartment window and repeated his threats."

"I threw slush, not rocks!" Michael protested to his lawyer. "And what *threats*? I did *not* tell her I wanted her dead! I quoted 'The Dead'!"

"Okay?" said his lawyer, a bitterly thin woman of fifty whose every sentence lilted up like a teenager's. "I don't know what that is?"

"'The Dead'? The short story? By James Joyce?"

His middle-aged-teenaged lawyer shrugged.

"This man, Gabriel, goes to a party with his wife, Gretta. After the party, Gretta tells him about a young man who stood outside her window in the rain, professing his love until he died of pneumonia. Gabriel becomes so unsettled by the story and by the depth of the young man's love that it sends him into a reverie of passion in the face of mortality. *That's* why I went to her apartment. Because of 'The Dead.'"

His lawyer cocked her head. "You want me to go into court and say you were inspired by some stalking manual called 'The Dead'?"

"'The Dead' is not a stalking manual. It's a classic."

"Okay? So is *Silence of the Lambs*? But that doesn't mean you get to go up to a woman and say, 'It puts the lotion in the basket,' and expect her to fall in love with you."

Michael was dumbfounded. After writing two novels that featured lawyers and courtrooms, after working on this television show about cops, after having a couple of run-ins with the law himself, he really knew nothing at all about the criminal justice system. All he could manage to say was, "I don't think you can really call *Silence of the Lambs* a classic."

There was the problem, too, of Michael's criminal record: a drug conviction in college, a DUI during the bad years of his marriage, and worst of all, the domestic violence charge from the worst days of his divorce. Michael explained how he'd discovered e-mails from his wife's lover and had confronted Meredith with the evidence at a restaurant. They became physical, wrestled and pulled each other's hair, and since Colorado law requires that at least one party be charged when police make a DV call, he was arrested. The charges were later dismissed, but the arrest still showed up on his record.

His lawyer seemed unimpressed by his version of the domestic violence, or for that matter, his Joycean defense for stalking.

And so, on the advice of his surly attorney, Michael pled guilty to second-degree criminal harassment and misdemeanor possession of cocaine, thereby getting the state to drop the resisting arrest charge. In this way, he avoided jail and retained the possibility of having his conviction set aside if he abided by the terms of his probation. The judge put him under six months house arrest and his probation officer fitted him with this home-monitoring ankle bracelet, his lawyer saying they could petition for release after three months as long as he hadn't violated the terms.

With this plastic shackle around his leg, Michael could leave only during daytime, and only after clearing it with his probation officer, to see his counselor, or for cleared trips to the market—things like that. "Otherwise, unless your apartment is on fire, if you so much as go out to the curb, this device will alert us that you're no longer in the apartment and you, my friend, will go to jail," his probation officer said.

He paced like a dog in a shelter. By the third day, he considered setting his apartment on fire. Two steps across the bedroom, one into the kitchen, three across the living room and one into the bathroom: how had he come to believe that paying $2,600 for 850 furnished square feet was a good deal? In Denver he could've rented a mansion for $2,600 a month; in Fort Dodge, Iowa, where he was born, he could own a whole neighborhood. This tiny space was insane. Kafkaesque. After four days, he took down all the art from the walls.

Michael's apartment was on the second floor of a walkup; he began haunting the one window that looked out on the street, staring out at the people below him. Michael watched two young women stretch for their morning jog against the iron railing on the stoop. He watched a bearded father tuck his son's long hair under a stocking cap before walking the boy to school. He watched until the father and the son turned the corner, until the girls jogged away, and then he turned from the window, tears welling in his eyes.

He hated how much he ached to see Jana. You barely know her, he told himself. *Doesn't matter.* You're fixating; she represents something else, some longing for another kind of life. For your own lost youth. *I don't care. If I could just talk to her, explain that I hadn't meant to scare her, that I was only pretending to be obsessed, that I was talking about "The Dead"* . . .

He googled her name to see if there was news. He checked her Facebook page and her Twitter feed, even though he knew for a fact that a publicist managed those accounts. He wrote long e-mails to her that he later deleted. If he tried to contact her, the judge had made clear, he would serve the rest of his time in jail.

The worst part was that Jana was only four blocks away. The producers had prepared them a list of available apartments and they'd apparently chosen places in the same neighborhood. He'd discovered this coincidence one day during a smoke break, when he asked where she lived. He almost swallowed his cigarette when she said, "Fort Greene."

"We're neighbors!" he'd said, and he saw something flash in her eyes.

Christ, clearly he'd seen something that just wasn't there. He thought of Tolstoy: "It is amazing how complete is the delusion that beauty is goodness."

Still, he didn't entirely blame her. Something else must have been going on that night. Yet he couldn't shake the feeling that he hadn't *entirely* imagined the moment between them, either, the closeness he felt. Even if she didn't feel exactly the same way, he wished he could make her see what an honest misunderstanding it had been.

He pulled down his copy of *Dubliners*, wondering what would happen if he just mailed it to her anonymously; maybe she would understand. But what if she saw it as another threat? He needed to explain himself. Christ, four blocks! He could run over there, ring her buzzer, leave the book inside her foyer! Four blocks! He looked at the black monitoring device plugged into the home phone jack. How long would it take before the company at the other end got a notification that he was gone? A minute? Two? And how long before the police showed up at Jana's apartment? He flicked at the black band on his ankle.

Jesus, was he going insane? Would he really endanger his freedom to give some girl he barely knew a book? Was he prepared, like Michael Furey, to face death merely to see her face again?

Oh, he could be so delusional sometimes— imagining that a young actress would be moved by a book. Some foolish nineteenth-century man adrift in the twenty-first. He had to remind himself that this woman wasn't in love with him; this was about his own feelings.

It seemed to be those very feelings that he was working so hard to protect, perhaps overprotect— the idea that the love he'd declared to her was proven by the sheer intensity of its declaration.

Look, I apparently misjudged how you might feel, he would say to her. *But I need you to know that* my *feelings, as I expressed them, were real, overwhelmingly real, not some deluded middle-aged crush, or some late-night lust.* He had this idea that the best way to explain the depth of his feeling was to have her read "The Dead."

When she looked up from the story, he would say to her, *I know I was intense the other night, Jana. I'm sorry. But if what I feel isn't love, then I don't think love exists.*

And then they would kiss.

He turned *Dubliners* over in his hand.

Michael reread his letter to her: "If what I felt for you that night is not love, Jana, then I am not sure love *can* exist."

He stared at the words. He imagined her opening the letter. And then he burst out laughing. "You're losing it," he said aloud. Christ, maybe he *was* a stalker. He'd begun to notice a pattern to his thoughts about Jana and what had happened that night: this need to justify his feelings inflated their rhetorical intensity, like a balloon blown up with its own deluded sentimentality. Eventually, the balloon popped, like now, in a moment of humiliated self-awareness.

"Interesting," said his court-appointed counselor, a man in his early sixties with gray hair and endlessly amused eyes. "So if self-awareness deflates the balloon, how can you stop blowing it up in the first place?"

"All I know," Michael said, "is that I wake up every day with this profound desire to explain myself."

"Explain? Or justify?" the counselor asked.

"Maybe. Look, I know I acted a little crazy. But I *really* felt something that night. Something I hadn't felt in, I don't know, a decade. Or ever. Something deep and transcendent. What am I supposed to do with that?"

The counselor flipped back a page in his notebook. "I've noticed you use words like that a lot. *Transcendent. Epiphany. Profound.* Almost religious terms. Are you religious?"

"No," he said. "I'm a writer."

The counselor laughed. "Can I ask, have you ever been to AA?"

"No," Michael said. "But I'm not an alcoholic."

The counselor was quiet.

Michael laughed. "There's really no way to say you don't have a drinking problem without sounding defensive or delusional, is there?" Honestly, he *had* been drinking more since he started the TV show—and twice he'd snorted stupid Freddy the Grip's discount blow. Fuckin' Freddy.

"Just think about it for the next time," the counselor said, uncrossing his legs to signal the session was over.

Michael took a cab home. He had the driver go past Jana's apartment. He looked up to her window. Blinds. Next time he could just have the driver stop and he could drop the book off. With a note.

Outside his brownstone, he took deep breaths. The spring air was thick with car exhaust, Greek meat cooking on the corner. He ran his hand along the iron rail of the stoop, the place those girls would put their ankles tomorrow to stretch, the place where the little boy would lean while his father tucked his bushy hair under his cap.

It was four o'clock in New York. Sixteen hundred miles away, in Denver, Michael's two sons would be starting their last hour of school. They were too old to have their hair tucked under their caps. Michael felt his eyes welling up again. Christ, what was the matter with him?

He keyed into his apartment, his charming

$2,600-a-month brownstone jail cell. He looked at the black monitor plugged like a phone into the wall. Its white electronic eye stared out at the world. When his cell phone rang Michael jumped, thinking for a moment it was the home monitoring system.

It was just Freddy the Grip. "Man. Hey. I just wanted to thank you, you know, for not bringing up my name in all this shit?"

"No problem," Michael said.

Days passed. He got another call, from his friend Patrick Martin, the television writer who had gotten him the job. They'd met years earlier, at a summer writing conference that included screenwriters, poets—all kinds of writers. They'd immediately hit it off. When Patrick had called out of the blue to say he was the show-runner for a new TV series and asked if Michael wanted to write for it, Michael had almost started crying.

"Just wanted to check in. You doing okay, man?"

"I'm fine, Patrick. A little humiliated."

"Everyone feels terrible."

"Can I ask … Jana? Is she—"

"I can't talk about that, Michael."

"Sure. No, I understand. I just wanted someone to tell her—"

Patrick interrupted, "Really Michael, I can't—"

"I don't suppose you have a copy of *Dubliners*," Michael asked.

"A copy of what?"

"*Dubliners*? The book of stories by James Joyce."

"No, I don't."

"Listen, if you could just get a copy of that book to Jana. Ask her to read—"

"Michael, I'll have to hang up if you keep talking about her. The producers sent a letter out. We aren't supposed to say anything about it. You know, if this ends up in court and it turns out you and I talked about it—"

"I was already in court," Michael said.

"You know what I mean, Mike. Like a civil suit. Workplace environment shit."

Jesus, he thought. A civil suit?

"I just called to say that we're using your pages for the episode ten-eleven swing, and they've decided to pay you for the whole season, which I figured would be good news for you. Your agent should be getting an email sometime this week."

He felt a burst of warmth for his old friend. "That's great, Patrick. Thank you. I'm gonna use that money to get back to Denver, be near my boys."

"I think that's a great idea," Patrick said. "And you know what, when this whole thing fades, maybe we could get you back in the room… everyone liked you. I mean, you never know."

"Thank you," Michael took a breath. He spoke quickly. "If you could just tell Jana to read that story. Tell her I wasn't saying I wanted her dead. It was—"

But Patrick had hung up before Michael could say *an homage*.

Michael stared at his phone in his hand. Homage? Was he really about to say *an homage*? Christ. *An homage?* His head fell to his chest.

Two nights a week, Michael talked to his boys back in Denver on Skype. Evan was ten, Tommy eight.

"Hey Dad!" they'd say, their voices so full of life and forgiveness it shocked him every time. Tommy had grown almost as tall as Evan, and Michael felt bad for his older son, who had his mother's small frame and pretty features. And suddenly he recalled the indignities that went along with being ten, and being eight, and he felt like the worst father in the world for not being there for his boys.

"You guys good?" he asked hopefully.

"Yup," they said every time. Their hair seemed both too long and too carefully combed. It should be tousled and cowlicked, messy from playing outside. The boys told him about school, about ski racing, about the dog they wanted to get.

"Tell you what, when I get there, we'll get a dog. How's that sound?"

He heard his ex-wife in the background, "Okay, let's wrap this up."

"Love you guys!" Michael always said at the end.

After the boys were gone, he'd stare at the computer screen for a few seconds more, at the electronic traces of them. Then he'd look for news of Jana on Facebook and Twitter. Or he'd start another e-mail to her. His e-mails always started the same way, with an apology, and then an explanation, for the hundredth time, of the plot of "The Dead." He always deleted them.

He watched the girls stretch on the stoop. Their legs were impossibly long.

Evan's face filled the computer screen. Tommy was at a friend's house. "Hey, Dad!"

"Hey Ev. You finish your homework?"

"I did all my math. Mom wants me to start on my hero project even though it's not due for two weeks."

"You can't let things go until the end, buddy. Start now, buy yourself some time later. Did you ever decide who you're doing?"

"I wanna do Adrian Peterson but Mom thinks Nelson Mandela would be a better hero. What do you think?"

Michael's voice cracked. "They're both great choices, buddy."

Routines developed. In the third week, Michael began turning off the wi-fi on his computer and his phone so that he could write without the temptation of going on the internet. Without the TV show to occupy his work hours, he returned to an unfinished novel he'd abandoned two years earlier. He made better progress on this book in two weeks than he had in the previous three years. The novel was set in the Pacific Northwest, at the turn of the century. Michael worked on it every day until noon, when he quit writing and did pushups and sit-ups until he was exhausted. Then he'd take a shower and, if he had permission from his probation officer, go to the store or to his counselor.

"I'm done feeling sorry for myself," Michael told his counselor.

"In my experience, no one's ever done feeling sorry for himself," his counselor said.

"Then it's okay if I bitch about paying twenty-six hundred bucks a month for a one-bedroom jail cell?"

"As long as you acknowledge whose fault that is."

"James Joyce's?"

"I don't know who that is," the counselor said

Michael looked at the clock on the counselor's desk. The time went so fast. "You asked me to think about AA. I did. And maybe I *am* fooling myself," he said, "but I really don't think booze is my problem."

"What's your problem?" his counselor asked.

"I have two," he said. "Longing and literature."

"You're right," the counselor said. "You *are* fooling yourself."

His novel started to take shape, like some figure in the distance, coming closer every day. It was about two brothers who go looking for their missing sister. He woke thinking of the characters, writing sentences in his mind. He'd always imagined the novel would really get off the ground once these two earnest brothers began having adventures. But he became interested in the sister's point of view. He found that she was living in a brothel in Corvallis, Oregon.

Writing from her point of view, he realized she hadn't been taken away; she had run away because life in a brothel was better than life on the ranch, where one of the brothers had been making advances toward her. It was a great realization: the brothers, these two character, chasing her across the West—he'd always assumed these men would rescue the sister and one of them was actually the person she was running from!

He told his counselor the development in his novel, finding the villain where he least expected it.

His counselor just stared at him, a wry smile on half his face.

"Yeah, I know," Michael said.

When did he stop obsessing about her? One day he just realized it had been a week since he'd visited her Facebook page or her Twitter account. Two weeks since he'd googled her. He never had the cab driver go past her apartment building anymore.

When he thought of her now, he was filled with shame for his foolishness, for his selfishness, for his deluded heart.

Then, one morning, six weeks into his home detention, with the spring sun breaking over the Brooklyn streets, he forgave even himself. He was sitting at the window, staring out. His eyes welled with tears, and this time he just let them spill over onto his cheeks. Couples laughed on the street below. Women walked dogs on shiny leashes. He thought of his own leash and wondered if he might actually miss the ankle bracelet after it was gone. It had saved his life in some way. He felt tethered to his better self by it, to a quieter self, free of the ambition and frenzied desire he'd lived with in New York the last few months.

That afternoon, on Skype, he apologized to Evan for not being there—"Sometimes we fool ourselves into thinking we belong somewhere we don't." He told his son that he'd never miss another game, another ski race, another spelling bee. He said that he'd be back as soon as he could. For good.

On the MacBook screen, Evan shifted uneasily on his bed. "Okay," he said.

"I love you, buddy," Michael said.

"Okay," Evan said.

Michael began to imagine his life back in Denver. He'd finish this novel and then he'd write a TV pilot; Denver would make a great setting for a show. He'd commit himself to being the best father he could be—start living for his boys.

His lawyer said she would petition the court for early release. They had a good chance of getting him out of his home detention early, especially if he was going home to Colorado.

Michael still looked out the window every morning, but it was less as a prisoner looking out on the yard than as an artist looking for inspiration. He felt the purest love for those girls who stretched on the stoop every day at 6:30 a.m. before going out to jog together. He named them—Lycra and Hoody. One day, as the weather warmed, he opened the window to listen to them laugh while they stretched. Hoody was telling some story of romantic entanglement that he caught in fragments. ("It was like being patted down at the airport.")

Michael laughed. He didn't know if he'd ever been happier. No, that wasn't right; he didn't know if he'd ever felt more at peace.

And that's when Freddy the Grip called.

The show had wrapped that day and everyone was scattering, heading off to new jobs, back to Hollywood, to their various homes. The powers that be seemed intent on a second season, so everyone was going away happy.

Michael was surprised by how well he took the news. "Well, I'm glad," he said. "Good people there. Look, you take care of yourself, Freddy, and maybe we'll work on something together in the future."

"Yeah," Freddy said. "That'd be cool. I thought I might come over with a bottle of whiskey— have one for the road."

Michael flinched. It had been almost six weeks since he'd had anything to drink. But before he could decline Freddy lowered his voice and admitted there was something else.

He had a letter from Jana.

It was a half-page letter, written on light blue stationery. She had the handwriting of a child. Michael's hands shook as he read it.

Dear Michael,

I am very sorry for so much trouble. (I am sorry for my English too.) I hope you understand. You scared me but I never mean for you lose your job. When I was a girl in Schaerbeek a man I meet and this man said he wants to take pictures for modeling. He said many things about my beauty and I will be a star. Then he took me to a house. He locked me to a railing and I could not leave for three days. The things he did I will never say. I thought he would kill me. He let me go and I did not tell even my mother. I pretended I have run away on my own because I did not want to say what this man did.

I did not think you would hurt me but my therapist Monica believes I am remind of this man. Monica says I will feel better if I write you this letter but not send it. But after I wrote I wanted to send it to you. I am sorry there was so much trouble. I always liked to smoke with you.

Jana

Michael looked up from the letter. He finished another glass of Jack Daniels and held his glass up for Freddy to fill it again. His breath felt short, electric. Christ—what if Tolstoy was wrong? What if beauty *was* goodness?

"I don't know about this," Freddy said. He set the portable power generator and the huge roll of phone cord on the table. "You sure you ain't building a bomb or something?"

"I told you what I'm doing," Michael said. He peeled off four hundred-dollar bills and handed them to Freddy. "Look, I didn't tell anyone where I got the coke, I'm not going to tell anyone about this."

They'd almost finished the whiskey when Michael had the idea. It hadn't been hard for Freddy to get the things Michael had asked for that night: a portable power generator with AC plug and a thousand feet of bulk phone cord. These were the advantages of knowing a crew member on a TV show.

Michael took one more pull of whiskey from the bottle. He unraveled the phone cord from its spool, looping it onto the floor of the apartment. When he got to the end, he plugged it into the wall jack. Then he unplugged the home monitoring station from its phone cord and connected it to the other end of the thousand feet of cord. He unplugged the monitoring station from the wall socket and plugged it into the Duracell PowerPack 300.

He held his breath as he waited for the ankle monitor or the phone station to register the break in signal, but it didn't seem to have caused any problem. The black monitor stared at him with that unblinking eye.

"Ha!" Michael yelled. His jail cell was now portable.

Freddy had seemed excited by the idea earlier but now he shifted uneasily. "Yeah," he said.

THE METAPHOR PROGRAM*
by BRIAN TURNER

so much depends
upon

the zero
and the one

amplified by Moore's
Law

at the Utah
Data Center.

* after "The Red Wheelbarrow" by William Carlos Williams

"I think I'm gonna take off now."

"Okay," Michael said.

He was glad to be alone for this.

This was it for him.

He would never again work on a TV show, never again be so close to the hot, throbbing center of life, of fame, never again be so close to a beautiful young girl.

We are meteors, burning up as we cross the night sky.

And for him, the time had come to set out on his journey westward.

He waited until 4 a.m., when he figured the streets would be empty. Right off he saw it was going to be tougher than he'd drunkenly anticipated. He looped the bulky phone cord over his left shoulder. In one hand he carried the heavy portable power station; in the other, the black phone monitor, which was plugged into the generator. He didn't have enough hands for the bottle of whiskey but that was probably for the best. After six weeks sober, he'd gotten drunk fast. He allowed loops of phone cord to fall off his shoulder as he backed down the steps of his brownstone, *Dubliners* tucked under his left arm.

The phone cord was light enough, but a thousand feet of it was awkward to carry. He unrolled it behind him slowly as he moved out

the front door, down the steps, and down the sidewalk. He tucked it against the curb so that it would be less noticeable. It was incredibly slow going. Where he crossed streets, he strung the phone cord across the pedestrian crossing. He went the long way so he wouldn't have to cross Lafayette, the busiest street between his apartment and Jana's.

He crossed Portland just as a cab turned and ran over the cord. He looked down at the phone monitor; the light hadn't changed.

It was a quiet, warm spring night. At four thirty in the morning even Brooklyn was dead. Michael slowly made his way past brownstones like his, laying loops of cord, walking a few feet, another loop, another few feet, another loop.

A young man and a lovely blond woman stood on a stoop, extending their 5 a.m. goodbye. The woman was barefoot, in a dress. The man wore a ball cap and was a step below and this made them the same height. He was holding her hand loosely, staring at some space between them. She nudged him and pointed to Michael, who was moving slowly down the sidewalk, dropping loops of phone cord.

"Hi," Michael said, trying to sound as normal as he could. He held up the battery pack and monitor for them to see. "I work on a TV show." The couple said nothing. "So…"

The load lightened as he dropped the phone

cord behind him. He stopped twice to set the power generator down for a short rest. On the way back he'd recoil the cord over his shoulder.

It wasn't until he turned the corner toward her place that he realized he would be at least a hundred feet short. Damn! He pulled the cord tighter, but it must have snagged on something, a mailbox or a light post. He risked breaking it. He'd have to go back, pull it off whatever had snagged it, maybe off all those curbs.

Michael had just started back when he glanced left and caught his own faint reflection in a street-level window. He wore a black jacket and black jeans and he carried the phone monitor and the personal power source like a man carrying shackles. His thin hair had grown longer, especially on the sides. He couldn't see his face in the window's reflection, but something about his slumping, middle-aged frame was sadly familiar. That's when Joyce's line came to him: *a ludicrous figure, a nervous, well-meaning sentimentalist, orating to vulgarians and idealizing his own clownish lusts.*

Michael slumped against the building on the corner. He and his reflection slid to the sidewalk. He was so close; he could *see* her building, her window on the dark third floor, not eighty feet away. He looked down at the black ankle bracelet and the small black phone monitor, plugged into the temporary power box.

He leaned back against the wall. The writer believes he is considering death, but the truth is mortality is the one with the final choice.

It was almost dawn on what looked to be a lovely spring day. The sun was just coloring the horizon but had not yet risen. Sun would soon be generous all over the city. It would rise on the dark fields of Central Park, on the tree-lined streets of Prospect Park, on the promenade in Brooklyn Heights; sixteen hundred miles west, it would eventually rise in Denver, seep through the window where his boys slept still in their twin beds. It would rise on Freddy the Grip and on Hoody and on Lycra and on the boy in the cap and on the boy's sweet father, all of them.

Michael could feel himself sobering. Still, he had come this far. He picked up the book, opened to the end, and cleared his throat. "One by one, they were all becoming shades," Michael read aloud, alone on a dark Brooklyn street. "Better pass boldly into that other world, in the full glory of some passion, than fade and wither dismally with age."

There was more, of course, but that was what he'd come to say. Michael stood, tucked the book back under his arm, and started back, looping the phone cord back over his shoulder as he went. The sun would rise on him, too, on a well-meaning sentimentalist slowly making his way home—the sun rising on all the foolish and the dead.

ONCE

by LAUREN GROFF

after "Wants" by Grace Paley

I saw my enemy at the beach. This was in the surf shack after a long day of sun, and she was waiting for her early bird crabcake special.

I said: Hello, Nemesis.

She said: What? That's not my name. Then she took a closer look and said, Oh. It's you.

You is not my name, either, but it's what she always called me. I never argue when disagreements hinge on semantics. So I sat and sent my little boys out to play in the sand. You'd think they had enough of it, having spent the whole day on the beach, but boys become men and I challenge you to show me a man who has tired of putting things repeatedly into one bucket or another.

The waiter came and I'll admit to flirting. Everyone is sexy at the beach, all sunburned and windblown and golden at the edges with sand. All but my enemy, who had clear tubes in her nostrils leading to a tank parked at her feet like a little pet. She was wearing a silk scarf on her head and although she'd always had the thin skin of the calorie-strict, her body had somehow turned gray as smoke. I put on my sunglasses because the sunset was making my eyes water.

When the waiter left, my enemy called out over the three tables between us: I see you haven't changed.

That stung. She'd been the mother of my first boyfriend. In the tiny town where I grew up, there were only two castes: those who belonged to the Country Club and the rest. The lowest of the rest were the people who worked at the Country Club, and I was the snack bar girl. I wore black eyeliner under my eyes, which back then was considered risqué. Even before she was the mother of my boyfriend, she had referred to me with her tennis friends as *La Poubelle*, which I'd taken as a sort of compliment until I went to the library to look the word up. So I seduced her son and she started calling me You.

The waiter put two globes of golden wine before me and said: Happy hour! Buy one get one free. He winked. Oh, the legendary generosity of the tip-dependent. It goes to show that although I have changed greatly, in fact, my most evident attributes have not.

My enemy stood and dragged her tank to my table to sit across from me. She said, Don't pity me, but I'm here, sick and alone, because of you. If my son's wife is a monster, it's because you ruined him forever for decent girls.

I said, Although I appear to be a professional woman, happily married and the mother of the two yonder tots, it's true that twenty years ago, when I was fifteen, I had such powerful sexual mojo that I could swerve the course of a man's life off the path of righteousness and into the thickets of evil.

She smiled. You always had a way with words, she said. Speaking of which, I read your first book. I waited. She shrugged and said nothing.

Well, she'd been in the poetry racket; nobody would expect her to stoop to contemporary fiction. In her study, she'd had a sizable row of literary journals with her bylines in them. I'd run my hands across the spines, marveling, when she was out of the house. She was also a librarian at the college a few towns away, in charge of the oddly complete selection of medieval courtly romances. Her son had gotten all As on his English papers, which had titles like, "Duessa: Good or Bad?" and "Duets: Love in The Chanson de Roland." Though I could still taste the Bag Balm he rubbed on his lips before kissing me, I couldn't remember his face. Her face I couldn't forget.

Her crabcake special came, but she made the waiter box it up. I've lost my appetite, she declared.

She stood and wobbled, then righted herself. Before she wheeled her tank away, Styrofoam clamshell in the other hand, she said, nodding at my boys who were socking one another with plastic shovels: I'm not surprised you've done well for yourself. You've always had such *grand* ambition.

From the first, the woman had had the ability to send a single word whipping like a gyroscope across the endless floors of my mind.

Ambition, well. Of course I had it, but where I come from, for a girl to show her ambition is like walking topless down the street: legal, perhaps, but not done. I had set my sights higher. Those nights long ago, my boyfriend would be strumming *In Your Eyes* on his guitar and I'd slip downstairs to the dim study and touch those journals and burn. I was going to take the literary world like a bull in a field of clover. I was supposed to vacation in the Mediterranean, not at a Florida condo with turquoise fountains ninety miles from where I'd live. I still think I have time to save the Amazonian jungles. The boys came and there were years of nursing and potty training and though the fires still crackled, much of the daily fuel I had to burn went to them. Still, I meant to translate Marie de France for some hip modern audience someday.

I sat for a while alone, those two goblets having gone to my head. I felt old and tired. My boys climbed onto my lap, and I didn't make them wash their hands and even let them eat my fries.

Something about how my enemy had looked when I came into the surf shack had struck me but I couldn't bring it to the fore. The beach does that. All day, metaphors had eluded me. There'd been a wash of dead jellyfish on the beach and all that had come to mind when I saw them glistening like that was: breast implants.

All of a sudden, it arrived. My enemy—skinny, in her scarf, dim against the sea—was like a wimpled lady I'd once seen in a tapestry, bent over her needlework. At the lady's feet was a dog that had the snub-nosed look of the oxygen tank. Oh, those pious ladies of the past, bending their heads over their fancy work, dreaming of grand loves, of lepers and white stags, thinking of their effort that would ripple on the walls and please distant generations when they were no more than dusty bones. Things spun, and it wasn't just the double wine.

Well, I reflected, if a questionable element came close to my boys, I'd scoop them into my maw and wing away like a pelican, too. I ordered another double wine and sang the baby to sleep in the dusk: *I see the doorway of a thousand churches.* I smiled at the waiter, at the ocean, at the couples eking in with their sun-spotted skin because, after all, I'm like all mothers and yearn to be known for more than just the one most obvious thing. What a distance I have to go before I'm better than I am.

MEN ON BIKES

by ROXANE GAY

after "Rape Fantasies" by Margaret Atwood

The way it's being talked about in the papers, you'd think the men in town had grown wings and all flown away. Better yet, you would think they had done something we could all be proud of. The news has been on the front page nearly every day for as long as I can remember. Nowadays, we just turn to the second page to hear of the rest of the world because the front page, that's reserved for our men and what they've gotten up to. No headlines about war or the economy or things politicians have said, nothing like that. Instead, every day, the front page talks about how eventually, every man in town ended up on a bicycle. This doesn't seem like something people should be talking about. There's nothing new or interesting about men on bicycles, right?

I suppose it's the drinking that got everyone riled up and righteous. I was playing poker with some of the other wives and having quite a good go of it, a healthy stack of chips in front of me—an ace and king of hearts in my hand and two aces showing on the flop. They were talking about how they were losing their husbands to bicycle maintenance and such—it's the craziest thing—lots of talk about gears and brake hoods and spokes and forks. It was like the men decided because they were riding bikes they were now bicycle experts. There was even a new section in the paper—ten weekly tips for keeping your bicycle in tip-top shape.

It started with Dean Shavers, the first to lose his job at the plant. He had seven kids, all under the age of ten, and sitting on the couch watching talk shows with those sticky kids crawling or running around him—it was maddening. The only time he had a moment's peace was after the older kids went to school and the younger kids went down for a nap. In the quiet of that precious hour or two, he cradled warm cans of beer, taking slow, careful sips until the younger kids woke up and the older ones came home, their furious energy now dulled and manageable.

Then his wife Marnie's car broke down and there was no money to fix it, so he had to take her to work and pick her up every day. Marnie still worked at the plant because she had nimble fingers and was real good with machines. It was like she understood them, her supervisor said during Marnie's annual review. Dean was mostly sober each morning when he took Marnie to work, but in the evening, when he was well into his case of Coors Light, his expanding gut soft and pliable against the steering wheel, he had a hard time finding his way to the place he had worked for nearly nineteen years.

Marnie mostly didn't say anything. Dean was a lazy drunk but he never got coarse with her or catted around with barflies. Marnie also knew men had their way with sorrow. It wasn't her place to get in the way of all that. Sometimes, as they lay in bed, Marnie would sigh as Dean sweated out the beer he spent all day drinking, their bedroom air thickening with yeast. She'd say, "This is not what we promised each other," and Dean would just grunt and pretend to be asleep.

The night of their anniversary, Dean picked Marnie up from work and they went to the Penalty Box for dinner and drinks, while Marnie's sister stayed home with the kids. Dean wore a clean pair of khakis and his favorite bowling shirt. Marnie changed in the locker room at work and wore the only nice dress she owned— black, simple lines, low scooped back. Dean whistled when Marnie slid into the car and leaned in to kiss her husband. He drew her close for a wet, boozy kiss, whispering, "You're gonna get it tonight," after they pulled apart. Marnie crossed her legs and laughed. "We'll see how long you stay awake, big boy."

Most of their friends were at the Penalty Box; there weren't too many options in town on a Friday night. After greasy burgers, Marnie played pool with Belinda Rucker, who went by Bindy and was the sexiest woman in town when she leaned over the pool table, her cue aimed carefully at a corner pocket. Dean sat at the bar with Bindy's husband, Tucker. Tucker Rucker went by Trucker and had also been laid off from the plant. It was late, so they shifted quietly from beer to gin to whiskey, giggling like little boys each time the bartender set fresh drinks in front of them. She was young and had perky breasts that seemed to wink as they swayed lightly beneath her tight T-shirt. Dean and Trucker talked about the terrible coffee at the unemployment office and the videos they were forced to watch each week, teaching them about new career paths they might pursue— office work, phlebotomy, sanitation. "My fingers are too damn big for most work," Dean slurred and Trucker nodded. They were both men with very big hands, could palm a bowling ball with room to spare.

By last call, Dean could barely keep his rheumy eyes open. He leaned heavily against Marnie as they walked to their car, listing from side to side. She tried to take the keys from her husband but he had too much pride. "I am a man," he said, "and I am gonna drive my woman home where I am really gonna give it to her." Marnie rolled her eyes. The only thing Dean was going to give her was a hard time as she rolled him into bed and tried to undress him. She knew exactly where the night was headed. They had been down this road before. Marnie tried again for the keys but Dean spun away and stumbled to the car. Marnie shouted, "You're not killing me tonight," pulled her coat around her, and began walking home

while Dean tried to fit the key into the lock. She took her time, muttering to herself about their worst anniversary yet, and planned on telling Dean, when he finally made it home, that they might not see their next.

In the morning, Marnie slowly opened her eyes and realized she was in bed alone. The house was quiet, which immediately set her on edge. She padded into the living room where five of her children were sitting in front of the television. Dean was nowhere to be found. It was several hours later when she finally checked her cell phone, having deliberately ignored it all night, and found several increasingly frantic messages from Dean begging her to come down to the police station to bail him out because "the pigs" had pulled him over. Marnie would have laughed, but knew they could hardly afford whatever the bail was, and then there would be a lawyer and who knows what else. She went on the back porch and lit a cigarette, ignoring the stern looks of disapproval from her children, their greasy faces pressed to the glass door. He can sit there for a little while longer, she thought. It was a warm day. The sky was clear. She enjoyed the sun on her arms for three cigarettes, and went down to the police station only when she was good and ready.

Dean was contrite when he saw his wife standing in the lobby, one hand on her hip, her lips stretched into a tight line. "I am so sorry," he said. "I should have listened to you." He wanted to say more but his mouth was sour and his head was thick and the looks Marnie was giving him were making it hard to think.

"You're damn right you're sorry," Marnie said. "This is the first and last time you will be arrested for a goddamned DUI. A DUI, Dean? Really?" She held out her hand, palm up. "Give me your driver's license."

Dean blinked. "What?"

Marnie snapped her fingers. "I did not stutter."

Dean sighed and reached into his pocket for his beat-up wallet, damp dollar bills and receipts spilling out. His hands trembled as he handed his wife his license. He needed a drink. She tucked the license into her bra and turned on her heel. "I'll let you know when you can drive again," she said, over her shoulder. "You can walk home."

Walk home Dean did, and people stared because we don't talk in this town, not really, even though this is a small sort of place. Marnie had a temper, we all knew that, but we couldn't imagine what Dean had done to be trudging home and looking so sorry.

That night, Dean went out to the garage he had been meaning to clean for months. Well, years, if he was being honest. With Marnie giving him the silent treatment and the kids looking at him suspiciously, it was the perfect time to organize the abandoned toys and hunting equipment and lawn games and his prized collection of dirty magazines—when *Playboy* was good, it was so very good. For a few minutes, Dean allowed himself the quiet pleasure of flipping through the glossy pages featuring women he would never dare touch but sometimes imagined when he was on top of Marnie, who was a looker herself, but different, because she had hair in certain places for one. These girls, they were so smooth, like dolls and yes, Dean realized it was kind of, maybe, abnormal to think of them that way but he did wonder what it would feel like to slide into one of these slick skin dolls. Oh he wondered. And then he stopped with all that because he was in enough trouble. The last thing he needed was Marnie finding him drooling in the garage, his dick sticking out of his pants.

After a few hours of steady work, the garage was finally starting to look like something they could park the car in. Dean was working up a masculine sweat and feeling pretty good about himself. Then he found his old ten-speed. It still worked. Dean took it for a lazy spin around the block and found that he could hold a beer in one hand and the handlebar with the other and still make progress. He was going to get around. Marnie could keep his damn driver's license. Maybe he would finally get in shape. Maybe he'd get some of those abdominal muscles Marnie was always nagging him about and then she would be the one pawing at him in the dark, her breathing stuttered and heavy.

ROOFERS*

by STEPHEN BURT

They pose no danger to themselves,
only to other people, and houses, and cars:

secure up there, they crouch and prowl like wolves,
and carelessly throw down whatever they wish to discard.

Tomorrow, we think, they are going to install
the rest of the tiles,

like rows of teeth, or seats in a concert hall.
Their acetone impugns the air for miles.

By evening a drizzle of nail,
screws, tacks, brads, inch-long scraps of electrical cord

and tar-scented plastic has fallen all over their lawn.
Someday the whole of our civilization will fail.

The empty house assumes its beams, its paste-encrusted crown,
its parallelograms of sky.

I wonder if they have to try
very hard, or very often, not to look down.

———————————————————

* after "The Armadillo" by Elizabeth Bishop

A few days later, Dean added a white wicker basket to the front of his bicycle because sometimes a man needed to carry things. Marnie stood in the driveway watching him work, arms across her chest. "This," she said, sighing, "is not what I had in mind when I confiscated your driver's license." Dean wiped his forehead and grinned at his wife. "We're going to be just fine, baby."

Trucker lost his license next. It was early morning and the previous night's drunk hadn't worn off and somehow, on his way to the unemployment office, he ran his truck right into the large oak in his front yard. Bindy came out, wearing nothing but her slippers and a slack robe, her heavy breasts loose against the silky material, which kind of turned Trucker on, but he didn't want anyone else getting any ideas. "Put on some clothes, woman," Trucker shouted from inside the truck. "Put on some damn clothes, but damn, you sure do look good."

Ignoring her husband, something she did often, Bindy went around to the driver's side, leaned through the open window with her breasts pressing uncomfortably against the door, and yanked the keys from the ignition. "You better find yourself a bike like your buddy Dean, because there'll be no more driving for you." Trucker shrugged because he was kind of confused and kind of turned on and he couldn't remember where he was supposed to be, so he stretched out along the front seat of the cab and turned the radio up, even though he had a headache, because it was Travis Tritt and he really liked that man's haircut, how it was feathered on top and long in the back.

When he sobered up, Trucker wandered over to Dean's house and Dean promised Trucker they would find him a bike, which they did, at the pawn shop, for only $25—older but red, Trucker's favorite color, and in fine working order. Later that afternoon, the pair pulled up to Trucker's house on their bikes. Bindy lay stretched out on a lawn chair in the driveway. She pushed her sunglasses to the top of her head as they pedaled around her. "What on earth is this?"

Trucker's bike had a little bell on it and he kept ringing it. "I got me a bike, woman. You can keep the damn truck."

Bindy laughed. "Don't worry, I will," she said. "Whatever you're up to, make sure you bike your ass home by dinnertime."

Trucker rang his bell three times and he and Dean, who was feeling remarkably fit, went on their way, wide grins spreading across their faces as they made their way around town.

Before long, all the wives in town had confiscated the keys and drivers licenses of their husbands. It was the right thing to do. They didn't want something terrible on their conscience while their men drank their way through complicated sorrows. "Drink and bike, don't drink and drive," Esther Rollins told her husband, Edgar, who complained that he was too damn old to be riding a bike like some damn kid. Esther, always an efficient problem solver, found Edgar an adult tricycle because she knew Edgar couldn't ride a bike and was too proud to admit it. At first Edgar was reluctant. "Look at this thing," he said, after it was delivered. "Everyone's going to make fun of me." Esther was unmoved. "Let them," she said. He was right. He was all legs, his knees jammed against his elbows as he hunched over to pedal. As he rode around, people often pointed and laughed. They weren't trying to be cruel, but Edgar on a tricycle was a spectacle.

The only bike Pete Lester could find was his daughter's pink Schwinn from when she was a little girl. Tricia, the daughter, was in her first year of college now. Pete couldn't even remember why they still had the bike, though he remembered teaching Tricia how to ride it, and how the first time she had wobbled for a few feet and then collapsed in a heap at the bottom of the driveway, screaming her head off because she had scraped her elbow. Pete's wife told him they weren't spending a dime on a new bike. He wanted to grumble about being a man and making the money, but he had been out of work for a good while and his wife wouldn't tolerate that kind of nonsense anyway. He was just going to have to make do. Pete looked ridiculous on the bike.

He knew it. Everyone in town knew it, but for whatever reason, they said nothing as Pete tooled around, a big brawny man on a little girl's bike. They all thought he rode that bike with dignity.

Bellamy Jones didn't even drink—couldn't stand the taste of beer or liquor—but he quickly tired of driving around alone while his friends pedaled by on their way here or there. One afternoon, Bellamy came home from his job as an insurance adjuster, handed his keys to his wife, Gina, and said, "I'm done with driving."

Gina frowned. "You are the clumsiest person I know. You have no business riding around on a bike."

Bellamy pointed out the front window. "If they can do it, so can I." He adjusted his blazer and strode confidently into the garage to make sure his bike tires had air. He promptly tripped over a floor mat. Gina decided Bellamy wasn't allowed to leave his house without elbowpads and kneepads and his bike helmet. It was worth it, though, to join his friends on their bikes, making their way here and there.

Much later, the women in town would agree that there was something in the air that year. It was strange, but what a beautiful sight it was at the end of a long day, all those big, brawny men, pedaling slowly on their bikes, one after the other in a never-ending line. I could cry just thinking about it. You can't understand how beautiful those men were.

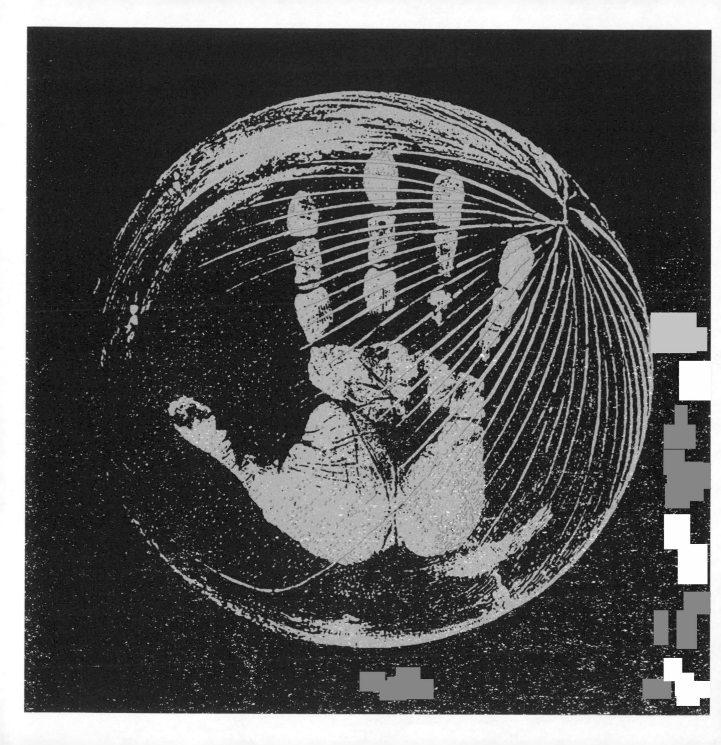

COMPANY

by NAMWALI SERPELL

after "Company" by Samuel Beckett

THE BRIGHTENING

We first saw the light on such and such a day. They told us it was coming, that we had knocked something loose from the sky. We suspected as much already. After centuries of medicine, of wanting life, life, life, there were too many of us. Too much survival. A genomic combination coincided with the greatest advances in medicine, leading to an unprecedented boom in population growth. What a healthy baby! Ten fingers and ten toes! Ten million billion fingers and toes! Another still, another of that other, yet another, countless others. The everchanging sum of those gone before, twenty-five thousand, seventy billion, the evermounting sum. So many to add to yesterday's, to yestermonth's, to yesteryear's. All of the structures we had built to separate our bodies, all of that reaching up and out we had done—all of that collapsed with the brightening.

The brightening happened one cloudless May day. They were at the swimming pool, his great-grandmother and her sister. This was before he was born, before his mother and his grandmother were born. His great-grandmother and her sister were still young girls, bold in their neon swimwear. The water was a paler blue against the pale blue sky. They lay on their backs, tossing in their warmth, tossing words and laughter around. Looking up at the pale blue sky and then at her sister's face, his great-grandmother broke the silence, asking if that sky was not in reality more distant than it appeared. Her sister replied with a detailed prayer to God to bless all they loved.

They dozed and did not notice when the sun spread to the edges of the horizon, brightness filling the sky like milk in a bowl. When they woke, everyone else was crouched under something. Everyone white clung to the shade, some of those bodies moaning and steaming. Shadowless sky above, the two girls looked over the dazzling land, straining to see across the blinding water, away across the expanse of light. Their eyes ached. His great-grandmother looked at her sister and asked, "Are you all right?" His great-aunt said, "I'm just fine. God is good. God is love." She wiped her fingers across her forehead, bursting a small cluster of blisters there.

THE CROWD

Soon, the night sky was the reverse of itself: instead of pinpricks in darkness, there were sooty spots in the general white. In the day, a mass of twisty clouds the color of ash. Above: glass towers protecting the rich from the ultraviolet light that still poured through the murk. Below: the crowd. No space between us. A roiling of limbs across the land like the uneven weave of a carpet. To eat: a river of pap oozing daily on the hour, just close enough to reach with a hand, just about separate from the river of shit.

He grew up in the West. He grew up in the crowd, on his back. Roll as he might, there was no other choice but to be prone or huddled with his legs drawn up within the semicircle of his arms and his head on his knees. Fumbling, half-blind, always with his mother. She stooped, cradling him from behind, or both lying on their sides at full stretch, face to face, their knees meeting and the hairs of their heads mingling.

She found a way to make sure he knew her always: a red triangle of cloth, her right breast slung in it. His eyes opened and closed, looked in hers looking in his, eyes in each other's eyes. He pressed his little nose against the rose-red pane of cloth and all became rosy.

He remembers the feel of her lips on his ear. His mother spoke all her knowledge into him, her voice a hot rush into his ear in the midst of the great murmur of the crowd. All the little that he knows of the world as it is and was before is colored by the sound of her voice. They stirred together, shifted and shuffled, and they shared between them any scraps other than pap.

One day she was gone and he didn't know if it was death. And so he went on, a notion to stir, stirring now and then, to turn on his side. On his face. And some days he would roll or be rolled on his back and if enough time had passed, he would open his eye a crack and see cloud, the waxen cope of sky. He sometimes caught a flash of blue and across it a bird once flew, its passing a wonder. It was the miracle of his life until the day he was recruited for the Company.

TRAINING

A voice comes to him in the dark.

"Move."

His leg kicks out. He groans. There is pressure on his hind parts. The voice comes again.

"It takes getting used to. Most of your life you have been barely able to move." He is uncertain whether this is addressed to him or to another sharing his situation.

"Where am I?" he frowns, hunching in.

"You are on the ship," says the darkness. He opens his eyes. Immeasurable dark. Contourless. Apart from the voice and his faint breath there is no sound.

After a while, he senses her circling him, but even that feeling takes time. How much time, he cannot say; there are no bells to mark the hour and it's hard to read sounds without the blaring murmur of the crowd. He learns. Her voice is quick and sharp; consonants clipped, vowels spinning with a burr. Lila. She is from the East. Same flat tone at all times. For its affirmations. For its negations. For its interrogations. For its exclamations. And the repetitiousness of her commands. Again and again.

Can he move? Does he move? Should he move? Crawl and fall. Crawl again and fall again. Try again, fall again, fall better. The mute count, grain by grain, one two three four. One knee hand knee hand two. Some relief that the days are no more when he writhed in vain. The arms unclasp the knees. The head lifts. The legs start to straighten. The trunk tilts backward. In time he can stand, unfurling from the crouch to which his limbs return automatically.

Training is hard. His body aches with all the moving. It's painful to feel so much air—volumes of it—between his knees and his fingers, but it reminds him of the bird. Soon he is greedy for it, for the food and water and air. And of course a certain activity of mind, however slight, is necessary for a new adjunct of the Company. He is wearied by such stretch of imagining. He learns and learns and learns, facts and facts and facts. Now it is time to work.

THE SHIP

There have been shimmers of light before, showing him life on the ship: the curve of a cup, the surface of the wafer-thin bread. When Lila stands near him, there is sometimes a brief spangle.

The ship functions via electro-epidermal contact.

"It's embedded in your nerves," Lila informs him. "You were asleep for the surgery. You just have to activate it."

She reaches for his hand. Just before they touch, he feels static in his fingertips and bright spidery lines crawl out between their palms. Their hands clasp and he sees her. Lila is a silhouette inside a dull glow, a small thin woman. Naked or covered? Naked. Ghostly in the glimmer.

In the infinitely faint light, he tries to make out the ship's form and dimensions. It is a hemispherical chamber of generous diameter—sixty feet? thirty?—its curved walls from above and from all sides equally remote from his position at dead center. The walls are the color of mirrors but do not reflect him. He tries to touch the nearest one and it recedes.

"Softly," Lila chides. She beckons and the wall comes at once. Still holding his hand, she puts her other palm to its surface, and a thin grid lights up inside it. She eases her hand through until her whole arm is swallowed by it. By the wall.

"Release my hand. Very slowly, just a little."

He unlocks his fingers a millimeter from hers, and the crackling light between their palms tangles brighter. A wide vibration grows around them, a broad chord moving up the scale to a consistent hum. A moment later that seems an eternity, her face appears, bathed in rainbow rays. The violet lips do not return his smile. The lights are on now. The ship is a giant bubble, a grid of light built into its skin. The place they are in swells slightly, flexes its checkered sides.

"This is the ship," says Lila.

THE TRIP

The ship is akin to an air bubble floating between tightly compressed strata of time. The first trip back in time seems to take no time at all. Lila hands him a pill and tells him to lie down on a ledge built into the wall.

"Sleep," she says, settling onto her ledge across from his, her feet dangling. She turns toward a diamondy pane and speaks into it:

"At 60 seconds and 30 seconds shadow hidden by hand. From 60 to 30 shadow precedes hand at a distance increasing from zero at 60 to maximum at 15 and thence decreasing to new zero at 30. From 30 to 60 shadow follows hand at a distance decreasing from zero at 30 to maximum at 45 and thence decreasing to new zero at 60. Seemingly endless parallel rotation round the dial and other variables and constants brought to light and errors if any corrected."

She turns back to him and smiles a quarter-smile and they grasp hands loosely in the gap between the ledges. This sparks the engines. The ship hums up its scale and the walls ripple, the grids of light pulsing like rain in the wind. He takes the pill and closes his eyes.

A voice comes to him in the dark.

"We're here," Lila says, her voice as groggy as he feels. He opens his eyes. She is standing, tapping at a wall in her mechanical way, sending numbers galaxying over it. "Suit up," she says over her shoulder.

He approaches the transparent greatcoat hanging beside his ledge. When he reaches for it, it flinches then inclines shyly toward him. He enters the coat inch by inch, easing in as if it's a pool of water. Goosebumps rise as it creeps cool and liquidy over his fingers, but the coat soon adjusts to his body temperature, his shoulders warm by the time it has covered his wrists.

At the wall, he leans forward with bowed head, his eyes closed, making ready to set out. Lila's hand slides up the back of his neck to cradle his skull. It feels like a comfort, maybe more. This is soon replaced by the familiar vacuum of panic as the encompassing surface of the wall presses into his nostrils. He shudders. Then there's a soft ripping and he can breathe. The wall slips over his eyelids.

"Just let them open," she says, "whenever you're ready. In any case, farewell." Her grip tightens on his scalp and she tilts his head forward and shoves him outside the ship.

THE VILLAGE

The hoods of his eyes lift and bare his corneas. Brightness flares, then dulls to a lemony light. The low sun shines on him from the east, flings his shadow all along the ground. Trees in the distance serrate the edge where earth meets sky. His ears pop and sounds clamor suddenly: birds screech like weapons, wind scrapes by. He shakes his head and blinks. He is to maintain eyes and ears at a high level of alertness for any clue, however small, to the nature of the place.

He sees a trail so he turns right and advances southward. He covers the ground, feet unerring. After some hundred paces, another sound: the choppy melody of people talking, a spotty version of the crowd's murmur. What language? Bantu? Erse?

He sees a group of dark-skinned men and women in the distance. He feels a surge of success.

AN EXCERPT FROM

SORRY TO DISRUPT THE PEACE

by PATTY YUMI COTTRELL

He was nine years old and I about to turn twelve, a repulsive time for me as I was just beginning to menstruate. Together, he and I had invented a game, because our adoptive parents were far too cheap to buy us board games or video games.

You each have the faculties to create your own games for fun, they told us. All you need is your imagination.

We made up a game called CONFESSION.

Do you ask for forgiveness of your sins? I said to him.

I played the priest, naturally, because I was older and more mature.

I want to confess my sins, Father. He bowed his head.

Go ahead, young man.

Last week I lied to our parents. I told them I had after-school baseball practice, but I didn't. It's not even the season for baseball, and besides, I'm terrible at it.

What did you do instead?

I went to the park with Max and we brought a magnifying glass. The sun was out, shining brightly, and there was a little boy there by himself. We snuck up behind him, grabbed his arms, and held him down against the gravel, Max rolled up the little boy's shirt,

and I burned his back with the glass. He had pale skin. Max and I watched the sunlight laser into it and burn him. I remember he had freckles and moles. We burned his skin with the sun. Before we let him go, I realized he was much younger than I thought, probably four or five years old. I think he wet himself, because he smelled like urine. And for this, Father, I ask for forgiveness.

Do you understand that lying is one of the gravest sins, I said, worse than stealing, worse than kidnapping?

I told him he would have to humiliate his body in some way, in order to atone for his sins and the harm he did to the little boy. He threw himself into a pile of leaves and rolled around, and he suddenly looked old, in the sun-dappled dark, and at that moment it occurred to me that one day we would both be dead, composting like leaves and garbage in the worm-ridden earth. After a few minutes of rolling around in the leaves, he sat up and asked if he was forgiven.

You're going to die at some point, I said, and it's over. It's really over. It doesn't matter if you're forgiven or not. It's made up, it's all pretend. Do you understand? It doesn't matter!

Sorry to Disrupt the Peace is available now from McSweeney's.

I saw my adoptive mother come up from out of nowhere like a shadow and she began to wipe his face with a brown greasy napkin from a fast-food restaurant.

Why do you have dirt all over your face? she said. What kinds of filthy things have you two been doing?

When she was done wiping my adoptive brother's face, she strode right up to me and struck me across the face.

No adoptive mother of mine! I cried as a red star spread its points across my cheek.

That morning, she had leaned over eleven-year-old-me to shove the tampon up my vagina, because I was unable to do it on my own, it was always a trial to get the tampon up and into my vagina without the feeling of something being torn. She and my adoptive brother were the people closest to me in life, based on the sheer amount of time we once spent together. That afternoon with them, I skulked in the shadows and ate a heel of stale crusty bread meant for feeding the ducks. I was full of competition; I have always experienced extreme fits of jealousy, the type of jealousy that destroys the peace.

He has accomplished his first task: find melanin. The villagers are coming toward him in a beeline. They carry hunting gear over their round shoulders and in their strong hands. One leans on a long staff, another carries an instrument—a lute? What year is it? They meander closer, involved in their talk, uninterrupted. When they reach him there is a swerve, a deliberate veer. They swarm around him unconsciously, like he is a tree in their path. He goes unseen, just as Lila promised.

A bird—black, hook-winged—swoops an arc over him. Miracle. His smile widens and expands down his body as if opening the front of him and now he runs, past the villagers, through them, barely feeling the breeze stirred by his greatcoat or the press of the ground against the bones of his feet.

POUND

When he stops, his face is wet and he is inside an enclosure of rustic hexahedrons made of logs. The light is thicker now, shadows seeping back into the things that cast them. The wind is gone, the birdsong softer, and he hears an odd sound. It is a rhythmic thudding—some kind of labor. He moves toward it, skirting the edge of a hut, and turns the corner.

A pallid creature covered in a thin layer of hair crouches on the ground facing away from him.

He creeps closer and sees that it is tied to a tree by a dirty rope around its neck. The thudding stops and the knobs in the creature's back spin as it twists and fixes him. A man. Elbows and knees angled, feet splayed ninety degrees. The open mouth is a cave in a craggy rockface, the straggling grey moustache like sparse shrubbery. Searching eyes, a hunted look in the red, round, cankerous face. The man turns back around. The thudding resumes.

Or maybe that's his own quickening pulse. Unlike the villagers, this pale man seems to sense his presence. He tiptoes around to see him more clearly. The man is beating at a sack with a thick stick. His hands are tight on the stick, his brow tight with concentration, but all else is slack— jaw, eyes, even the genitals which sweep useless in the dust as he beats and mutters, beats and mutters. A single word. *Pound.*

"Pound. Pound. Pound."

Whatever is inside the sack grows wetter as it flattens. A dog barks. The villagers are approaching, bringing with them chatter and clatter and a smoky smell. The pale man pauses his work and curls his body over the sack. The villagers swarm around them both, but while they sidestep his invisible form again, several of them knock into the tethered man, one so forcefully that he tips over into the dust. Quick leave him.

THE MISSION

66 WWhy do we have to go back?" he asks in one of the pauses between his gushes of vomit. A side effect of re-entering the ship. He pants with the throb and thrust of puking.

"I do not know who that white man is," Lila gives him a sidelong glance, a trace of emotion in her voice. Her black eyes and hair flash as she paces. Signs of distress. "He might be the officer we lost on the last mission from A to Z. Or from another mission, from the North. It could be Hodgkin, Percival, Pott, Haitch, Coote, Haddon, Dante. I do not know. It can be verified, but it's too soon to say. Either way, he is not supposed to be here. He is a contaminant."

"Contaminant?" he spits.

"Think about it. You and I are here to harvest pigment. If that man has inseminated even *one* source of melanin, finding pure stem cells will be impossible." She parts the ship's wall like a curtain and vanishes behind it.

Pigment. He lies on his ledge, tasting the sick in his mouth, thinking on Lila's skin. Purple brown. Like his own but cast in shadow. The same pigment, though, dark. Dark as his mother's, dark as her mother's. Dark as his great-grandmother and her sister, lying out by the pool while the whites had to run for the shadows on the day the sun stepped closer. Dark skin marks you as lucky, as a descendant of those who had the evolutionary advantage when the brightening came. The rich and the descendants control everything. He suspects Lila comes from that strata. But he is a crowd-born descendant, black as basalt, poor and fertile. Recruitable. What an addition to the Company!

FLY

He finds Lila tapping at a wall, her eyes skittering, pinpricked by the shifting constellation.

"We have to go back to our origin point," she repeats. "The mission is over." Her panic manifests as a kind of thresher, chopping up her words and motions. They seem logical, just smaller and faster.

She points him to his ledge and leans over him. He feels on his face the ends of her long black hair stirring in the still air. She orders his mouth open, places a sleeping pill inside, and lies on her ledge. He swallows and shuts his eyes and tries to taste Lila's finger on his tongue. Their hands reach out for each other, clench, unclench to start the ship.

When he wakes, she is kneeling beside him, eyes wet and worried. They are back where they came from. What will the Company do? They suit up and move to a wall and halt with bowed heads on the verge of it. Then they grasp hands to ignite the grid and Lila dives forward with enough force to expel them both.

Moonless starless night. A roaring. By the time he opens his eyes, his feet have turned to cinder. But it is not hot. He looks over at Lila's feet, black and furred. He thinks for a moment that this is the true color and texture of her skin—it is the first time he's been outside the ship with her.

Something crispy and light and dry scurries between their loosely clasped palms. He looks up and feels a terrible scratching against his corneas. He can barely make out the black bits whirring around like scraps of burnt wood. The wind dies. Together the black bits come to rest, an immense twitching lake cloaking everything. Millions of them, tessellated, their wings and eyes iridescent as an oil slick.

"Flies," he says, and just as he opens his mouth, they rise.

BACK

Lila drags him back into the ship with her. He coughs flies from his mouth. They make curt zipping noises as they hit the floor of the ship. Lila vomits first. When he's done, he feels dizzy and weary. He tries to listen to her, his eyes closed, his body scooped out like a swimmer. She tells him they made an exact return journey, back to the very day of their departure.

"What does it mean?" he asks. "Everything's different. There's no crowd. There's no... people."

Lila's back is to him. She tracks lines on a wall with a finger. Doodling. Devising it all for the Company. The Mission: might not the future be improved? By retrieving something from the time past? But what if the trip trips a change? That is the hazard built into the Mission.

"You must have affected something," she says. "In the village. Something crucial."

"How?" he stutters. Nothing has occurred to make this possible. "The villagers didn't see me. They walked right past me." She looks at him. They both know that Pound, somehow, sees him.

"He's tied to a tree," he mumbles. "He can't do anything." But he still feels regret at having brought it about, and at not knowing how to dispel it.

"We have to go back." Lila's elbows are propped on her knees, her head in her hands.

"Can't we travel to another time? Earlier maybe?"

"The Company gave us one origin," she shakes her head, "and one destination. A to Z."

He doesn't bother asking why. Who would resist the temptation to reset the destination? An image of his mother's breast in a red sling flicks in his mind.

"We have to go back to the village."

He nods. Outside the ship, the time they are from has become no-space.

They go back. They take their pills, they lie on their ledges, they go back from A to Z. There is a great uneasiness, speechless misgivings about irreversible decisions, about conjuring something out of nothing. Every now and then he wonders in the back of his mind if the woes of the world are all they used to be. In his day.

All is much the same at Z. They pass a month at the village, maybe more. Lila scans old ship logs, taps listlessly at a wall, speaks tonelessly into it: "Unadvisedly consigned him. Need for company not continuous. How current situation arrived at unclear. No that then to compare to this now. As then there was no then, so there is none now. Observing how revocable its flights. To achieve its object, persist till the converse operation cuts it short."

He leaves Lila to these perplexities. He contrives to chart the area however roughly, ranging far and wide, walking the little winding back roads. Nothing changes. Birds utter their patterns and animals make small local movements, surviving. The trees loom with their silent growing, and at noon the sun blasts wide and down. He sits a while, listening.

By the banks of a stream, he lets the delicate earth rise between his sinking toes and touches the reticulated parts of flowers. He sniffs at insects. He can name a few. He learned about them from his mother, as they moved with and in the crowd. He is engrossed by the faint whiff of memory in even the newest things. Listen to the leaves, his mother whispers, and so he listens to the leaves in their trembling shade, and he hoards it in his memory with the rest.

Sometimes he remembers to follow Lila's directive to observe Pound, who remains tied to a tree. He sits and watches the pale man pound and murmur and catch animals within reach. A rat, a hedgehog. The villagers continue to ignore Pound, streaming around his body like water around a rock. Pound is their pet. They feed and stroke and taunt him. They are keenly interested in his bowel movements. They play out their dramas with him—children ride him or make him gambol around his tether, men kick at him, women cry in his ear. Pound says "pound," or shouts it. The villagers swim their lives around him.

SYNCOPE

One day, he finds himself alone with Pound. It is afternoon. Sleep and heat hang over the deserted village like a spell. He is leaning against a tree, examining the sharp fold of a blade of grass. Pound is squatting under the fat sun, shoulders hunched, patches of hair like a plague on his body. For some reason, their eyes lock and the look between them seems to swell with mutual seeing.

Pound suddenly breaks into a dead run directly at him. He is already on his feet, backed against a tree, when the rope catches at Pound's throat and the creature's feet fly forward and lands with a yelp. It is a shock to see Pound fall but then laughter and relief flood his gut and he bends at the waist, hands on knees. When he lifts his head, Pound is turning in his crouched circle, banging his fists on the ground, muttering.

That evening, he tarries in the remains of light before heading back the way he came. Setting out across the fields in the young moonlight, he smiles to himself as he rehearses the story he will tell Lila. Pound's misadventure. He glances behind and cuts through a hedge. He finds the wobble in the air, the warp where the ship is parked, and vanishes himself through its wall. Home! He peels his greatcoat off and, as the vomit begins to rise, Lila hands him a pail.

"How was your day?" she says.

"Well," he says and spits into it and looks up. Pound is standing behind her. Flesh gleaming, eyes bright as coins. The creature is naked but for a loose necklace of rope. The frayed end where he must have gnawed through dangles over his sternum. As Pound raises his arms, he yells out a warning but it's too late. The blow of Pound's fist catches Lila hard on the shoulder. She staggers forward and stumbles onto her hands and knees.

He leaps after them and, just as Pound's hand

reaches Lila's ankle, he locks his forearm around Pound's neck and his other arm around Pound's chest and pulls back, constraining him. Lila scuttles away. He tightens his grip. Pound stops, stands perfectly still, then coughs a stream of vomit down his front, a sticky mess clumping down over his chest and the arms wrapped around it. He recoils and Pound, feeling the slight slack, flings his head backward. He hears the dull impact of Pound's crown against his forehead, the strike unwavering. His mind closes as the window of a dark empty room might close.

RAPE

He wakes to an odd sound, a rhythmic knocking. He feels around. He is tied to something, manacled invisibly. It is pitch-black. He is back in the timeless dark, in the void. His face feels too large for his face. He realizes his eyes are not open because they cannot open. He has been beaten.

He wakes the next time to Pound's voice. It is groaning. "Pound. Pound. Pound." He is overhearing a communication not intended for him, overhearing a confidence.

God is love. Yes or no?

What visions in the dark of light! What visions in the shadeless dark of light and shade!

He dreams of bitter bright coins and his mother's red breast. He dreams of a sea of melanin.

Outer and inner dark. Which of the two is better company?

Voices come to him in the dark.

One says "pound," or sometimes "code."

"No," the other voice says. "No," it says again and again.

NO SPACE

Pound grows stronger. He tightens the ropes with which he has bound his two prisoners; he distributes bread and water between them; he gives them pails to do their business and empties them daily. This is the most excruciating thing: those wafts of villainous smell. When, as he sometimes does to void the fluid, he opens his eyes, darkness lessens. But his eyes do not meet Lila's. The taste of her slim finger in his mouth? Long since dulled by fatigue and discouragement. He views his suffering as he would a stranger's.

Pound has cleaned himself up. The creature remains bootless but now wears old tramping rags, a topcoat once green stiff with age and grime, the waist of his trousers unbuttoned. This suggests Pound is familiar with the ship, the whereabouts and workings of its storage space, its bathroom. But he cannot make it go. Pound taps bluntly at the wall, growling with irritation when it does not respond as he wishes, slamming his palm against it—it gives, swallows his hand whole. Where to go?

Pound rapes Lila every once in a while. After

some days—weeks? there is no time, no bell or sun to mark the hours—the violence dissipates. Her struggles, her refusals become subdued, softening to a whimper, a moan. She is changing. Better a sick heart than none. What kind of imagination is this? Is it his hunger or hers that mutates her sounds? Is it his dread or hers that lends to her clipped, burred voice that ill strain of desire?

DEFEAT

Confusion too is company to a point. A movement of sustained horror or desire or remorse or curiosity or anger and so on. He is still tied up on the floor. Why not just lie in the dark with closed eyes and give up? His hand. Clenching and unclenching. He thinks he hears a buzz, a live fly mistaking them for dead.

He marks time by the waxing and waning of Lila's monthly blood, that alien smell. She has had three cycles by the day he wakes to find her sitting on her ledge, her hands free. Pound mutters and taps at the wall. Lila rubs her wrist, ignoring them both. He is close enough to see that the edges of her lips are streaked with white. Parched? Has the creature's skin come off in her mouth?

Pound turns, marches over, grabs her by the hair, and drags her to the wall.

"Code," he barks.

She obeys immediately, her fingers quicksilver. She reaches automatically for Pound's hand to ignite the engine but he cringes warily and she shakes her head. She comes over to where he is tied and reaches for his hand. Her presence makes the mush, the stench in his pail, newly unbearable to him. He shuts his eyes.

When he opens them, Pound is sitting with Lila in front of him. There is a pause. Then Pound smiles as gentle as a priest and reaches forward and joins their hands—his and Lila's. Light simmers up between them and the time ship yawns awake. As the vibration grows and fills the place they are in, Pound rises with unexpected grace. He stands tall and laughs with triumph.

COLLUSION

Lila is late. She blooms, thrills with sex. She is a whole new being, there is love in her eyes. He cannot but wonder if she has not sunk to her knees. At first he leaves them to do their business, bowing his head till it can bow down no further. Then he turns his back. Eventually—the temptation—he finds himself watching, his hands on his pubes in that dead-still rainbow light.

Lila smiles loose and sloppy, her lip catching on a tooth. She whimpers and moans, differently. But—is it a clue?—she has not told Pound about the sleeping pills. Wherever Pound has decided that they are traveling, the trip from here to there will take as long as it takes. The trip feels all at once over and ongoing and to come. How best to pass the time? They pass the time with sex and watching.

There comes a day when Pound, spent from an orgasm, reaches forward with his white hand and joins their black hands again, setting off a spritz of light. This is Pound's version of a joke. An old act, a new context. But no-one laughs when Lila's thighs open wide and he enters where Pound just left, his thrusts making flashes. Who made that happen? He is too delirious to know and they are all of them in motion. At one point, Lila moves aside to let Pound look.

Little by little, the craving for company revives. Between debauches, he sits huddled in the same dark as his creature, devising games to temper the nothingness. Pound is companionable if not downright human. The lower the order of mental activity, the better the company. Up to a point.

He draws a line on the checkered floor and Pound adds one to it and he adds another. They draw lines to make boxes, and then they separate the segments and lay them side by side. Most diverting! They play with their grubby fingers while they wait for the ship to land. The journey continues, lapped as it were in its meaninglessness.

SOLO

Lila, untied in the corner, natters to herself. "Oblong now rhomboid," she says. "Erect locomotion, occipital bump aforesaid. Halving distance between it and homologous hand. All the way from calcaneum to bump of philoprogenitiveness. Rectigrade into the bargain. The obvious answer not far to seek, the most helpful another matter."

"The temptation is strong to decree," she says.

"Inexplicable premonition of impending ill," she says.

ARRIVAL

The only word they exchange these days is *pound*. Even Lila just says "pound" now, a joke that he himself started, he can't remember when. It became habitual and finally the rule, the one constant. The ship makes its caterpillar journey from time to time. Its shuddering grid casts flickers like fish swimming in and out of coral. Pangs of faint light and stirrings still.

A voice comes to him in the dark.

He opens his eyes. Lila sits before him, her belly resting on her thighs. The skin on her upturned face is bumpy and splotchy. Her lips are no longer violet. His eyes descend to the breasts. He does not remember them so big. To the abdomen. Same impression. Devised deviser devising it all for the Company. He feels a sudden dread: the unpleasantness of labor and delivery, the ship strewn with red placentae.

"Sleep," Lila says matter-of-factly.

He looks over her shoulder. Pound is slumped against a wall, vomit clumped on his topcoat. Hope slowly dawns that the creature is dying. It is over at last. Over!

Lila explains, her flat tone unchanged: a ground-up sleeping pill sprinkled over Pound's bread. She waited until they got back to the origin, back to A from Z. They both know why she left his bread untouched. She needs him to activate the wall. Her ruby lips do not return his smile.

He grabs her hand and the light of their skin grows angry bright. Together, naked, holding hands, they stumble to the wall of the ship and fall through.

THE BRIGHTENING

When first the brightening came, white skin grew tattered and hung like lace from the body, and the world smelled of thin singed hair. When the brightening came, black folk cackled at their own casual blisters. When the brightening came, only the darkest survived. Tanning beds became beds. Melanin became more valuable than any currency, the center of the stock market, the heart of the economy. Melanin was extracted and bought and sold and transfused. It turned out to be temporary; if you weren't born with it, it faded under the ultraviolet, like everything else. Skins burned slowly under the calamitous sky.

His back to the ship, he lets go of Lila's hand. He raises his head and opens his eyes. Whiteness on the ground, everywhere he looks, an endless vista. All is quiet and still. No, not still—shuffling. What is it? A white pasture of snow, but it is not cold. Afrolic with lambs, alive with flocks? What animal this time has conquered the earth? What effect have they wrought with their dabblings?

He hears Lila laugh at his elbow and moves away, making to strike out. He steps into softness but when he bears down, twigs snap under his weight. Not twigs. Bones. At the sound, a hundred thousand million billion eyes slide open, red spots stippling the white. The pale forms shuffle closer, pressing against him, muffling. He makes to retreat but feels a soft press against his back, pinning him. He cannot see the warp. He cannot see Lila.

As he struggles, the white around him rises, a tender, insistent tide. Every once in a while, something tumbles up or down beside him. He tries to turn his head and feels an infinite plush against his cheeks, a void in his nostrils. Light dying. Soon none left to die. No. How much better in the end their labor lost, and silence. Just before all company is snuffed, he remembers it, the gentle word his mother gave him for this. His breath palls. Rabbit.

AND SO ON

by KIESE LAYMON

after "Hills Like White Elephants" by Ernest Hemingway

Two weeks ago, on the third Thursday of March, sixty-four black folks changed the world. Then they disappeared. Then they changed the world. Then we disappeared. Chanda Stewart, my roommate and colleague, was the eighth of those black folks. Nella Mae Cade, my student and research assistant, was the ninth. Doug E. Brovani, Chanda's boyfriend was the first. I was the tenth. You are the eleventh.

And so on. And so on. And so on.

Emergency Chanda texted forty-five minutes after my first class. I was in office hours. *Sorry didn't come home last night. Lunch at Feverly's in 20 minutes. Can't talk. Something is really wrong. Just come.*

For most of February, when Chanda didn't come home, I knew she was spending the night with Doug E. Brovani. When I moved to Middletown, Massachusetts, from Alabama five years ago, I mentored Doug E. Brovani in a program for juvenile delinquents. I adored little Dougie's revolutionary imagination and his ashy bowlegs until Chanda started fucking him six and a half weeks ago.

Chanda swears up and down that Doug E. Brovani is a porn star. And I'm steady trying to tell her that having 1,089 Twitter followers and awkward consensual sex with a few white women filmed on an iPhone 2 in his fake Timberlands, blue knee brace, and yellow wristbands makes you a porn participant, not a star. Chanda knows this. Chanda knows most everything. But you know how it is: you can't tell some folks, no matter how brilliant they are, nothing that they aren't ready to hear.

I'm not a star in any part of life. I am a 32-year-old, broke, black assistant professor at one of the most elite northeastern liberal arts colleges in the United States. I'm honestly the Doug E. Brovani of academia. Unlike Doug E. Brovani and me, Chanda Stewart is the blackest, most affirming star you'll ever meet. She's the type of black star who says, "Loving life. Pulling it together. How about you?" every single time you walk up on her. So when Chanda Stewart texts *Something is really wrong. Just come*, you know that something or someone black and wonderful just died.

But black death or not, I literally didn't have the money to be eating at Feverly's four days before payday. Feverly's was the bougiest place on or around campus, next to our faculty meetings. I'd been to better versions of Feverly's back home in Alabama, but those better Feverly's were sprinkled with black or Chicano cooks, dishwashers, and busboys. Damn near all the faces in Feverly's, including the patrons, the servers, and the folks in the kitchen, were long, and white, and bored. A notch or two beneath the empty chatter and the ding-dinging of forks on empty plates, folks like Chanda and you and me heard three words over and over again.

Wow. So good.
Wow. So good.
Wow. So good.

Our campus sits in the valley of what folks in Middletown call the White Hills. Watching campus from Feverly's, especially around noon, the campus looks like it's cupped in a shaded force field. Rising above the force field are the pointy tops of the brick castles where students commit felonies, write, and read parts of books. The illest thing about Feverly's was that the door to the restaurant was covered in these dusty beige and maroon bamboo beads that my grandmother had covering her closet.

Wow. So good.

I walked up and saw Chanda sitting at one of

the six tables outside. "Hey," I said, before she stood up and hugged me. "How you?"

"Loving life," she said and sat down. "Trying to hold it together. How about you?"

"You invited me to Feverly's and it ain't payday," I told her. "Plus, you're doing that thing where you just smile with your mouth. Your eyes way too big to fake smile. What's wrong?"

A former student of Chanda and mine named Eliza was our waitress. I had given Eliza a B+ in her Intro to Lit Crit course the previous semester. That made her hate me. I told Eliza I was okay with just seltzer water. "Y'all do unlimited refills for lunch, right?" She ignored my question and took Chanda's order of rum and Coke, and this appetizer-sized beet burger that cost damn near twenty dollars.

"You spending close to forty dollars on one appetizer and a mixed drank?" I asked her. "Why didn't you come home last night?"

Wow. So good.

"We broke up," she whispered across the table.

"You and Dougie Brunson, aka Doug E. Brovani, aka let-me-fuck-you-with-some-new-wristbands-on?" I said low enough so only she could hear.

"Don't play," she said, and looked around. "And please stop talking so loud."

"I'm not playing. What happened? Wait. Why are we meeting at Feverly's to talk about this?"

"Dougie's been different ever since what happened to Brittney."

A little over a week ago, Doug E. Brovani's twin sister, Brittney Brunson, was shot and arrested in the middle of Main Street by Middletown police. When the cops approached and asked Brittney for her ID, one of the cops said he saw Brittney pull out a gun. She actually pulled out her ID and a box cutter to protect herself. Brittney's primary job was working the cash register at the cafeteria on campus. She spent her nights literally cutting boxes open at the new Stop & Shop off of Dave Avenue. The bullet ruptured her spleen and she's been in the trauma center at St. Francis ever since.

"Dougie and I stayed up all night talking about what the college and police would do if there was a mass occupation by young people in the community."

"Over what happened to Brittney?" I asked her.

"Over what happens to all of us."

"All of us or all of them?"

"All of them, I guess."

"All of who though?"

"People like Dougie and his sister, and his cousin, and his friends," Chanda said. "And our cousins, and our nieces and our nephews. Shit! Us, too, if we didn't live in this make-believe world."

"But we do live in this make-believe world."

"How many times has security asked to see your ID when you were sitting in your office?"

"I don't know how many times," I told her. "But the difference between security and police stepping to me is a loaded Glock. They can come in my office everyday all day as long as they can't handcuff and shoot me in my stomach."

"Whatever," she interrupted. "It was so fucking weird. Dougie wouldn't stop asking all these questions last night."

"Wait. So, that's what y'all do at night? Y'all just ask and answer questions? I thought your little Dougie was a pornstar."

"That's what we did for some of last night," she said and looked over both shoulders. "So he's bringing me home this morning, and right across from our building, this injured baby deer is straining to cross the street."

"So?"

"So I asked him to stop because the baby is just straining to get into the grass."

"Did he stop?"

"He did. He stopped and actually parked the car in our lot."

"Car? Whose car was Dougie driving?"

"His aunt's boyfriend's car."

"Shame," I said. "Then what?"

Wow. So good.

"Then nothing," she said. "I'm on the side of the road, trying to help this dying fucking baby deer and he's just in his car watching me. Just watching me."

Eliza brought my seltzer water, Chanda's rum and Coke, and the twenty-dollar beet burger. "It's usually not free refills for lunch," Eliza said while looking at Chanda, then glancing over my shoulder, right at you. "I'll hook you up."

"Appreciate that," I told her, and rolled my eyes. "So wait. Did dude ever get out of the car or not?"

"Nope. When I walked over to the car, he said that he thought it would look suspicious if people at my job saw him helping me, given what's about to happen later today."

"What's about to happen later today?"

"I don't know," she said. "He told me that I needed to be here at twelve-thirty to witness it. I think it's some kind of revolution."

"Chanda Stewart, you're saying you invited me to expensive-ass Feverly's because your twenty-three-year-old porny boyfriend told you to be here to witness the revolution at twelve-thirty?"

"He's not my boyfriend anymore," she said. "And that's not the only reason. We need to talk about something."

Wow. So good.

"Wait," I said. "Did he stay in the parking lot watching you walk into our building? That's what I'm asking."

"I didn't want to turn around. I just wanted to get far away from him and take a shower."

"This Trump shit got everyone thinking they

starting a revolution," I told her and laughed into my napkin. "Damn near every kid at our school swears that they leading the next revolution. Don't you hate yourself so much less every second you're away from that dude?"

Chanda looked up and locked into my eyes. "I don't hate myself at all," she said. "Who you think you're talking to? Do you say that to Nella Mae?"

Wow. So good.

"Why you talking so loud? What does this have to do with her?" I asked her and looked around to see how many students were sitting next to us. "Wait. Did you take a shower after touching that deer?"

"No," she said and finished her drink. "That's not what I needed to wash off."

Wow. So good.

I went in my book bag and faked like I was looking for a pen. "Listen," she said, inching closer to the table and reaching for my hand. "You have anything you want to say?"

Though Chanda and I technically had real sex once, we have never been in love. But everyone thinks we are. We like it that way. It keeps folks out of our business. We tried to do the black-academics-fall-in-love-at-a-rich-white-school-and-have-bougie-ass-gluten-free-kids thing when we first met. Chanda was curious, nervous, fine as all outdoors, and, unlike most of us

black professors on campus, not easily impressed by white folks. Actually, she wasn't impressed with white folks at all. I'd never met a black person in the academy like that. No matter who your black ass was, or what you looked like, or where you were from, Chanda Stewart invested in the work of loving you until you gave her three or four reasons not to. And I'm talking about *love*-love, not *fetishize*-love, or *tolerate*-love, or that *intellectual* black love that could get you on CNN twice a year. I'm currently working on *love*-loving black folks like that, but like you, I'm too desperate, and afraid of white supremacy to be good at it.

Wow. So good.

"You gonna tell me what you're getting at," I told Chanda as her student brought her another drink. "Wait. Did she come by your office today?"

"Nella Mae? She did."

"So. Did you talk to her?"

"I did."

"What did she say?"

"I can't tell you that."

"You pick now to be ethical about what our students say to us in private?"

"She talked about eating too much sauce at the Red Robin," Chanda laughed and took a huge gulp of her drink. "She talked about this boy who won't stop staring at in her Creative Writing class."

Fourscore and seven years ago our fathers brought forth on this continent a new nation, conceived in liberty and dedicated to the proposition that all men are created equal. Now we are engaged in a great civil war, testing whether that nation or any nation so conceived and so dedicated can long endure. We are met on a great battlefield of that war. We have come to dedicate a portion of that field as a final resting-place for those who here gave their lives that that nation might live. It is altogether fitting and proper that we should do this. But, in a larger sense, we cannot dedicate, we cannot consecrate, we cannot hallow this ground. The brave men, living and dead who struggled here have consecrated it far above our poor power to add or detract. The world will little note nor long remember what we say here, but it can never forget what they did here. It is for us the living rather to be dedicated here to the unfinished work which they who fought here have thus far so nobly advanced. It is rather for us to be here dedicated to the great task remaining before us—that from these honored dead we take increased devotion to that cause for which they gave the last full measure of devotion—that we here highly resolve that these dead shall not have died in vain; that this nation under God shall have a new birth of freedom; and that government of the people, by the people, for the people shall not perish from the earth.

—*Abraham Lincoln, from "The Gettysburg Address," 1863*

Don't believe the main stream (fake news) media. The White House is running VERY WELL. I inherited a MESS and am in the process of fixing it.

—*@realDonaldTrump, February 18, 2017*

"Really? What's his name?"

"She didn't say. She talked about these bizarre text messages her mother keeps sending her at four in the morning when Nella Mae's with her new boyfriend."

Wow. So good.

"Really?" I asked and took the first sip of my seltzer water. "That's weird. What's his name? Can you tell me? Is he one of your clients too?"

"I don't have clients," she said and finished her third rum and Coke. "I have students."

Chanda's not technically a shrink on campus, but instead of paying salary and benefits for a new certified counselor, the administration agreed to pay her an additional $5,000 a year if she took on some informal counseling responsibilities. In addition to those counseling responsibilities, Chanda teaches three sections of the most popular course on campus, Radical Love in the Age of the Neoliberal Inner Prize: (E)racing Gender, Sexuality, Geography and You in the United States. Now, all the black kids, and all the brown kids, and all the trans kids, and all the poor-as-fuck white kids go to her when they feel blue. A quarter of them take my African American Lit classes when they want to feel something else.

"Nella Mae told me that they've been seeing each other for three months," Chanda said. "She said that it's supposed to be a secret."

"Really? What's his name?"

"Yeah. I asked her if the idea to keep the relationship a secret was her idea or her boyfriend's."

"What she say?"

"She said it was both of theirs."

"Really?"

"Yeah. But I don't believe her. Has she been acting strange in your class?"

"Naw," I told her. "Not really. I mean, she's a strange kid. You know that." We looked at each other and looked towards the tops of the castles. Behind the castles, way far away, way past the White Hills, were these dark mountains. "What's technically the difference between a mountain and a hill?"

"You mean a mountain and molehill?"

"Naw, I mean a mountain and a real hill. There ain't no mountains in Alabama. But there are a lot of hills. Y'all have all kinds of mountains in North Carolina, don't you? Technically, what's the difference?"

Wow. So good.

"Perspective," she said.

"Perspective what?"

"The difference between mountains and hills is perspective. Let me ask you something. You think of Nella Mae as a kid? Do you get what I'm saying? I know she's your research assistant, so you probably see her in a different light, right? We all have those students who are like family."

"I mean, she's the best student I've ever taught. There's nothing she can't write."

"Right. She mentioned something about her new boyfriend convincing her that they should both try not to look in the mirror for a whole week then write about what they see."

"Whoa. That's weird. Why?"

"Yeah. Whoa. She said something about a conversation they had about bodies and reflections. She talked about you a lot, too."

"Really?"

"Yeah, she said your class changed her life, and the way you talk about Bambara and Hemingway was genius."

"She said genius?"

"She said genius."

Wow. So good.

"That's cool?"

"You're not telling the class that you think that guy stole your book idea, are you?"

"Nope," I told her. "Not at all."

"Good. I think you're obsessed."

"With her?"

"Are you? I didn't mean Nella. I meant obsessed with believing that guy actually plagiarized you for his book. But can we talk honestly about Nella? Are you obsessed?"

"Stop. Are *you* obsessed? You're the one who keeps talking about her. And I'm not obsessed with that dude or the book. I wrote that book first. He saw it, copied it. And he got credit. It is what it is."

"What is it?"

"I just told you what it is."

"You know, I tell you this all the time and you never listen. But when we don't get treatment we need, and we don't admit that we're sick, we infect the people around us. You might be infecting people right now because you won't admit you're sick."

"I'm not sick, though. Are you?"

"Probably," she said. "I tell people close to me though. And I do all I can to not infect anyone, especially students. Especially students. That's just not fair. I'm being serious. Don't you think you should see someone?"

"You brought me to Feverly's in front of all these white people to tell me that I'm sick? Chanda, you trippin'."

"No," she said and put her napkin in her empty plate. "I brought you here to tell you that you don't eat the hearts out of people you care about, especially when there's no way to satisfy your appetite."

"Appetite for what?"

"For control."

"I don't get it," I told her.

"You do get it," she said. "That's what's really wrong. You get it. Would you ever inappropriately approach a white girl student the way you…"

"I wouldn't inappropriately approach any…"

"Hell no, you wouldn't. Just stop. Treat us the way you would treat them."

"What are you talking about? Now you're a student?"

"When you're bad," she said, "you kinda are the worst. Nella Mae said that the way you talk about secrets in the book has opened her heart to different ways of connecting with herself."

"Okay, so why are you talking to me about this again?"

"Nella Mae said you accused her of writing something. Did you?"

"I didn't accuse her at all," I said. "I asked her if she knew who wrote something in a blue book and slid it under my door."

I went in my backpack and pulled out this blue book. "So yeah, someone slipped this under the door." I handed it to Chanda. "And when I opened the door, the person was gone."

Name:
Subject: I Know What You're Doing
Instructor: Chanda's Boyfriend
Section: in his lies
Date: Today
Grade: (F)u(c)ke(d)

The yellows and greens and browns and blues still ooze but Rachel Jeantel, Korryn Gaines, Michael Brown, Sandra Bland, Trayvon Martin

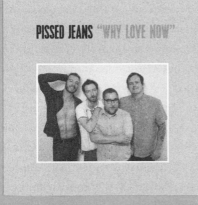

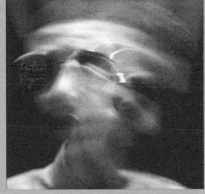

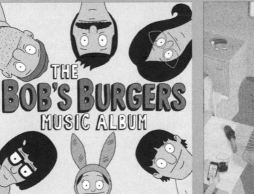

and I are getting closer to the edge of that subdivision. We're almost free. But inside, something is growing. And something is dying. And my professor is laughing.

Someone is dying. And my professor is laughing.

"This is not good," Chanda says. "Dude, what are you doing to that girl?"

"What do you mean? I have no idea who left this."

"Stop."

"I mean, I have an idea, but I'm not sure."

"So some girl puts this under your door, calls you 'Chanda's boyfriend,' and you weren't even going to tell me?"

"I was gonna tell you. But you didn't come home."

"You will say anything," she said. "What does the 'in his lies' part mean?"

I moved my chair closer to Chanda's. She smelled like coffee and body shop perfume. "So, you're asking me about the 'in his lies' line?" I asked her and touched her finger. "I don't know. Weird that it's in lower case, huh?"

"Stop being shady," Chanda pulled away from me. "You know Nella Mae wrote this. What does she mean by 'inside something is growing?"

"I don't know that she wrote this." I told her. "You met with her today. What do you think?"

"I thought your new thing was honesty no matter what." She finished her fourth rum and Coke. "Why haven't you called her by her name all day?"

"Is Eliza not charging you for all those dranks?"

"Stop changing the damn subject. Be honest."

"You be honest," I told her.

Chanda went in her bag and pulled out a journal. "I wrote this down," she said. "Nella Mae said that she's in love and she knows it's stupid but there's nothing she wouldn't do for her boyfriend because even though he's in a situation with a woman that she characterized as a 'long twisted goodbye,' she knows that he would do anything for her."

Wow. So good.

"Whoa."

"That's all you have to say? Whoa?" She threw a piece of ice at my chest.

"What else do you want me to say?" I asked her. "It doesn't sound like the person who wrote that shit in the blue book is so in love. Does it?"

"What are you saying? That's exactly how that sounds. I want you to tell me the truth. Nella Mae wanted me to know what you're doing. Are you going to the doctor with her?"

"No, I'm not," I told her. "I'm glad she could talk to you."

"Listen." She grabbed my hand and squeezed my middle finger. "Seriously. You have to stop.

You are letting this place fuck you up. You can't do this." Chanda looked at her watch. "We can talk about this later. Angle your chair this way," she said. "It's 12:30."

Out of the corner of my left eye, I saw Doug E. Brovani walking down the middle of the street with what looked like at least sixty young black folks around him. They all had on black hooded sweatshirts that read IT MUST BE THE LAND on the front and AND SO ON on the back. Every one of them had an axe in one hand and a shovel in the other.

There were big heads and small heads. There were weaves, fades, and braids. There were long arms and short arms. There were chucks and Js. No one was smiling. No one was frowning. No one said a word. There wasn't a leader. They knew where they were going.

Chanda dipped the tips of her middle fingers in the melting ice and looked at me. "Oh Jesus," she said. "Oh Jesus. Are they…"

"Heading to campus?" I said. "Hell yeah, that's exactly where they're headed. What do we do?"

There were no more forks ding-dinging on empty plates. No more robotic *Wow. So good*s. No more truths bent, snared, broken, and shared between Chanda Stewart and me. There were lots of standing white folks on their cell phones taking pictures and talking to other white folks on their cell phones about a group of young black folks from Middletown about to risk it all to change their world.

"Choose sides," Chanda finally said.

"Choose sides?"

"Choose sides, or run for our lives," she said looking directly in my eyes. "Either way, tonight the riots begin."

"Wow. For real?" I asked her, and looked over at you. "You gonna break out old-ass Tracy Chapman lyrics now? Now? With your boyfriend leading a massive crew of niggas in black hoodies to your job? Fuck. Trippin'."

Chanda Stewart and I just sat there. And we looked at our people. And we just sat there. And we looked at our people. And we looked at each other until we looked past ourselves, past our lies, past the castles, past the hills, past the fading summits of every mountain. Then we gathered our things, asked you if you wanted to come with us, and slowly, very slowly, we chose sides and followed our people deep into the center of the white world we knew far too well.

Sixty-four black folks were about to change the world. And we are going to be honest. And it will be too late. And someone white is going to wonder why the verbs never agree when they kill us how they killed us. And I am going to tell you the truth. And I am going to tell her the truth. And we were going to be honest. And so on. And so on. And so on.

IF YOU'RE HAPPY AND YOU KNOW IT

by MEG WOLITZER

after "A Perfect Day for Bananafish" by J.D. Salinger

Winter in the city had been brutal, everyone said; this was the word they kept using as they stood around the lobby of the hotel in Miami, waiting to check in. After being relieved of their luggage, all the guests were handed little cups of ice water with chunks of fruit floating in it, and some of them seemed slightly overcome by the gesture, as though it were one of special kindness and charity and not simply good business.

The girl in 609 had recently arrived with her new husband, and immediately sent him off to the beach, where he had needed to go all winter. His skin was whiter than anyone's. "I call him the milkman," Jen said to her parents a little while later on Skype, which she was able to use as soon as she had agreed to the hotel's outrageous internet terms. Three days for fucking forty-five dollars. She knew that if she paid for the internet, she would want to use it all the time to justify the cost. She had inherited that from her parents who, on Jen's birthday, used to sit on the sofa for a couple of hours watching her play with her new toys, making sure she was playing with them hard enough, and long enough.

The sun and the beach and the margaritas by the pool were all waiting for her, but she wasn't ready for them, not yet, not today. Instead, having quickly downed her glass of fruited water and claimed her room key, she was now connected and fat-faced in the lens of her laptop's camera, skyping with her mother and father, who sat in their suburban living room over a thousand miles away in the middle of the cold snap, straining toward the screen and their daughter. Behind them she could see the edge of the painting she'd always disliked as a child: the one of the juggler with the head that was too large for its body, and not intentionally.

As they faced one another, the mother said, "What is he doing? Right now, I mean."

"He's on the beach, I think."

"You *think,* or you *know?*"

"I think. Therefore I am."

"What?" said her father.

"Never mind."

"Did you eat yet, Jen?" he asked.

"We just got here, Dad. In the lobby they gave us water with little pieces of mango in it. It was very nice. Tonight we're going to have dinner in the hotel restaurant and just take it easy."

"Is he taking the Klonopin?" her mother asked.

"Mom, I don't know. I just know that he needs to be outside on the beach. He's been so overworked with that app."

"Everyone is overworked," said her father. "I'm overworked."

"And *I'm* overworked," said Jen. "And now I have to worry about him, too."

"Oh, a great father he'll make," said her mother.

"What? I'm not pregnant!"

"Well, you might want to be, one of these days," said her mother. "You never know. The desire just sneaks up and hits you over the head, and then there's no turning back."

"Mom and Dad, I have to go. I need to lie down a little before dinner. I'm hanging up now."

Of course, she knew she could not hang up, not really, because she wasn't on the phone. And maybe after the call ended, while she lay drowsing on her side of the hotel bed, her mother and father would sit waiting in front of the screen of their blank computer until she returned to them. Jen watched now with some small but bracing satisfaction as her parents' faces were suddenly made to disappear.

That night, at a baby grand piano in one of the hotel's lounges, a guest sat and played as if he were the hired entertainment. People began to gather around the young man, both adults and children. Chloe, age four and staying with her babysitter in a room that connected to her parents' room, 811, asked Moira if they could stay and listen, and the sitter said yes.

He was talented, Moira saw. At first, he played the songs that the adults wanted—the mainstream music that had been flooding through their heads all those years before parenthood came in and swept over them like a virus: Billy Joel, Elton John, the Eagles. How many hits had the Eagles had? A thousand?

Then the children started making requests. A boy came right up to the man and screamed in his face, "'This Old Man'!"

"What?" said the piano player. "I couldn't hear you."

"'This Old Man'!" the boy cried again.

"Now that's a little unkind of you. I'm not exactly *old*," said the man. "My AARP card won't arrive in the mail for another, oh, twenty-six years."

But when Chloe walked up and gently tugged on the sleeve of the piano player's linen shirt, and whispered to him, "Can you play 'If You're Happy and You Know It?'" her voice was husky and endearing, and the man looked at her with tenderness.

"Now that's a good name for a song," he said quietly. "Because it's entirely possible that I *am* happy and I don't know it. It had never occurred to me before that that could be the case."

Chloe tilted her head like a sparrow. "How you not know you are happy, man?" she asked.

The pianist put a hand to his breast. "Young miss, you are breaking my heart," he said. "No one calls me man except other men. The kind of men I have nothing to say to. 'Thanks, man,' this kind of guy will say, and I hate that. Usually he's eighteen and lives in Williamsburg. But a little girl has never once called me man, nor has she inquired about my happiness. I am in bliss right now. Not connubial bliss; that, I am *not* in. No, not at all, alas, though I am squarely *connubed*."

He played the desired song for her, with new lyrics, and all the children obediently sang along. "If you're happy and you know it… shout 'Brazil!'" Then, "If you're happy and you know it… shout 'police!'"

Moira realized that he himself did not know what he was going to sing at the end of a line until the moment he sang it. He was a little wild, she noticed, a little too invested in all this. At one point later in the evening, as the children were being peeled away by sitters and parents to return to their hotel rooms, Chloe started peppering him with suggestions for the song that they were no longer singing.

"What about," she said, "shout 'lamp!'"

"Pardon?" he said, confused at first, but then understanding. "Ah, 'lamp,'" he told her. "Well, it'd be a little rhythmically *challenging*, but perhaps that's not a bad thing."

"Or, or, what about, shout 'escalator,'" she said.

"You are monomaniacal, little one," he murmured with affection.

POEM ON THE OCCASION OF A WEEKLY STAFF MEETING*

by MATTHEW ZAPRUDER

Across the deep eternal sky
a thousand changing shapes flit by,

i.e. clouds, or so I have always called them.
But how is it I have never

among my incessant coffee refills
and insectivorous travels

among the cubicles in search
of individual wrapped chocolates

and conversations asked you
if you in my heart detect

several as I do in yours
of the adorable qualities

of broken folding chairs?
Or why we build desired outcomes

on the spots where old ones stood?
I call this meeting to order:

item one let's go to lunch and order
wild boar. Let's have an old world chat

about the original action items.
O fuck the fluting on the donuts!

I feel totally Anglo Saxon!
I want for once in my life to whip

around an actual halberd gleaming
in the sun and win

a great victory versus the air!
Here is my project update:

the file cabinet is watching
over the particles

safely asleep in a beam,
and nothing into our building

has at last so gently crashed
leaving us bored and fortunate.

I move our faces
around this highly polished table

to each other look
almost familiar

so let us slip into the light
blue sleeve this afternoon

so gracefully carries
the next few hours in

and together forget
what our great task is.

---

* The first two lines of this poem are taken from "A poem on the occasion of the consecration of Sandford and Shippon Churches," by Rev. F. Wilson Kittermaster, 1855

And then Moira decided that it was time to break this up, and she peeled Chloe away. The little girl tried to ignore her even as she was being physically removed from her spot beside the man.

"Or shout… 'Chloe!'" tried Chloe in desperation. And within moments the man was suddenly peeled away from the piano, too, by a young, pretty, if angry-looking woman.

"All right, all right, Jen," he said as she took him by the hand.

From room 811, the following day, Elissa texted the sitter: *I see u both on the beach.*

What, Moira wrote back. *Are you here.*

No. Gary and I are still in the room. Look up.

The sitter looked up toward the curving black glass wall of the hotel, and dutifully counted eight storeys, but there were far too many windows, and the sun fuzzed and blackened the view so that it was like looking into a limousine.

Cant see a thing.

Did you put SPF on her, wrote Elissa, quickly adding, *And can you please make sure you get the back of her neck.*

In the location of the handheld device, question marks had gone the way of so many other non-essentials in recent years. Elissa, the mother, seemed to exist inside that flat wafer of a phone that the babysitter was asked to carry on her person at all times. "Not in the *water*, I hope?" Moira had said when they made this request.

"Obviously not in the water," said the jovial father, Gary. But Elissa gave him a look, like, Why not in the water, Gary?

They were older parents, in their forties when Chloe was born "with the help of modern technology," as Elissa had confided to Moira. Chloe was their one and only. Elissa had a hard time separating from her, and sometimes in New York City she would "coincidentally" bump into Moira and Chloe, as if she didn't know they went to the park every Tuesday after school or the ice cream parlor on Fridays. Moira could often feel the presence of the mother on the street, perceptible through the kind of microwaves that were constantly being transmitted between women and the women who worked for them.

It did not seem as if Elissa was worried that Moira would *do* something to Chloe. She wasn't like those mothers who hid video recorders inside large, expressionless teddy bears, said, "Bye! I'm going out for the entire day," and then at night sat zealously watching the tape in the bedroom with their husbands as if it were some kind of mommy porn.

It just seemed as if Elissa simply could not bear to be away from Chloe. It was a little sick, maybe, but it was not uncommon. Children were protected like dauphins now, kept close by sitter or parent. Moira knew another sitter on the Upper

East Side, a Polish girl named Magda, who had been hired for inexplicable reasons. The mother was by the little boy's side every moment of every day. They made a good-looking threesome, the slender mother, the young, strong sitter, and the contented child, who had every reason to think he was the center of the universe.

Elissa was not so bad. But bad enough.

"Try to have a good time," Gary had been saying to his wife since they arrived. Yesterday, waiting on line in the hotel's enormous lobby to check in after the flight from JFK, he'd said it twice. Then, holding up the cup of water with the little pieces of fruit floating in it, he said, "Nice touch." He clicked his glass against Elissa's, and told her, "I want us all to have a good time. We won't get away on another trip for months. Don't hover over Chloe and Moira. Try to let Chloe have a good time without you; it's important that she learns to separate."

"I'm already having a good time," Elissa told him. "See, look at me!" She took a big swig from her glass and chewed on a hunk of mango. She and Gary smiled at each other and it was like a brief clearing of cloud cover, when you were able to see the weather that was meant to dominate.

Elissa Benedict, looking down at the beach from high above, did not want to be a panicky mother who shadowed her child. She did not want to be

obsessive. There had once been another, more relaxed side to her, but it had been allowed to atrophy in the four years since Chloe's birth, and here it was again, valiantly trying to come through; and maybe, over the next few days in Miami, it could.

She did not want to be horrible.

"Moira, I want to go in!" Chloe said, and though Moira thought to ask her to say 'please,' she immediately decided it wasn't really necessary. Of course Chloe wanted to go in; Moira wanted to go in too. Here in Florida, the trip was off to a very good start. There had been singing last night, and pancakes this morning, and now Elissa, reassured that Moira had things under control, had finally stopped texting. Chloe was sweetly easy, and Moira was enjoying the sun. They entered the water together, hand in hand, a tall young Irish woman with the red-gold hair and freckle-spattered arms, and a tiny pink child.

Moira could feel someone behind her and she thought, Oh Christ, it's Elissa again, doing a sneak attack. But she turned to see a young man standing there. Familiar. Nice-looking, but with the kind of skin that would burn and blister if he didn't cover himself in a very high SPF. She realized it was the man who had been in the hotel lounge the night before, playing the piano.

While behind the piano he had seemed a little eccentric and wound up, in daylight he looked a bit worse, as if he hadn't gotten much sleep, and his fingers were twittering on the sides of his legs.

Moira didn't know this man, but looking at him on the beach in all his milky-skinned glory, separated from the piano that had given him reflected luster, her immediate instinct was to shield Chloe from him. At that moment he said, "Oh, hello," to the little girl, who at first did not recognize him. She squinted at him and licked her lips nervously. "It's *me*," he said. "The man from last night who is apparently happy but, sadly, doesn't know it. You remember, don't you?"

Then Chloe smiled, and her smile was so startlingly wide and clear—an expression that had rarely made an appearance for Moira, or for her mother or father—that Moira had the impulse to neatly insert herself between the two of them, blocking his view of the child, and soon Chloe seemed to forget she had ever spoken to this man. The night around the piano receded like a fever dream.

Throughout the long day on the beach, whenever the man tried to approach her, Moira was there, making sure it didn't happen.

"I found a shell that looks like your ear," he said in the general direction of Chloe, but Moira came closer and snatched it from his hand.

"Thank you," she said. "It's pretty." And he was much too polite to tell her it wasn't meant for her.

Late in the afternoon, when the sun was slung low and many of the people on the beach had gone back inside to nap, or fuck, or skype, or check the news, or just talk like the old days, Chloe and Moira remained on the beach. The little girl was deep in the architectural throes of building a sandcastle with an even younger child, three-and-a-half-year-old Taylor. Moira was right beside them, half lying down but vigilant, her head tipped up to the granular light. The man lurked again; he had been gone for hours, off with his wife, who had dragged him away much as she had done the night before, but here he was again.

"I was walking along the sand," he said to Chloe now in a chatty, regular voice. "And what did I see? A flat-faced marital crab. Do you know of such a creature?"

Chloe was not listening; she and Taylor were in the middle of a loose, free-associative conversation about the castle they were building, with its lumpy, unturreted top, its punched-in "windows." They did not know that it was all futile, that the tide would destroy it—or maybe they did know. Chloe was a New York City child, after all, versed in some of the complicated things of the world; she had already had the word *tsunami* explained to her in preschool. What would the wreckage of a sandcastle on a beach mean to her?

"Do you know of such a creature?" the man asked Chloe again, but since Moira was there between them, the child was not even aware she was being spoken to.

That a grown man, however otherwise unhappy or misunderstood, should befriend Chloe, a *preschooler,* and speak to her with intense, exclusive interest, and that he might imagine this could be considered charming and winning by the adults in their midst, was something from a romanticized view of the world. A lost world. Certainly not this world that Moira had joined when she moved to New York City from Killeshandra, Ireland. A young, innocent child and a grown, troubled man—a stranger—did not go together, and yet somehow he thought they did. In his thinking they were *both* innocent, neither one ruined by grunting needs, like most people. Not run over like a soft castle, all flooded and gummed up with seawater.

No, Moira thought, he would never have a friendship with Chloe because he would never get near enough. He would not get to tell her a fantastical story that she might be haunted by for a long time. Even a brief and seemingly innocuous moment in the Disney movie *Frozen* had somehow haunted the little girl. Chloe didn't need his ideas in her head; no one did.

But he was still talking. "The flat-faced marital crab is mostly seen among other flat-faced crabs," he said. "It is never seen alone. If you want to see one alone you have to get through an entire wall of crabs that look just like it. But all these crabs are highly critical, that's the thing. So if you go to their sea-cave for a meal, they will stare at you the entire time with eyes that can be found on the ends of their eye-stalks.

"The family will not allow you to just come in and be yourself, because the truth is, they never wanted anyone new in their midst to begin with. No one could fit the bill, and if you even try, you will be struck down and made to feel discouraged and anxious. The flat-faced marital crab is both weak and critical, a bad combo. It also has the ability to scuttle. But it doesn't scuttle, not really. It likes to stay stationary and watch others scuttle around it. It gets sun sometimes, but often it stays inside and bathes in the rays of a blue, artificial star that glows almost as powerfully as the sun. If you stare at that star too long, it will make you go blind in a different way. Blind *inside*. The flat-faced marital crab is tender, yet suddenly withholding and cruel, faulting you for its family's disapproval. This can feel crushing. But the flat-faced marital crab is kind of crushed too, having been raised in this kind of stifling environment, so a little sympathy is definitely in order."

He rattled off more of his story, which might've gone on for hours, Moira thought. Everyone else was exhausted, but not him. She imagined that upstairs right now, Elissa and Gary, who had gone swimming on their own, and had also gone "exploring," as Gary had put it, were probably napping together post-coitally. Here was the sun, and here was the sand, not to mention their very own child, who had been wanted with such a depth of desire that machines had been brought in to whir and shake and create a cocktail of stretching sperm and egg. And then, finally, after the cocktail had taken and something began to emerge, a giant claw had come down, as in one of those machines you could find in arcades—a clumsy claw in a glass box that you have to manipulate like a derrick in order to get it to lift the thing and bring it to you, as it had been brought, in its swaddling, to Elissa and Gary. And so loved, so deeply loved. Sweet Chloe, with her happiness and her tiny bikini bought in a store on Madison Avenue. And her kind, unflappable father, and anxious, well-meaning mother.

"Then the crab finds a way to make all the creatures in its midst crazy," the man continued. Despite herself, Moira was listening closely. "They are stunned into madness!" he said. "They hardly know what to do. They stay on shore, clutching at themselves and groaning. They take Klonopin, but it only makes them feel fuzzy the next day and, like all the benzos, might possibly lead to dementia later in life. The poor creatures grow weak and pale. All they do is walk in smaller and smaller circles, subsisting on a diet of ice-water with cubes of mango in it."

"Mango?" said Chloe, the single word having somehow been isolated from all the others and hauled in by her. She looked up for the briefest moment, but then Taylor said something to her and Chloe quickly returned to what they'd been doing.

"Eventually the tide takes the creatures," he went on, "and pulls them out to sea. It's the saddest thing imaginable. It could make you cry forever."

The man had so obviously longed to tell this story to the little girl, but the little girl had not heard almost any of it, and that was a relief. What would she have made of it? Which parts would have clung to her and reappeared in her dreams at night? Moira knew about men who gave off a certain stripe of irregularity; there had been one in her town when she was a child. Thomas O'Grady, who worked in the grocer's. He had frightened her once, coming past with a box of carrots and grazing the top of her thigh with his own clumsy claw. For a long time, whenever she thought about it, that thigh had burned.

"You'll keep a close eye on Chloe?" Elissa had asked, and of course Moira had said she would. Chloe and Taylor got up now and ran off to the edge of the water, abandoning their castle in advance of its destruction. Moira started to get up and follow them, but then she stopped herself. They were smart, Chloe and Taylor; they knew when to bail. She watched them from a distance with her sharp eye beneath its golden lashes, and the man watched, too. Now the little girls were up to their knees in the waves, emitting the kinds of shrieks that come only from children, for whom happiness and fear exist in great supply, and in as close proximity as ocean and shore.

THE ARGENTINE ANT

by T.C. BOYLE

after "The Argentine Ant" by Italo Calvino

he baby had been ill, we'd exhausted our savings and our patience, too, and were equally weary of the specialists who seemed to specialize only in uncertainty and of the cramped noisy conditions of our apartment in student housing, so when the chance came to rent the place in Il Nido we jumped at it. We'd never been that far south, but my uncle Augusto had lived in this particular village during the happiest period of his life and had never stopped rhapsodizing about it—and since the rent was a fraction of what we were paying for our apartment and my fellowship would provide us with a small but steady income for the coming year, there was nothing to stop us. Provided that the baby stayed healthy, that is. At sixteen months, he was a fine, sturdy-looking child, whose problem—a super-sensitivity to touch, which might have been dermatological in origin or perhaps neurological, depending on which specialist you talked to—seemed to be improving as he grew into the squat stance of his chubby legs. Would there be specialists in this flyspeck of a fishing village on the tip of the southern peninsula? Pediatricians? Neurologists? Dermatologists? Not likely. But in a way, that would be a relief, since his condition was hardly life-threatening and the various diagnoses and explanations for it were more worrisome than the condition itself. No, what our son needed was to get out from under the impress of our dreary northern clime, with its incessantly dripping gutters, and into the sunshine where he could bask and thrive—and, no small consideration, so could we.

A Signora Mauro was the landlady, and our connection with her was through my uncle, who'd rented the house from her twenty years back when he was between marriages and working on a novel that was never published. I don't remember anything of the novel, portions of which he'd read aloud to me and my sister when I was a boy and he was occupying the guest room over the garage, but I recall vividly his portrait of the village and the tranquility he'd found there, though, in retrospect—in light of what fell out, that is—I suppose this was fiction too.

My wife and I questioned nothing. This was an adventure, pure and simple. Or more than an adventure: an escape. We took the train and then a succession of buses, the last of which deposited us in front of Signora Mauro's rambling house in the village, and all the time the baby was well-behaved and my wife, Anina, and I stared out the jolting windows and dreamed of a long period of respite in our lives, she no longer trapped in a minimum-wage job as a temporary secretary and I free to work on solving the projective algebraic problem known as the Hodge conjecture and thereby winning the one-million-dollar Millennium Prize, a sum that would set us up handily for some time to come. Did I have unrealistic expectations? Perhaps. But I was twenty-eight years old and terminally exhausted with the classroom and academic life, and it is a truism that mathematicians, like poets, do their best work before thirty. So we packed our things, boarded the express, and found ourselves on Signora Mauro's doorstep in the sun-kissed embrace of Il Nido.

The house we were to rent was on a bluff overlooking the sea and it was crowded between two others—both, like ours, modest single-story structures of two or three rooms. Signora Mauro, exhibiting traces of a former beauty that was now for the most part extinct but for the low-level radiation of her eyes, found two men to help carry our things up the parabolic hill to the house on the bluff and spent the next quarter hour showing us the essentials—how to light the gas stove and regulate the temperature of the refrigerator and such—before nudging me to hand over a few crumpled bills to each of the workmen and then vanishing down the hill, looking satisfied with herself.

It took no more than half an hour to put away our things—clothes, books, baby paraphernalia, a box of kitchen items Anina had insisted on bringing along though the house had come furnished and the essentials were all in place—and get a quick impression of the living space. There were three rooms, kitchen, bedroom, sitting room, as well as an indoor bathroom featuring a grand old claw-footed tub big enough to bathe armies, and the casement windows in back gave onto a narrow elongated garden (or former garden: it was dried up and skeletal now) that ended in a low hedge and another fifty feet or so of scrub that fell away to the ocean below. "Look, Anina," I called, pushing through the back door and out into the yard, "there's space for a garden! We can grow tomatoes, squash, cucumbers. Beans, beans, too."

My wife, so reticent in public, so proper (humorless, was how my mother put it), was anything but in private. She took a critical view and always seemed to see things for what they were while I tended to romanticize and hope for the best. I watched her come out the door to me, after having set the baby down in his carrier at the foot of our new bed, where he'd promptly fallen asleep. She was grace incarnate, the wafting streamers of her hair caught up in the breeze she generated, her hips rotating in the earthy way that defined her, and her lips parted as if in passion, but what she said wasn't at all graceful or passionate. "You call this a garden? It's nothing but stones and leached-out soil."

"The house has been sitting empty—what do you expect? Some seeds, a little water, manure—"

"Where's the water? I don't see any water."

I snatched a look around me. There was a birdbath—or former birdbath—set beside the central path that bisected the yard, the blistered remnants of a wheelless bicycle that looked as if it had been there since Uncle Augusto's time, and a rusted watering can snarled in a tangle of yellowed vines, evidence that the garden had once been provided with water. "There"—I just now looked behind me to the whitewashed wall of the house to discover the faucet and a length of ancient hose coiled beneath it. I pointed. "What do you call that?"

She didn't say a word but just walked back up

the path to the house, bending to the hose bib as if to twist open the valve and prove me wrong, when she pulled up short and let out a low exclamation. "My God," she said, the voice dwindling in her throat. "What is *that?*"

What it was—and I hurried across the yard to see for myself—was a black sinuous ribbon of ants emerging from the ground beneath the hose bib to flow up the wall of the house and vanish into a crevice where the stucco met the overhang of the roof. I didn't react at first, rooted in fascination over this glistening display of coordination and purpose, a living banner composed of thousands, hundreds of thousands of individuals in permutations unfathomable (though already I was thinking in terms of algorithms). "Ants," I heard my wife declare. "I hate ants."

Without going into detail about her unhappy undergraduate romance with a biologist at the university who happened to be ten years her senior, married, and a myrmecologist to boot, I'll just say that when she snatched up the hose and leveled it on that column of ants, she saw nothing fascinating about the creatures—quite the opposite. The hose flared, a stream of water jetted out, and the ants fell away, only to mass at the base of the wall, realign themselves, and start climbing again, this time in two separate ribbons that converged just above the locus of the spray.

"That won't help," I said. "It's only temporary."

My wife abruptly shut off the faucet. "You'll have to go into the village for poison then. Some sort of powder, what is it? My father used to use it. You sprinkle it along the base of the walls—"

"We can't use poison here, are you crazy?" I said, thinking of the baby, and in that very moment a high sputtering scream echoed from the depths of the house. We stared at each other in horror, then my wife dropped the hose and we both bolted for the bedroom to discover that the floor had been transformed into a sea of ants— dislocated ants, angry ants, ants that had fled the wet and come to the dry—and that the baby, all considerations of skin tone aside, was black with them.

The irony wasn't lost on me. Here was a child whose condition one specialist likened to the feeling of having phantom ants crawling all over him, and now the sensation was real and the ants no phantoms. He threw back his head in his extremity, screeching till we thought his lungs would burst while I lifted him out of the cradle and my wife tore off his terrycloth pajamas, balled them up and employed them in frantic, quick jerks to swipe the ants from his torso and limbs. They were everywhere, these ants, foaming in miniature waves over our sandals to work their way between our toes and even scurried up our fingers and arms where we came into contact with our son. When finally we'd succeeded in brushing him clean, I went for the broom and attacked that roiling black horde with a pestilential fervor until many thousands of them, crushed and exuding their peculiar acidic odor, were swept out the door and into the courtyard. The baby, whimpering still, was in my wife's arms as she rocked with him, cooing little nonsense syllables to soothe him, and the remaining ants retreated into a crevice where the tile of the floor joined the wall. "This is intolerable," my wife spat, spinning and rocking, but with her eyes fixed on me like a pair of tongs. "We can't live here. *I* can't live here—not like this."

I told her, in a quiet voice, though I was seething too, that we really had no choice in the matter, as we'd already put down a deposit and first and last months' rent, and that I had my desk to set up and my work on the prize to do if we ever hoped to rise to the next level.

"The prize?" She threw it back at me. "Don't make me laugh. You're going to become a millionaire by solving an all but impossible problem that every other mathematician in the world is probably working on right this minute—without ants? In real houses, in university offices, with air conditioning, polished floors, and *no insects* at all!"

This stung. Of course it did. Here we hadn't been in our new home—in our new life—for more than an hour and already she was questioning the whole proposition, and worse, my abilities, my intellect, my faith in the exceptionalism that set me apart from all the others. I'd been close to a solution—it had floated there, just out of reach for months now, a matter of discovering and applying the right topology—and I knew that if I could just have these months of tranquility here by the sea to focus my mind, I could do it. I dropped my voice still lower. "I'm going to try."

A long moment transpired, I standing there in the doorway to the bedroom, she bouncing the baby, before she turned to me again, conceding the point but obstinate still, upset, her nerves frayed by the move and the baby's fragility and everything given figurative expression in these swarming insects that didn't even belong here, migrants from across the sea in South America. "All right," she said, biting her lower lip and swinging round on me with the baby as if she'd taken him hostage, "but you'd better find a solution to *this* problem, to these, these *pests*, before you even think about sitting down at that desk."

We hadn't eaten, either of us, and as it was now late in the afternoon, I thought I'd walk down to the village to pick up a few things for a quick meal—bread, cheese, salami, a fiasco of wine, milk for the baby—and take the opportunity to inquire about whatever non-toxic powders and sprays might be available for application, anything to discourage the ants—especially after dark. I had a grim vision of tossing all night in a strange bed as the ants boiled up from a crack in the floor and made a playing field of the expanse of my flesh. And my wife's. I could already foresee hanging the baby's cradle from a hook in the ceiling like a potted plant—ants couldn't fly, could they? Or not this species anyway. In any case, I'd just started up the flagstone path for the front gate when I heard music (jazz violin, sensuous and heartrending over the rhythmic rasp of the bow) drifting across the yard from the house next door and a low murmur of voices punctuated by laughter. On an impulse—and out of a feeling of neighborliness, that too—I changed direction and made my way to the low hedge that separated our property from that of the house next door and peered over.

I was immediately embarrassed. Here were my neighbors, a man and woman in their forties and dressed in swimsuits—he in trunks and she in a two-piece that left little to speculation—staring up at me in surprise. They were seated at a glass-topped table, sipping Campari and soda, and they both had their bare feet propped up on the two unused chairs in the set of four.

She was dark, he was fair, and they both looked harmless enough—in fact, once over their initial surprise they both broke out in broad smiles and the woman, whose name, I was soon to learn, was Sylvana, cried out, "Hello, there! You must be the new neighbor." And the husband: "Come join us. You must. I insist." And then the wife: "No need for formality—just hop over the hedge. Here, come on."

I was dressed in khaki trousers and a rayon shirt I'd rolled up to the elbows, nothing formal, certainly, but here they were all but naked, so I put away my scruples and vaulted the hedge. I came away with a handful of ants where I braced myself atop the vegetation to swing my legs and hips over, but it was nothing to eliminate them with a covert clap of my hands. Neither husband nor wife rose, though the wife shifted her (very shapely) legs to prop her feet on the same chair as her husband's, making room for me. I sat and we made our introductions—he was Signor Reginaudo ("Call me Ugo")—and soon I was enjoying a cool Campari with ice and a slice of lemon.

How long was it before I began itching? Minutes? Perhaps even seconds? Both the Reginaudos let out a little laugh. "Here," Sylvana said, a flirtatious lilt to her voice, "put your feet up beside mine—"

It was then that I noticed that the legs of the chairs—and the table as well—were anchored in old pomodoro cans filled with what I presumed to be water, and it was my turn to laugh. "The ants," I said, and suddenly we were all laughing, a long riotous laugh shot through with strains of relief, frustration, and commonality, a laugh of friendship and maybe desperation, too. Nodding his head and giggling till he had to steady himself with a deep draught of his Campari and a hyperactive pounding of his breastbone, Ugo repeated the noun, the plural noun, as if it were the most hilarious term in the language.

This was succeeded by an awkward pause, during which I became aware of the violin again and we simultaneously sipped our drinks, trying not to look too closely at the stems, leaves, fronds, and petals that surrounded us as if in some miniature Eden for fear of spoiling the illusion. Every blade of grass, every stone, every object in that yard was animated by a dark roiling presence as if the earth itself had come to life. Sylvana gave me a look caught midway between mortification and merriment and I heard myself say, "We have ants next door, too," and then the three of us were howling with laughter all over again.

"This is a fact of life here in Il Nido," Ugo began, once he'd recovered himself (again, with a gulp from his glass and a rapid thrust of one

fist to his breastbone), "but we've devised ways of dealing with it."

I lifted my eyebrows even as Sylvana shifted her feet so that her sun-warmed toes came into contact with mine and rested languidly there.

"Hydramethylnon," he pronounced, giving me a tight grin. "That's the ticket."

A frown of irritation settled between his wife's eyebrows. "Nonsense. Sulfluramid's the only way to go."

Ugo shrugged, as if to concede the point. "Azadirachtin, pyrethrum, Spinosad, methoprene, take your pick. They're all effective—"

"At first," Sylvana corrected.

Another shrug. He held out his palms in a gesture of helplessness. "They adapt," he said.

"But we stay one step ahead of them," Sylvana said. "Isn't that right, darling?" Her tone was bitter, accusatory. "One step ahead?"

Ugo pushed himself impatiently up out of the chair, his fair skin showing a pink effusion of sunburn across the shoulders and into the meat of his arms. "What is this, a debating society?" he demanded. "Come, friend, follow me out to the shed and I'll give you a good healthy sample of them all—and you can decide for yourself which is best."

I was on my feet now, too, gazing down on the gap between Sylvana's breasts and the long naked flow of her abdomen, which, I have to admit, stirred me in spite of myself.

"Come," Ugo repeated. "I'll show you what I've got."

"But what about the baby?" I gazed from him to Sylvana and back again even as I felt the itch start up in my feet and ankles. "He gets into everything. Worse: everything goes in his mouth."

"That's a baby for you," Ugo said. "But this stuff's harmless, really. Even if he—is it a he or she?"

"He."

"Even if he somehow gets into it, it won't do him any harm—"

"Ha!" the wife exclaimed, stretching her legs so that I could see the muscles of her inner thighs flex all the way up to the tiny patch of cloth that covered the mound where they intersected. "And it won't harm the ants either. Least of all the ants."

Though I felt a bit tipsy from the effects of the alcohol on an empty stomach, I had no problem vaulting the hedge with two large shopping bags full of various cans of insect powder Ugo had insisted I take, including one labelled ANT-AWAY and another called ANTI-ANT. When I entered the house to tell my wife what I'd discovered, I saw that both she and the baby were asleep, Anina stretched out diagonally across the bed and the baby tucked in beside her, and perhaps because I wasn't exercising the soberest of judgment, I spread a healthy dose of Anti-Ant along the base of the outside walls, and, for good measure, dumped a can of Ant-Away (active ingredient malathion, whatever that was) atop it. I didn't see any ants in the house and I suppose I didn't really look all that hard for fear of what I'd uncover, but instead made my way back down the hill to the grocery.

This was an old-fashioned grocery, dimly lit, kept cool by the thickness of its ancient walls and smelling strongly of the meats and cheeses in the refrigerated cases—provolone, with its potent smoky aroma, above all else. It was a pleasant smell, and as I pushed my cart through the deserted aisles and made my selections, I began to feel at home, as if everything were going to work out as planned and the solution to all our problems were at hand. I selected the wine, found milk and butter in the cooler and a dry salami hanging from its string in the front window, added bread, cheese, olives, artichoke hearts. Once I'd concluded my business, I wheeled the cart up to the checkout counter, behind which waited a solitary woman in a stained white apron. We exchanged greetings, and as the woman rang up my purchases I couldn't help inquiring if she knew of a reliable product for ant control. At first I thought she hadn't heard me, but then she lifted her eyes to mine before dropping them again. "Signore," she said, her voice no more than a whisper, "here we don't talk of such things."

"Don't talk of such things?" I repeated incredulously. "What do you mean? I see that you carry several ant powders, including Anti-Ant, and I just wanted to ask if you find it effective? If it's the best product, that is. And safe. Is it safe?"

She just shook her head, refusing to look up from the counter as she wrapped my things, then shifted her eyes furtively to my left and I saw that we were not alone. A man stood there beside me, not young, not old, wearing some sort of official uniform—matching trousers and shirt, which bore an insignia patch on one shoulder. He wore his hair long and slicked back beneath an undersized cap in the same hue as his clothing and he was giving me a quizzical smile. "And you are—?" he asked, his voice a kind of rumble that rose on the interrogative.

I introduced myself and we shook hands.

"Ah, of course," he said. "I should have known—you're the new tenant of the Mauro place, am I correct?"

"Yes," I said, "we just moved in—today, in fact. And I was just, well"—I shrugged by way of adducing the age-old relation between the sexes—"my wife sent me down here to the grocery to pick up a few things. For our first meal in the new house." I shrugged again, as if to say, You know how it is.

"I'll be there first thing in the morning," he said. "Would six be too early?"

I gave him a look of bewilderment. "I'm sorry," I said. "And who are you, exactly?"

He straightened up then and perhaps I was imagining it but his heels seemed to click as if ready for action. "Forgive me," he said, digging a card out of his shirt pocket and handing it to me. "Aldo Baudino," he said with a bow. "Of the Argentine Ant Control Corporation."

I wanted to question him further—*Ant Control? Six in the morning?*—but the woman behind the counter was shaking her head and jerking her eyes toward the door, trying to warn me off, trying to tell me something, but what? I thanked her, paid, bade them both farewell and went out the door sans further comment.

Arriving at home, just as I swung open the gate and started up the path, I was startled by a shriek that all but stopped my heart. I dropped my packages and broke into a run. At that moment the door flung back and Anina came down the steps with the baby clutched to her and I saw in an instant what had happened: the baby was dusted all over with the ant powder and there was a greenish crust of it round his mouth where he must have crawled across the floor to ingest it. "The doctor!" Anina cried. "We have to get him to the doctor!"

My heart was pounding and I felt nothing but guilt and horror: how could I have been so stupid? What were ants, a plague of ants, every ant in the world, compared to this? But where was the doctor and how would we find him? We didn't have a phone—or we did, but it hadn't been connected yet—and the only thing I could think of was the Reginaudos. They would know. Without a word—and here Anina must have thought I'd lost my mind—I veered right and sprang over the hedge into their yard, expecting to find them still seated at the table with their feet up, sipping Campari. They weren't there. Ants boiled up around my feet and I saw then that a whole swift roiling river of them was heading for our house, as if the powder had attracted rather than repelled them. Anina shrieked again. And then I was pounding on the Reginaudos' door, peering through the glass and shouting for help.

A moment later, Ugo appeared, looking annoyed—or perplexed, perhaps that's a better word. "Yes?" he said, pulling back the upper half of the Dutch door to his kitchen. "What is it, what's all the commotion?"

"The baby!" I could barely get the words out—and now, even as I noticed that Ugo was wearing a pair of rubber galoshes and that the concrete floor of the kitchen seemed to be glazed with half an inch or more of water, Anina was there beside me, jabbering excitedly and holding the baby out in evidence.

That was the tableau we presented, the four of us—and the ants, of course. The baby, for his part, seemed calm enough, grinning a broad greenish grin and clinging to his agitated mother as if nothing were amiss, as if ant poison were no more a concern than lime Jell-O and every bit as irresistible. Ugo waved a dismissive hand. "I see he's been into the Ant-Away," he said. "But not to worry, it's nothing. No more harmful than sugar and water."

My wife just stared at him, her eyes—her beautiful olive eyes—so swollen they looked as if they would burst. "What do you mean, it's nothing? Can't you see? He's eaten ant poison!"

And here came Sylvana, still in her skimpy two-piece, sloshing bare-footed across the floor. "I told you," she called out, "it's harmless."

But my wife wouldn't be assuaged—and nor would I, though I was trying to make sense of this. Why would anyone market an ant powder that was harmless, unless it was harmless only to humans and fatal to the insects? But if that were the case, then why were there so many of them?

Finally, leaning over the frame of the door as a single column of ants worked its way down along the wall to join the phalanx heading for our house, Sylvana said she'd call the doctor if we really insisted, "But he'll do nothing, believe me. He's seen it before, a hundred times. You want my advice? Give the kid a tablespoon or two of olive oil and let him bring it up."

"No," my wife said, shaking her head emphatically, and I realized, absurdly, that she hadn't even been introduced yet. "The doctor."

Both the Reginaudos exchanged a look and shrugged, and then Ugo sloshed across the kitchen to where the phone hung from the wall. I turned to my wife, ignoring the boots and the soaked floor and what they implied. "Anina," I said, "this is our neighbor, Sylvana. Sylvana, my wife, Anina."

The baby grinned and stuck a green finger in his mouth.

"Pleased to meet you," Sylvana said, extending her hand.

The doctor came on foot, toting his bag up from the village below. He was a jaunty, bowlegged man of indeterminate age, though I figured him to be twice as old as I, if not more. "Ah, you must be the new people," he exclaimed, pushing through the front gate as I came up the path to meet him, followed by an anxious Anina clutching the baby in her arms. "And this," he said, slipping a pair of reading glasses over the bridge of his nose and bending to the baby, "must be the patient." He held out

his arms and Anina handed the baby over. The doctor hefted him, then clucked his tongue in the way of doctors everywhere—even specialists—and stated the obvious: "I see he's been into the Ant-Away, eh?"

This was the signal for Anina to pour out her concerns to him, beginning with the story of awakening to find that the baby had crawled down from the bed and somehow managed to push open the screen door that someone had carelessly left ajar (and here she shot me a look), then segueing into the medical issues we'd had with the child over the past six months and ending with a long unnecessary coda about our trip down from the north and our surprise—shock, really—over finding the house infested with ants.

The doctor wasn't really listening. He was shuffling his feet and whirling about with the baby thrust high in his arms, cooing baby talk as our son, giddy with the attention, peeled back his lips in a wide green smile and cried out his joy. It was then that I realized that all three of us were unconsciously shuffling about—motion the only thing to discourage the ants underfoot—and I found myself giving in to impatience. "But the baby," I said, trying to get the doctor's attention as he cooed and spun, "is he all right?"

"Oh, he's fine," the doctor assured me, handing the baby back to Anina. "A little malathion never hurt anybody." The birds were settling into the trees by this time and the sun sat low in the sky. My stomach rumbled. It had been a long day and still we hadn't eaten. "And you, little mother," the doctor said, focusing on Anina now, "feed him nothing but pastina for a day or two and examine his diaper carefully. If the result is in any way greenish, you must bring him to my offices; if not, forget the whole business and feel blessed because there isn't a thing in the world wrong with this little fellow." And here he leaned in to mug for the baby. "Isn't that right, Tiger?"

"But aren't you going to examine him?" My wife, usually so reserved with strangers, was in a state, I could see. She'd practically attacked the Reginaudos and now here she was making demands of the doctor—and this was only our first day in town.

Shifting from foot to foot in a kind of autonomous tarantella, the doctor just grinned. "No need," he assured her, "no need at all," and already he was swinging round to go. "Just remember," he called over his shoulder, "pastina and a close scrutiny of the diapers."

Furious and muttering to herself—I distinctly heard her spit out the term *quack*—Anina spun round and stamped back up the path and into the house, murdering ants all the way, while I followed the doctor to the gate to see him out. "What about your fee?" I asked, pulling open the gate for him.

He seemed to shiver all over and he brusquely swiped one pantleg against the other. "No need to worry about it now," he said, grinning and twitching as the sinking sun made a lantern of his deeply fissured face, "I'll send a bill tomorrow." He held out his hand and I took it. "*Specialists,*" he pronounced, and for an instant I thought he was going to spit in the dirt, but he merely squeezed my hand, swung his bony shoulders round, and headed back down the track to the village below.

It was then, just as I plucked the paper bags of groceries up off the ground, almost idly brushing the ants from them and thinking of dinner and a glass of wine—some surcease to all the turmoil of the day—that I heard a *pssst-pssst* from the hedgerow that divided our southerly neighbor's property from ours and turned to see a man beckoning to me from the shadows there. He was squat, big-bellied, with an enormous head and eyes that seemed to absorb the day's remaining light till they glowed like headlamps.

He was known only as "the Captain." He was a foreigner, from Mexico, and he'd formerly been enforcer for one of the narcotics gangs until he was shot three times in the abdomen and his wife, who'd been sitting beside him in their convertible while they were stopped at a red light, was killed by yet another bullet meant for him. Now he was retired and—according to the Reginaudos, who'd filled me in on the details and warned me against him (they called him an extremist)—he didn't get out much. Which, I suppose, was only understandable.

I crossed to the hedge and offered him a *buona sera*, but he didn't return the greeting or bother with introductions. He merely said, "The Reginaudos? Don't trust them. She's a slut—and come to think of it, so is he. All they do is throw down their powders and lie around screwing all day."

I lifted my eyebrows, though I wasn't sure if he could read my expression in the fading light. I wasn't especially happy—I didn't want to hear criticism of my neighbors or get caught up in pitting one against the other, and the ants, naturally, had begun to discover me standing there with the bags of groceries in hand—but I was polite, polite to a fault. Or so Anina claimed.

"You want to know how to deal with this scourge? Huh? I mean, *really* deal with it, the final solution and none of this pussyfooting? Here, step over the hedge and I'll show you."

The Captain didn't use powders or sprays. He used traps of his own devising. Baited wires suspended over coffee cans filled with gasoline, into which the ants, in their frenzy, would drop singly and sometimes by the dozen, as well as electrical connections timed to give a fierce jolt to a rotting fish head or scrap of stinking meat every thirty seconds. For the next half hour, though I wanted only to go home, sit down to dinner, and devise some sort of plan to keep my own ants out of the bedroom for the course of a single night, I patiently followed him around and forced out little noises of approbation over one device or another, so exhausted I could barely make sense of him through his vertiginous accent.

"This is the Argentine ant," he said at one point, "and I don't know if you quite comprehend what that means. They are invaders"—and here he paused to give me a sharkish grin—"like me. But they're from the true south, from the jungle of the Americas, where you have to fight without quarter every minute of every day even to have a prayer of staying alive. They've outcompeted the native ants everywhere they wash up, destroyed them, devoured them. You know what these ants are like?"

I shook my head.

"Like the cells of your body, each ant a single cell and all working in concert, one thing, one living organism, and the queen is the brain. My plan is to starve her by taking her workers away from her in the way you cut up a corpse, piece by piece." There was a silence broken only by the snap of electricity and the faint hiss of ants dropping into cans of gasoline. "Here," he said, and he gestured toward one of his suspension traps, "take as many of these as you like—it's your only hope."

In the morning, at first light, after having spent an all but sleepless night at war with the ants (resorting finally to encircling the bed with a frangible wall of green powder, despite fears for the baby), I was awakened by a noise in the garden. I arose, pulled on my slippers, and went to investigate, crushing ants underfoot all the way across the bedroom, through the kitchen, and out the back door. I saw a figure there, bent to the wall of the house, and though my mind wasn't as clear as I would have liked, it took only a moment to identify him—the undersized cap, the slicked-back hair, the shoulder patch—as the Ant Man, come as promised. Or threatened, if you prefer. "Good morning," I said, irritated and relieved at the same time—here was intrusion, here was hope.

He didn't look up. "You have a problem," he said. His voice rumbled like a tremor in the Earth.

"A problem?" I said, throwing it back at him. "Isn't that stating the obvious? Don't we all, as you say, *have a problem*? My question is, what are you going to do about it?"

Down on one knee now, working the dirt with a trowel, he glanced over his shoulder and gave me a sardonic smile. "My intention," he said, speaking slowly, his voice a rolling fervent peal, "is to eliminate that problem. Come. Look here."

I bent closer.

"You see this?" I saw now that he had set a clay saucer in a depression he'd made in the soil where it came into contact with the wall of the house. There was something in the depths of the saucer, a thick amber substance that glistened in the early-morning light as if it were a precious gift. "This is my special formula—honey, yes, but laced with an insecticide so fast-acting and fatal that you'll be ant-free here within the week. I guarantee it."

"But what of the baby?" I said. "Won't the baby—?"

He made a small noise in the back of his throat. "This is for ants, not babies," he said. "If you're so anxious, why not keep the infant inside—you can do that, can't you? Don't you think it's worth the effort, considering the alternative? Wake up. This is the planet earth we live on—and it has its terms and conditions like anything else."

"Yes, but—"

"Yes, *nothing*. Just do as I say. And these traps the Captain has given you"—he made a rude gesture toward the traps I'd set up in the garden the night before—"don't you think gasoline is fatal to babies, too? Eh? Or don't you think at all?" And now he rose, giving me a hostile look. "Amateurs," he said, jerking his chin first toward the Captain's house, then the Reginaudos'. "Do you really suppose that eliminating a few thousand workers will have any effect at all? No, you have to get the queen, you have to entice the workers to bring her this incomparable bait, to feed it to her and worry over her as she withers and desiccates and the whole stinking horde goes kaput. You're a mathematician, aren't you? Or so I've heard—"

I nodded.

He held me with his acerbic eyes, then nodded back, as if we were in agreement. "Do the math," he said, and then he bent to set the next saucer in the ground.

A week went by. Several times during that week, and at the oddest hours—dawn, midnight—Signor Baudino appeared to refill his saucers, a secretive figure who became almost as much an annoyance as the ants themselves, which, despite his promise, seemed even more abundant than ever. We slept little, though I finally resorted to setting the four posts of the bed in their own pomodoro cans of water, and that gave us a measure of relief, though Anina and I tossed and turned, dreaming inevitably that the swarms had overtaken us and gnawed us right down to our meatless bones. For the baby, even his waking hours were a kind of nightmare, the ants attacking him the moment we released him from his cradle, and when I look back on that period I have a vision of him itching himself, his former condition complicated now

Great Speeches from History vs. the Tweets of Donald J. Trump

I have no fear about the outcome of our struggle in Birmingham, even if our motives are presently misunderstood. We will reach the goal of freedom in Birmingham and all over the nation, because the goal of America is freedom. Abused and scorned though we may be, our destiny is tied up with the destiny of America. Before the Pilgrims landed at Plymouth, we were here. Before the pen of Jefferson scratched across the pages of history the majestic word of the Declaration of Independence, we were here... If the inexpressible cruelties of slavery could not stop us, the opposition we now face will surely fail. We will win our freedom because the sacred heritage of our nation and the eternal will of God are embodied in our echoing demands...

—*Martin Luther King, Jr., from*
"Letter from Birmingham Jail," 1963

The so-called angry crowds in home districts of some Republicans are actually, in numerous cases, planned out by liberal activists. Sad!

—*@realDonaldTrump, February 21, 2017*

by a melding of the imaginary and the actual so that he could never be sure what he was feeling, just that it was a perpetual harrying of the flesh, and I felt powerless to console him. I see Anina, too, growing more sullen and combative by the day and blaming me for all our problems, as if I had any control over this plague in our midst. The Reginaudos stopped by to offer advice and yet more powders and sprays, and the Captain, unbidden, twice slipped into the yard to set up his gasoline traps. For my part, I felt as harried as my wife and infant, trying gamely to pursue my work at a desk set in cans of water and scratching my equations across a page only to see them devolve into streams of ants that were as insubstantial as the ones crawling through my dreams.

On the seventh day, a Monday, Anina came to me at my desk, the baby clasped in her arms. "This is fraud," she informed me, her voice rigidly controlled but right at the breaking point.

I glanced up, noticing a thoroughfare of ants descending the wall before me—or no, they were ascending. Or no, descending. Descending and ascending both. I'd been lost in concentration, in another world altogether, and now I was back in the world of existence. "What is?"

"The contract. The old lady." And here she spat out Signora Mauro's name as if it were a ball of phlegm. "She never once mentioned the ants—and the ants negate that contract, which was made under false pretenses, fraudulent pretenses. This isn't paradise, it's hell, and you know it!"

I was being berated and I hardly deserved it or needed it either. I was going to throw it back at her, going to say, Can't you see I'm working? But in that moment the truth of it hit me. She was right. We'd come to the end of pretense. "Get your handbag," I said.

She just glared at me. The baby twisted his mouth and began to cry.

"We're going down to the village to see Signora Mauro. And demand an explanation."

The landlady's house, which we'd scarcely noticed the day we stepped off the bus, was a long low meandering structure with an intricate web of iron grillwork out front that must have dated from the Renaissance. It was situated in the better part of town, surrounded by imposing villas, the vegetation lush, the air so fresh it might have been newly created. My wife threw back the gate and marched up the walk to the front door, where she jabbed at the bell with a vengeful thrust of her finger. A moment passed, the two of us framed there beneath a trellis shaped like an ascending angel, the baby for once quiet in my wife's arms. Anina drew in an angry breath, then depressed the doorbell again, this time leaving her finger in place so that the bell buzzed continuously. Finally, the heavy oaken door eased open just a crack and a maid the size of a schoolgirl stood just behind it, gaping up at us. "We've come to see the Signora," I said.

The maid's face was like a wedge cut from a wheel of fontina. Her eyes were two fermented holes. "The Signora is not at home to visitors today," she said.

"Oh, but she *is*," my wife countered, forcing the door open and striding into the foyer as I followed in her wake.

We found ourselves in a dark echoing space, the only light a series of faint rectangles that represented the margins of the drawn shades. Furniture loomed in the darkness. There was a smell of dust and disuse. To this point, I'd been swept up in my wife's fervor, but now, standing there in the gloom of a stranger's house—a house we'd forced ourselves into, uninvited—I began to have second thoughts. But not Anina. She raised her voice and called out, "Signora! Signora Mauro! We've come to see you—we *demand* to see you. Right this moment!"

There was a stirring at the far corner of the room, as if the shadows were reconstituting themselves, and then a match flared, a candle was lit, and Signora Mauro, in a widow's colorless dress, was standing before us. "Who are you?" she demanded, squinting through the glare of the candle.

"We've come about the lease," I said.

"It's a fraud," Anina added, her voice rising. "The conditions," she began, and couldn't go on.

"Vermin," I said. "It's infested with vermin and you never said a word about it."

Signora Mauro's voice was the voice of a liar and it came to us in a frequency that wasn't much more than a liar's rasp: "I know nothing about it."

"Ants," my wife put in. "The ants." At the mention of his nemesis, though he could hardly have been expected to know the term, the baby began to squirm and gargle.

"You've got to keep things clean," Signora Mauro said. "What do you expect, with your filthy ways? I've got a mind to double your rent for abusing my property. And don't think I haven't had reports—" Even as she spoke I could see that she was twitching in some way, furtively scratching, rubbing one leg against the other, flicking a hand across her hips and abdomen.

I threw it back at her. "What about you? What makes you impervious?"

"Me? I don't have pests here. I keep a clean house. Scrupulously clean." Again she twitched, though she tried to suppress it.

"But you do," I said. "I know you do."

"I don't."

"We want out of this contract," Anina said. "We demand it."

The Signora was silent a moment. I could hear her drawing and releasing her harsh ragged breath. "Demand all you like, but I'll take you to court—and you'll never see a penny of your deposit, I guarantee it."

"No," I said, surprising myself by taking a step forward—what was I going to do, attack her?— "we'll take *you* to court." Even as I said it, I knew I was bluffing. She had the power, she had the position, she had our first and last month's rent and absent the house on the bluff we wouldn't even have a roof over our heads.

"Go ahead," she said, her voice jumping an octave as she squirmed in her clothes and stamped her feet on the carpet that must suddenly have come alive there in the dark. "I'd like to see that. I really would."

In the sequel, Anina, my sweet Anina, transformed now in her rage and grief beyond all recognition, shoved me roughly aside, stormed out the door and slammed the iron gate behind her so furiously the entire house seemed to shake. I was left there in the gloom to make an awkward bow and bid the old woman a good afternoon before hurrying after my wife. When I reached the street, I jerked my head right and left, in a panic over what she might do next—I'd never seen her like this, violence erupting from her like a lava flow, and I was afraid for her and the baby,

too. The street was busy enough, pedestrians and vehicles alike making their way from one end to the other, and at first I couldn't find her in that shifting chaotic scene, but finally I made out the unmistakable rotating motion of her hips as she veered left down a side street at the end of the block. I ran to catch up.

By the time I turned into that block, she was already at the next, swinging, descending toward the section of town where the fishermen lived in their ancient stone houses amidst a petrol station and a few tumbledown canneries that once processed the sardines that had become rarer and rarer over the course of the years. "Anina, what are you doing?" I called, but she ignored me, her shoulders dipping over the burden of the baby in her arms, her legs in their faded blue jeans beating double time along the walk. Then I was beside her, pleading with her—"Let's go home and talk this over, there's got to be a solution, calm yourself, please, if not for me, then for the baby"—but she just kept on going, her mouth a tight unyielding slash in a jaw clenched with rage.

We went down another street, then another, until finally I saw where she was headed—a warehouse just a block from the sea, a place of concrete block and corrugated iron that had seen better days. As I followed her up the walk to the front door, still pleading, I spotted the hand-lettered sign over the lintel—THE ARGENTINE ANT CONTROL CORPORATION—and at the same time became aware of the smell. And the ants. The smell was of rot, of the spoiled fish heads and lumps of offal the Captain might have used for bait, and the ants were swarming over the walls in such legions they must have been six inches deep. Anina tried the front door—locked—and then began pounding on the metal panels, dislodging ants in great peeling strips like skin. "Come out of there, you son of a bitch!" she shouted. "I know you're in there!"

I snatched at her arm, shook her, and now the baby had gotten into the act, bellowing till he was red in the face. "What are you doing?" I demanded.

There were tears in her eyes. The baby howled. "It's true what they say, don't you see? He claims to be doing a governmental service, this Ant Man, but in fact he's breeding them. Don't you get it?"

"No," I said, "frankly, I don't. Why would he do a thing like that?"

She gave me a look of contempt and pity, a look for the fool blind to the realities of life. "If the ants are eliminated, so is his job. It's as clear as day. He's not baiting the insects, he's *feeding* them!"

Of course, that couldn't be. I saw that distinctly. And I saw that through no fault of our own we'd been distracted from our path in life, that we'd become disoriented and at odds with each other. And all for what? For *ants*? I still held onto her, my grip firm at her elbow, and even as the idea came into my head, I swung her around, the baby still mewling, and began guiding her down the street to where the sea crashed rhythmically against the shore. We made our way amongst the rocks to the pale bleached sand of the beach and I just held her for a long moment, the baby calming around the deceleration of his miniature heartbeat, the sun a blessing on our upturned faces.

In that moment, the solution to the Hodge conjecture came to me, or the hint of a solution that would next require pencil and paper, of course, but the intuition was there, a sudden flashing spark in my brain that made everything come clear. It was an abstraction, yes, but math was the purest thing I knew, a matter of logic, of progression, of control. The ants were nothing in the face of this. We could learn to live with them. We *would*. I took a deep breath and looked out to sea, Anina and the baby pressed to me as the surf broke and receded and broke again. Here was a gathering force that predated everything that crawled on this earth, the waves beating at the shore until even the solidest stone was reduced to grains, each a fraction of the size of an ant and each lying there inert on the seabed, stretching on, clean and austere, to infinity.

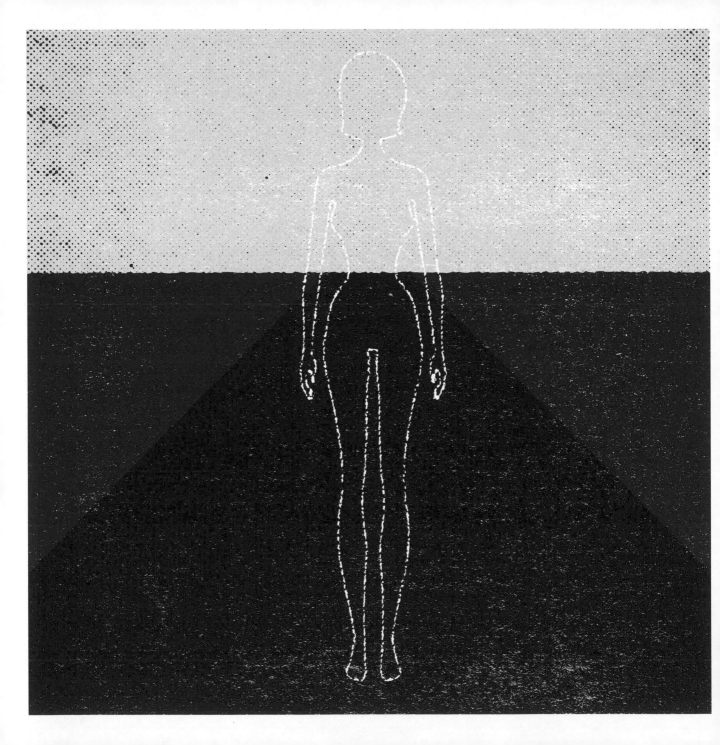

ONE HOUR, EVERY SEVEN YEARS

by ALICE SOLA KIM

after "All Summer in a Day" by Ray Bradbury

hen Margot is nine, she and her parents live on Venus. The surface of Venus, at that time, will be one enormous sea with a single continent on its northern pole, perched there like a tiny, ridiculous top hat. There is sea below, and sea above, rain continually plummeting from the sky, endlessly self-renewing.

hen I am thirty, I won't have turned out so hot. No one will know; from a few feet away, I'll seem fine. They won't notice the dandruff, the opalescent flaking of my chin. They won't know that I walk hard and deliberate, like a '40s starlet in trousers, in order to compensate for the wobbly heels of my crummy shoes. They won't see past my really great job. And it will be a great job, really. I will be working with time machines.

When Margot is nine, it has been five years since she has seen the sun. On Venus, the sun comes out but once every seven years. Margot's family moved to Venus from Earth when she was four. This is the main thing that makes her different from her classmates, who are just a bunch of trashy Venus kids. Draftees and immigrants. Their parents work at the desalination plants, the dormitory facilities; they plumb and bail, they traverse Venus's vast seas in ships and submersibles, and sometimes they do not come back.

To her classmates, Margot will never be Venusian, even though she's pale and clammmy like a Venusian, and walks and talks like a Venusian—with that lazy, slithering drawl. Why? First finger: she's a freak, quiet and standoffish, but given to horrible bursts of loud friendliness that are so awkward they make everyone hate her more for trying. Second finger: her dad is rich and powerful, but she still isn't cool. The Venus kids don't know it, but it isn't her wealth they hate. It is the waste of it. The way her boring hair hangs against her fresh sweatshirts. The way

she shuffles along in her blinding new sneakers. Third finger, fourth, fifth, sixth, seventh, eighth, ninth, tenth fingers, and all the toes, too: in her lifetime, Margot has seen the sun and they haven't. Venus kids are strong and mean and easily offended. They know there's a thing they should be getting that they're not getting. And that the next best thing to getting something is no one in the whole world getting it.

When I am thirty, I will have gotten my first boyfriend. He'll be a co-worker at the lab and I won't have noticed him for the longest time. Big laugh, right? You would think that, as some nobody who nobody ever notices, I'd at least be the observant one by default, the one who notices everyone else and forms complex opinions about them, but no, I will be a creature spiraled in upon myself, a shrimp with a tail curled into its mouth.

Late night at work, a group of people will be playing Jenga in the lounge. The researchers love Jenga because it has the destructive meathead glamour of sports but only a fraction of the physical peril. Anders will ask me if I want to play and I'll shake my head, hoping it looks like I'm too cool for Jenga but also bemused and tolerant, all of this hiding the truth, which is that I am terrified of Jenga. I'm afraid of being the player who causes all of the blocks to fall. Because that player is both appreciated and despised: on the one hand they absorb the burden of causing the Fall, thus relieving everyone else of said burden, but on the other hand they are responsible for ending the game prematurely, killing all the fun and potential, not to mention the Jenga tower itself—the spindly edifice that everyone worked so hard together to create and protect.

The guy who will be my first boyfriend will push a block out without any hesitation. He won't poke at it first, he will go straight for the block, and I will watch as the tower wobbles. It won't fall. As he takes the dislodged block and stacks it on his pile, he will make eye contact with me, a carefully constructed look of surprise on his face—mouth the shape of an *0*, eyebrows pushing his forehead into pleats.

When Margot is nine, the sun comes out on Venus. Her classmates lock her inside a closet and run away. They are gone for precisely one hour. When her classmates finally come back to let Margot out, it will be too late.

When I am thirty, I will have been at my great job, the job of working with time machines, long enough to learn their codes and security measures (I've even come up with a few myself), so I will do the thing that I didn't even know I was planning to do all along. I will enter the time machine, emerging behind a desk in the school I attended when I was nine. Water droplets will condense on the walls. There is no way to keep out the damp on Venus. The air in the classroom will taste like the air in a bedroom where someone has just had a sweaty nightmare. I will hide during all of the ruckus, but don't worry: I will work up the courage. I will stand and open the closet door and do what needs to be done. And I will return!

When Margot is nine, the sun comes out on Venus. Her classmates lock her inside of a closet and run away. She hears someone moving outside. Margot's throat is raw but she readies another scream when the door opens. A golden woman stands in the doorway, her face dark, her hair edged with gilt. Behind her the sun shines through the windows like a fire, like a bombing the moment before everybody is dead. "Wouldn't you like to play outside?" the woman says.

When I am thirty, I will live on Mars, the way I've always dreamed I would. I will live in the old condo alone, after my mother has moved out, and I will become a smoker the moment I find a pack my mother has left behind. It will feel wonderful to smoke on warm and dusty Martian nights. It will feel so good to blow smoke through the screen netting on the balcony and watch it swirl with the carmine dust. Many floors down, people will splash in the pool of the condo complex, all healthy and orange like they are sweating purified beta-carotene and vitamin C.

It is the sight of these party people that will spur me to spend a month attempting to loosen up and get pretty. I will have a lot of time on my hands and a lot more money after my mother moves out. I will learn that there are lots of things you can do to fix yourself up, and that I hadn't tried any of them. Makeup, as I learn it, is confusing and self-defeating. I'll never understand why I have to make my face one flat uniform shade, only to add color back selectively until my old face is muffled and almost entirely muted, a quiet little cheep of itself. I will learn all of this from younger women at the department store, younger women who are better than me at covering up far nicer faces. I will also get some plastic surgery, because I will be extremely busy; I don't have time to be painting this and patting that! I will have lost so much of my time already.

When Margot is nine, the sun comes out on Venus and she is on the verge of getting pushed into the closet when a woman appears out of nowhere and starts screaming at the kids. They scatter and run. Margot is trapped, backing into the closet that she had been fighting to stay out of. The woman approaches. She is tidy, flawless even, but her face droops and contorts like a rubber mask without a wearer. "Recognize me," says the woman.

When I am thirty, Sana, the new researcher at the lab, will tell me what she's been writing in that notebook of hers. After her first day of work, Sana will have written down her observations about everybody: summaries of the kind of people we all are, predictions about what we might do. After working at lab after lab and traveling the worlds, Sana will be confident about her ability to nail people down precisely. She is nice, though. When I ask her what she wrote about me, she'll reply, "I'm not sure about you yet. You are a tricky one. It will take some time to see." I'll know that that means I have the most boring entry with the fewest words.

Sana will be one of those who believe that you cannot find your own timeline. You will not be able to access it, to travel back in time to change your life. You can go into other universes and mess the place up and leave, but not your own. We will both know of the many who have tried to find their own timestreams; all have failed. Sana will say, "The universe does not allow it to happen because we cannot be the gods of ourselves," and this is about as mystical as Sana will ever get.

When Margot is nine, her parents refuse to take her out of school. She asks and she asks and they don't hear. Margot's father is high up in the Terraforming division, which has both an image problem and a not-being-good-at-its-job problem. Her parents tell her that it helps them that she attends regular school with the kids of their employees' employees' employees' employees' employees. It doesn't matter that Margot hasn't exactly been the best PR rep.

A while back, the students had studied the Venus Situation in Current Events. The teacher played a video, which showed the disaster as it was happening, everyone in the control room yelling, "Fuck!" The fucks were bleeped out incompletely. You could still hear "fuh." 1,123 people had died moments after the Terraformers pressed the button. The Terraformers had been trying to transform Venus from a hot gassy mess into an inhabitable, Earth-like place. What actually happened was that everything exploded, the blast even sucking in ships from the safe zone. After the space dust had cleared, they did not find a normal assortment of continents and oceans and sunlight and foliage: what they found was one gross, sopping slop bucket of a world. A Venus that was constantly, horribly wet. A Venus that,

to this day, rains in sheets and buckets, a thousand firehouses spraying from the sky. Iron-gray and beetle-black and blind eye-white: these are the colors of Venus. Forests grow and die and grow and die, their trunks and limbs composting on a wet forest floor that squeaks like cartilage.

The teacher had stopped the video. "Margot's father is part of the new Terraforming division," she said. "He is helping us make Venus a better place to live." The teacher was too tired to smile, so she made her mouth wider. She had been drafted, had come from New Mexico on Earth. She despaired of her frizzing hair and her achy knees, and she missed her girlfriend a lot, even though it was sad to miss someone who didn't love you quite enough to follow you somewhere shitty. But, not a ton of lesbians on Venus. The teacher was tired of going out on lackluster dates where she and the other woman would briskly concur that, *yes, we are both interested in women, that is why we are on this date*, maybe not in those words exactly, but you get the drift, and then sometimes they would go home alone and sometimes not.

One kid had turned around and given Margot the finger. Behind her, a girl leaned forward and whispered something like "maggot." The children in the classroom whispered in their slithering voices, things about Margot, things about her father who was so bad at his job, things about

Venus. Then someone said, "Who said penis?" and laughter rose and exploded outward like a mushroom cloud. "You know who likes penis?" a boy said in a high, clear, happy voice, as if he had just gotten a good idea. "Your dad."

When I am thirty, I will visit other time-streams. It will almost feel like traveling into my own past, but not quite. Sometimes there will be big differences: shirts, the configurations in which the children stand, the smell of lunch on their breaths. But there will also be the differences I can't see. I could stay in one event cluster until I died and I still wouldn't have seen it all. In one timeline, a single hair on a girl's head might be blown left. In another, blown right. A whole new universe, created just for that hair. The hair was the star of the whole goddamn show but the hair was not egotistical about it at all. It would simply, humbly change directions when the time came. But always: children will come in; children will run out.

When Margot is nine, her parents are carefully, jazzily, ostentatiously in love. Enraptured by each other and enwrapped in money, their love cushioned against the world and Margot. Native Martians for two generations, their families had come from China and Denmark and Nigeria and South Korea. The people do sigh to watch Margot's parents walk hand in hand—they are lovely alone and sublime together, a gorgeous advertisement for the future, except to see them is to know that the future is the present, it is here, and isn't that a happy thing?

This pressure is beneficial to their relationship; they perform a little for the world and for Margot, and most of all for themselves; they grin at each other competitively; their real feelings are burnished until they blaze. She has never seen them in sweatpants, whereas Margot herself often changes into pajamas the moment she gets home, which makes Margot's mother laugh and pat her face and tell her how extremely Korean she's being. At the dinner table, her parents feed each other the first bite. Sometimes this is yet another competition, a race to construct the perfect tiny arrangement of food, and sometimes it is a simple moment of closeness that doesn't make Margot want to barf yet (she's not old enough) but induces in her narrow chest a weird, jealous, proud feeling. She is certain that, someday soon, she will be able to create a role for herself and join them in their performance.

When I am thirty, I will be too tall for my parents to make jokes over my head. They'll have to look me in the eye when they do it. Or the back of my head.

I will call my mother and she won't pick

up, over and over again. Catching myself in the viddy reflection, I'll be scared by my face. How perfectly slack and non-sentient it is when nothing prompts it into action. It will remind me of my father's face when I watched him alone in the dining room a few weeks before his disappearance. I had woken up in the middle of the night and crept out of my room to get a glass of water. I needed to be quiet, because at night the house stopped being mine. Sometimes it belonged only to my parents. Sometimes the grayscale walls of our aggressively normal house looked alien, as too-smooth as an eggshell, and then the house seemed to belong to no one.

I peered around the corner into the dining room and saw my father sitting at the table alone. He sat still, staring at his computer. Nothing moved. I was frightened but fascinated to see my father this way, all flat surface. Suddenly he reached up and pinched his upper arm hard, on the inner part where it really hurts. He pinched *hard*, and then he *twisted* hard, and the tiny violence of his fingers was so at odds with the nothing expression on his face that I wanted to laugh. I pressed my hands to my mouth and tiptoed quickly back to bed.

But who could say what the significance of that single memory was, or whether it was significant at all? The record will show that he had faked everything, and had been good at it. My father behaved weirdly the night I spied on him; that is true. So maybe that does mean something. But his mind, a very strange place indeed, must have been even stranger when the rest of him was normal: him at dinner, taking a first bite; him at work, making everyone feel special as he told them exactly what to do.

When Margot is nine, the sun comes out on Venus. All rain stops and the sun comes out for an hour, and for that hour everyone can pretend that Venus turned out okay. Because this gracious, lovely celestial event happens every seven years, some of the kids sorta, kinda remember the last time the sun came out. When they talk about it, they sound like old people reminiscing: they chatter on about how the sun smelled like warming butter and glittered on their skin. Other kids don't remember anything. And then there's Margot. She had been four instead of two the last time she saw the sun, which makes a difference—it's like having a brain made of clay instead of dough. She knows how the sun is a discrete object in the sky and, also, that it is everywhere, like air. And she knows that, like air, you can breathe the sun in and even taste it a little, but it doesn't taste like butter or sprinkle sparkles onto your face, that's just stupid. She has tried to tell this to the other kids, but only makes that mistake once. Margot stares out the window, brimming. Her parents had been letting her paint gold x's on the wall to count down the days. They laughed about it. Just paint. Margot is looking forward to being warm. She is looking forward to opening her mouth and letting the sun fill her stomach (which is one idea she doesn't find stupid, no; she believes it will happen).

The teacher leaves the room for a moment. No one has been able to concentrate on lessons today, after all. Someone prods Margo in the back and she turns, still smiling. A ring of kids closing in on her, shivering in the tank tops and shorts and sandals that they put on that morning in preparation. They look like skinny old stray cats. It occurs to Margot that there is nothing she can say. She's amazed by their cruelty, but not surprised. Hasn't she done so much to earn it?

When I am thirty, I will lose my boyfriend. He will have asked me many times, over the course of many weeks: "Is there anything I can do to make you happy?" He'll even get down on his knees, a move that will strike me not only as melodramatic but also aggressive and mean, yes, mean, because the way he does it, it's not the action of a supplicant, it's the action of a bully who wants to force my hand by slumping to the ground so aggressively like this, far before the situation warrants it. I will be harsh in my gloom and he harsh in his cheer. He'll say again,

"Is there anything I can do to make you happy?"

I will think that the answer is yes—although I don't know what the thing would be—and he will think that the answer is no.

When Margot is nine, the sun comes out on Venus, and the teacher runs into the classroom. She looks from child to child and knows that she has gotten there just in time. Though still troubled by her encounter with the strange woman, she puts her arm around Margot and another child and says brightly, "Let's go! We don't want to miss a single second." They go out into the day.

Afterward, in the post-sun future, life is a little easier. Now all of the kids have seen the sun; it's not something that Margot owns and they don't, and so Margot is allowed to develop into less of a loser. After all, you only need a little bit of space to not be a loser, a few hours in the day of not being teased. I'm telling you, you'd be surprised. You'd be shocked at what miracles can happen.

When I am thirty, most of my old classmates will have added me to every conceivable social network. They won't remember anything from when we were nine, and I'll be relieved. I'll think that's sweet. I will be asked to look, listen, gubble, like, pfuff, [untranslatable gesture], post, re-post, and blat for their sakes, and sometimes I will.

After all, I will have the time, plenty of time for everyone, after my mother moves out. At that point, we'd lived together for ages. Early on, she would sometimes come into my room at night, desolate and weepy, telling me how she needed to kill herself and asking for my reassurance that I would be fine without her. I was nine, ten, seventeen, twenty-three, and always I'd say to myself, What is required here? Reassurance given, so she'd at least calm down, or reassurance withheld, so she would decide to not kill herself?

Other times my mother could cook; she could be funny while we watched televised vote-in talent shows, and able to imitate just about anybody in her good/bad/perfectly not-too-cruel way; she could offer to take me shopping with my money because I had forgotten to cultivate a sense of style because I was working, but only with my money, so that we could stretch the money that was left after my father disappeared, and after I attended school and got full scholarships that indentured me to a corporation for five years post-graduation.

At first, it was hard for her to turn down invitations and skip social events. I'd come home angry, slamming doors and dropping my bag like I was thirteen, even when I was seventeen, twenty-three, twenty-seven. Then I'd see her on the couch looking like the dropped bag and I'd go make her a drink. I would have one too. Each of us just one, or two. And then I would proceed with my life's work of putting her in a good mood, and, failing that, dragging her up from wailing despair, silent despair, mumbling despair. "Daughter, you are all I have," she would say in her deep, beautiful voice—part Nigerian and English and Martian and not at all Venusian. Part of me liked hearing that, both the sentiment and the grand sound of it, like we were in some BBC miniseries, and part of me hated the non-specificity of *daughter*, as if I could be anyone and not me in particular, plus the implication that I, the *daughter*, was the leftover quantity, and not one anyone would keep by choice. And she hadn't. My poor mother.

Soon no one invited me to things and I was too busy anyway; soon I was in the groove of our shared routine and remembered nothing else. And in the groove I grew up twisty, quiet and distracted and money-grubbing and unibrowed. No matter: I did good for us. I took care of my mother, I got better and better jobs once I was released from my contract, and, when I was twenty-nine, I bought us a condo on Mars. It was nothing like the wonderful places my mother had lived in when she was younger, but it was reminiscent of them, with its higher-than-absolutely-necessary ceilings and the modern fixtures that hid their functionalities behind unhelpfully smooth surfaces.

Whether we turn to the declarations of the past, or to the professions of the present, the conduct of the nation seems equally hideous and revolting. America is false to the past, false to the present, and solemnly binds herself to be false to the future. Standing with God and the crushed and bleeding slave on this occasion, I will, in the name of humanity, which is outraged, in the name of liberty, which is fettered, in the name of the Constitution and the Bible, which are disregarded and trampled upon, dare to call in question and to denounce, with all the emphasis I can command, everything that serves to perpetuate slavery—the great sin and shame of America! "I will not equivocate—I will not excuse." I will use the severest language I can command, and yet not one word shall escape me that any man, whose judgment is not blinded by prejudice, or who is not at heart a slaveholder, shall not confess to be right and just.

—*Frederick Douglass, from "The Hypocrisy of American Slavery," 1852*

Any negative polls are fake news, just like the CNN, ABC, NBC polls in the election. Sorry, people want border security and extreme vetting.

—*@realDonaldTrump, February 6, 2017*

It was moving into this condo, I believe, that spurred my mother to start working out and getting into therapy and, finally, to move out; but who knows, it's not like I saw her look upward at the ceilings and down at herself, down at the gorgeous young orange people and back up at herself. My mother moved out. Five months after that she wouldn't even take any of my money. At first she called often and I would be there for her or I would go over there to fall asleep on her couch. Then I was the one calling her, every missed call a slasher film in which the very worst had happened, inflicted by someone else or herself.

I will call my mother again. She won't pick up. One more time. Then I will go out to smoke on the balcony. It will be the best thing about living here alone.

When Margot is almost ten, she and her mom move to a tiny apartment on Mars. Margot loses her favorite sneakers in the move. She throws a quiet tantrum, drums her feet on the floor. Ordinarily, Margot's mom would enjoy seeing such liveliness in her, would encourage it by laughing and grabbing Margot's hands and dancing until Margot could no longer resist. But Margot's mom is in bed, covers over her face, still wearing her shoes and her Martian jackal-collar coat.

For them it had been a long rocket trip, and

before that, a long and extremely bad month. A month ago, a young woman in a boxy neoprene business suit had visited their house. On their doorstep she squeezed rain out of her hair and asked if she could have a moment of Margot's mother's time. She said her name was Hilda. She was immaculately composed, her makeup like a bulletproof vest.

Hilda had told them that their father put the whole Venus Project in jeopardy. But this meant nothing to Margot's mom; she couldn't care less about the Venus Project. Her husband had disappeared, and that's what mattered to her. Margot's dad had disappeared, and her mom absolutely did not give a shit about the Venus Project.

It wouldn't be that hard to kill yourself on Venus. Margot has thought about it. You just walk out of your door and keep walking, don't change a thing. Sure, you could do that on any planet, but on Venus death would be fast, and it would be predictable: drowning or sea monster.

Her mom questioned all their friends, searched his files, demanded that the authorities scour the oceans, and then paid contractors to continue searching—until she ran out of money. Because that was the thing, there wasn't much money left. When it came to money, Margot's dad had lied in every way possible, about the getting of it and most certainly about the spending of it.

Margot and her mother left Venus after that.

When I am thirty, my mother will viddy me, looking great. She'll have just gotten the hand rejuvenation surgery that she'd been saving up for. "Check it out," she'll say, waving springy teenage hands that look like they could repel water. She'll tell me that things have been great since she moved out. She likes her job at the archive. She likes that her younger coworkers will tell her all the work gossip because they think she's old and harmless but still fun enough to confide in. Sometimes she's the subject of the work gossip, like the time she went out on four dates with a researcher who had frequented the archive more and more since she started working there, haunting the checkout desk with increasingly unnecessary requests. My mother has even gotten back into painting, where she was on a hotter track decades ago, when she was younger than I will be now. She'd studied at Martian Yale and won a big prize and everything.

I'll remind her that I haven't heard from her in a long time.

My mother, who usually apologizes so sweetly, whose apologies are heartfelt and devastating but ultimately goldfish apologies, the kind that are forgotten six seconds later, this time will not even say sorry. "There's been so much going on," she'll say. "The most wonderful thing has happened. Your father is alive." She'll tell me that she rehired a private investigator on Venus, who has found a man who looks like my father working on a research submersible. There is a photo. Seeing it, I won't be able to tell whether it's him, one way or another. I will have so many things to say that they will get stuck, like too many people trying to crowd through a narrow door. My mom will just look at my face, which she can tell I've changed, I can tell.

"I'm going to Venus to find him," she'll say. "I've given notice at the archive."

"You can't," I say. "You just moved out." My new face will not move around as much as my old face, for which I will be grateful.

"Please, darling. I'm going. We're not going to be able to talk again for a while, so let's make this nice."

In my opinion, all my mother has to do is get better and stronger and never call me. Even if she acts like a high school best friend who thinks you're a dork but puts up with you because she loves being worshipped and always hangs up first, that is still all I want and all that is required of her, and the words crowd together and all that will come out is another strangled:

"You can't."

My mother will shake her head. She will laugh, looking everywhere but at the screen, at me. "You think that I like everything, that I'm having such a fabulous time and this is the best that can be expected," she'll say. Then she'll look at me. "All of it's nothing."

When Margot is nine, the sun comes out on Venus and a woman bursts into the classroom and starts punching the kids. She is not very good at it and the children quickly overpower her. To Margot, this is the height of unfairness: that an adult would bend from her looming height to attack children, so Margot shouts and fights back, too. The others look at her with a new respect. The woman coughs, dabs her bloody nose with the back of her hand, and disappears. By the end of that day the children will have witnessed two miraculous events, and they will never forget either one. Over beers, they will meet at least once a year when they're in their twenties, once every two years in their early thirties, and so on, the connection degrading but never really disappearing.

When I am thirty, I will give up trying to be pretty. I will give up on trying to have fun. I will decide, instead, that what I need to do is erase myself and then proceed on a new, normal path. Late one night—so late that no one is hanging around, playing Jenga, drinking from beakers, what fun—I will open the door to the lab. Time machines are so beautiful in the moonlight. They look like what they are, like pearls, like eggs you can crawl into and sleep inside until it's time to be born.

I will initiate a program that I cooked up myself. It will take many attempts, but I have so much time after giving up on having a smiling boyfriend, even skin, rosy lips, a mother who calls, friendly eye contact with just about anyone. Those things, I will come to realize, are cosmetic. What I need to fix is far, far back, before I got twisted and grew wrong, my little gnarled life, the lives of everyone around me warped around it.

Eventually I will do it: I will find my own timeline. After three days without sleep and only one change of underwear and a tender pink groove worn into my left middle finger by my pen, I will type a new code into the time machine. I will fold myself inside, close my eyes gratefully, and when the egg shudders me into a new universe I will already know something is different. Something is right.

When Margot is nine, the sun comes out on Venus and her classmates let her out of the closet only after they've come back from playing outside. She tries to make her face ready for them, to steel herself, but when they open the door, it all comes undone.

When I am thirty, when Margot is nine, I open the door and she opens the door.

I open the door and I remember opening the door. I will be nine, thirty staring right at nine. It is almost more than any human being can endure. I am nine and I am seeing the woman in front of me who I know to be myself and it is changing my life: I grow fuller and happier and even stranger as I stare at my nine-year-old self. I remember that, when I was nine, a woman appeared out of nowhere to stop the children from shutting me in the closet on the day that the sun came out. Because at the moment I am telling the children to go, because the sun will be coming up soon, and I take myself by the hand and I lead myself out of the classroom, through the tunnel, and it is exactly as I remember: I look up at the woman leading me by the hand and her eyes are closed. My eyes are closed. I feel wonderful, and I just want to rest for a moment; I'm dizzy; I'm skating around a shrinking loop and things are moving very quickly now.

I search for what I know, and one thing I know is this: my father is still lost or dead somewhere on Venus. My mother still searches for him. I know I can help them, maybe with the right word to one of them, or myself, at the right time. The right action taken. This life is a good one, but all is not well. Now that I'm here, there is so much left to do.

I can see it all, my whole life, a complex tower of blocks—I can reach out and grab any block I choose; I can make the tower wobble. I can feel my mind growing stranger by the minute.

SLEEPY

by CHRIS ABANI

after "Sleepy" by Anton Chekhov

I died when I was ten. I struggled through cerebral malaria, the child killer. My mother told me this story so I would never forget that I had overcome death; regardless of what followed in my life, I would have that knowledge. She lay my body out and washed me lovingly, humming a hymn. She was crying. She told me all this; how else would I know it? But I somehow have some memories of my own from the event. Flashes that her soothing story smooths into an even narrative. It is my visceral memories that brought the story alive for me, made me remember the wetness of her tears on my face. Not the water she washed me with, just her tears. She dressed me in my white first communion dress; white socks; white shoes with white butterfly ties in my nappy hair. She laid me out on a mattress in the living room and lit a ring of white candles around me. Stop, my father tried to tell her. Stop and let the undertakers do their job. But my mother ignored the two men standing in the solemn black suits by the front door, haunting the scene like angels of death. This is what she told me, but it feels like I could hear it all, see it all, feel it all—the soft pull of the washcloth, the prickling evaporation of water liked by breeze, the rub of talcum, the gentle ease of lotion. Even now I am both the flicker of candlelight and the uneven breeze outside.

"Kemi, Kemi."

My eyes flutter open. It's young Jessica, one of the kids for whom I nanny. Go away, I want to say. I'm so tired, so tired. Why am I raising someone else's kids when I'm only sixteen, still a kid myself? Between six-year-old Jessica and Joe, the baby, I get no sleep.

"What is it Jessica?"

"I want to go home now."

I smile at her pouting, entitled white face. I look around the park. It is full of people at lunch in this sunny, spring, New York afternoon. Baby Joseph is still asleep in his stroller. Everyday in the park, I dose his milk with Benadryl. Then I try to sleep. I look at my watch. I can eek out another fifteen minutes I think.

"Go show me what you learned on the monkey bars," I say.

She pouts.

"No, I want to go home."

"Your mom is sleeping," I lie. "Show me how good a monkey you are."

"You're the monkey," she says and stamps her feet.

"Jessica!"

She walks back to the bars. I close my eyes. Sleep, sweet sleep.

"Kemi!"

My eyes snap open.

"You're not even looking," she accuses.

"I'm looking."

Jessica starts to swing across the bars as I begin to doze.

"Kemi!"

This is a scream of pain. I wake with a start. Jessica is on the floor under the bars, her knee scraped.

"Shit," I mutter. This will be bad if her mother notices. She'll never let that go and her husband will hit me for sure. As he says, blood for blood.

I try to soothe her. I pick her up and she folds into me, burying her head into the crook of my neck. She is difficult and rude to me and I forget that she is still only a child; a baby really.

"I fell and you didn't catch me," she sobs.

It's time to go home.

"Come on Jessica," I say, getting off my bench. As I bend to clip Jessica's walk leash on her, she touches my face.

I pull away and straighten up. "Let's go home and get you some lunch."

As I leave the park, I look back at my bench as if expecting to see myself still sitting there, but a different self, one who is still hopeful and not so tired.

The family I work for lives in a big house in a leafy suburb. The house is big enough to remind a person how lonely wealth and success are in America. In Nigeria, this house would be full. Of relatives, hangers on, and an ever expanding extended family, full of commotion, of conflict, of love, laughter, anger and the business of living. In Nigeria, success makes you less lonely.

This couple is odd. The husband works all hours for a hedge fund and I sometimes only see him when he is arriving late or leaving early. He treats me like furniture, to be ignored or used in a utilitarian way. He speaks to me in clipped directives. Fetch. Give. Put. Don't. And he always gets my name wrong—Camdy, Kamy, Carly, Karma. Then it's—stupid. Listen. Fool. Ass.

The wife uses me as a shield from her husband, her children, her confusion about herself, and, at every opportunity, she never fails to humiliate me. She doesn't work but is busy on multiple fundraising committees dedicated to solving the world's problems and always says, We have to help those less fortunate than us, don't we, Kemi? As they say in Nigeria, let me not tell you about yourself and I don't.

She pops her head out of her home office and yells at me.

"Kemi, can I have a sandwich when you're done feeding Jessica?"

"Yes, ma'am," I say.

"Oh and Kemi, did you do the laundry yet?"

"Yes, ma'am."

"Good, good."

As I feed Baby Joe, I realize Jessica has gone to see her mother and I count out the beats in spoonfuls of baby food shoveled into Joseph's mouth. There it is, three spoons in.

"Kemi, take Jessica. I have to work!"

"Jessica," I call. "Let your mother work. She's busy saving the world's children."

"Kemi!"

I put down the jar of baby food and walk to her office.

"Come on, Jessica," I say, pulling the reluctant Jessica behind me. As we leave, Mrs. Jones asks: "Aren't you forgetting something?"

"Ma'am?"

"My sandwich. And remember this time to cut the crust off the bread."

"Yes, ma'am."

"And Kemi—"

"Yes, ma'am?"

"Don't ever sass me again or Mr. Jones will hear about it."

I nod and lower my head like a dog. Like the dog they have made me.

In the kitchen, Joe has started crying. I sigh. When he gets like that he doesn't stop. He can go on for days, testing even the most patient person. I try to calm him as I settle Jessica down at the kitchen table with a piece of paper and colored pencils.

"But I want to work with mommy," she whines.

"Jessica," I snap and the steel in my voice silences her.

Half an hour later, Joe is still crying and Jessica is yelling.

"Shut up, Joe! I hate you, Joe!"

I ignore her and keep trying to soothe the baby. I hope he tires out and falls asleep soon. I have dinner to prepare. Mr. Jones doesn't like it when his food isn't ready on time. Last time he slapped me across the face, a cruel satisfied smile curling his lips as he watched blood bead the side of mine.

"Kemi, shut that child up!" Mrs. Jones yells from her office.

"Mommy yelled at you," Jessica says, smiling.

I ignore them both and keep rocking Joe. I want to give him more Benadryl but I'm afraid I'll kill him with an overdose. But if I don't get rest soon—God help me.

Mrs. Jones comes into the kitchen. She is dressed in her coat. She looks really angry.

"Really, Kemi, why can't you do your job and keep these kids quiet! I have to go out now to get any work done. Be sure to go to the store and pick up fresh produce for dinner. And while you're out, get the dry cleaning too."

I hear the front door slam and she is gone. Two infants and a list of chores. I sigh. I'm so tired. A nap would be a great gift. I return to hushing the baby but he won't stop and I am almost in tears. My life wasn't always like this. Is this what I came back from the dead for?

Even through death I swear I could sense mother's purpose, her resolute dedication to this task of seeing me across. The weight of the cold pennies closing my eyes was the weight of her guilt and sorrow. I must have felt it, why else would I have come back? But it was not until she gently worked the cotton wool up my nostril that I stirred, my nostrils twitching like a bunny. Then I exploded into a sneeze that sent the copper pennies ringing across the floor and everyone, even my mother, running for the bright sunlight outside. Later, with a trembling voice, my mother reassured me, reassured herself: "You're like a character from a fairy tale. I know who you are, you're Peter Pan and you have an everlasting life. Just like Peter Pan.

"You're like a character from a fairy tale. I know who you are, you're Peter Pan and you have an everlasting life. Just like Peter Pan."

There were so many things I could have said, but I knew she needed this to be a fairy tale, a children's story, a harmless miracle.

"Just like Peter Pan," I whispered and touched her face.

From then on, nothing was the same. Death will do that. Once its wings have grazed your life, it is only a matter of time before its shadow swallows you up. And so, two years after I died and came back from the dead, my parents were both killed in a car accident. My grandmother spat at my feet that day, said, Life gives nothing it doesn't take back in double value. She believed my resurrection was the curse that took them, and so I was sent to live with an aunt and uncle in Lagos. That city of noise and surrender, a city made almost entirely of sound and the endless haggle of people and landscape. But it grew quieter in my new home on Victoria Island where the sea on one hand and the expensive and extensive landscaping on the other muted the sounds. To live a middle class life in that city was a strange contradiction. Daily, on the way to school, or market, or church, the city and its relentless cacophony and desire filled me. But in the shady hush of Victoria Island, I lay in the backyard under trees and let the sun pattern my face through the leaves. My aunt watched, always, with a relentless fear and who can blame her? Who would not fear the undead, and so I was sent to America to live with her sister. Why not? My aunt was still to have children and who wants a ghost hanging around their children? To be sixteen and to have died and come back is truly a curse, especially when it costs you your parents. I would send me away too if I were her.

And so I came to America and a life of poverty and depression. My American aunt is poor and can barely make the rent on her dirty studio apartment. Between school, where she is studying to be a nurse, and her job as a nurse's assistant at an old peoples home, she is barely eking out a living. I found out about my job from her friend who was the nanny before me, but who just got married to a Nigerian doctor and was moving on to better things. And now I am living with a family too rich and too busy to be human. With slight variations, even with my parent's dead, this rich life was my life in Nigeria. Yet now *I* am the domestic. And I am exhausted. I was not cut out for this kind of life. And this baby that won't stop crying. I dream of setting him free and watching him fly out of a window into the night, like Peter Pan.

Kemi. Kemi.

Someone is calling my name in my mother's voice and I cannot tell if I am awake or dreaming. Everything is becoming a blur.

Jessica is tugging on my arm. She is yelling my name. I snap back to the present and I realize why. I am holding Joseph over the edge of the stairs. Rocking, still rocking him, but the danger is clear.

"You'll hurt him," she says.

"Sorry," I mumble.

Proud Supporter of McSweeney's

"It's okay. I won't tell mommy if you read me a story."

I look at her and I want to punch her. Not that fucking story again. Over and over until I want to cry. But I am startled and so I say, "Yes, I will."

I don't know how I got up here from the kitchen. Slowly I make my way down the stairs, the ever-present Jessica, like a faithful puppy, trails me. She is at that age: questions. Endless questions. What makes the moon shine so bright? Where does the tooth fairy come from? Why do clouds look fluffy and are they God's cotton balls? Where do babies come from? Where do we go when we die? What does it mean to die? Why does Mommy think Daddy has a hoe? Is Daddy gardening? And why and why and why? It took all of my willpower not to yell at her.

"Go get your coat on. We have to go to the store," I say.

"I don't think Mommy meant for me to go to the store with you. That's your job. I'm not a servant."

I stop in my tracks. I want to smack her but instead I try reasoning.

"I can't leave you alone while I go to the store."

"I'm grown, I can look after myself."

"You're right. You can take care of the bogeyman who lives under your bed all by yourself," I say and turn to walk away.

I feel, rather than see, her hesitate. I've barely got Joe in the stroller before she turns up, wearing her coat.

"You're still my servant," she says.

I say nothing, trying to soothe Joe who is still crying at the top of his lungs.

"Can't you shut him up," Jessica says.

"Let's go," I say and head out the front door. I don't bother to secure her with the child leash.

"Teething?"

I look up from the organic kale I'm sorting. The woman is hovering over Joe. She is about sixty, white, gray hair in a bun like a storybook grandmother.

"I don't think so," I say.

"Yours?"

"That's my brother," Jessica says. "Kemi is just our servant."

"Little girl…"

"My name is Jessica."

"Well, Jessica, you are very rude," the old lady says.

"And you're old. Mommy says old people should die and not be a burden." I ignore the exchange and select the kale I need and move on to the carrots.

Later, outside the store, I try to give Joseph his binky to shut him up, but he doesn't. I haven't slept properly in a month now and I'm faint. The pavement is buckling. I lean against the wall and steady myself. Jessica is playing dangerously close to the edge of the road. I want to call out, but a part of me also doesn't want to call out. A young hipster leads her back to me.

"She with you?" he asks.

I nod. He gives me a look and moves on. It's time for the cleaners.

When I get home, the husband is there. He is sipping on a beer and rummaging for snacks. He turns on me.

"Where have you been?"

"Store and dry cleaners, sir," I say. He likes it when I call him sir. Tames his cruel streak.

"What's wrong with Joe?"

"I don't know, sir. Once he starts crying he won't shut up. For days at a time."

"Well it's your job to figure out a way to shut him up. Jesus, I can't think."

He slams out into the living room and Jessica follows.

"Daddy, is Kemi our slave?"

"We don't call them that anymore," he says.

I tune them out and begin to prep dinner, trying not to lose my mind as Joe cries. I pause while I'm chopping onions and look at him, and I feel something creep over me so strong I have to put down the knife and turn away from him.

Dinner is almost ready when Mrs. Jones comes in.

"Kemi, why can't you get Joseph to shut up?" she says from the door.

"I'm trying, ma'am."

"Honey," Mr. Jones calls from the living room. "Can you get me another beer?"

"I just walked in, honey. Besides, why can't Kemi fetch it. Kemi fetch a beer for Mr. Jones, and a shot of Bourbon straight for me."

She joins her family in the living room. I take the drinks in to them. Jessica is sitting on her daddy's knee and Mrs. Jones is sitting across from him.

"Do you really have to go out again tonight?" she asks her husband.

"Don't start, Debbie," he says. "Not in front of the help."

I stop at the door.

"Would you like me to bring Joseph in?" I ask.

"Lay the table and set the dinner up then take him upstairs to your room with you."

I nod and leave the room.

It is quiet up in my room. It's a converted attic at the very top of the house. Noise doesn't carry up here, or from here down to the rest of the house. I used to like it up here when I first arrived. It was peaceful then. An escape. But as the days passed it became a prison, a cell at the top of a tower, one I could never escape from.

And then Mrs. Jones had a crib moved in so

Joseph could sleep up here with me. And that was when the crying started, and it hasn't really stopped. Months. I slept so little the first week that I lost all depth perception and broke a lot of china. But the symptoms have stopped and now all I have are the tears and the endless tiredness.

Two weeks after the baby moved in I began to fantasize about my own death. Wondering what it would have felt like to die with my parents in that crushed metal fireball. I remembered my grandmother's words about life never giving what it didn't take back doubled.

It feels like I am sleeping but I am not. I am just so tired that most sensation has stopped except for the pounding in my head. Joe's endless shrill. I pace with him. I rock him. I sing to him. I coo to him. I read to him. I beg him. I pray for silence, whispering words into his ear like an incantation or a spell. But none of it works. He just won't sleep.

I wander the planes of my mind as I sit in the rocking chair Mrs. Jones placed thoughtfully in the corner. I return to my childhood, to playing with the village kids, chasing the cattle egrets by the river, romping through the grass, my feet sinking into unseen cow dung. And always the scrubbing and telling off I would get when I got home. Mother would have the servants boil the water to scalding temperatures, then she would stand me in the bathtub and scrub me with a rough loofah until it felt like my skin would bleed, all the while warning me about the village kids who were dirty and beneath me.

"You're too good to play with them," she would say. "Your father is an important man. You must always comport yourself with that in mind."

I hated those baths and yet now I long for them with the innocence of a child, with a need too great for words. Then I'm crying. Not just silent tears like before, but body shaking animal sounds of pain. It is so sudden it shocks Joe into silence for a moment. But then, as soon as I fall into soft whimpers, he begins to scream again and this time he is squirming.

I stand up and pace. I try to croon through my tears. Nothing works. And then I hear my name being called in my mother's voice again.

By the window. Kemi. By the window.

The voice is saying over and over. I cross to the window and open it.

"Mama," I call.

Silence.

I look out into the night and then I look down at Joseph.

"Do you want to fly, Joseph? Like Peter Pan? Do you want to be free? A cattle egret breaking for the sky?"

Joseph just screams. When I close the window he has flown away and I am crumpling to the floor into a blessed darkness. Into sleep.

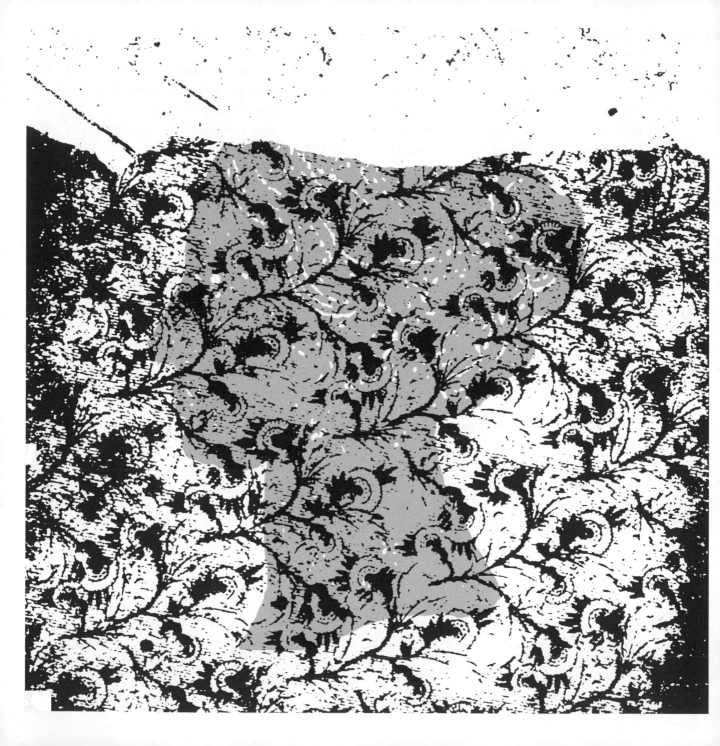

THE YELLOW WALLPAPER

by TOM DRURY

after "The Yellow Wallpaper" by Charlotte Perkins Gilman

n the ferry to the island, Jane stood watching a pod of seals sunning themselves on black rocks in the water. She counted them. Nine seals. Something in the light on their backs reminded her of a Labrador retriever she'd had as a child, and she lifted her hands to her face at the memory.

She and her husband, John, were renting a place on the island for the summer while carpenters worked on their house on the mainland. John was a doctor and very popular at the hospital where he worked. They had even given him a Vespa for his birthday. He thought that Jane had a case of mild depression and the island would be the place for her to rest and recover and breathe the air.

The ferry docked and they stood waiting by their car. "You have to be strong to exercise, and hungry to eat," he said. "But you don't have to be anything to breathe. You breathe automatically."

SUSPENSE*

by STEPHEN BURT

A way of holding things up, as the Zakim Bridge
holds up the cables that hold up
the nearly horizontal wedge and grids
that hold the boxed-in traffic in its variable
progress north to Somerville.

It holds us taut. It stretches out our days.
Without its gates and levels, we would slip
too rapidly off and onward, towards the end
which is the only end
no storyteller knows, or disobeys.

---

* after "Proem: To Brooklyn Bridge" by Hart Crane

"I know how breathing works," said Jane. Though when she thought about it, she didn't, not really.

She believed that John loved her and wanted to look out for her, but sometimes she had to admit that he got on her nerves. She would raise a shoulder at his advice and feel like a bad person for doing so. John said that such feelings were natural for someone with her condition. They had been married four years and had a baby son.

From the ferry slip, they drove to the house where they would be staying. It reminded Jane of a place you would see in a movie about an English family who'd had money at one time but no longer did. When you looked closely, everything seemed a little run-down. The house was moss-colored with dark green woodwork and stood above the road on some number of acres with gardens and greenhouses and a dock on the bay.

The rent was lower than they had expected because no one had lived in the house for a while, and Jane wondered if something had happened there to keep people away, but the real estate lady said no, the place was only tied up in a fight over inheritance.

"We see this often," she said, the impartiality of her voice suggesting that family disappointments were a secret known only to realtors.

John and Jane disagreed about where their

bedroom would be. She wanted to sleep in the little room downstairs with the garden out front and the roses growing around the windows. He said there would not be enough circulation or light there.

The room that he liked was upstairs. It took up most of the second floor and there were seven windows and all the sunlight and air that anyone could possibly stand. The room was empty except for an old sleigh bed that seemed to be nailed to the floor.

"All we have to do is bring furniture from downstairs," said John. "In fact, I will get started on that right away."

"I don't know if I can write here."

"Okay. We've talked about this."

She was the author of a series of young adult novels about teenage changelings who were cast out by society and devoted to each other and the adventures that came their way, but John had asked her to take the summer off. He did not want her touching pen to paper. And he had reason. She had become very low finishing the latest changeling book.

"I found you on the floor," he said.

"What's wrong with the floor? We would fall on the ground without it."

"You don't have to read, you don't have to write. The only thing you have to worry about is yourself."

"And you think that will help."

"I know it will."

She would read and write anyway that summer, just in secret, when no one could see her. She was reading an epic of Iceland called *The Elder Edda*, which kept asking a question that she liked: *Do you know yet, or what?*

John furnished the room with bedside tables, armchairs, a dresser, a mirrored vanity, and an assortment of lamps he found around the house, and there they made their bedroom.

There were good points and bad points to the room, in Jane's opinion. Standing before the windows, she felt she had stepped into a painting. There were meadows of gold and green, a winding road rising, a garden with ragged hedges, and an arbor covered with vines. The greenhouses ran parallel to the east, magnificent and sad with broken windows. She liked the greenhouses in disrepair because they made the place seem haunted, and she thought it should be haunted.

One night when the moon was in the window, Jane and John were sitting up in bed playing Crazy Eights and she said that she'd felt a hand touch her arm.

"You're sure of that?" said John. "Maybe it was the wind. I feel the wind. But I don't feel any hands."

She laid her cards on the bedspread and placed

her right hand on her left arm, over and over. "No," she said. "It was a hand."

He got out of bed and closed the windows.

Jane thought that children must have lived in the room at one time. There were grates in the windows and iron rings in the walls and an accordion gate at the head of the stairs. Scarred and faded, the wallpaper was a sad shade of yellow, like stained sheets left out in the rain and sun to recover as they might.

The wallpaper had a floral pattern that seemed to have been designed by someone suffering from aesthetic dementia. Jagged leaves, buds, and vines careened across the walls stabbing each other like fighters in an alley. And just when Jane thought she knew where they were going, they went somewhere else. It was no wonder that the children would have scratched at the wallpaper with their little fingernails. If she lived in the house all the time she might do the same.

John went to work on the mainland all day, returning on the night ferry or sometimes staying in the city to look after his patients. She knew that some of his patients had terrible troubles that made hers seem minor. He reminded her if she forgot. But what she had didn't have to be the worst thing in order to be something.

She felt tired most of the time. Her breath would run quick and shallow for no reason, as if she was afraid of something she didn't understand. She cried easily and her eyes were often red. She had even cried on seeing the seals on the rocks and remembering the old dog who had been her childhood companion.

The simplest things, she found difficult. When she called the grocery store in the village, someone would say hello and she would get scared and hang up. Probably they knew the calls were coming from the house that used to be empty. An empty phone call from an empty house.

Many times, she could not think of a reason in the world to get out of bed.

After three weeks on the island, John had made a schedule for every part of Jane's day, and what she could and couldn't do. He did this for his patients. They appreciated it, and so should she.

She could:

Sleep or rest.

Ride her bicycle around the property.

Walk around the property.

Not ride the Vespa around the property.

Sit on the dock of the bay.

Not swim, as the currents might carry her out to sea.

Eat as much as she liked, even more than she liked, rare meat and fresh greens being best.

Drink two glasses of red wine a day.

Listen to country music or the soft sounds of Island 106.1.

Beyond these accepted activities, she had not much else to do. She would have liked to go to a movie, but *Carnival of Souls* was playing, so that was out. John's sister, Jenny, was staying in the house—in the room that Jane had wanted, as it happened—and she did all the cooking and cleaning. This seemed to make Jenny happy beyond compare. Jane would hear her downstairs, scrubbing, mopping, singing.

A girl named Mary, who lived on the island, took care of the baby. The baby was such a darling. He didn't know anything, or need to. He was only beginning to understand who everyone was and that things that went away would come back. Every afternoon, Jane and Mary, carrying the baby, would walk in the garden and sit for a while in the shade of the arbor. The baby ran soft syllables together in an excited voice, as if leading a tour. Jane asked Mary about the people who'd lived in the house, but Mary didn't know. Sailing and storms that might keep her from sailing seemed to be her only interests.

One night, Jane told John that she wanted her cousin and his wife to visit from Gloucester. Henry built wooden boats and Julia designed lighting for theaters, and they were the funniest and most loving couple. They would get a kick out of the house. They would make it seem harmless. That's just what they were like.

"You used to see them a lot," said John. He was reading a newspaper he'd brought back from the mainland. "Clubs and bars and falling down and staying out all night. Which got you where?"

"Tell me," she said.

He turned the page in a patient way that made her want to take the newspaper from his hands and tear it into tiny pieces.

"I think you know."

After finishing her latest book, she had spent ten days in the hospital. There she painted pictures and did yoga, ate lasagna and hash browns and rice pudding. One thin pillow made for the very best sleep. She still slept exactly as she had on the ward, always on her right side, returning to blessed blankness. Her roommate in the hospital had played the violin in the common room. "I'm making the best music of my life," she would say.

Jane left John reading the newspaper, and went upstairs to their room. The children of her imagination really had done a number on the place. The floors were pitted as with an ice pick and the sleigh bed seemed to have been used for archery practice. But this was their home for now and she felt good just knowing she was about to lie down. She had been sleeping a lot since they moved in. She got into bed, and pulled *The Elder Edda* out from under the mattress. The Norse god Odin knew a spell for men's sons who wanted to be doctors.

One morning, John stood before a mirror, sawing a tie through his collar trying to get the ends right. Jane lay on her side with her hands pressed together beneath her cheekbone. This was a traditional position of rest, yet it was surprisingly uncomfortable.

"This wallpaper is a living nightmare," she said.

"Give it up, Jane."

"You said we could take it down."

"And we could. We could do that. But it would cost a lot. I talked to some island guys. And besides, first it's the wallpaper, then the grates, then the chairs and tables, then I don't know what. Your problem is not with the things in this room."

"I need your help."

He came to the bed and knelt beside it. "Let's pretend that we're like other people," he said. "If you don't like the wallpaper, don't look at the wallpaper. I don't. Jenny doesn't. Walk away from it."

Jane listened to what he said. It was only wallpaper, made by someone somewhere, long ago, someone dead now, in all likelihood. There was not that much reason to worry about it. She reached out and messed up his hair. "Now you look like you," she said.

He got up and brushed his hair and put on his jacket. "Oh, and I meant to tell you. Seems like I might have to stay in town tonight."

When he had gone, she turned on the radio. A band named Cake was playing a song that asked the musical question, "Ruby, are you contemplating going out somewhere?"

They had visitors for the Fourth of July— not the dangerously entertaining Henry and Julia, but Jane's mother and sister. They pretended that Jane was all right, they pretended not to notice everything wrong with the house. They sat with John and Jane and Jenny and Mary and the baby on the veranda, watching fireworks over the bay, orange embers drifting down and going out.

All that weekend, Jane didn't have to do one thing but eat and drink and sit down and stand up and engage in conversation about things like tennis and horses and streetlights. Still, she was worn out when everyone had gone and she and John were alone at the table in the dining room.

"Maybe I will go on a trip," she said.

"Oh yeah? Where will you go?"

"To see Henry and Julia."

"Well, what if you pass out on the train and wind up in Newfoundland?"

"I don't think that will happen."

"And, say you did get to Henry's, say you did, and then you had one of your spells. We don't want them to think of you that way. We want them to remember you as you were."

"Jesus, John, I'm not dead."

"You didn't let me finish."

But he had finished, she thought. He'd made a mistake and said what he meant. Hot tears formed like pearls in her eyes and ran down her face.

"Do you see what I mean?" he said.

He picked her up and carried her upstairs and laid her down on the bed. He read a true crime novel aloud until she sank back, as if her body would disappear into the mattress.

"If something happened to you, I don't know what I would do," he said.

She woke in the darkest part of night. The wallpaper looked better now, silver not yellow. And as she studied the pattern, her eyes softened and something unusual happened. The figure of a woman appeared in the wall as if coming up from water. The woman stood for a moment, getting her bearings, and began pacing back and forth. Sometimes she would stop and touch the tangled vines of the pattern from the inside. Jane got out of bed, crept to the wall, and put her palms on the wallpaper.

"Who are you?" she whispered.

Instead of answering, the woman faded into the wall and was gone. Probably Jane should have stayed quiet. She waited for the woman to come back, but there was only the wallpaper now and after a while she went to bed.

"Do you want a Trazadone?" said John.

I am certain that my fellow Americans expect that on my induction into the Presidency I will address them with a candor and a decision which the present situation of our people impel. This is preeminently the time to speak the truth, the whole truth, frankly and boldly. Nor need we shrink from honestly facing conditions in our country today. This great Nation will endure as it has endured, will revive and will prosper. So, first of all, let me assert my firm belief that the only thing we have to fear is fear itself—nameless, unreasoning, unjustified terror which paralyzes needed efforts to convert retreat into advance. In every dark hour of our national life a leadership of frankness and vigor has met with that understanding and support of the people themselves which is essential to victory. I am convinced that you will again give that support to leadership in these critical days.

—*Franklin D. Roosevelt, from his inauguration speech, 1933*

Happy New Year to all, including to my many enemies and those who have fought me and lost so badly they just don't know what to do. Love!

—*@realDonaldTrump, January 22, 2017*

"I want to leave."

"Our house isn't ready. You know this. We have no place to go."

"I think I'm losing my mind."

"You might wish that. It's tempting. Sometimes I wish I could lose my mind."

"Maybe you have."

As a girl, she had sensed that things had a life or character beyond their appearance. Her imagination was strong and did not listen to her. Her parents' bed was an airplane; a chair by the bed, a mountain; an orange light on the dresser, the sun. And the unknown relatives in a photograph on the wall were ghosts who would stare straight into her eyes, as if she had done something bad and they knew what.

John had said she would get used to the room, and it turned out he was right about that, as well as everything else. By August she felt happy there. The wallpaper was still gross in daylight, that would never change, but every night she would see the women—there seemed to be more than one—and she'd learned that if she did not bother them, they would stay. They walked around, hands on hips or turning their heads in idle boredom. Sometimes they took hold of the pattern and shook it the way children rattle the wire fences of playgrounds. Jane was glad, now, when John stayed away. Maybe he was sleeping with someone else. Whatever kept him busy, and left her alone with these women.

Sometimes, during the day, one or two of the women would get out—not just out of the wall, but out of the house. Jane didn't know the rules, but this was unexpected. She would see them from the windows, creeping on all fours down the garden paths, through the meadow, along the foundations of the greenhouses. They would hide when someone came along, which was understandable, because it was a rather strange way of getting around.

One hot afternoon, after baby time in the garden, Jane walked up the meadow in a T-shirt and cutoffs. The grass felt good on her bare feet. She closed her eyes and stood in the wind with her face to the sun. She breathed. If only John could see her breathing. And when she opened her eyes, she saw a woman loping through the grass on long arms and legs. Jane froze, not in fear but in wonder. "Do you know yet, or what?" the woman said.

Jane walked to the house without looking back and went upstairs to her room, where she found Jenny with her hand brushing the wallpaper.

"I wouldn't do that if I were you," said Jane.

"Jesus Christ, don't scare me like that."

"Creepy, isn't it?"

"It's just all this yellow dust," said Jenny. "You should do the laundry once in a while, you would see what I mean. And it'd be really really helpful to me if you guys would stop leaning against it."

"We don't lean against it. I have no idea what you're talking about."

"Oh well. I guess at least we won't be here much longer."

"Yeah, too bad."

Jenny looked at Jane, a flash of sympathy in her eyes. "You're getting stronger, aren't you?"

"I could lift you right up off the ground."

"Well, I don't know about that," said Jenny. "I'm not quite as light as I used to be."

Jane put her hands on either side of Jenny's waist and lifted her away from the wallpaper. Jenny gave a little shout and, held aloft, broke into laughter.

"Oh no, Jenny's flying," said Jane.

"Okay, but really."

Jane set her back on her feet. "You don't weigh anything."

"Why thank you," said Jenny. "It's so nice to see you in a good mood."

"I saw an unusual seal today," said John. He and Jenny and Jane had finished supper and were sitting at the table in the late, green light from the garden.

"Unusual how?" said Jane.

"Well, generally, as we know, seals stay close to the rocks," said John. "I've been watching them.

Observing their habits, so to speak. There's not much else to do on the ferry. And I believe they're uncomfortable in open water. But not this one. He was swimming around like he didn't care where he was."

"That was Chomper," said Jane.

"Who?"

"My dog."

"You're so funny," said Jenny.

"No really. I saw him before. He loves to swim."

John moved his wine glass in a lazy circle and took a drink. "I hope I would know the difference between a dog and a seal."

"We all hope that," said Jane. "You're what keeps Jenny and me alive. Don't you think so, Jenny? You are the wind and the rain and the interstate highway system."

The dining room was quiet then. A church bell in the village rang. A shining green fly buzzed across the room and came to rest on Jane's glass. John and Jenny began to laugh. Apparently, Jane had made the cleverest remark of the summer. Or maybe it was the fly. Whatever it was, they couldn't stop laughing. Their faces nodded and bobbed above the table. Jane watched how they laughed and tried to do the same.

Then came bad weather, as predicted by Mary. Three days of fog and hard rain. Everything in the house turned damp and the wallpaper buckled and began to smell. Not the musty and melancholy odor of an old house by the water, but something harsh, like paint thinner maybe. Jane woke up to the smell, and it followed her everywhere. Her head ached to be rid of it. She washed her hair in the shower and in the rain and that helped for a while. She thought about burning the house down, but wouldn't have known how to go about it.

It was the second to last night in the house on the island. They'd begun to pack and the furniture from the bedroom had mostly been moved back downstairs. The only things left were the sleigh bed, a table, and a lamp. John called around seven o'clock and, to no one's surprise, said he would be staying on the mainland. At supper, Jenny offered to sleep in Jane's room and Jane said that was thoughtful but she would be all right on her own. She listened to the radio until ten o'clock and then turned out the light and waited with her arms and hands arranged carefully on the covers.

When moonlight came through the windows, one of the women appeared. And this time she did not fade away when Jane came near. Instead she pointed to a place high on the wall where Jane dug in with her fingernails and ripped a strip of the wallpaper down to the baseboard. The tearing paper made a clean sandy sound like clogs on a beach. She touched the uncovered plaster, which was rough and wiry and crumbled beneath her hand. Now the woman was looking elsewhere on the wall, and Jane pulled away another piece of the wallpaper. Together they worked in this way late into the night.

When Jenny brought breakfast in the morning, she stood holding the tray and staring at what had happened in the room. Jane sat on the floor in her nightgown with her back to the wall, surrounded by plaster dust and long curling scraps of wallpaper.

"What have you done?" Jenny said.

Jane smiled and spread her arms in the air.

"I told you I didn't like it."

Jenny set the tray on the table. "Well me neither," she said, "but John will…"

"Yes he will."

"Come downstairs, Jane. The sun is back. Please. It's a beautiful day and you need to get out of this room."

"I'm feeling a little tired."

"Well, I can imagine. My goodness, what you have done to yourself. Will you at least eat something?"

Jane got up and had a bite of toast.

"They're gone," she said.

"Who is?"

"You know. Them."

When Jenny left, Jane locked the door and threw the key out the window. Most of the wallpaper was on the floor, but there were patches clinging and she scratched at them patiently with red and broken fingernails. When she looked out the windows she saw a woman creeping in every one. They had all come from the wallpaper, and she felt that she had too. The large cold room sparkled with sunlight. When the walls were as bare as they were going to get, Jane began to creep like the women did, around and around the room.

John got home from work at sundown. Jane heard the car door and his city shoes scraping the walk. He talked to Jenny for a moment and then came running up the stairs.

"Let me in," he said.

"I'm sorry, doctor. I can't."

"What are you doing?"

"Breathing."

"Do you want me to break down the door?"

"I think enough damage has been done here."

"I mean it, Jane."

"Go away."

There was a big splintering sound when he forced the door and a smaller banging one when the doorknob hit the wall. She paused and looked at him over her shoulder.

"Get up," he said. "What is wrong with you?"

"You don't even know who I am."

He opened his mouth but for once could not keep talking. The color left his face, his eyelids batted rapidly, and he fell down into the room. She looked at him with interest for a while and began creeping again, slowly at first and then faster. Her rounds were the same as before except now, when she came to the doorway, she had to crawl over John lying in it.

After dark, Jane stood up, left the room, and went down the stairs. Jenny leaned on the kitchen counter talking on the telephone. Seeing Jane, she took the phone and hurried into the pantry and closed the door.

"Goodbye," called Jane. "Thanks for everything."

She left the house and walked slowly down the steps. Hearing music, she followed the sound across the garden and down through the trees to the dock. A radio played on a boat, barely rocking in the water. At the end of the dock, she untied her hair, crossed her hands over her head, and dove into the water. She surfaced and swam toward the jetty. She had almost forgotten what a strong swimmer she was. The water was cold and the air colder still. There were no currents. There was nothing to be afraid of. When she reached the jetty, she climbed up onto the dark rocks. Her chin trembled and she tucked her hands under her arms. Out in the water, the night ferry headed back to the mainland with windows so bright that the passengers inside might have been dancing.

EMILY RABOTEAU is the author of *The Professor's Daughter*, a novel, and *Searching for Zion: The Quest for Home in the African Diaspora*, winner of a 2014 American Book Award. Her short fiction has appeared in *Tin House*, *The Missouri Review*, *The Gettysburg Review*, *StoryQuarterly*, *Callaloo*, *Transition*, *Narrative*, *Best American Short Stories*, *Best American Mystery Stories*, *Best African American Short Stories*, and elsewhere. Honors include a Pushcart Prize, the *Chicago Tribune's* Nelson Algren Award, and literature fellowships from NYFA, the NEA, and the Lannan Foundation. She teaches creative writing at the City College of New York, in Harlem, and is at work completing a novel entitled *Endurance*.

NAMWALI SERPELL is a Zambian writer. Her story "The Sack" won the 2015 Caine Prize for African writing. It first appeared in the *Africa39* anthology, a 2014 Hay festival project to identify the best African writers under 40. She received a Rona Jaffe Foundation Writers' Award in 2011. Her first published story, "Muzungu," was selected for the *Best American Short Stories 2009* and shortlisted for the 2010 Caine Prize. Her first novel, *The Old Drift*, will be published by Hogarth Press in 2018.

T.C. BOYLE's latest novel is *The Terranauts*. His new collection, *The Relive Box and Other Stories*, the first since the publication of the second volume of his collected stories, *T.C.*

Boyle Stories II, in 2013, will be published in October and will include "The Argentine Ant."

KIESE LAYMON is a black southern writer from Jackson, Mississippi. He is author of *Long Division*, *How to Slowly Kill Yourself and Others in America*, and the forthcoming memoir, *Heavy*. He is a Professor of English and Creative Writing at University of Mississippi.

MEGAN MAYHEW BERGMAN is the Associate Director of Bennington's MFA program. She is the author of *Birds of a Lesser Paradise*, *Almost Famous Women*, and a forthcoming novel, *The Exhibition*. Bergman's story is excerpted from *Almost Famous Women*. Copyright © 2015 by Megan Mayhew Bergman. Published by Scribner, an Imprint of Simon & Schuster, Inc. Reprinted with permission.

ROXANE GAY lives and writes in the Midwest.

LAUREN GROFF has written a story collection and three novels. She lives in Gainesville, Florida.

RICK MOODY is the author of six novels, three collections of stories, a memoir, and a collection of essays on music. He writes regularly about music for The Rumpus, and is an occasional Life Coach at LitHub. He has released six albums of songs, most recently including *The Unspeakable Practices* with Kid Millions of Oneida (Joyful Noise Recordings). He's presently at work on a memoir.

MARY MILLER is the author of two story collections, *Always Happy Hour* and *Big World*, and a novel, *The Last Days of California*.

ROBIN TERRELL is a writer living in Prague. She blogs about virtual work at Global Mobile Worker, is a contributor to FastCompany on gender partnership, and is a proud member of the Prague Writers Group.

MATTHEW ZAPRUDER is the author of four collections of poetry, most recently *Sun Bear*. *Why Poetry*, a book of prose, is forthcoming from Ecco Press in summer 2017. He teaches in the the MFA Program at Saint Mary's College of California, and is Editor at Large at Wave Books. He lives in Oakland, CA.

KIMBERLY HARRINGTON is a copywriter and creative director, a contributor to McSweeney's Internet Tendency and Funny or Die, and is the co-founder and editor of parenting humor site RAZED. She's currently working on two books at the same time because she loves feeling frustrated.

BRIAN TURNER is a poet (*Here*, *Bullet* and *Phantom Noise*) and memoirist (*My Life as a Foreign Country*), and his publications and appearances include *National Geographic*, *Harper's* magazine, Vulture, the BBC and NPR, among others. He directs the MFA program at Sierra Nevada College and lives in Orlando, Florida.

REBECCA LINDENBERG is the author of *Love, an Index* and *The Logan Notebooks*. She wrote this poem while traveling on the gift of an Amy Lowell Fellowship. She's a member of the poetry faculty at the University of Cincinnati, and the Queens University of Charlotte Low-Residency MFA Program.

STEPHEN (also STEPH or STEPHANIE) BURT is Professor of English at Harvard and the author of several books of poetry and literary criticism: a new book of Stephen's own poems, *Advice from the Lights*, will be published by Graywolf in 2017.

MEG WOLITZER is a novelist whose works include *The Interestings*, *The Ten-Year Nap*, and *The Wife*, among others. Her short fiction has appeared in *The Best American Short Stories* and *The Pushcart Prize*.

WILL BUTLER plays in the band Arcade Fire. His dad is a geologist. His mom plays the harp.

NICK JAINA is an itinerant writer and musician. His memoir *Get It While You Can* was a finalist for the 2016 Oregon Book Award.

JESS WALTER, a former National Book Award finalist, is the author of eight books, most recently the #1 bestseller *Beautiful Ruins* and the story collection *We Live in Water*. He lives in Spokane, Washington with his family.

ALICE SOLA KIM's writing has appeared or is forthcoming in places such as *Tin House*, *The Village Voice*, Lenny, BuzzFeed Reader, and *The Year's Best Science Fiction and Fantasy*. She is a winner of the 2016 Whiting Award, and has received grants and scholarships from the MacDowell Colony, Bread Loaf Writers' Conference, and the Elizabeth George Foundation.

TOM DRURY is the author of five novels. His short stories have appeared in *The New Yorker*, *A Public Space*, *Ploughshares*, *Harper's*, and other publications. In 2015 he was awarded a Berlin Prize Fellowship from the American Academy in Berlin, and he currently lives in Berlin.

CHRIS ABANI'S prose includes *The Secret History of Las Vegas*, *Song for Night*, *The Virgin of Flames*, *Becoming Abigail*, *GraceLand*, and *Masters of the Board*. His poetry collections are *Sanctificum*, *There Are No Names for Red*, *Feed Me the Sun*, *Hands Washing Water*, *Dog Woman*, *Daphne's Lot*, and *Kalakuta Republic*. He holds a BA in English, an MA in gender and culture, an MA in English, and a PhD in literature and creative writing.

ANTHONY MARRA is the *New York Times* bestselling author of *A Constellation of Vital Phenomena*, longlisted for the National Book Award and winner of the National Book Critics Circle's John Leonard Prize, the Anisfield-Wolf Book Award in fiction, and the Barnes and Noble Discover Award.

WAJAHAT ALI is a father of two caramel-mocha-skinned babies with Arabic names. He occasionally writes when he gets time, which is never.

GARY BURDEN has been drawing continuously since age six. His early career included cover designs for Joni Mitchell's *Blue*, as well as albums by Steppenwolf; Three Dog Night; The Mamas and the Papas; Crosby, Stills & Nash; The Doors; Judee Sill; Jackson Browne; and countless others. Burden is now enjoying the great pleasure of working with current singer-songwriters like Conor Oberst, Jim James, and My Morning Jacket.

ARIEL S. WINTER is the author of the novels *Barren Cove* and *The Twenty-Year Death*, which was a finalist for The Los Angeles Times Book Award, the Shamus Award, and the Macavity Award, as well as the children's picture book *One of a Kind*, illustrated by David Hitch. He lives in Baltimore.

PATTY YUMI COTTRELL'S work has appeared in *BOMB*, *Gulf Coast*, and *Black Warrior Review*, among other places. Her debut novel, *Sorry to Disrupt the Peace*, is available now from McSweeney's. She lives in Los Angeles.

KEVIN MOFFETT is the author of two story collections and a collaborative novel, *The Silent History*. He teaches at Claremont McKenna College and in the low-residency MFA at the University of Tampa.

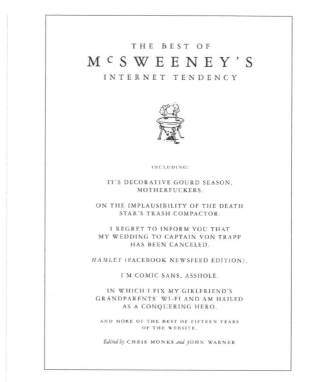

"The first bona fide literary movement in decades."
—Slate

THE BEST OF McSWENEY'S
edited by Dave Eggers amd Jordan Bass

To commemorate the fifteenth anniversary of the journal called "a key barometer of the literary climate" by the *New York Times* and twice honored with a National Magazine Award for fiction, here is *The Best of McSweeney's*—a comprehensive collection of the most remarkable work from a remarkable magazine.

"{The Best of McSweeney's Internet Tendency} is just like those chocolates that hotels put on pillows, if the chocolate were laced with acid." —Michael Agger, The New Yorker

THE BEST OF McSWEENEY'S INTERNET TENDENCY
edited by Chris Monks and John Warner

Every year or so, we collect some of the site's better material and attempt to trick readers into paying for a curated, glued-together version of what is available online for free. This collection is the best and most brazen of such attempts.

"*Irresistible… its intelligence, its honesty and, above all, its compassion provide a kind of existential balm*
—Curtis Sittenfeld, The New York Times

ALL MY PUNY SORROWS
by Miriam Toews

All My Puny Sorrows is the latest novel from Miriam Toews, one of Canada's most beloved authors—not only because her work is rich with deep human feeling and compassion but because her observations are knife-sharp and her books wickedly funny. And this is Toews at her finest.

"*This dynamite collection of stories has it all—Chile and Belgium, exile and homecomings, Pinochet and Simon and Garfunkel—but what I love most about the tales is their strangeness, their intelligence, and their splendid honesty.*"
—Junot Díaz

MY DOCUMENTS
by Alejandro Zambra

Zambra's remarkable vision and erudition is on full display here; this book offers clear evidence of a sublimely talented writer working at the height of his powers.

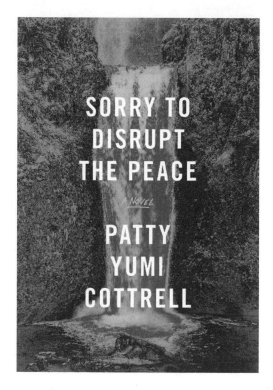

*"Unflinching, unforgettable, and animated
with a restless sense of humor."*
—Catherine Lacey, author of Nobody Is Ever Missing

SORRY TO DISRUPT THE PEACE
by Patty Yumi Cottrell

A bleakly comic tour de force that's by turns poignant, uproariously funny, and viscerally unsettling, this debut novel has shades of Bernhard, Beckett, and Bowles—and it announces the singular voice of Patty Yumi Cottrell.

"In Dada's wild amalgam of quest story, social satire, and comic shtick, you won't catch Savicevic offering tidy diagnoses. You won't care, thanks to prose that glints like the sea in the distance."—The Atlantic

ADIOS, COWBOY
by Olja Savičević

This American debut by a poet from Croatia's "lost generation" explores a beautiful Mediterranean town's darkest alleys. By the end of the long summer, the lies, lust, feuds, and frustration will come to a violent and hallucinatory head.

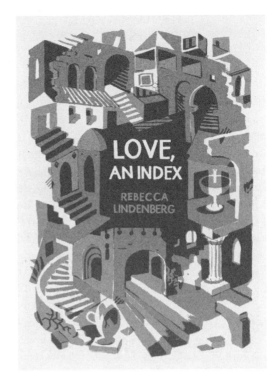

"A delightful, endlessly inventive read."
—The San Francisco Chronicle

ONE HUNDRED APOCALYPSES AND OTHER APOCALYPSES
by Lucy Corin

Lucy Corin's dazzling collection is powered by one hundred apocalypses: a series of short stories, many only a few lines, that illuminate moments of vexation and crisis, revelations and revolutions. *One Hundred Apocalypses and Other Apocalypses* makes manifest the troubled conscience of an uneasy time.

"An A-to-Z collection of poems that are passionate, plainspoken, elegiac, and lyric as they capture the moments of a life shared." —Vanity Fair

LOVE, AN INDEX
by Rebecca Lindenberg

A man disappears. The woman who loves him is left scarred and haunted. In her fierce debut, Rebecca Lindenberg tells the story—in verse—of her passionate relationship with Craig Arnold, a much-respected poet who disappeared in 2009 while hiking a volcano in Japan.

Awake Beautiful Child .... Amy Krouse Rosenthal; Ill. Gracia Lam

Lost Sloth .... J. Otto Seibold

The Expeditioners I .... S.S. Taylor; Ill. Katherine Roy

The Expeditioners II .... S.S. Taylor; Ill. Katherine Roy

Girl at the Bottom of the Sea .... Michelle Tea

Mermaid in Chelsea Creek .... Michelle Tea

NONFICTION

White Girls .... Hilton Als

In My Home There Is No More Sorrow .... Rick Bass

Maps and Legends .... Michael Chabon

Real Man Adventures .... T Cooper

The Pharmacist's Mate and 8 .... Amy Fusselman

Toro Bravo: Stories. Recipes. No Bull. .... John Gorham, Liz Crain

The End of War .... John Horgan

It Chooses You .... Miranda July

The End of Major Combat Operations .... Nick McDonell

Mission Street Food .... Anthony Myint, Karen Leibowitz

At Home on the Range .... Margaret Yardley Potter, Elizabeth Gilbert

Half a Life .... Darin Strauss

VOICE OF WITNESS

Throwing Stones at the Moon .... Ed. Sibylla Brodzinsky, Max Schoening

Surviving Justice .... Ed. Dave Eggers, Lola Vollen

Nowhere to Be Home .... Ed. Maggie Lemere, Zoë West

Refugee Hotel .... Juliet Linderman, Gabriele Stabile

Patriot Acts .... Ed. Alia Malek

Underground America .... Ed. Peter Orner

Hope Deferred .... Ed. Peter Orner, Annie Holmes

High Rise Stories .... Ed. Audrey Petty

Inside This Place, Not of It .... Ed. Ayelet Waldman, Robin Levi

Out of Exile .... Ed. Craig Walzer

Voices from the Storm .... Ed. Chris Ying, Lola Vollen

HUMOR

The Secret Language of Sleep ... Amelia Bauer, Evany Thomas

Baby Do My Banking .... Lisa Brown

Baby Fix My Car .... Lisa Brown

Baby Get Me Some Lovin' .... Lisa Brown

Baby Make Me Breakfast .... Lisa Brown

Baby Plan My Wedding .... Lisa Brown

Comedy by the Numbers .... Eric Hoffman, Gary Rudoren

The Emily Dickinson Reader .... Paul Legault

All Known Metal Bands .... Dan Nelson

How to Dress for Every Occasion .... The Pope

The Latke Who Couldn't Stop Screaming .... Lemony Snicket, Lisa Brown

The Future Dictionary of America .... Various

The Best of McSweeney's Internet Tendency .... Various; Ed. Chris Monks, John Warner

I Found This Funny .... Various; Ed. Judd Apatow

I Live Real Close to Where You Used to Live .... Various; Ed. Lauren Hall

Thanks and Have Fun Running the Country .... Various; Ed. Jory John

POETRY

City of Rivers .... Zubair Ahmed

Remains .... Jesús Castillo

x .... Dan Chelotti

The Boss .... Victoria Chang

TOMBO .... W. S. Di Piero

Of Lamb .... Matthea Harvey, Amy Jean Porter

Love, An Index .... Rebecca Lindenberg

Fragile Acts .... Allan Peterson

The McSweeney's Book of Poets Picking Poets .... Various; Ed. Dominic Luxford

COLLINS LIBRARY

Curious Men .... Frank Buckland

Lunatic at Large .... J. Storer Clouston

The Rector and the Rogue .... W.A. Swansberg

MᶜSWEENEY'S WOULD LIKE TO THANK THE FOLLOWING DONORS FOR THEIR BOUNDLESS GENEROSITY. YOU MAKE OUR WORK POSSIBLE.

A. Dupuis • A. Elizabeth Graves • A. Haggerty • A. Lee • A. Reiter • Aaron • Aaron Cripps • Aaron Davidson • Aaron Flowers • Aaron Mcmillan @Ericrosenbizzle • 826 Fan • A.A. • Aaron Quint • Aaron Rabiroff • Aaron Richard Marx • Aaron Sedivy • Aaron Stewart • Aaron Vacin • Aaron Wishart • Abbey • Abigail Droge • Abigail Keel • Abigail Kroch • Adam Alley • Adam Angley • Adam Baer • Adam Batty • Adam Blanchard • Adam Cady • Adam Colman • Adam Esbensen • Adam Hirsch • Adam J. Kurtz • Adam Keker • Adam Kempa • Adam Mueller • Adam O'Riordan • Adam Shaffer • Adam Wager • Adam Weiss • Adam Zaner • Addison Eaton • Adeline Teoh • Aditi Rao • Adriana Difranco • Adrienne Adams • Adrienne Kolb • Adrienne Spain Chu • Adscriptum.nl • Agatha Trundle • Aida Daay • Aiden Enns • Aimee • Aimee Kalnoskas • Akiko K • Alaina Roche • Alan Federman • Alan Keefer • Alana Lewis • Alana Stubbs • Alanna Watson • Alessia Rotondo • Alex • Alex Andre • Alex Atkinson • Alex Daly • Alex Field • Alex Grecian • Alex Haynes • Alex Khripin • Alex Motzenbecker • Alex Power • Alexa Dooseman • Alexa Huyck • Alexa Pogue • Alexander Birkhold • Alexander Carney • Alexander F. Myers • Alexandra Cousy • Alexandra Kordoski • Alexandra Phillips • Alfie • Alfredo Agostini • Ali Procopio • Ali Sternburg • Alice Armstrong • Alice Christman • Alice Curtis Cline • Alice Freilinger • Alice Gardner Kelsh • Alice Mccormick • Alice Quinn • Alicia Kolbus • Alicia Mullen • Alijah • Alina Shlyapochnik • Alisa Bonsignore • Alisa Morgan • Alison Benowitz • Alison Huffman • Alison Lester • Alison Michael • Alison Thayer • Alissa Elliott • Alissa Sheldon • Alistair Bright • Alisun Armstrong • Allan Weinrib • Allen Eckhouse • Allen Rein • Allie Carey • Allison • Allison Arieff • Allison B. Bransfield • Allison Downing • Ally Kornfeld • Allyson Fielder • Altaire Productions • Alvin Tsao • Alyson Levy • Amalia Durham • Amanda & Keagan • Amanda Bullock • Amanda Canales • Amanda Duling • Amanda Durbin • Amanda Niu • Amanda Roer Duling • Amanda Uhle • Amanda Wallwin • Amandeep Jutla • Amazing Grace! • Amber • Amber Bittiger • Amber D. Kempthorn • Amber Murray • Amro Gebreel • Amy • Amy Blair • Amy Brownstein • Amy Henschen • Amy Lampert Pfau • Amy Macauley • Amy Marcus • Amy Ponsetti • Amy Rosenthal • Amy Shields • Amy Wallace • Amy Ware • Amy Welch • Amy Wolfner • Ana Cr • Ananda V.h. • Andi Biren • Andi Winnette • Andra Kiscaden • Andre Kuzniarek • André Mora • Andrea Biren • Andrea D'tonio • Andrea Dahl • Andrea Lunsford • Andrea Pilati • Andrea Sammarco • Andrew Bailey • Andrew Bannon • Andrew Benner • Andrew Blossom • Andrew Cohn • Andrew Crooks • Andrew Durbin • Andrew Eichenfield • Andrew Eisenman • Andrew Glaser • Andrew Glencross • Andrew Gurnett • Andrew Hirshman • Andrew Holets • Andrew Jensen • Andrew Kaufteil • Andrew M. Jackson • Andrew Macbride • Andrew Mason • Andrew Mclaughlin • Andrew Mcleod • Andrew Miles • Andrew Noonan • Andrew Patton • Andrew Perito • Andrew Rose • Andrew Rosen • Andrew Sachs • Andrew Stargel • Andrew Steele • Andrew Stratis • Andrew Watson • Andrew Yakas • Andrew Alan Ferguson • Andy Banks • Andy Barnes • Andy Dobson • Andy Que • Andy Steckling • Andy Steele • Andy Waer • Andy Yaco-Mink • Angel Logue • Angela Hunter • Angela Johnson • Angela Johnson • Angela Lau • Angela Petrella • Angela Saunders • Angelo Delsante • Angelo Pizzo • Angie • Angie Boysen • Angie Holan • Angie Newgren • Anisse Gross • Anja R. • Ann Giardina Magee • Ann Gillespie • Ann Gillespie • Ann Mcdonald • Ann Mckenzie • Ann Morrone • Ann Sieber • Ann Stuart King • Anna Bond • Anna Calasanti • Anna Luebbert • Anna March • Anna Stroup • Anna Wiener • Anna-Marie Silvester • Annalisa Post • Anne Connell • Anne Fougeron • Anne Gaynor • Anne Germanacos • Anne Holland • Anne Lebaron • Anne Petersen • Anne Shelton • Anne Tonolli Cook • Anne

Wheeler • Annemarie Gray • Annette Toutonghi • Annick Mcintosh • Annie Ganem • Annie Logue • Annie Lynsen • Annie Neild • Annie Porter • Annie Ross • Annika Shore • Anonymous × 9 • Antares M • Anthology Llc • Anthony "Tony" Schmiedeler • Anthony Clavelli • Anthony Devito • Anthony Effinger • Anthony Ha • Anthony Marks • Anthony Myint • Anthony St George • Anthony Teoh • Anthony Thompson • April Fry Ruen • April Ruen • Arianna Reiche • Ariel Hartman • Ariel Zambelich • Arielle Brousse • Arlene Buhl • Armadillo & Dicker • Arthur Hurley • Arthur Strauss • Arturo Elenes • Ash Huang • Asha Bhatia • Ashima Bawa • Ashley • Ashley Aguirre • Ashley Kalagian Blunt • Ashley Otto • Ashraf Hasham • Atsuro Riley • Audrey • Audrey Butcher • Audrey Fennell • Audrey Yang • Augusta Palmer • Christopher Robin • Ayni • Azro Cady • Balz Meierhans • Barbara Barnes • Barbara David • Barbara Demarest • Barbara Kirby • Barbara Passino • Barry Traub • Basil Guinane • Beau Bailey • Becca • Becky • Beckyjo Bean • Beejieweejie • Bekah Grim • Beki Pope • Ben Ames • Ben Blum • Ben Crowley • Ben Gibbs • Ben Goldmam • Ben Hughes • Ben Larrison • Ben Matthews • Ben Pfeiffer • Ben Zotto • Benjamin Elkind • Benjamin Han • Benjamin Jahn • Benjamin Liss • Benjamin Novak • Benjamin Peskoe • Benjamin Petrosky • Benjamin Russell • Benjamin Small • Benjamin Southworth • Bernadette Segura • Bernard Yu • Berry Bowen • Bertis Downs • Beth Ayer • Beth Chlapek • Beth Daugherty • Beth Duncan • Beth Mcduffee • Betsy Ely • Betsy Henry Pringle • Betsy Henschel • Betsy Levitas • Betsy Pattullo • Betty Jane Jacobs • Betty Joyce Nash • Bill Bonwitt • Bill Crosbie • Bill Frazier • Bill Hughes • Bill Manheim • Bill Owens • Bill Rising • Bill Spitzig • Bill Weir • Billy Moon • Billy Taylor • Billy Tombs • Bindi Kaufman • Birch Norton • Birchy Norton • Blair Roberts • Blake Coglianese • Blaz • Blythe Alpern • Bob • Bob Blanco • Bob Den Hartog • Bob Sherron • Bob Slevc • Bob Wilson • Bonnie Garmus • Bookman • Boris Glazunov • Boris Mindzak • Boris Vassilev • Bosco Hernandez • Bourbonsmartypants • Brad Feld • Brad Kik • Brad Marcoux • Brad Phifer • Bradley Clarke • Bradley Flynt • Bradley Harkrader • Bradley Mcmahon • Brandon Amico • Brandon Bussolini • Brandon Chalk • Brandon Flammang • Brandon Forsyth • Brandon Wynn • Brenda A Vogan • Brendan Dowling • Brendan James Moore • Brendan Mcguigan • Brenna Field • Brent Emery • Brett Anders • Brett Goldblatt • Brett Klopp • Brett Silton • Brett Yasko • Brian Agler • Brian Bailey • Brian Bowen • Brian Cassidy • Brian Chess • Brian Cobb • Brian Cullen • Brian Dice • Brian Dillon • Brian Eck • Brian Gallay • Brian Godsey • Brian Green • Brian Grygiel • Brian Guthrie • Brian Hiatt • Brian James Rubinton • Brian Knott • Brian M Rosen • Brian Meacham • Brian Pfeffer • Brian Pluta • Brian Turner • Brian Z Danin • Brianna Kratz • Brianna Suzelle • Bridget • Brinda Gupta • Brittany • Brittany Carroll Jones • Brittany Medeiros • Brnnr • Bronwyn Glubb • Brooke Haskell • Brooke Lewis • Brooke Prince • Brownstone BBQ • Bruce G Gordon • Bruce Gordon • Bruce Greeley • Bruce King • Bryan Alexander • Bryan Curtis • Bryan Waterman • Bryce Gorman • Bryn Durgin • Brynn Elizabeth Kingsley • Bsj • Buffalo Architectural Machine • Buffy • Buttocks • C Broderick • C. Odal • C.d. Hermelin • C.j.winter • C.m. Tomlin • Caedlighe Paolucci • Caitlin • Caitlin Fischer • Caitlin L. Baker • Caitlin Van Dusen • Caitlin Webb • Callie Ryan • Calvin Crosby • Camaro Powers • Cameron David • Candice Chiew • Capelessst • Cara Beale • Cara J Giaimo • Cara Mchugh • Cari Hauck • Carisa Miller • Carl Grant • Carl H. Hendrickson Jr • Carl Jacobsen • Carl Salbacka • Carl Voss • Carleton Smith • Carley Phillips • Carlos Parreno • Carly • Carmel Boerner • Carol Anne Tack • Carol Davis • Carole Sargent • Caroline • Caroline Carney • Caroline Moakley • Caroline Pugh • Carolyn Anthony • Caryn Lenhoff • Cassie Ettinger • Catastrophoea • Cate Trujillo • Caterina Fake • Cath Keenan • Cath Le Couteur • Catharine Bell • Catherine • Catherine Chen • Catherine Coan • Catherine Flores Marsh • Catherine Hagin • Catherine Jayne • Catherine Keenan • Catherine Leclair • Catherine Shuster • Catherine Smith • Cathi Falconwing • Cathryn Lyman • Cathy Nieng • Catie Myers-Wood • Cb Murphy • Cece • Cecile Forman • Cecilia Holmes • Cecilia M Holmes • Cecilia Mills • Cedric Howe • Celbridge Rob • Celeste Adamson • Celeste Hotaling-Lyons • Celeste Roberts-Lewis • Cesar Contreras • Chad Gibbs • Chad Gibbs

• Chairs And Tables • Char Kuperstein • Charibdys • Charis Poon • Charlene Ortuno • Charles • Charles Bertsch • Charles D Myers • Charles Dee Mitchell • Charles Irby • Charles Lamar Phillips • Charles Pence • Charles Spaht, Jr. • Charley Brammer • Charlie B Spaht • Charlie Garnett • Charlie Hoers • Charlotte • Charlotte Locke • Charlotte Moore • Cheesybeard666 • Chef Ben Bebenroth • Chelsea Bingham • Cheng Leong • Chenoa Pettrup • Cherisse Datu • Cheryl • Cheryl Flack • Chester Jakubowicz • Chris • Chris Baird • Chris Brinkworth • Chris Bulock • Chris Clancy • Chris Cobb • Chris Duffy • Chris Foley • Chris Hogan • Chris Kleinknecht • Chris Maddox • Chris Martins • Chris Niewiarowski • Chris Ohlson • Chris Preston • Chris Remo • Chris Roberts • Chris Roe • Chris Saeli • Chris Sandoval • Chris Schmidt • Chris Warack • Chrissy Simonte Boylan • Christen Herland • Christi Chidester • Christian Gheorghe • Christian Lovecchio • Christian Rudder • Christian S. • Christian Smith • Christina Dickinson • Christina Erickson • Christina Grachek • Christina Macsweeney • Christina Schmigel • Christine Allan • Christine Chen • Christine Delorenzo • Christine Evans • Christine Langill • Christine Luketic • Christine Lyons • Christine Ogata • Christine Rehm • Christine Ross • Christine Ryan • Christine Tilton • Christine Vallejo • Christopher Benz • Christopher Carver • Christopher Fauske • Christopher Fox • Christopher Greenwald • Christopher Harnden • Christopher Hinger • Christopher Knaus • Christopher Madden • Christopher Maynard • Christopher Mclachlan • Christopher Naccari • Christopher Sarnowski • Christopher Soriano • Christopher Stearly • Christopher Strelioff • Christopher Todd • Christopher W Ulbrich • Christopher Wright • Christy Brown • Christy Fletcher • Christy Rishoi • Chrysta Cherrie • Cindi Hickman • Cindi Rowell • Cindy Foley • Cindy Lamar • Cirocco • City Tap House • Claire Boyle • Claire Burleson • Claire Swinford • Claire Tan • Clare Hyam • Clare Louise Jones • Clare Wallin • Claudia • Claudia Milne • Claudia Mueller • Claudia Stein • Cleri Coula • Cleri Coula • Clint Popetz • Clive Thompson • Cloe Shasha • Cmg • Cns • Cody Hudson • Cody Peterson • Cody Williams • Colby Aymar • Colby Ray • Colin • Colin Nissan • Colin Urbina • Colin Winnette • Colleen Bright • Collin Brazie • Colton Powell • Connor Kalista • Conor Delahunty • Corey & Meghan Musolff • Corinne Caputo • Corinne Marrinan Tripp • Cortney Kammerer • Cory Gutman • Cory Hershberger • Cory Hershberger • Courtney A. Aubrecht • Courtney Hopkins • Courtney Nguyen • Craig Clark • Craig New • Craig Short • Cris Pedregal Martin • Crystal • Curt Sobolewski • Curtis Edmonds • Curtis Rising • Curtis Sutton • Cyd Peroni • Cydney Stewart • Cynthia Baute • Cynthia Foley • Cynthia Yang • D • D Cooper • D Miller • D. Whiteman • D.a. Pratt • Daan Windhorst • Dale Sawa • Damfrat • Damian Bradfield • Damien James • Damon Copeland • Damon-Eugene Rich • Dan Ashton • Dan Carroll • Dan Colburn • Dan Grant • Dan Haugen • Dan May • Dan Mckinley • Dan Money • Dan Pasternack • Dan Pritts • Dan Rollman • Dan Schreiber • Dan Spealman • Dan Stein • Dan Winkler • Dana K • Dana Skwirut • Dana Werdmuller • Dani D • Daniel • Daniel A. Hoyt • Daniel Bahls • Daniel Beauchamp • Daniel Berger • Daniel Dejan • Daniel Edwards • Daniel Erwin • Daniel Feldman • Daniel Grossman • Daniel Grou • Daniel Guilak • Daniel Hoyt • Daniel Khalastchi • Daniel Levin Becker • Daniel Morgan • Daniel Ness • Daniel Ridges • Daniel Tovrov • Daniel Wilbur • Danielle Bailey • Danielle Gallen • Danielle Granatt • Danielle Jacklin • Danielle Kucera • Danielle Lavaque-Manty • Danika Esden-Tempski • Danny Richelson • Danny Shapiro • Danyl Garnett • Darby Dixon Iii • Darcie Thomas • Dargaud-Fons • Darko Orsic • Darlene Zandanel • Darrell Hancock • Darren Higgins • Daryl Dragon • Dash Shaw • Dave • Dave Baptist • Dave Curry • Dave David • Dave Forman • Dave Haas • Dave Lucey • Dave Madden • Dave Polus • Davi Ferreira • David • David • David + Kami • David Andrews • David Baker • David Bradley • David Brett Kinitsky • David Brown • David Burns • David Charlton • David Chatenay • David Cornwell • David Desmond • David Dietrich • David E Baker • David Eckles • David F. Gallagher • David Frankel • David Galef • David Givens • David Givens • David Goldstein • David Guerrero • David Hodge • David J. Whelan • David James • David K • David Karpa • David Kneebone • David Knopp • David Kurz • David L Gobeli • David Leftwich • David Lerner

• David Levy • David M • David Macy-Beckwith • David Mccarty • David Nilsen And Melinda Guerra • David Peter • David Pollock • David R Lamarre • David Rodwin • David Sam • David Sanger • David Sievers • David Springbett • David Strait • David Sundin • David Thompson • David Wolske • David Wright • David Zaffrann • David Zarzycki • D.b. Ramer • De_hart • Dean • Dean O'donnell • Deane Taylor • Deb Olin Unferth • Debbie Baldwin • Debbie Berne • Debbie Millman • Debby Weinstein • Deborah Conrad • Deborah Urban • Deborah Wallis • Debra Bok • Demeny Pollitt • Dena Verhoff • Denae Dietlein • Denise Sarvis • Denise Witherspoon • Dennis Caraher • Dennis Gallagher • Dennis Marfurt • Derek Van Westrum • Designers & Books • Devon Henderson • Diana Behl • Diana Cohn • Diana Funk • Diana M. • Diana Tomchick • Diane Arisman • Diane B Kresal • Diane Fitzsimmons • Diane Holdgate • Diane Lederman • Diane M. Fedak • Diane S. • Diane Wang • Dianne Weinthal • Dianne Wood • Dillon Morris • Dinika Amaral • Dirk Heniges • Dom Baker • Dominic Lepper • Dominic Luxford • Dominica Phetteplace • Don Smith • Donald Deye • Donald Schaffner • Donald Solem • Donald Woutat • Donna Copeland-Fuller • Donna Fogarty • Doreen Kaminski • Doro • Dory Culver • Doug • Doug Dorst • Doug Green • Doug Mayo-Wells • Doug Messel • Doug Michel • Doug Moe • Doug Schoemer • Doug Taub • Doug Wolff • Doug Wykstra • Douglas Andersen • Douglas Candano • Douglas Hirsch • Douglas Kearney • Douglas Mcgray • Dov Lebowitz-Nowak • Dr. Demento • Dr. Hornet • Dr. Meredith Blitzmeyer • Drew Atkins • Drew Baldwin • Drew Sussman • Duane Murray • Duane Murray • Dustin Mark • Eap • Ed Freedman • Ed Krakovsky • Ed Riley • Ed Rodley • Ed Sweeney • Edie Jarolim • Edinblack • Edward • Edward Crabbe • Edward Lim • Edwina Trentham • Eileen Considine • Eileen M Mccullough • Eileen Madden • Eitan Kensky • El Chin • Elaine Froneberger • Elana Spivack • Elda Guidinetti • Eleanor Cooney • Eleanor Horner • Elia Wise • Elinor Wahl • Elisa • Elisa Harkness • Elisabeth Carroll • Elisabeth Hammerberg • Elisabeth Seng • Elise Persico • Elizabeth Alkire • Elizabeth Allspaw • Elizabeth Averett • Elizabeth Carmichael-Davis • Elizabeth Chang • Elizabeth Craft • Elizabeth Dalay • Elizabeth Davies • Elizabeth Engle • Elizabeth Gemmill • Elizabeth Gray • Elizabeth Green • Elizabeth Hom • Elizabeth Hykes • Elizabeth Keim • Elizabeth Macklin • Elizabeth Miller • Elizabeth Pfeffer • Elizabeth Ray • Elizabeth Redick • Elizabeth Rovito • Elizabeth Siggins • Elizabeth Smith • Elizabeth Taylor • Elizabeth Weber • Elizwill • Ella Haselswerdt • Ellen Goldblatt • Ellen Line • Ellen Tubbaji • Ellia Bisker • Ellia Bisker • Ellie Flock • Ellie Turzynski • Ellyn Farrelly • Ellyn Toscano • Eloy Gomez • Elsa Figueroa • Elske Krikhaar • Elyse Rettig • Ema Solarova • Emilce Cordeiro • Emily Bliquez • Emily Bryant • Emily Cardenas • Emily Carroll • Emily Diamond • Emily Donohoo • Emily Friedlander • Emily Goode • Emily Harris • Emily Kaiser Thelin • Emily Lynch • Emily M. • Emily Morian-Lozano • Emily Olmstead-Rumsey • Emily Raisch • Emily Schleiger • Emily Schuck • Emily Wallis Hughes • Emma Axelson • Emma Axelson • Emma D. Dryden, Drydenbks Llc • Emma Roosevelt • Enrico Casarosa • Epilogue • Eric • Eric • Eric • Eric Botts • Eric Brink • Eric Brink • Eric Donato • Eric Farwell • Eric Harker • Eric Heiman • Eric Hsu • Eric Johnson • Eric Kuczynski • Eric Larsh • Eric Mauer • Eric Meyers • Eric Muhlheim • Eric Perkins • Eric Potter • Eric Prestemon • Eric Randall • Eric Ricker • Eric Ries • Eric Schulmiller • Eric Segerstrom • Eric Tell • Eric W • Erica Behr • Erica Lively • Erica Nardello • Erica Nist-Lund • Erica Portnoy • Erica Seiler • Erick • Erick Gordon • Erik Henriksen • Erik Pedersen • Erin • Erin Ambrozic • Erin Badillo • Erin Barnes • Erin Corrigan • Erin Eakle • Erin Mcgrath • Erin Senge • Ernesto Gloria • Erwin Wall • Esme Weijun Wang • Ethan Nosowsky • Ethan Rogers • Euan Monaghan • Eva Funderburgh Hollis • Eva Thompson • Evan Brooks • Evan Orsak • Evan Regner • Evan Rosler • Evan Williams • Eve Bower • Evelyn Tunnell • Everett Shock • Evil Supply Co. • Evonne Okafor • Experiencing Life To The Fullest-Da Wolf • Eylem Ezgi Ozaslan • Ezra Karsk • F.p. De L. • Faisel Siddiqui • Fanny Luor • Farnaz Fatemi • Fawn • Felicia • Femme Fan1946 • Fengypants • Fern Culhane • Fernanda Dutra • Fiona Hamersley • Fiona Hartmann • Flash Sheridan • Fotios Zemenides • Frederic

Jaume • Fran Gensberg • Frances Lopez • Frances Tuite • Frances Tuite • Francesca Moore • Francis Desiderio • Frank Drummond • Frank Lortscher • Frank Riley • Frank Ruffing • Frank Turek • Franklin • Franklin Friedman • Freddi Bruschke • Freddy Powys • Frederick De Naples • Frederick Fedewa • Free Expressions Seminars And Literary Services • Frin Atticus Doust • Fualana Detail • Full Gamut Consulting • Gabe Gutierrez • Gabe Mcgowan • Gabriel Pumple • Gabriel Vogt • Gabriela Melchior • Gala Grant • Galen Livingston • Garth Reese • Gary Almeter • Gary Almeter • Gary Beckerman • Gary Chun • Gary Gilbert • Gary Rudoren • Gary Rudoren • Gavin Beatty • Gaye Hill • Gayle Brandeis • Gayle Dosher • Gayle Engel • Genevieve Kelly • Geoff "Not-So-Mysterious-Benefactor" Brown • Geoff D. • Geoff Smith • George Hodosh Associates • George Mcconochie • George Mitolidis • George Veugeler • George Washington Hastings • Georgia • German (Panda) Borbolla • Gerrit Thompson • Gertrude And Alice Editions • Gibby Stratton • Gieson Cacho • Gina • Gina B. • Gina Smith • Ginny • Girija Brilliant • Gisela Sehnert • Gitgo Productions • Glorianne Scott • Gopakumar Sethuraman • Gordon Mcalpine • Grace Levin • Graeme Deuchars • Graham Bell • Greg Grallo • Greg Johnson • Greg Lavine • Greg Lloyd • Greg Prince • Greg Steinberg • Greg Storey • Greg Versch • Greg Vines • Greg Weber • Greg Wheeler • Greg Williams • Gregory Affsa • Gregory Hagan • Gregory Stern • Gregory Sullivan • Griffin Richardson • Guillaume Morissette • Gunnar Paulsen • Guy Albertelli • Gwen Goodkin • Haden Lawyer • Haiy Le • Hal Tepfer • Haley Cullingham • Haley Williams • Hank Scorpio • Hannah Mcginty • Hannah Meyer • Hannah O'regan • Hannah Rothman • Hannah Settle • Hannelore • Hans Balmes • Hans Ericson • Hans Lillegard • Hans Zippert • Hans-Juergen Balmes • Harold Check • Harris Levinson • Harry Deering • Harry J. Mersmann • Harry Mersmann • Harry White • Haruna Iwase • Hassan Fahs • Hassanchop • Hathaway Green • Heather Bause • Heather Boyd • Heather Braxton • Heather Flanagan • Heather Forrester • Heather Guillen • Heckle Her • Hedwig Van Driel • Heidi Baumgartner • Heidi Meurer • Heidi Raatz • Helen Chang • Helen Kim • Helen Linda • Helen Tibboel • Helena • Hemant Anant Jain • Hilary • Hilary Leichter • Hilary Rand • Hilary Sasso-Schleh • Hilary Van Dusen • Hillary Lannan • Holly • Holly Iossa • Holly Kennedy • Houston Needs A Swimming Hole! • Howard Katz • Howeverbal • Hugh Geenen • Hypothetical Development Organization • Ian • Ian Benjamin • Ian Casselberry • Ian Chung • Ian Delaney • Ian Foe • Ian Frederick-Rothwell • Ian Glazer • Ian Harrison • Ian Joyce • Ian Prichard • Ian Shadwell • Ilana Gordon • Iliana Helfenstein • Ingrid Kvalvik Sørensen • Ioana Popa • Irene Arntz • Irene Hahn • Isabel A • Isabel Pinner • Isabella • J.F. Gibbs • J.G. Hancock • J. Wilson • J.A. López • J.B. Van Wely • J.J. Larrea • J.L. Schmidt • Jack Amick • Jack Dodd • Jack Stokes • Jack Thorpe • Jackie Jones • Jackie Mccarthy • Jackie Yang • Jaclyne D Recchiuti • Jacob Davis • Jacob Haller • Jacob Lacivita • Jacob Leland • Jacob Zionts • Jacqueline Utkin • Jacquelyn Moorad And Carolyn Hsu • Jade Higashi • Jaime Young • Jaimen Sfetko • Jake • Jake Bailey • Jamal Saleh • James Adamson • James And Rasika Boice • James Brown • James Chesky • James Crowley, Jr • James E Wolcott • James English • James Manion • James Merk • James Mnookin • James Moore • James Newton • James O'brien • James Osborne • James Park • James Roger • James Roger • James Ross-Edwards • James Trimble • James Vest • James Woods (Not The Actor) • Jamie Alexander • Jamie Campbell • Jamie Campbell • Jamie Tanner • Jamie Zeppa • Jamon Yerger • Jan Greene • Jan Yeaman • Jane Clarke • Jane Darroch Riley • Jane Gibbins • Jane Jonas • Jane Kirchhofer • Jane Knoche • Jane Nevins • Jane Whitley • Jane Wilson • Janet Beckerman • Janet Beeler • Janet Fendrych • Janet Gorth • Janet M. Fendrych • Janet Marie Paquette • Janice & Cooper • Janice Dunn • Janice Goldblatt • Janie Locker • Jared Quist • Jared R Delo • Jared Silvia • Jaron Kent-Dobias • Jaron Moore • Jarry Lee • Jason • Jason Bradshaw • Jason Chen • Jason File • Jason Gittler • Jason Hannigan • Jason Kirkham • Jason Kunesh • Jason Levin • Jason Martin • Jason Martin • Jason Riley • Jason Rodriguez • Jason S • Jason Seifert • Jason Sobolewski • Jason Sussberg • Jasper Smit • Jasun Mark • Jay • Jay Dellacona • Jay Price • Jay Schutawie • Jay Traeger • Jayveedub • Jbflanz • Jd Ferries-Rowe

• Jean Carney • Jean Haughwout • Jean Prasher • Jean Sinzdak • Jean T Barbey • Jeanette Shine • Jeanine Fritz • Jeanne Weber • Jeanne Wilkinson • Jeannette • Jeannie Vanasco • Jeanvieve Warner • Jed Alger • Jedidiah Smith • Jeff • Jeff • Jeff Albers • Jeff Anderson • Jeff Caltabiano • Jeff Campoli • Jeff Chacon • Jeff Dickerson • Jeff G. Peters • Jeff Garcia • Jeff Greenstein • Jeff H White • Jeff Hampl • Jeff Hayward • Jeff Hilnbrand • Jeff Hitt • Jeff Jacobs • Jeff Klein • Jeff Klein • Jeff Magness • Jeff Neely • Jeff Omiecinski • Jeff Peters • Jeff Stiers • Jeff Stuhmer • Jeff Trull • Jeff Vitkun • Jeff Ward • Jeffrey Brothers • Jeffrey Brothers • Jeffrey Brown • Jeffrey Garcia • Jeffrey Meyer • Jeffrey Parnaby • Jeffrey Posternak • Jeffrey Snyder • Jen Alam • Jen Burns • Jen Butts • Jen Donovan • Jen Jurgens • Jen Lofquist • Jenn De La Vega • Jenni B. Baker • Jenni Baker • Jennie Lynn Rudder • Jennifer • Jennifer Aheran • Jennifer Anthony • Jennifer Cole • Jennifer Cruikshank • Jennifer Dait • Jennifer Day • Jennifer Dopazo • Jennifer Grabmeier • Jennifer Howard Westerman • Jennifer Kabat • Jennifer Kain Kilgore • Jennifer Laughran • Jennifer Marie Lin • Jennifer Mcclenon • Jennifer Mccullough • Jennifer Mcfadden • Jennifer Ratcliffe • Jennifer Richardson • Jennifer Rowland • Jennifer Ruby Privateer • Jennifer Westerman • Jennifer White • Jennifer Wolfe • Jenny Cattier • Jenny Lee • Jenny Stein • Jenzo Duque • Jeremiah • Jeremiah Follett • Jeremy Cohen • Jeremy Ellsworth • Jeremy Fried • Jeremy Peppas • Jeremy Radcliffe • Jeremy Rishel • Jeremy Smith • Jeremy Smith • Jeremy Van Cleve • Jeremy Walker • Jeremy Wang-Iverson • Jeremy Welsh • Jeremy Wortsman • Jerry & Val Gibbons • Jerry Englehart, Jr • Jerry Krakoff • Jerry Pura • Jess Chace • Jess Fitz • Jess Higgins • Jess Kemp • Jess L. • Jess Mcmorrow • Jess Voigt • Jesse Brickel • Jesse Hemingway • Jessi Fierro • Jessica • Jessica • Jessica Allan Schmidt • Jessica Bacho • Jessica Bifulk • Jessica Eleri Jones • Jessica Fiske • Jessica Ghersi • Jessica Hampton • Jessica Martinez • Jessica Mcfadden • Jessica Mcmillen • Jessica Mcmorrow • Jessica Partch • Jessica Poulin • Jessica Shook • Jessica Spence • Jessica Stocks • Jessica Suarez • Jessica Vanginhoven • Jessica Yu • Jessie Gaynor • Jessie Johnson • Jessie Lynn Robertson • Jessie Stockwell • Jett Watson • Jezzka Chen • Jijin John • Jill • Jill Cooke • Jill Ho • Jill Katz • Jillian Mclaughlin • Jillian Mcmahon • Jim And Loretta • Jim Haven • Jim Kosmicki • Jim Lang • Jim Mccambridge • Jim Mcelroy • Jim Mckay • Jim Moore • Jim Redner • Jim Stallard • Jim Taone • Jimmy Orpheus • Jincy Kornhauser • Jjamms Hoffman • Jo Ellen Watson • Joachim Futtrup • Joan Basile • Joan Greco • Joann Holliday • Joann Schultz • Joao Leal Medeiros Hakme • Joddy Marchesoni • Joe Callahan • Joe Dempsey • Joe Kukella • Joe Kurien • Joe Romano • Joe Stuever • Joe Williams • Joel Bentley • Joel Kreizman • Joel Lang • Joel Santiago • Joey & Berit Coleman • Joey Hayles • Johanna Pauciulo • Johanna, Finja, & Charlie Degl • John & Minda Zambenini • John Artrock77 • John Baker • John Bannister • John Bearce • John Borden • John Bowyer • John Cahill • John Cary • John Charin • John Debacher • John Ebey • John Gialanella • John Hawkins • John Hawkins • John Hill • John Justice • John Karabaic • John Keith • John Kornet • John Lang • John Mcmurtry • John Muller • John Onoda • John P Monks • John P Monks • John P Stephens • John Pancini • John Plunkett • John Poje • John Pole • John Prendergast • John Repko • John Ricketts • John Sarik • John Semley • John Terning • John Tollefsen • John Tompkins • John W Wilkins • John Walbank • John-Fletcher Halyburton • Johnston Murray • Jokastrength • Jon Englund • Jon Folkers • Jon Senge • Jon Stair • Jonas Edgeworth • Jonathan Brandel • Jonathan Deutsche • Jonathan Dykema • Jonathan Fretheim • Jonathan Jackson • Jonathan L York • Jonathan Meyers • Jonathan Van Schoick • Jonathan Wenger • Jordan Bass • Jordan Bell • Jordan Campo • Jordan Campo • Jordan Hauser • Jordan Katz • Jordan Kurland • Jordan Landsman • Jordana Beh • Jorge • Joseph • Joseph Buscarino • Joseph Edmundson • Joseph Fink • Joseph Marshall • Joseph Miebach • Joseph Pred • Josh "The J-Man" Kjenner • Josh Houchin • Josh Mason • Josh Rappoport • Josh Tilton • Joshua Arnett • Joshua D. Meehl • Joshua Farris • Joshua Harris • Joshua Lewis • Joslyn Krismer • Jowi Taylor • Joy • Joyce • Joyce Hennessee • Jozua Malherbe • J.P. Coghlan • Jeremy Radcliffe • Jt Chapel • Juan Mapu • Jude Buck • Judi L Mahaney • Judith • Judy B • Judy

O'karma • Judy Schatz • Julena Campbell • Julia • Julia • Julia Bank • Julia Buck • Julia Fought • Julia Henderson • Julia Kardon • Julia Kardon • Julia Kinsman • Julia Kochi • Julia Meinwald • Julia Pohl-Miranda • Julia Slavin • Julia Smillie • Julia Streit • Julia Strohm • Julia Strukely • Julian Gibbs • Julian Orenstein • Juliana Capaldi • Julianne Rhodes • Julie • Julie Fajgenbaum • Julie Felix • Julie S • Julie Schmidt • Julie Stampfle • Julie Vick • Julie Wood • Jumpsaround • June Speakman • Justin Barisich • Justin Foley • Justin Guinn • Justin Katz • Justin Owen Smith Stockard • Justin R. Lawson • Justin Rochell • Justin Wilcox • Justin A. • Justo Robles • K. Edward Callaghan • Kaat • Kai Van Horn • Kaitlyn Trigger • Kali Sakai • Kane E. Giblin • Kara Richardson • Kara Soppelsa • Kara Ukolowicz • Kara White • Karan Rinaldo • Karen • Karen Enno • Karen Gansky • Karen Gray • Karen Hoffman • Karen Holden • Karen K. • Karen Stilber • Karen Unland • Karin Gargaro • Karin J. • Karin Ryding • Karl Gunderson • Karl Petersen • Karla H. • Karla Hilliard • Karolina Waclawiak Derosa • Karrie Kimbrell • Kaspar Hauser • Kat Lombard-Cook • Kat Marshello • Kate • Kate Aishton • Kate Berry • Kate Brittain • Kate Bush • Kate Fritz • Kate Kapych • Kate Ory • Kate Semmler • Kate W. • Kate Webster • Kath Bartman • Katharine Culpepper • Katherine • Katherine Buki • Katherine Harris • Katherine Love • Katherine Minarik • Katherine Sherron • Katherine Tweedel • Katherine Weybright • Katherine Williams • Kathleen • Kathleen Brownell • Kathleen Fargnoli • Kathleen O. • Kathleen O'gorman • Kathleen Ossip • Kathleen Seltzer • Kathleen Stetsko • Kathryn Anderson • Kathryn Bumbaugh • Kathryn Flowers • Kathryn Holmes • Kathryn Kelley • Kathryn King • Kathryn Lester • Kathryn Page Birmingham • Kathryn Price • Kathy Harding • Kati Simmons Knowland • Katie • Katie • Katie Chabolla • Katie Dodd • Katie Jewett • Katie Lewis • Katie Linden • Katie Love • Katie Mcguire • Katie Y • Katie Young • Katielicious • Katmcgo • Katrina • Katrina Dodson • Katrina Grigo-Mcmahon • Katrina Woznicki • Katryce Kay • Katy Carey • Katy Orr • Katy Shelor Harvey • Katya Kazbek • Kayla M. Anderson • Kaylie Simon • Keiko Ichiye • Keith Cotton • Keith Crofford • Keith Flaherty • Keith Morgan • Keith Van Norman • Kellie • Kellie Holmstrom • Kelly • Kelly Browne • Kelly Conaboy • Kelly Conroe • Kelly Cornacchia • Kelly Doran • Kelly Heckman • Kelly K • Kelly Marie • Kelly Miller-Schreiner • Kelly Wheat • Kelsay Neely • Kelsey Hunter • Kelsey Rexroat • Kelsey Thomson • Kelsie O'dea • Kemp Peterson • Ken Flott • Ken Krehbiel • Ken Racicot • Kendel Shore • Kendra • Kendra Stanton Lee • Kenneth Cameron • Kerri Schlottman • Kerry Evans • Kev Kev Meister • Kevin And Kim Watt • Kevin Anderson • Kevin Arnold • Kevin Ashton • Kevin Camel • Kevin Cole • Kevin Cosgrove • Kevin Davis • Kevin Eichorst • Kevin Felix • Kevin Freidberg • Kevin Gleason • Kevin Hunt • Kevin Johnson • Kevin Keck • Kevin Lauderdale • Kevin Mccullough • Kevin Mcginn • Kevin Mcginn • Kevin Mcmorrow • Kevin O'donnell • Kevin Spicer • Kevin Vognar • Kevin Wynn • Kevin Zimmerman • Khalid Kurji • Kickstarter • Killer Lopez-Hall • Kim • Kim Baker • Kim Ku • Kim Sanders • Kim Wishart • Kimberley Mullins • Kimberley Rose • Kimberly Grey • Kimberly Hamm • Kimberly Harrington • Kimberly Nichols • Kimberly Occhipinti • Kimberly Rose • Kira Starzynski • Kirsten Zerger • Kitkat • Kitz Rickert • Kj Nichols • Knarles Bowles • Knut N. • Kom Siksamat • Kori K. • Kris Majury • Kris S. • Krista Knott • Kristan Hoffman • Kristan Mcmahon • Kristen Ann Tymeson • Kristen Brooks • Kristen Easley • Kristen Miller • Kristen Reed • Kristen Reed • Kristen T Easley • Kristen Westbrook • Kristi Vandenbosch • Kristin M. Morris • Kristin Mullen • Kristin Nielsen • Kristin Pazulski • Kristin R Shrode • Kristina Dahl • Kristina Harper • Kristina Rizga • Kristine Donly • Kristine Donly • Kristy Kulp • Kristyn Dunn • Krisztina Bunzl • Krystal Hart • Kuang-Yi Liu • Kunihiro Ishiguro • Kurt Brown • Kurtis Kolt • Kyle Dickinson • Kyle Garvey • Kyle Jacob Bruck • Kyle Lucia Wu • Kyle Prestenback • Kyle Raum • Kylee Panduro • Kyra Rogers • L.n. • Landy Manderson • Lang Thompson • Langston Antosek • Lani Yamamoto • Lara Kierlin • Lara Struttman • Larisa Shambaugh • Larry Doyle • Larry Farhner • Launa Rich • Laura • Laura • Laura Bauer • Laura Bennett • Laura Bostillo • Laura Buffington • Laura Celmins • Laura Dapito • Laura Farris •

Laura Hadden • Laura Howard • Laura Nisi • Laura Owens • Laura Schmiedicke • Laura Scott • Laura Stevenson • Laura Thomas • Laura Vigander • Laura Weiderhaft • Laura Williams • Laurel • Laurel C • Laurel Chun • Laurel Fedder • Laurel Flynn • Laurel Hall • Lauren Andrews • Lauren Groff • Lauren Isaacson • Lauren O'neal • Lauren Peugh • Lauren Powers • Lauren Rose • Lauretta Hyde • Laurie Bollman-Little • Laurie Ember • Laurie L Young • Laurie Major • Laurie May • Laurie Young • Lawrence Bridges • Lawrence Porricelli • Layla Al-Bedawi • Leah • Leah Browning • Leah Dieterich • Leah Mallen • Leah Murray • Leah Swetnam • Leanne Stremcha • Lee • Lee Ann Albury • Lee Brumbaugh • Lee Harrison • Lee Roe • Lee Smith • Lee Syben • Lee Trentadue • Leigh Vorhies • Leila Khosrovi • Lene Sauvik • Lenore Jones • Lenore Rowntree • Leonard • Leone Lucky • Les Edwards • Lesley A. Martin • Leslie • Leslie Bhutani • Leslie Cannon • Leslie Kotzas • Leslie Maslow • Leslie McGorman • Leslie Mclinskey • Leslie Woodhouse • Lester Su • Lewis Ward • Lex Leifheit • Lian Fournier • Lila Fontes • Lila Lahood • Lillian Rachel Taft • Lily Mehl • Linda Cook • Linda Given • Linda Ocasio • Linda Ostrom • Linda Parker Gates • Linda Schroeder • Linda Skitka • Linda Troop • Linda Weston • Lindsay Hollett • Lindsay Mcconnon • Lindsay Morton • Lindsey • Lindsey Darrah • Lindsey Eubank • Lindsey Shepard • Lindsey Spaulding • Linn Elliott • Linne Ha • Lisa Berrones • Lisa Brown • Lisa Ellis • Lisa Janowski Goode • Lisa M. Geller • Lisa Pearson • Lisa Ryan • Lisa Thaler • Lisa Vlkovic • Lisa Winter • Living Life To The Fullest • Liz Benson • Liz Crain • Liz Flint-Somerville • Liz Nord • Liz Weber • Liza Behles • Liza Harrell-Edge • Lloyd Snowden • Logan Campbell • Logan Hasson • Logan Wright • Lois Denmark • Lora Kelley • Loredana Spadola • Loren Lieberthal • Lorenzo Cherubini • Lori • Lori Blackmon • Lori Cheatle • Lori Dunn • Lori Felton • Lori Fontanes • Lori Hymowitz • Lorie Kloda • Lorin Oberweger • Lorna Craig • Lorna Forbes • Lorraine Dong • Lotus Child • Lou Cove • Louis Loewenstein • Louis Mastorakos • Louis Silverman • Louisa • Louise Marston • Louise Mccune • Louise Williams • Luca Maurer • Lucas Foster • Lucas Hawthorne • Lukas Drake • Luke • Luke Benfey • Luke Burger • Luuly Tran • Lyn Walker • Lynn Farmer • M Robertson • M. Koss • Madeleine Watts • Madeline Jacobson • Mae Rice • Maggie Rotter • Maggie Stroup • Magnanimus • Maia Pank Mertz • Mainon Schwartz • Maitri Sojourner • Majelle • Major Solutions • Manca G. Renko • Mancinist • Mandy Alysse Goldberg • Mandy Brown • Mandy Kinne • Manion • Mara Novak • Mara Zepeda • Marc Atkinson • Marc Beck • Marc Lawrence-Apfelbaum • Marcella Forni • Marcello • Marcia Hofmann • Marco Buscaglia • Marco Kaye • Marcus Cade • Marcus Liddle • Margaret Bykowski • Margaret Cook • Margaret Grounds • Margaret Harvey • Margaret Kelly • Margaret Landis • Margaret Lusko • Margaret Newman • Margaret Peters • Margaret Prescott • Margaret Wachtler • Margo Taylor • Margot Atwell • Mari Moreshead • Maria • Maria • Maria Alicata • Maria Cunningham • Maria Faith Garcia • Maria Sotnikova • Maria Verloo • Mariah Adcox • Mariah Blackard • Mariah Blob Drakoulis • Marian Blythe • Marianne • Marianne Germond • Marie Dever • Marie Harvat • Marie Hohner • Marie Knight • Marie Marfia • Marie Meyer • Marielle Smith • Marina Meijer • Marinna Castilleja • Mario Lopez • Maris Antolin • Maris Kreizman • Mark • Mark • Mark • Mark Aronoff • Mark Beringer • Mark Bold • Mark Brody • Mark Dezalia • Mark Dober • Mark Dudlik • Mark Durso • Mark Fisher • Mark Fritzenschaft • Mark Gallucci • Mark Giordono • Mark Helfrich • Mark Himmelsbach • Mark Kates • Mark Levine • Mark Macleod • Mark Mandel • Mark Movic • Mark Novak • Mark Ramdular • Mark Reitblatt • Mark Riechers • Mark Ryan • Mark Southcott • Mark Van Name • Mark Weatherup, Jr. • Mark Wilkerson • Markus Wegscheider • Marlin Dohlman • Marlo Amelia Buzzell • Marna Blanchard • Marrion K • Marsha Nunley • Marsha Soffer • Marshall Farr • Marshall Hayes • Martha • Martha Benco • Martha Linn • Martha Pulleyn • Martin Berzell • Martin Cielens • Martin Gelin • Martina Radwan • Martina Schuerpf • Martina Testa • Marty Anderson • Mary • Mary Atikian • Mary Beth Hoerner • Mary Byram • Mary Christa Jaramillo-Bolin • Mary Dumont • Mary Durbin • Mary E I Jones • Mary Elizabeth Huber • Mary F Kaltreider • Mary Gioia • Mary Krywaruczenko • Mary Larson • Mary Lukanuski • Mary Mann • Mary Mannison •

Mary Melville • Mary Nieves • Mary O'keefe Bradley • Mary Williams • Mary Z Fuka • Mary-Kim Arnold • Marya Figueroa • Marybeth Gallinger • Maryelizabeth Van Etten • Mason Harper • Mateo Sewillo • Mathias Hansson • Matt • Matt • Matt Adkins • Matt Alston • Matt Bouchard • Matt Conner • Matt Davis • Matt Digirolamo • Matt Fehrenbacher • Matt Gay • Matt Greiner • Matt Kelchner • Matt O'brien • Matt Slaybaugh • Matt Slotkin • Matt Werner • Matthew • Matthew Clark • Matthew Edwards • Matthew Grant • Matthew Honeybeard Henry • Matthew Latkiewicz • Matthew Ludvino • Matthew Morgan • Matthew Morin • Matthew Mullenweg • Matthew Rhoden • Matthew Robert Lang • Matthew Sachs • Matthew Smazik • Matthew Storer • Matthew Swatton • Matthew Wild • Matthew Wood • Mattie Armstrong • Maureen • Maureen Mcbeth • Maureen Van Dyck • Maureen Van Dyck • Max Elman • Maxime • Maximilian Virkus • Maxine Davies • May Ang • May-Ling Gonzales • Maya Baratz • Maya Munoz • Mayka Mei • Mayka Mei • Mayra Urbano • Mbhsing • Mc Macaulay • Mckenzie Chinn • Meagan Choi • Mebaim • Meg Ferguson • Meg Palmer • Meg Varley Keller • Megakestirsch • Megan • Megan • Megan Dowdle • Megan Marin • Megan Murphy • Megan Orsini • Megan Reigner-Chapman • Megha Bangalore • Meghan Arnold • Meghan Smith • Meghan Walker • Meghann Farnsworth • Megin Hicks • Meimaimaggio • Melanie Paulina • Melanie Wang • Melia • Melia Jacquot • Melissa • Melissa Boilon • Melissa Locker • Melissa Stefanini • Melissa Weinstein • Melissa Yes • Mellena Bridges • Melynda Nuss • Meredith Case • Meredith Davies • Meredith Payne • Meredith Resnick • Mette-Marie Katz • M. Garvais • Mi Ann Bennett • Micaela Mcglone • Michael Angarone • Michael Ashbridge • Michael Avella • Michael Barnstijn • Michael Bebout • Michael Birk • Michael Boyce • Michael Denning • Michael Donahue • Michael Eidlin • Michael Gavino • Michael Gillis • Michael Gioia • Michael Glaser • Michael Greene • Michael Hall • Michael Harner • Michael Ireton • Michael Kidwell • Michael Laporta • Michael Legge • Michael Lent • Michael Marsicano • Michael Marx • Michael Mazur • Michael Moore • Michael Moorhouse • Michael Moszczynski • Michael O'connell • Michael Olson • Michael Patrick Cutillo • Michael Sciortino • Michael Sean Lesueur • Michael Thompson • Michaela Drapes • Michaelle • Micheál Keane • Michel Ge • Michelangelo Cianciosi • Michele • Michele Bove • Michele Fleischli • Michele Hansen • Michele Howard • Michelle • Michelle • Michelle • Michelle Akin • Michelle Badash • Michelle Castillo • Michelle Clement • Michelle Cotugno • Michelle Curtis • Michelle Floyd • Michelle Matel • Michelle Nadeau • Mickey Bayard • Micquelle Corry • Miguel Duran • Mik • Mike • Mike Benner • Mike Etheridge • Mike Golay • Mike Lee • Mike Levine • Mike Mcvicar • Mike Munsell • Mike Smith • Mike Thompson • Mike Zuckerman • Mikel Wilkins • Miles Ranisavljevic • Milind Kaduskar • Mimi Evans • Misha Renclair • Missy Manning • Mitch Major • Mitchell Hart • Mo Lai • Moise Lacy • Moishe Lettvin • Mollie Brooks • Molly • Molly • Molly Charnes • Molly Grpss • Molly Guinn Bradley • Molly Mcardle • Molly Mcsweeney • Molly Murphy • Molly Ohainle • Molly Taylor • Mona Awad • Monica Beals • Monica Fogg • Monica Tomaszewski • Mono.kultur • Morningstar Stevenson • Moshe Weitzman • Moss • Muckdart • Mudlarque • Mudville • Murray Gm • Murray Steele • Mygreensweater.com • Myron Chadowitz • Myrsini • Mythmakers • Nadia Ibrashi • Nadine Anderson • Nai-Wen Hu • Nakiesha • Nakiesha Koss • Nalden • Nancy C. Mae • Nancy Folsom • Nancy Friedman • Nancy Goldberg • Nancy Hebben • Nancy Jamieson • Nancy Jeng • Nancy Keiter • Nancy Riess • Nancy Rosenberg • Nancy Rudolph • Nancy Smith • Naomi Alderman • Naomi Firestone-Teeter • Naomi Pinn • Nara Bopp! • Nat Missildine • Natalie • Natalie • Natalie • Natalie Gruppuso • Natalie Hamilton • Natalie Strawbridge • Natalie Ung • Natalie Villamil • Natasha Boas • Nate Arnold • Nate Corddry • Nate Merchant • Nathan Chadwick • Nathan Pyritz • Nathan Rostron • Nathaniel Weiss • Navjoyt Ladher • Neal Cornett • Neal Pollack • Ned Rote • Neda Afsarmanesh • Neil • Neil Blanck • Neil Rigler • Neil Shah • Nelly Ben Hayoun • Nesher G. Asner • Newtux • Nic Barajas • Nicholas Almanza • Nicholas Bergin • Nicholas Herbert • Nicholas Maggs • Nicholas O'neil • Nicholas Van Boddie Willis • Nicholas Walker • Nicholson Baker • Nick • Nick Brown

• Nick C. • Nick Cooke • Nick Fraenkel • Nick Kibodeaux • Nick Miller • Nick Peacock • Nick Plante • Nicky Montalvo • Nicolas Llano Linares • Nicole Avril • Nicole Carlson • Nicole Elitch • Nicole Flattery • Nicole Howard Quiles • Nicole Mandel • Nicole Pasulka • Nicole Rafidi • Nicole Ryan • Nicole Yeo • Nicoletta • Nicoletta Beyer • Nicolette Blum • Nigel Dookhoo • Nigel Taylor • Nigel Warren • Nighthawk • Niina Pollari • Nikil • Nikki H • Nikki Thayer • Nil Hafizi • Nils Normann • Nina Drakalovic • Nion Mcevoy • Nirav • Nitsuh Abebe • No • Noah Miller • Noah Slo • Noelle Greene • None • Nora Caplan-Bricker • Nora L • O. Dwyer • Ofpc Llc • Ola Torstensson • Oleg • Oliver Emanuel • Oliver Grainger • Oliver Kroll • Oliver Meehan • Oliver Mooney • Omar Lee • Owl • P. E. Zalinski • P.M. • Pamela Marcus • Pamela Pugh • Pamela Rooney • Papermantis • Parashar Bhise • Paris Ward • Parker Coddington • Pascal Babare • Pascalle Burton • Pat Jenatsch • Pat Wheaton • Patience Haggin • Patricia Baas • Patricia Bindert • Patricia Iorg • Patricia Miller • Patricia Parker • Patrick • Patrick Cates • Patrick Cox • Patrick Dennis • Patrick Ducey • Patrick M. Freebern • Patrick Maier • Patrick O'driscoll • Patrick Rafferty • Patrick Schilling • Paul • Paul • Paul Bielec • Paul Bloom • Paul Boxer • Paul Braidford • Paul Cancellieri • Paul Curtin • Paul Debraski • Paul Degeorge • Paul Durant • Paul Dutnall • Paul Eckburg • Paul Ferraro • Paul Ghysbrecht • Paul Kohlbrenner • Paul Lasch • Paul Littleton • Paul Mikesell • Mike Sell • Paul Moore • Paul Nadeau • Paul Rosenberg • Paul Studebaker • Paul Upham • Paul Van Zwieten • Paula Palyga • Pauls Toutonghi • Pax • Payton Cuddy • Pedro Poitevin • Peggy Stenger • Penny Blubaugh • Penny Dedel • Peri Pugh • Perii & John Owen • Pete Mulvihill • Pete Smith • Petel • Peter • Peter Blake • Peter Bogert • Peter Bradley • Peter Brian Barry • Peter Fitzgerald • Peter Gadol • Peter Gerhardt • Peter Hoddie • Peter Hogan • Peter Maguire • Peter Mcnally • Peter Meehan • Peter Paul • Peter Platt • Peter Quinn Fuller • Peter Rednour • Peter Roper • Peter Woodyard • Phil Dokas • Phil Fresh • Philip Kor • Philip Kors • Philip Maguire • Philip Platt • Philip Scranton • Philip Wood • Philip Zimmermann • Philippa Moxon • Phillip Henderson • Phillip Johnston • Phyllis Tankel • Pia Widlund • Pierre L'allier • Pierre L'allier • Poilleux • Prisca Riggle • Priscilla Riggle • Priya Sampath • Prmes • Pro • Quim Gil • Quinn • Quinn Formel • R. Mansolino • Rachael Klein • Rachel All • Rachel Bartlett • Rachel Beal • Rachel Brody • Rachel Didomizio • Rachel Droessler • Rachel Fershleiser • Rachel Newcombe • Rachel Pass • Rachel R. Rdriguez • Rachel Sluder • Rachel Smith • Rachel Unger • Rachele Gilman • Radovan Grezo • Rami Levin • Rana • Randall Imai • Randolph Baker • Ravi And Kaela Chandrasekaran • Ray Adams • Raymond Desjarlais • Raymond Khalastchi • Raymond Zhou • Raysha Gallinetti • Rbeedee • Rea Bennett • Reality Connection • Rebecca • Rebecca • Rebecca Bame • Rebecca Calvo • Rebecca Ha • Rebecca Harlow • Rebecca M • Rebecca Martin • Rebecca Rubenstein • Rebecca Scalio • Rebecca Scalio • Rebecca Schneider • Rebecca Schneider • Rebecca Serbin • Rebecca Wilberforce • Reean • Reed Johnson • Reese • Reese Kwon • Reid Allison • Reina Castellanos • Renée Reizman • Renton Wright • Rich Hjulstrom • Rich Scott • Richard Busofsky • Richard Byrne • Richard Cripe • Richard Light • Richard Marks • Richard May • Richard Meadow • Richard Nisa • Richard Parks • Richard Rutter • Richard Sakai • Richard Sakai • Richard Stanislaw • Richard Stroud • Richard Tallmadge • Richard Winter • Rick Cox • Rick Lo • Rick Redick • Rick T. Morrison • Rick Webb • Riley • Riley • Rivkah K Sass • Rk Strout • Rkt88edmo • Rob Atwood • Rob Callender • Rob Colenso • Rob Knight • Rob Mishev • Rob Neill • Rob Wilock • Robby Sumner • Robert Amerman • Robert Archambault • Robert Biskin • Robert Brandin • Robert Brown Glad • Robert Denby • Robert Dickau • Robert Doherty • Robert Drew • Robert E Anderson • Robert Fenerty • Robert George • Robert Hilton • Robert Jacklosky • Robert Macke • Robert Okeefe • Robert Rees • Robert St. Claire • Robert Wilder • Robin Nicholas • Robin Olivier • Robin Ryan • Robin Smith Peck • Roboboxspeaks • Rob W • Rochelle Lanster • Ron Calixto • Ron Charles • Ron Sanders • Ron Wortz • Ronald Neef • Ronnie Scott • Rory Harper • Rosalie Ham • Rosanna Yau • Rose • Rosie Cima • Ross Goodwin • Rosy Capron • Rotem Shintel • Roy Mcmillan • Roy Mcmillan • Ruari

Elkington • Russ Maloney • Ruth Franklin • Ruth Madievsky • Ruth Wyer • Ryan + Lucy • Ryan A. Millager • Ryan Abbott • Ryan Bailey • Ryan Barton • Ryan Curran • Ryan Hetherington • Ryan Molony • Ryan Pitts • Ryan Stenson • Rye Sour • S.P. Garrett • S. Tayengco • S. Grinell • Saelee Oh • Safwat Saleem • Sage Dahlen • Sairus Patel • Sal Macleod • Sally • Sally Brooke • Sally Jane Weed • Sally Macleod • Salpets • Sam • Sam Barrett • Sam Brightman • Sam Hockley-Smith • Sam Skrivan • Sam Sudar • Sam Sweeney • Sam Wright • Sam Zucchi • Sam Zuckert • Samantha • Samantha Armintrout • Samantha Bloom • Samantha Grillo • Samantha Hunt • Samantha Krug • Samantha Netzley • Samantha Schoech • Samia Haddad • Samir Shah • Samuel Cole • Samuel Douglas Miller • Samuel Preston • Sandra Delehanty • Sandra Edwards • Sandra Spicher • Sandy Cooley • Sandy Guthrie • Sandy Stewart • Sanford Nathan • Sara Arvidsson • Sara Corbett • Sara K. Runnels • Sara M • Sara Mouser • Sara Rowghani • Sara Satten • Sarah • Sarah • Sarah • Sarah • Sarah Aibel • Sarah Bacon • Sarah Bownds • Sarah Brewer • Sarah Burnes • Sarah Carter • Sarah E Klein • Sarah Elizabeth Ridley • Sarah Frazier • Sarah Getchell • Sarah Hotze • Sarah Hutchins • Sarah Johnson • Sarah Lavere • Sarah Lincoln • Sarah Litwin-Schmid • Sarah Lukachko • Sarah Maguire • Sarah Mundy • Sarah Rosenshine • Sarah Scire • Sarah Stanlick Kimball • Sarah Tiedeman Gallagher • Sarah Towle • Sarah Walker • Sarah Weissman • Sarita Rainey • Sasquatch Watch Company • Savannah Adams • Savannah Cooper-Ramsey • Scooter Alpert • Scott A. Harris • Scott Bateman • Scott Callon • Scott Dagenfield • Scott Elingburg • Scott Farrar • Scott Ferron • Scott Malagold • Scott Mcgibbon • Scott Olling • Scott Paxton • Scott Rinicker • Scott Shoger • Scott Snibbe • Scott Stanfield • Scott Stelter • Scott Stelter • Scott Suthren • Scott Thurman • Scott Underwood • Scott Wahl • Scott Williams • Sean • Sean Baker • Sean Beatty Oaktown Ss • Sean Boyle • Sean Carr • Sean Harrahy • Sean Jensen-Grey • Sean Kelly • Sean Langmuir • Sean Mcindoe • Sebastian Campos • Sebastianfidler • Sebastien J Park • Segundo Nallatan Jr • Serjio • Seth Casana • Seth D. Michaels • Seth Fowler • Seth Reiss • Shane P. Mullen • Shane Pedersen • Shane Tilton • Shane Ward • Shannon Christine • Shannon David • Shannon Dunbar • Shannon Kelly • Shari D Rochen • Shari Rochen • Shari Simpson • Sharon Lunny • Shaun Bossio • Shaun Pryszlak • Shauna Sutherland • Shaunda Tichgelaar • Shawn Calvert • Shawn Calvert • Shawn Hall • Shawn Lee • Shawn Liu • Shawn Lucas • Sheenagh Geoghegan • Sheila Mennis • Shelby Black • Shelby Kling • Shelley Vinyard • Shelleyboodles Gornall • Shelleysd • Shelly Catterson • Sheri Kenly • Sheri Parsons • Sheri Sternberg • Sheridan Fox • Sherry Suisman • Shevaun Lewis • Shield Bonnichsen • Shih-Lene Jee • Shira Geller • Shira Milikowsky • Shoshana Paige • Simon • Simon Bird • Simon Groth • Simon Harper • Simon Hawkesworth • Simon Kuhn • Simon Nurse • Simon Petherick • Simon Pinkerton • Simon Smundak • Siobhan Dolan • Sisyphus • Smilner • Smivey • Solange Vandermoer • Solenoid • Somedaylee • Somrod Creative • Sona Avakian • Songeehn Choi • Sophie Malone • Sophine • Soraya Okuda • Spencer Coates • Spencer Nelson • Spencer Tweedy • Ssk • Stacey Pounsberry • Stacy Murison • Stacy Ryan • Stacy Saul • Stan Smith • Stanley Levine • Stef Craps • Stefanie Pareja Reyna • Steph Hammell • Steph Widmer • Stephan Heilmayr • Stephanie • Stephanie • Stephanie Anne Canlas • Stephanie Arman • Stephanie Goode • Stephanie Mankins • Stephanie Morgan • Stephanie Murg • Stephanie Wagner • Stephanie Wan • Stephanie Wu • Stephen Angelette • Stephen Beaupre • Stephen Benzel • Stephen Berger • Stephen Bronstein • Stephen Bryce Wood Jr • Stephen Fuller • Stephen Hahn • Stephen Hairsine • Stephen Kay • Stephen Littell • Stephen Mallory • Stephen Murray • Stephen Northup • Stephen Paul • Stephen Schifrin • Stephen Shih • Stephen Shocket • Stephen Smith • Stephen Tabler • Stephen Williams • Steve • Steve Beaven • Steve Berkovits • Steve Caires • Steve Clancy • Steve Conover • Steve Jackson • Steve Kern • Steve Kindrick • Steve Lewis • Steve Maher • Steve Marian • Steve Mockus • Steve Payonzeck • Steve Rivo • Steve Smith • Steve Sweet • Steve Thornbury • Steve Tsuchiyama • Steve W. Jones • Steven Canning • Steven Danielson • Steven Elias • Steven Friedman • Steven Friedman • Steven Hemingray • Steven Hudosh • Steven Jay Athanas • Steven Kindrick • Steven Lowry • Steven Marten • Steven Morley • Steven

Powell • Stewart Davis • Stuart Macdonald • Stuart O'connor • Stuart Rosen • Sue Diehl • Sue Naegle • Sue S • Susan • Susan Auty • Susan Barrabee • Susan C. • Susan Clements • Susan Cooke • Susan Cormier • Susan D. • Susan Davis • Susan Eichrodt • Susan Fitzgerald • Susan Hobbs • Susan Hopkirk • Susan Ito • Susan King • Susan Loube • Susan Miller • Susan Morrissey • Susan Mosseri-Marlio • Susan Schorn • Susan Spradlin • Susan Strohm • Susan Yuk • Susanna • Susanne Durkin • Susanne Durkin-Schindler • Susheila Khera • Suzanna Zeitler • Suzanne Scott • Suzanne Scott • Suzanne Spencer • Suzanne Wilder • Suzi Albertson • Suzie Baunsgard • Syafii • Sydney Blackett • Sydney Morrow • Sydney Sattell • Sylvia Tran • Sylvie L. • Syncione Bresgal • Szienceman • T Cooper • T S Plutchak • T. L. Howl • T.m. Ryan • Tabitha Hayes • Tamar Shafrir • Tamara Zver • Tami Loeffler • Tami Wilson • Tangerine0516 • Tanya F • Taryn Albizzati • Taylor Baldwin • Taylor F. • Taylor Kearns • Taylor Pavlik • Taylor Smith • Taylor Stephens • Tdemarchi • Ted Jillson • Tedder • Teresa Hedin • Teresa Sweat • Terna • Terrence Hayes • Terri Arnold • Terri Coles • Terri Leker • Terry Morris • Terry Wit • Tershia D'elgin • Tess Kornfield • Tess Marstaller • Tess Swithinbank • Tessa Holkesvik • Thanh Tran • The Creature • The Duke Of Follen Street • The Haikooligan • The Lance Arthur • The Nyc Cooper Clan • The Shebooks Team • The Tomato Head, Inc • The Typewriter Revolution • Thedammtruth.com • Thempauls • Theo Plocg • Theresa • Theresa C Kratschmer • Thientam Nguyen • Thierry / On The Road To Honesty • Thomas Barron • Thomas Belote • Thomas Demarchi • Thomas Green • Thomas Kiraly • Thomas La Farge • Thomas Moore • Thomas Moore • Thomas Pluck • Thomas W. Conway • Thomas Weverka • Thousand • Tieg Zaharia • Tiff Chau • Tiffany • Tiffany Cardoza • Tiffany Holly Lyon • Tiffany Peon • Tiffany Tseng • Tim Gaffney • Tim Keogh • Tim Larrison • Tim Lash • Tim Perell • Tim Ruszel @ Ruszel Design Company • Timothy Blackett • Timothy Clark • Timothy Johnstone • Timothy Mey • Timothy N. Towslee • Timothy Paulson • Tina Burns • Tina F. • Tinderbox Editions • Tirza Ben-Porat • Tobias Carroll • Tobin Moss • Tod Story • Todd • Todd • Todd Abbott • Todd Barnard • Todd Bever • Todd Fell • Tom Fitzgerald • Tom Garbarino • Tom Gonzales • Tom Head, Ph.d. • Tom Hood • Tom J Clarke • Tom Joiner • Tom Keekley • Tom Marks • Tom Skoda • Tom Steele • Tom W. Davis Iii • Tomasz Werner • Tony Puccinelli • Tony Solomun • Tori Bond • Tracey A Halliday • Traci Ikegami • Tracy Cambron • Tracy Middlebrook • Travis Burton • Travis Gasser • Trevor Burnham • Trey Kuchinsky • Tricia Copeland • Tricia Psarreas • Triscuit Vallejo • Trisha Bunce • Trisha Weir • Tristan Telson • Troy Goertz • Troy Napier • Tttt • Tucker Christine • Turner Partain • Turtlepants • Tyler Cazes • Tyler Cazes • Tyler Cushing • Tyler Munson • Tyler Robertson • Tyler Smith • Uccf • Uncle Doug • Under Construction Dvd.com • Uttam Kumbhat Jain • V Hollingsworth • V. • V. Stoltz • Vaia Vaena • Val Emmich • Valerie Gprman • Valerie Seijas • Valerie Sonnenthal • Valerie Woolard • Vanasa Bowden • Vanessa Allen • Vanessa Kirker • Vaughn Shields • Veena • Vera Hough • Vernon • Veronica V-V • Victor Jih • Victor Kumar • Victoria Bartelt • Victoria Davies • Victoria Evert • Victoria Marinelli • VII • Vika • Viken • Viktor Balogh • Vinay • Vincent Hsieh • Vinson Cunningham • Virginia E Mead • Virginia Killfoile • Vitor Neves • Vivian Wagner • W.C. Beck • Waipo5kathryn Blue • Wayfarer • Wayne Gwillim • Wendi Aarons • Wendy Ju • Wendy Koster • Wendy Molyneux • Wendy O'neil • Wes Wes • Whitney Isenhower • Whitney Pape • Wiebke Schuster • Will Brodie • Will Cavendish • Will Johnson • Will Mellencamp Leubsdorf • Will Ramsey • Will Skelton • Willa Köerner • Willh • William • William • William Amend • William Donahoe • William Farley • William Hatt • William Kirchner • William Mascioli • William Noonan • William Ross • William Smith • William Van Zandt • William Woolf • Willliam Merrill • Winnie Dreier • Winston Finlayson • Wire Science • Www.smltalk.com • Wythe Marschall • Xiangyun Lim • Yahaya Baruwa • Yang Dai • Yani Robinson • Yeekai Lim • Yew-Leong Wong • Yodiez • Yosef • Yoshihiro Kanematsu • Yotta Sigma • Yuen-Wei Chew • Yukiko Takeuchi • Yvette Dezalia • Yvonne Mains • Yvonne W • Zabeth Russell • Zach • Zach Blair • Zach Lascell • Zach Lipton • Zachary Amundson • Zachary Beamer • Zachary Doss • Zack Daniels • Zack Peercy • Zain Khalid • Zainab Juma • Zalfer • Zanne Cameron • Zoe Laird

McSweeney's exists to champion ambitious and inspired new writing, and to challenge conventional expectations about where it's found, how it looks, and who participates. We're here to discover things we love, help them find their most resplendent form, and place them into the hands of empathic, engaged readers.

Founded in 1998, McSweeney's is an independent publisher based in San Francisco. As well as operating a daily humor website, we publish a short-story quarterly (this one!) and an ever-growing selection of books.

THERE ARE SEVERAL WAYS TO SUPPORT MCSWEENEY'S:

Memberships & Donations
visit *www.mcsweeneys.net/donate*

Volunteering & Internships
email *interns-sf@mcsweeneys.net*

Subscriptions & Online Bookstore
visit *store.mcsweeneys.net*

Books & Quarterly Sponsorship
email *kristina@mcsweeneys.net*

To learn more, please visit *www.mcsweeneys.net/donate* or contact Director Kristina Kearns at kristina@mcsweeneys.net or call 415.642.5609.

All donations are tax-deductible through our fiscal sponsorship with SOMArts, a nonprofit organization that collaborates with diverse artists and organizations to engage the power of the arts to provoke just and fair inclusion, cultural respect, and civic participation.

SOMARTS
CULTURAL CENTER